His body shook. His jaw stretched wider than seemed possible, and Amerind anticipated his shriek. Instead, there emerged a series of snapping sounds, like chicken bones breaking one by one. His jaw slipped off-kilter. His body shook harder, his breaths came in mad gasps. He began vibrating so hard that she couldn't really see him anymore, every part of him a cracking blur. Then as quick as that, it ended—in one final, brutal snap.

The body sagged down, deflated, deliquescing before her eyes . . .

THE PURE COLD LIGHT

GREGORY FROST

AVON BOOKS • NEW YORK

THE PURE COLD LIGHT is an original publication of Avon Books. This work has never before appeared in book form. This work is a novel. Any similarity to actual persons or events is purely coincidental.

AVON BOOKS
A division of
The Hearst Corporation
1350 Avenue of the Americas
New York, New York 10019

Copyright © 1993 by Gregory Frost
Cover illustration by Gregory Frost
Published by arrangement with the author
Library of Congress Catalog Card Number: 92-97298
ISBN: 0-380-76774-0

First AvoNova Printing: May 1993

AVONOVA TRADEMARK REG. U.S. PAT. OFF. AND IN OTHER COUNTRIES, MARCA REGISTRADA, HECHO EN U.S.A.

Printed in the U.S.A.

RA   10   9   8   7   6   5   4   3   2   1

For Barbara and the Poot . . . Home.

Acknowledgments

The author wishes to thank: Steve Mohl of AVI for technical support; Mark Tatuli, Ed Sherry, and Peter Lollelman for imaging; Steve Beuret of Videosmith, Inc., for items of the console; Bill Kent for the lunches that launched it; Uwe Luserke for deutsch support during rough spots; Martha Millard for remarkable fleetness; and, in far too many ways to name, Michael Swanwick, whose sagacity forever enlightens.

Contents

Prologue

Covenant of
the Arc

Heffernan would never appreciate that magnetism was what killed him.

The alarm klaxon honked twice in the tiny lunar shack, so loud that he fumbled his coffee cup and seared a stripe across his thighs. He hopped to his feet, shouting "Son of a *bitch!*" and prying the wet pant legs away from his skin. He had been absorbed till then in a movie on the monitor—a Bette Davis film called *Jezebel*—but shut it off, cut the overheads, and pressed his face against the cold window. Outside, an empty hopper came sliding smoothly by, silent as a ghost.

The mass driver on which it rode looked like the track for the world's dullest roller coaster ride: two aluminum rails stretched straight to the horizon like a big zipper closing the lunar surface. Every couple of seconds a magnetically levitated payload—what everyone called a cannonball—shot off down the length of the right rail and out of sight, to the far end of the driver, where it finally launched its payload at just over two KMPs into space. The empty hopper rode the left rail back around, past the modular shack to where it loaded up again. Heffernan thought magnetic levitation was just swell—at least, he had till now. Once launched, the cannonballs traveled on a precisely aligned trajectory for sixty thousand kilometers to a collection point near one of ScumberCorp's orbiting factories, where they dropped right into a funnel-shaped net as broad as the whole lunar facility. The process was computer-controlled, and everything depended upon the precise instant that the hopper hit the switch and ejected its payload. But lunar soil had a slight magnetic charge to it; twice previously within the last five years, despite the system's built-in damping, a charge had built up in the hopper, a magnetic tug sufficient to throw off its speed just the tiniest bit. With mass driver propulsion, any variation in speed meant that instead of those cannonballs zooming straight into the net, they peppered the black sky like a shower of meteors. That was why Heffernan lived eight hours a day in solitary confinement—to monitor trajectory and correct any problem before it became a problem. It was a cushy job and he'd had it for nearly two years. He couldn't remember the last time he had spent more than ten seconds of any eight-hour stretch monitoring the arc of the cannonballs. Nothing had ever gone wrong before. "Why is this happening on *my* shift?" he asked the sterile landscape.

Another hopper ripped silently past him. He followed it as best he could, watched the tiny speck of its payload shoot into the sky. Without glancing away, he toggled the monitor switch along the sill; blue numbers appeared in the window glass—a precise measurement of the payload's trajectory. The wrong numbers. "Skewed," he said bleakly. "Gone to hell. It's skewed, and I'm screwed." He turned to the console, started running the recorded disk back . . . and back . . . and back, seeking the point at which the parabola returned to normal, counting the number of mis-guided launches with growing alarm. As the disk ran on without change, James Heffernan began to grind his teeth. When the parabolic arc shifted back, he stopped the disk.

Two hundred eighteen of the twenty-kilogram ilmenite cannonballs had been flung into the wrong part of the void. The trajectory had begun to drift about the time he had sealed up his dry suit and gone down the tunnel for his first cup of coffee. He'd gone for two more after that, all without noticing anything amiss. Why hadn't the alarm gone off *before*? This thing had been out of whack for hours without a beep. What sort of margin of error had it been *set* for? Already he was trying to put together a defense. He would need a good one.

He had no choice but to shut down the mass driver. Somewhere, in other rooms of other buildings in SC's lunar factory, more alarms were now going off.

The speaker on the wall popped to life. Goertel, his shift director, shouted, "Heffernan, what the fuck is going on out there? You've shut down!"

He explained about the belated alarm, the parabolic angle that had slowly drifted from true. He named the number of off-target shots. "The balls just got by me, is all."

"Did I hear that? 'Got by you'?" Heffernan could picture Goertel's face gone grape with anger. "Well, let's just see if you get your balls by *me*." The speaker popped dead. He sank down into his chair. If he could have, he would have melted through the floor.

The whole length of the track would need to be inspected. The lost man-hours on this and the other end were—for him at least—incalculable; budget projections sucked into the vacuum. Somebody had to take the heat. He knew already who it would be. Goertel had to answer to the *strungatz*—the suitboys who had never set foot off Earth and who thought a mass driver was the Catholic who parked the choir bus. The only way to save his job and his ass would be to take a lunar skimmer and chase down the errant ilmenite by himself, on his own time, for no pay. Volunteer work. Right now . . . before they ordered him to do it anyway. Wearily, he got to his feet and reached for his suit.

Four hours later he had retrieved eighty-two of the cannon-balls—about all that the skimmer's bay net could handle.

He was coming in on automatic when he found the site. He never would have noticed it at all except that something flicked past the windshield while he was daydreaming about suitboy murder. Whatever the glittering thing was, it had zipped out of sight by the time he pulled himself up against the glass. Not a sign of it.

Seeing his own blue-lit face in the glass, he decided it must have been an optical illusion—light from the maneuvering system display reflecting off the white of his eye, which in turn had reflected in the windshield and created the falsely perceived object. Happened all the time with his helmet faceplate, which was enough to convince him; he did not want to report anything in the first place. But, as the impression had been of something shooting up and over him, he naturally gazed down to see where it had come from.

Beneath him lay the moon's back side. Craters like lunar acne spotted the surface below as far as he could see—a thousand times more than on the face. Craters.

And one anomaly.

Unable to believe what he saw, Heffernan mashed his face up against the glass to peer over the nose of the skimmer just as the anomaly twinkled out of sight. Grabbing the control stick, he thumbed off automatic and nudged the ship down for a closer look.

In the shadow of the Cordillera Mountains stood a cluster of objects—he wanted to call them buildings but they looked more like enormous budding flowers. "Flowers in a vacuum?" he muttered at the preposterous idea. He could not say just what they were. Lights dotted the edges, running in sequence. He circled the structures, and decided that they reminded him of shiitake mushrooms, too.

Not far to the north were the landing pad lights of a second installation, which he knew to be the site where Stercus Pharmaceuticals refined raw Orbitol. The flower-buildings below had to be brand new. He couldn't figure how there hadn't been a whisper of scuttlebutt about them.

Abruptly, he realized that the people below would have been tracking him all the while. He was going to catch hell for being there instead of hauling in his payload. Now there would be even more trouble if he didn't report something. They would want to know what he was covering up. He trembled at the thought of an interrogation. The bastards would try to link him to some rebel subversion—they always did.

He hastily put in a call to Goertel, who was in the shack, supervising the check on the mass driver. Heffernan babbled a description of the weird structures. Goertel responded oddly. He didn't get excited; he didn't get angry. He got very quiet, something he had never done before, and gently told Heffernan to wait.

Five minutes passed without a reply. Heffernan began to sweat more than his suit could handle. If he had put his helmet on, the faceplate would have been flashing red. What was Goertel doing? Going through the corporate ranks with this?

A curt voice he didn't know made him jump when it spoke. "Pilot of SCS one-niner-five, return to colony base instantly. Acknowledge." He swallowed. "Fuck me," he muttered, then replied dully into the mike, "Copy."

"Land at Cargo Dock E to unload. Repeat, Cargo Dock E as in Edgar. Acknowledge and repeat."

Heffernan acknowledged the instruction. He imagined the corporate chucklehead who would meet him in the dock— a pink-faced suitboy who hadn't gotten to grind anyone into protein paste lately, who would read him the riot act, then slap him with a fat fine for deviating from his course. Christ, they *would* send him down for this; the structure had to be an SC operation, something experimental, part of the infamous "black budget" that everybody pretended did not exist.

If he'd had enough fuel, he might have tried for the closest Ichi-Plok *factorb*. As it was, he didn't have a prayer.

The landing pad lights flashed on and off in sync with computer display number three; the landing was automatic. Heffernan sat with his helmet on, ignoring the red square flashing in the lower right corner of the glass. He stared at the horizon indicator, his brain shocked to numbness, his stomach gurgling like an aerated drinking fountain.

Cargo Dock E lay at the farthest point from the main colony enclosures. The building itself, covered by a thick layer of lunar soil, looked like a buried cheese log on the moon's surface.

By the time the skimmer set down on the circular pad, the doors to Cargo Bay E had opened. Its crew would have been rudely rousted from their normal off-duty pastimes to unload the ilmenite he had recovered. On top of everything else, the dockers would now hate his ass. He wanted to die.

He pressed the pads at his wrists to seal the dry suit, then bounced back to the belly of the skimmer. A conical mesh bag twice his height contained the retrieved payloads, each one big as a packing crate.

He opened the hatch and cranked down the gangway. The ramp into the open cargo dock lay empty before him. There should have been a half dozen or more people there. There was no one. The inside of the dock glowed golden. The hatches stood snugly sealed. A vertical stack of canisters stood just at the edge of the ramp, where the floor flattened out.

"Son of a bitch," he muttered in furious despair. The corporate motherfuckers were going to make him haul the payloads all by himself.

He walked down the short gangway, grumbling fearfully. He could see one electric cart, parked up behind the canisters. He slogged up the ramp to get it, feeling like a third-stage Orbitol junkie—shunned, rejected, and all but invisible. His faceplate flickered crimson with information about his blood pressure and adrenaline level, which he ignored. The sweat breaking out everywhere told him everything anyway.

At the entrance to the cargo bay, his helmet radio abruptly clicked and hissed. He paused, leaning on the stack of eight canisters while he glanced around, expecting that someone was about to say something to him. Idly, he considered the labeling on the canisters: hydrazine. Nothing surprising in that. Hydrazine abounded on the Moon—a very useful form for storing nitrogen gas.

Like everyone else in the SC lunar facility, Heffernan had routinely been instructed in first aid regarding hydrazine's many noxious properties. Inhaled, it caused pulmonary edemas; spilled on the skin, it created unspeakable chemical burns while being rapidly absorbed as a poison into the body. Since he didn't work directly with the stuff, he had never thought much about it, and paid hardly any attention to that part of his first aid training. Not that there was much he could have done in any case.

He pushed away from them, taking a bounce down the ramp, when his radio clicked again. Now, for all his fear, he was getting annoyed at being jerked around.

He skidded to a stop and turned back angrily just as the canisters detonated.

In the first instant, the explosion was silent, like something witnessed through the window of the lunar shack. Then the blast caught him in a fist as big as Creation. His helmet roared. The faceplate shattered into him. He flew, punched like a nail through the side of the skimmer, and burst, ruptured in freeze-dried agony against the eighty-two netted cannon-balls.

1

Fat Farm in Space

Much later, after the fallout resulting from her exposé had settled, Thomasina Lyell would tell interviewers that the journalist in her had recognized unerringly, the first time they met, that she would encounter the man called Angel again.

The meeting itself was sheer accident; no one could have predicted it. Her presence on the orbiting Geosat station that day had nothing to do with him.

Lyell was exercising for a fifteen-year-old girl.

She pumped away at a good clip on her assigned stationary bicycle, right side up or maybe upside down or sideways; she couldn't say for sure. TV screens, pressed together like the quoins of an enormous vacuum-grown gem, hung in the center of the workout room, dozens of them, at every angle, to accommodate viewers on all the cycle machines in the gravityless environment, no matter what surface they might be bolted to. There were no windows, and the single exit door sealed snugly and invisibly in the left wall. The only constant point of reference was *toward the screens*, where every TV, at whatever angle, displayed the loud opening credits of "The President Odie Show."

Over two dozen floating lipoid athletes—Lyell nestled in among them—pedaled and heaved upon their machinery. They stared slackly at the screens to forget themselves, to escape the excruciation of weightless workout by shutting off their brains and acquiescing in scripted idiocy. Odie and Vice President Schnepfe felicitously dished up a story as lurid as a plate of intestines.

"Normally, you know," chimed the president, "we just have on board your and my favorite celebrities. And we *do* have with us the juggling prime minister of Lithuania later, so

7

don't switch satnets on me yet, folks. But our *first* guest—
I gotta tell you, this woman's story really moved me. I think
Schnepfe had a movement, too." Laughter, spattered applause,
a brief cut to Schnepfe, making hyperthyroid fish-eyes over the
joke. "This is Mrs. Akiko Alcevar, a widow and a registered
voter," said the president of the tiny Oriental woman at his
side. His digitized voice emerged again, out of the ensuing
applause, beguiling, insidious, a snake in sharkskin. "Or is
Akiko a widow? What you're about to hear may sound like—
well, like the kind of headline you'd expect to get from Alien
News Network or some other overproduced smegma—but it's
staggering, honest-to-*gawd* reality time. For you certainly,
hey, Akiko?" She nodded somewhere between Odie and the
camera, her lack of resolution injecting just the right amount
of believability into the performance. Lyell pedaled hell-bent,
trying hard to ignore it but trapped by the program's contriv-
ance of mystery. Usually, Odie and Schnepfe just bored her
to the point of self-immolation. This was not their characteristic show.

The screen filled with the president's face, which glistened,
his pores brimming like rain-fed puddles. "Maybe for *you*,
too . . . because Mr. Andre Alcevar, Akiko's ex and a former
Orbitol junkie—who went all the way to Orbitol decay—has
reappeared *from the beyond*! Don't believe me? See for yourself, yeah, yeah." The background exterior washed away like
topsoil; beneath it lay Odie's documentation—two enormous
photos side by side that the president and Mrs. Alcevar now
appeared to be walking across, studying them intently beneath
their feet. Both pictures were, of course, out of focus.

Lyell thought that the one on the right could as easily have
been a portrait of the Loch Ness Monster as of the late Andre
Alcevar. She'd worked with bad imaging in a few missing
persons hunts, but not *that* bad. She couldn't see why Odie
had gotten so revved up about it. His ratings must be down.
Elections *were* only eight months away. Time for bread and
circuses.

Her attention drifted from the screen to the individual faces
puffing away at crazy quilt angles. In weightlessness faces
tended to inflate, so that all those in the room looked as if
they had Esquimau forebears. None of the faces, puffed up or
not, belonged to the girl she was hunting. None she'd spoken

to had been able to offer Lyell any help in locating Tamiami Trayle. Nonetheless, she touched her arm just above the elbow and, by turning her head smoothly from side to side, began recording them all.

The girl had run away from home. Her parents—her father most aggressively—had hired Lyell to find her and bring her back. A credit trace had revealed that Tamiami had shuttled up to the Geosat, suggesting that she was dead serious about getting away from her family. But Geosats as salvation were a pipe-dreamed nightmare. Runaways of all demeanors, hungry for some kind of temporary security before their parents' credit disks filled up or were turned off, jockeyed for jobs that hadn't been there to begin with. Lyell had combed the docks, hunted through boutiques, food kiosks, and virtual-sex shops—most of them ScumberCorp franchises, finally narrowing her search to the station's arms. The arms didn't spin as the core of the Geosat did, and therefore had no gravity. A handful of business ventures had figured out how to utilize zero-g profitably; mostly the arms represented storage space, and dutifully she inquired at every cargo office. When she had eliminated every place else on the satellite, Stardance Weightless Weightloss remained. She checked herself in for the full treatment.

Thomasina Lyell, private investigative journalist—*pijin* for short—had gleaned a wealth of information about SWW in two days. The main thing she'd discovered was that the Stardance staff had an obsession with group dynamics. They wanted the customers bound by a reductive identity, a collective impetus to burn off fat. It was this group bonding that was interfering with her quest. Clients associated strictly with their own group. Other groups—and there were at least three she knew of—had no contact with them at all. Tamiami, if she were here, was in some other group, watching some other bank of TVs.

Odie's two unfocused photos of the late Mr. Alcevar had now been incrementally and dramatically enhanced. They appeared to reveal the same face. Scornfully, Lyell shook her head, fanning droplets of perspiration into the air.

Any video artist with a stylus could have executed the entire enhancement effect—including the odd lumps on the right-hand face—in under half an hour. The time had long since passed where fraud looked any different from truth. Nevertheless, here was the president of the United States presenting the argument that a man had actually returned from the far side of death. Or what was supposed to be death, since no one truly knew what Orbitol decay was.

She finished her slow pan of the room, then resignedly reached over and gripped her left arm again, pressing her fingertips against the switch that shut off the nose ring cam on her right nostril. Its lens had the appearance of a perfect star sapphire glistening against her dark skin. She could have produced a compilation disk of all the grotesquely distorted faces that had squashed up close to adore it.

She leaned down and applied herself strenuously to an all-out sprint. The session was nearly over, not more than a few minutes left. She didn't need the workout particularly but wanted the endorphin high. She had always been large-boned and the slightest bit plump, and already in four days she had worked off all her excess weight. Everyone lost weight at Stardance. Everyone.

Lyell had one alternative remaining. Over the past two days, she'd struck up a tense association—it could hardly be called friendship—with the group trainer, whose name was Nance, in the hope of getting a look at the lists of the other squads. The whole business was requiring extraordinary finesse. As was the case with so many people on the Geosats, Nance had hired on with Stardance in the fervent hope of hitching a ride to the Moon or Mars colonies. She was not about to screw up her chances by allowing some Earth-bound investigator to take a peek at confidential data. What she was willing to do was meet Lyell away from the weight loss center—on the main ring of the spinning station—and to listen and, maybe, to talk.

The bell chimed and the TV screens went dead, signaling the end of the exercise period. Lyell wondered how things had turned out for Akiko Alcevar and her ridiculously resurrected hubby. With a certain amount of self-reproach, she hoped that Nebergall was recording it so she could find out. Her whole life she had had a weak spot for nonsense like that.

One by one the group unbelted from their cycle harnesses and grabbed the rungs of zero-g ladders to pull themselves toward the door. To Lyell it was like watching the migration of mutant Galapagos tortoises, their bodies marked with almost identical rings and swatches of sweat. A pond of sweat had developed just above her breasts; none on her legs, another oddity of weightlessness.

The door slid open on cue. Lyell caught hold of an overhead rung and swung behind the pack to the exit. Nance stood braced outside the doorway, a "drop-dead" look on her freckled face as the bodies bobbed past. She acted as if she didn't notice Lyell.

Sound trilled through the green corridor beyond—a peaceful susurration of waterfalls, a soothing twitter of jungle birds. The group thinned out as exhausted individuals returned to their cubicles to strip down and rinse off in a shower bag before gathering for the small noon meal. Lyell decided she had savored enough nasty diet pastes for the rest of her life.

She continued past her cubicle, moving hand over hand into the reception area of Stardance. The pop-eyed male secretary strapped in behind the desk realized her intentions when she didn't slow down. "You know, that's very ill-advised," he called after her. "Have you consulted your trainer? You only hurt yourself when you stray."

"If I can't hurt myself, who can I hurt?" she called back. The clear doors with the red SWW logo slapped across them opened, and she swung on into the main tube.

Even as Lyell stuck her feet into two foot cups on the automatic beltway down the center of the tube, she broke out in a new sweat. Anticipation of the return to gravity settled upon her like a batwinged phobia.

The belt moved her along past mostly blank doorways, empty compartments. *Flotation Dreams*, a gel-sleep therapy center, was the only other thriving weightless business on this arm.

The belt deposited her in front of a rotating air lock. Grasping the rails on each side, she bobbed inside and then dangled as the inner door performed a countdown. When it slid back, a wide second doorway dropped into place and Lyell stepped through onto the spinning hub of the platform wheel. Instantly, the pressure of half an atmosphere clutched at her like an invisible slime. She clung to two more rails while vertigo threatened her. It passed in a moment, leaving her to other ailments.

Her feet seemed to be melting into the floor and in response, her legs knotted up hard as stone. Her breasts tugged heavily at her rib cage. She tottered along like a sailor trying to adjust her sea legs to land after years upon the waves. Instinct propelled her. Signs guided her to the elevators.

She wiped the salty sting of sweat from her eyes; she was unused to its tickle running down her face. Probably, she now realized, she should have taken a shower first and changed into dry clothes; but she could never have run the gauntlet from weightlessness to this demoralizing shuffle a second time.

Her left calf cramped up. She hopped into a waiting elevator car, clumsily pressed "D" to the debarkation deck, then doubled over and grabbed her leg. Groaning, she dug her thumbs into the agonizing clutch of muscle. The elevator car rumbled unsteadily up the shaft.

D-deck consisted of little more than shops along a tubeway—movie libraries, bookwalls, spicy take-away foods—the sorts of places that could fit into confined niches. Lyell had hit them all on her hunt.

She bought a taco on her way to the lounge. The extruded meat had undoubtedly never been alive, but that didn't matter. The beans were real, the green sauce tangy and hot. After days of bland paste, the big flour taco was pure manna.

People glanced curiously at her as she limped past. Escapees from the weight loss academy would be few. Most of the layover clientele wouldn't know or care that it even existed.

She finished the taco, licked her fingers, then wiped them on her sweat suit. The spice made her sniffle. On Earth it would have been enough to send her clawing for a liter of water.

The deck echoed with the sound of piped-in gentle rain. She lingered for a moment at a windowall. The view, effected by mirror and fiber systems, was of the Earth below. She identified clouds delineating the southern trade winds off the tip of Brazil. She smiled, and wondered how, after seeing a view like this, the likes of Nance could elect to flee that world forever. There would always be a percentage of humanity who did not mind letting everybody else clean up after them. In fact, she decided as she looked over the crowd in the corridor, a large percentage.

She walked on. The Way-Station Lounge, where she was to meet Nance, lay at the far end of the tube, near the docking stems. It was no bigger than the other shops, but, with the liquors concealed in their containers behind the wall, most of the space was given over to small tables and chairs, enough for fifteen or so people if nobody farted—for which reason alone there would not be any carbonated drinks on hand.

She ordered up a glass of cold *pertsovka*. It was touted as the most popular drink among the platform crews, and Lyell understood why immediately—she could taste it even over the afterburn of taco sauce. Vodka and hot peppers. "The spice of life," she said to the Oriental bartender after she took her first tentative sip. He wore a red name tag: Skip. She wondered if he thought he was on his way to Mars, too. Sure, they would need bartenders on Mars.

She moved over to one of the small tables and sat down to wait for Nance. For a while she continued massaging the last of the charley horse out of her leg.

If the lounge had been much larger or busier, she might have missed the three who arrived after her: two men, with a third man pressed between them. She sized up the relationship that way from the contrasting attitudes of the three. In the mirror behind the bar, the two on the end—one pale, freckled redhead and one dark-skinned black—wore the expressions of men looking forward to their drinks. The man between them was another matter.

What he was thinking could not be judged easily. The right side of his face—over the bridge of the nose and down the cheek—couldn't be seen beneath a metal headpiece and lens. Hospitals used such electronic calottes, she knew, in cases where brain circuitry needed rerouting around damaged tissue. Accident victims, for instance. The impression hardened when he failed to respond to the bartender's query. The redhead nudged him. He shook his head. He'd been listening after all but wanted nothing.

Lyell's glance fell to his hands, but he wore no manacles. Nevertheless, she assumed he was a prisoner. Having served three months in the penal colony of Corson's Island, she recognized the unmistakable look—a face that had used up its defensive expressions of self-esteem and denial, body language of a captive overwhelmed by the machinery of justice. The man was darkly handsome—or would have been without the headgear. His blue jumpsuit looked as though he had slept in it for days—and all at once Lyell realized that she was looking at a Moon colony uniform, and she idly pretended to scratch her elbow, switching on the nose-cam. Maybe the weight loss gig wouldn't be a complete failure after all.

The man in the middle caught her staring at him. He glanced back at her indifferently, then past her, out the lounge doorway, at nothing. He hadn't killed anyone or he *would* have been shackled, and probably not allowed to enter inhabited platform areas during layover no matter how much his officers wanted a short one. Something else, then. A mystery. . . .

Lyell downed the rest of her vodka. The pepper burned lovingly in her throat. She got up and went to the bar. "I'll have another," she told Skip.

The black man beside her made the next step easier. He looked at her and said wryly, "What did you do, jog through the park?"

Thomasina stared smilingly into his eyes, to tell him how attractive she found him. She let her gaze slide to the one in the middle as if by accident. "You're out of the Moon colony, aren't you?" she asked. Peripherally, she saw Skip hesitate and glance up from the drink nozzle.

The black man nodded, but with a vaguely disquieted look as if he wished now that he had kept his mouth shut.

"SC miners, I'll bet."

"Well." He sipped his drink, caught between the desire to leave and the desire to enjoy what he was paying Geoplatform prices to savor. He tried to ease out of it. "Isn't everybody?"

She laughed lightly, which was what he'd wanted. "I just wondered what it was like up there, you know, as compared to down here." He started to answer but she continued, "I mean, you talk to anybody on the platform here, there isn't anybody can imagine why colonists would go *back* to Earth."

"Who said we were?" sneered the redhead.

"Oh, come on. You didn't come all this way to drink on a *company* platform."

"You're awfully nosy, lady."

She gave a coquettish pout to her expression—it felt so good being able to use her face again—to keep the nearer man in sympathy with her. She would get good sharp close-ups of all three of these men. "It's just that we don't see many workers on their way down from the Moon to the Earth."

"So what are you, the Welcome Wagon? We're dropping our friend off. He's cycled down. People do that."

She pretended to study the man in the middle for the first time. "You look like you had an accident."

The other two became noticeably more edgy but they needn't have worried, because the one in the middle said nothing, just stared somewhere out the door.

"What's your friend's name?"

"Do you mind if we finish our fucking drinks without being bothered by you?" asked the redhead.

"Hey, lighten up, now," the man beside her warned him. "Lady, don't get me wrong, but we've got a twenty-minute layover and we'd prefer to relax one little last time before we have to deal with the stink of Philly air again. You see what I'm saying?"

"But you can't mean you're going to *my* hometown, to Philadelphia? Well, of course you are, you're with ScumberCorp. You and Mr.—"

"Rueda, his name's Angel Rueda," the redhead blurted out, "and he's not being talkative today, which is his prerogative. Why don't you try it yourself?"

She stiffened indignantly, took her drink, and walked back to her small table. She took her time with the second drink, letting the camera do all the work while she ignored the trio altogether.

Nance arrived, gave the trio a cautious look, then sat beside Lyell. "All right," she said immediately, "who the fuck are you, lady, and what do you want with Tami?"

Lyell pretended to have been aware of this from the start. "You know where she is," she said.

Nance said something else but Lyell didn't catch it. Her attention had been snagged by the trio, leaving.

She glanced their way casually, as if she had already forgotten them, to find Angel Rueda staring at her with the strangest look in his one dark eye. It stayed with her long after he and his escort had disappeared down the tubeway.

It was a look of something like forlorn hope.

2
Life in the Pit

Amerind Shikker arrived in the subterranean world of the disued subway concourse against her will, trussed up naked in scraps of her clothing and thrown down the steps into the darkness. Her neighbors—her "friends"—were the culprits. They thought she'd gone crazy, and maybe they were half right. She'd killed a man, cut his dick off. He had shown her who he was, was why.

He was an Orbiter for sure. He had the burn marks on his temples where he fired the injector gun, so she would have known anyway. But the fucker's right leg had vanished from the knee down, which became apparent when he crouched next to her and his pant legs, too short to begin with, pulled halfway up his calves.

He didn't have any socks, and he didn't have any right leg, either.

His left leg was raw with flea bites. The right just wasn't there. She wondered if the fleas had been erased, too. His shoe looked to be empty; she could see straight through to the tear in the sole.

He hadn't liked her seeing that, and that was when he had begun his singsong ditty about "not bein' a kid, and not bein' a skipper." She supposed, with that leg, he likely couldn't skip if he wanted to.

Amerind knew something of Orbitol and its long-term effects—enough to stay away from it.

"What the hell you muttering?" she had asked the john.

"I'm your fun-loving man," came his reply. He was grinning by then, an off-kilter smile, and she ought to have known better; but she needed the business.

" 'course you are, sweetie."

"Jack the Ripper," he had announced with pride.

Amerind had never heard of him but didn't say so. He'd paid, and she needed the money. She didn't care if he was fresh off a prison isle in the Atlantic. A lot of her clients were.

He'd settled over her face and sunk in as far as he could go. He wasn't very big. His dirty fingers grabbed up her tits, began kneading. He was rough, but she'd known rougher. She didn't understand his true intention until she felt the cold shock of his blade against her rib. He was trying to slice her tit off. Without hesitation, she dug furiously under her pillow and pulled out her flick-knife. He was cackling and trying to saw up under her tit; his dull blade carved a fire in her side, at once icy and hot. His butt and legs squashed her movement, trapping her other arm; she wrestled but couldn't get past them. She bent her wrist till she thought it would break, slid her blade up under his pants, right across her nose, and stabbed hard. Blood, hot and black, jetted all over her face. Jack began shrieking and clawing at himself, but she couldn't budge the bastard. His blood poured out in a torrent and she was drowning. The Ripper twisted one way and Amerind, still holding onto the slick knife, twisted the other. He toppled headfirst onto the cardboard floor beside her blankets. His blood sprayed feathery across the trembling wall of her little box. Coughing, choking, she spat out blood and his excised member. It bounced off his skull and rolled along the floor beside him like a little gray sausage link.

While the bastard Ripper shrieked and twitched in the final moments of his life, Amerind's neighbors poked their heads in through the ratty curtain. Their faces seemed to swell up at the sight of her, all naked and bloody. The Ripper's disease had spread to them, she could tell, and Amerind yowled and swiped her knife at the fiends before they could finish cutting her up. They backed off out of sight, but not for long.

The curtain lunged at her. It tore off its nails, grew hands that reached for her, and two bodies slammed into Amerind and pinned her to her bed. Maybe she stabbed one of them. She couldn't be sure. The curtain twisted them all up. But they got the knife away from her.

Their hands swarmed all over her, shredding the curtain with her knife, taking her skirt, her sheets, making bindings and a gag. Ripper's blood, thick upon her, hid her own flowing wound. She kicked and writhed and screeched like a banshee, looking like something equally fantastic.

They hoisted her and carried her through the narrow aisles of Box City, up and down the black slate walk, past the Liberty Bell, and into the street. Her flesh in the daylight was sallow where it wasn't bloody.

From out of the foamboard and plywood and plastic shacks, people emerged, drawn by the noisy parade. She saw their breath smoke like fires, their faces stinging pink in the chill morning air.

A cheering, crazy crowd accreted. She, like a flayed sacrifice, hung up ahead of it all. Appropriately, her black hair glistened with blood.

By the time they reached 9th and Chestnut Streets, Amerind had recovered her senses and was pleading for her life, but the gag kept her protestations mute, and, besides, the matter of disposing of her had become a festival. She did not hate them for it exactly. She thought this might be God's fit punishment for the times when she had taken part, when she had urged other hands to throw other sacrifices into the Snake Pit. That was what they called the unknown depths of Market East Station.

All kinds of stories existed about what lurked down there, on various levels, in endless tunnels, in dark recesses where no sane citizen—not even derelicts such as themselves—would venture. Graffiti glyphs on the walls shouted spraypaint warnings of the contaminating madness down there.

If only they would let her explain . . . but they flung her down the steps as if she were a sack of garbage. She tumbled and rolled, struck her elbow and cried out at the pain, struck her head and lost consciousness.

To those above, watching, the bluish dark of the Snake Pit swallowed her whole. Everyone cheered.

Amerind awoke to hands as delicate as bat wings softly caressing her. The darkness was so pure that she thought she had been blinded, and in a panic she tried swatting at the hands. Her right arm hardly moved, and that little motion slashed the perfect darkness with lightning bolts of agony. The gentle hands withdrew. A moment later the wick of a lumpish candle flared to life beside her.

She found herself inside a box hardly larger than the one she had been thrown out of, except that this one had a funny little barred window and a bench. She was lying beside the bench.

Holding the candle was a man she at first took to be wearing black livery. Then she realized that she was looking through most of him.

Seeing her astonishment, he tried to reassure her with a smile, but this was complicated by the absence of most of the left half of his face. "I fixed your arm," he explained softly, too embarrassed to look at her directly. He took a brown cloak off a hook by the window and wrapped himself inside it; his invisible body took on substance; folds of drapery outlined a spindly torso. It was a kind of magic trick—hey, presto! and now you see him.

"It's fractured," he said, "the ulna, just behind the wrist. Lucky that's all, the way the topsiders threw you." She wondered if he'd been watching the whole time. He floated nearer, his one blue eye wide as if with hysteria. "I'll f-find you some clothes, how would that be? My name's G-Glimet." When he moved the candle aside, she saw the ancient scars at his temple and knew that he wasn't a ghost.

Glimet was the most decayed Orbiter she'd ever seen.

He had been reduced to his right arm and shoulder, and the right half of his head and neck. Any sane man would have sought rehabilitation long before that, she thought. Most anybody would have turned back when their toes and fingers went, but not Glimet. Clearly he was forging ahead into uncharted territory.

She had been told that final-stage Orbiters simply vanished like ghosts, like smoke. Until then, their bodies maintained some tenuous connection to this world. She'd met plenty such in her line of work. Some offered to let her feel their "missing" limbs—she had only acted on the offer once, the first time. Her fingers, waving through the air, had pressed into something spongy that she couldn't see, that wasn't there. Just remembering the sensation made her skin crawl. She had been scared for a month afterward that the change was contagious, that any day her body would start to rot out of existence the same way. She'd asked everyone who knew, or pretended to know, all about it. Ex-Orbiters told her tales, like old seafarers: it was sticking your hands or feet in cold cooking grease, and forever after you had to drag yourself through thick jelly that you could never see or get away from one inch. It slowed them all down, and made some go crazy. But then if you stuck on a sock or a glove, there were the missing toes and fingers again, like out of that magic hat—here and not here.

The extremities went first. And usually, once their toes or fingers began to disappear, they got themselves weaned off the shit in a hurry. *She* would have. She had never seen anything like this piece of a man, this floating ghost. How long it must have taken him to end up this way. How many Orbits. Did it ache so good that he couldn't be without it? There would be visions, wouldn't there? Christ, how the stupid fuckers all babbled about their visions.

Without drawing closer, Glimet offered her the hissing candle, placing it carefully on the bench above her. Then, true to his word, he set off in search of clothes. She watched him float in slow lurches, as if walking underwater.

The moment he was gone Amerind worked her way up to a sitting position, discovering that she had no clothes, nothing to cover her grimy, blood-drenched nakedness but the shreds of cloth she'd come wrapped in. She couldn't leave if she wanted to.

Tilting toward the candle, she carefully lifted her wounded breast and found that her savior had pressed a thick piece of batting there to stanch the bleeding. Glimet might be crazy, but at least he wasn't bad. The gash throbbed but she wasn't about to peel off the batting. She leaned back, and took stock of her surroundings.

What place was this long tall box? The walls were rough wood with a few flakes of green paint still attached. There was a narrow shelf below the barred window, and half a dozen cans—most without labels—stacked on it. Outside the bars she couldn't see anything. The walls showed holes where things had been screwed into them once, but all those things were gone, maybe to make more room. It would be cozy for one person. With all the thermal blankets Glimet had stuffed in the box, it was downright warm.

Amerind found herself trembling with the effort of sitting up. She gathered the covers around her, burrowing down into them, and drew her knees up halfway. The candle threw wavering shadows past her.

Her trembling grew after awhile to a body-racking shiver. She couldn't make it stop. She hugged her knees to her belly; her teeth began clacking together. The world peeled back. Her thoughts fumbled muzzily along, slowing, drifting. The shaking drained from her limbs, leaving her limp with exhaustion.

She was nearly asleep when Glimet returned. He set aside the discarded clothes he had brought her and floated closer to lay his right hand across her shiny forehead. Hot. Sweat had made stripes in the blood on her face.

He tried to smooth her hair back, but it had stiffened into knotty clumps: she had bled from her scalp. His fingers tangled, tugged. She winced, but was too exhausted and confused to do more than mutter. He leaned over her.

She had high cheeks and long lashes beneath full, thick brows. Deep lines around her eyes. More than that he couldn't tell, except that he found in her face an illusive perfection. He patted her hair lightly so as not to snarl his fingers again.

Glimet couldn't remember when he'd last been with a woman. A couple of times in the early days while he was orbiting, but that had been years back. His body didn't seem much interested in the notion now. Sex had no importance on the other side. To get all the way to there—that was all that mattered.

He fitted his palm over his eye and sat back on the blankets and rugs. A crooked smile bent his face. He did not notice as he began to jabber about the Other Place.

He took his hand away and reconsidered Amerind. "Maybe you'd wanna go with me," he said. "I-I would take you, sure I would. You're so beautiful, sure. But you haven't even started, have you? You've never flown, and I've almost finished." He hovered over her, his single eye round with inspiration. "I know what," he said. He nodded to himself, then blew out the candle. Dreamily, she sensed him lying down against her back.

He stared into a world that Amerind Shikker had never seen. The deep darkness offered a perfect canvas against which to view it. "Would you like to?" he asked, although she'd said nothing. "Maybe there's a way." But she had already fallen asleep.

3

Gansevoort & the Gang of Four

Everyone was watching him; they just weren't looking. Emerging from his cubicle, Ton Gansevoort immediately, nervously, scanned the whole office. No one looked up; no one even glanced his way. He had become invisible against the tan dividers, the desks and cabinets and ergonomic furnishings. That was how he knew that they knew that he'd been ordered upstairs.

"Hold all my calls, Cheryl," he told his assistant as he swept past her. "Cancel everything." He didn't want to see her expression, no matter what it was. He heard the twist of humiliation in his voice. Shame scorched his cheeks.

One morning during his second-grade year of school, little Ton had shat himself in the middle of class. Unable to conceal the fact—too afraid to raise his hand and excuse himself to the bathroom—he'd locked up, scalded with shame. The sweetly awful stench had permeated the entire classroom. The teacher, a cold, mean-spirited old bitch named Battlecourt, had only to look at him to identify the culprit. In front of everyone she demanded to know if there was something he wanted to share with them, as if shitting in his pants were a part of "Show and Tell." *Everyone* had known. Their eyes had stabbed him in the back like a hundred poisoned arrows.

He had read somewhere that moments of such absolute terror could alter brain chemistry, actually change the path of neurotransmitter flow forever. He was living proof. Second-grade mortification fed the flames of adult terror, as autonomic as his heartbeat, leaping as it did from the pit of his soul.

He dissembled as best he could by concentrating on his reflection in the brown marble floor tiles; but at the doorway he couldn't help turning to survey the room.

Still no one looked up. They must have sensed his radiating shame from the doorway. They needed for him to leave so that, behind his back, they might lift their heads, trade their knowing glances, and begin their scheming—forging quick *quid pro quo* relationships in preparation for any sudden restructuring of the department. He imagined their salivating in anticipation of his decline.

Beyond his coworkers—beyond the blue-tinted, etched-glass cubicles in which they dwelt—green floor-length curtains separated a broad row of high windows. He looked out upon a familiar view of the tower in which he resided (it was one of his favorite jokes that he could keep an eye on himself from either vantage point). He wished that he were across the plaza now, in his cramped apartment, hiding safely.

Excommunicated, he walked out into the *conveyidor* and stepped onto the metal belt. Only one lift serviced the COs' suite, totally private and set back from the rest of the offices. He watched other faces passing him on the opposite belt, faces he hardly knew. Many of the men sported the new, studded, high ruff collars. Gansevoort was sadly behind the times where fashion was concerned. He never felt quite comfortable in his work clothes. He wished now that he had bought a new wardrobe, if only to look smart before the four officers, as if the right attire might somehow salvage his career. ("We were going to fire you, old man, but now that we've seen what a sharp dresser you are, we've decided to turn over the reins of the company to you.")

Recent rumors abounded that ScumberCorp had been divesting itself of unsatisfactory subsidiaries—Lopango Chemicals and Ars Gratis Entertainments definitely, and maybe a half dozen other companies whose true ownership couldn't even be ascertained. Such gossip always hinted at layoffs and personnel cuts. He believed, if there were to be layoffs, they would start in the very core of personnel, in Human Resources itself. What better way to clean house than to dismiss that threadbare local HR Manager, Gansevoort? He was the obvious target—the COs could smell the shit in his pants from all the way up on the top floor, twenty-five years away.

He rode the conveyer as if it carried him to the guillotine, and spent the time combing through his life, zeroing in on an endless string of mistakes, certain that each one contributed to his doom. He had never felt competent in his job: he had always suspected there were hidden quotas he'd failed to fill, competitors he should have enticed into the company, job duties he'd carelessly overlooked. He didn't know what he'd done, but he knew he was guilty of something and always had been, since at least the second grade if not from before birth. If he had been on his way into heaven, Ton Gansevoort would have talked himself into hell.

The belt delivered him to the main foyer. There he confronted a glass and gold construct of the SC logo into which was built a display case containing four heads—three males and one female—Gotoh, Sherk, Kosinus, and Rajcevich. *Extraordinarily* realistic LifeMasks of the four COs. Their beautiful eyes followed his approach.

To his mind the company logo looked like a snake about to eat its own tail.

The heads began to speak. "Mars Colony," said the first, the Japanese face.

"If not today, then tomorrow," the second, Kosinus, added.

"Sure," Gansevoort muttered.

"If not this generation, then the next," the head of the third man proposed.

Gansevoort knew the speech; he couldn't remember a time when they hadn't been promising to take mankind to glory. He recited along with the head of the woman, Rajcevich: "A new world will open to us and return mankind to greatness. On Mars."

She smiled at him, expressing her pride in his knowledge, as if he were her son.

He passed the logo as the fourth head began a long recitation of the company's many successes. Without an audience, the speech cut off after a few seconds, and the heads rested again.

The masks had been in place for over twenty years. Gansevoort couldn't imagine what the Gang of Four (as nearly everyone called them) looked like now. He would find out, he figured despondently, all too soon.

A woman named Fulrod ran the officers' private lift. She was a wizened little gnome really, a fairy-tale troll guarding a bridge; she'd been squatting there in her little blue glass booth since the Declaration of Independence had been signed. Possibly she wasn't even real. Her head like a dish antenna tracked his approach. Her severe haircut uncovered her jug ears. He thought he saw them twist like surface-search radar antennae.

In the voice of his second-grade teacher, she said, "You're expected, Mr. Gansevoort." Then she smiled. He almost burst into tears.

She must have hit a hidden switch, because the deco-crafted door of the lift slid aside on cue.

Gansevoort passed her, his lips in a paralyzed curl, desperately making a great show of being in control and at ease. It was at times like these that floor tiles buckled to trip you, or furniture shifted to snag your trousers, or the elevator cable snapped and the car sheared your body in two just as you were stepping in.

He took his place in the redwood-paneled car. His knuckles had gone white; if he hadn't already chewed his nails down, they would have dug into his palms. The door rolled smoothly shut. There was almost no perception of movement, just a single flashing green light in the panel.

The door opened again, upon a foreign scene—walls of *fusuma* design, all constructed of pale mounted rice paper, sliding panels enclosing this small room like the chamber in the heart of a maze; shift the panels and change the true path. Black glacé leather cushions lined the wall to his left, separated in the middle by a sunken rock garden full of bulbous, even phallic, cacti. Huge needles. The floor was bare wood.

At the far end of the room, another man sat with his shoes off, his legs folded. He held a cup and saucer. A red-glazed teapot stood on a small table in front of him. He was wearing a black suit, a high, studded red collar, and a multicolored silk scarf. He was slender, with a leonine profile accentuated by the straight fall of blond hair off the back of his head. So still was he that he might have been a piece of ornamentation. Gansevoort shuddered.

This is my replacement.

"Mr. Gansevoort," a voice called, disrupting his preoccupation. The voice came from behind the sliding rice paper screens. "Come in, sit down." He stepped out of the elevator car. "Ah, your shoes, if you would." He took them off, leaving them beside the stranger's expensive ones. His right blue sock had a small hole in it over the big toe, and he cringed. How much could they see?

He chose a cushion this side of the cactus, away from the other man but not so far away as to appear intimidated—at least, that was his rationale in selecting it. He was sure he lacked the flexibility to adopt the position the other man sat in, but he folded up his right leg to hide the hole in his sock.

The voice asked him if he wanted some tea but he declined. Tea went straight through him, and he didn't want to have to raise his hand and excuse himself in the middle of a meeting as important as this. His body prickled with renewed sweating.

The voice said, "Mr. Gansevoort, we want to introduce you to Mr. Mingo." He leaned out past the cacti to see if they meant the other man. Expressionless, the blond Mingo nodded slightly to him.

"Mr. Mingo is a troubleshooter for the company, specializing in Human Resource problems."

Oh, Christ, thought Gansevoort, *here it comes.*

"It was our original intention to say nothing of his arrival to you, but Mingo insisted we bring you in, as you will be—technically at least—his acting superior."

Gansevoort leaned forward again and took another look at the other's sharp, supercilious profile.

"In reality, of course, he's answerable only to us, and we anticipate you won't even know he's in place most of the time, which is the way someone in Mingo's position prefers it."

"He's an efficiency expert? You're planning to make cuts in personnel?"

"As few as possible," replied the voice. He thought he overheard a soft chuckle. He wondered which one of the males this was, which mask matched the voice. "However, he may require of you some staff; in fact he does already need—what?—half a dozen?—security people, for a small operation on SC Plaza level."

"Ah, well, that should be no problem. We have lots of idle security people." He could hardly keep from trembling with excitement. They weren't going to *fire* him, they were singling him out for a special assignment!

"No problem, you say. Glad to hear it. There, you see, Mingo was right. Should point out—yes, I should—that your salary will be raised a full six percent to compensate you for any extra work you might have to do. It's in the nature of Mingo's explorations that he may conceivably need your assistance, or intervention, at inconvenient hours. You understand?"

"Oh, certainly, sir. Anything." He meant it, too. Not only *not* fired, but promoted! "I don't know what to say."

"Say that we can rely on you completely as we have for so long."

He jumped to his feet. "Sir, you can!"

"Well, good. Fine."

Wouldn't everyone be buying him drinks tonight? The whole office would want to hear the details of *this* meeting. But, hold on, maybe that wasn't such a hot idea. If Mingo were scoping out personnel, he wouldn't do himself any good by spreading stories to that effect, even true ones. If it got back to Mingo . . . He'd have to say *some*thing, though, if he wanted to keep speculation from spreading. The call-up was too extraordinary to dismiss out of hand without all sorts of remonstrations from disgruntled coworkers. Just tell about the promotion, sure. Make himself sound important. He'd been doing such a terrific job that they'd wanted to tell him personally—

"Mr. Gansevoort!"

"I'm sorry?"

"If you would sit down, there's a further related matter we must discuss with you." He sat and the voice asked, "What do you know of *Xau Dâu*?"

He hesitated to answer while he tried to guess how much he was supposed to know versus what gossip had passed through his office. Guardedly, he replied, "I suppose, what everyone knows. Does this . . . involve them?"

A new voice broke in. It was the woman, Rajcevich. "The subject is not his concern."

"We agreed Jean—"

"We did *not*, unless my opinion counts for nothing. How do we know he won't spread what he hears to everyone. We've never used him before. I haven't even studied his file yet."

"You won't, will you, Gansevoort?"

"No, *never*," he said. He almost drew an "X" over his heart but stopped himself.

"See? Thoroughly reliable."

"Oh, Kosinus, you're preposterous. Who is this man? A middle manager, for God's sake—his life's ambition is to keep his weight down! I'm telling you, this breach of protocol will come back upon us."

"Madame thinks her name is Cassandra," observed a third, accented voice, which opened the floor to competitive bickering.

"People in the colony are already suspicious, Huston—"

"—Bickham and Ichiban-Plokazhopski wait like two mountains—"

"—we'll surpass all competition when this is over. The angel—"

"I tell you, Jean, he's completely *reliable*."

"—knows nothing!"

In the midst of it, Gansevoort sensed more than saw Mingo unfold himself and rise to his feet. He stepped to the cactus arrangement and snapped a particularly long needle off the tallest succulent. He smiled apologetically at Gansevoort, as if the bickering were somehow his responsibility. He had the palest blue eyes, and curving white lashes like the spines of a flytrap. Swinging about, he took two quick steps to the nearest sliding screen. His arm whipped across it. The caterwauling ceased, immediately replaced by squeals and shouts. One of the males shouted, "Mingo!" as a large polygon of rice paper uncurled from the center of the screen and fluttered to the ground. Through the hole Gansevoort saw hulking shadows against an intaglioed ceiling. A moment later a new screen slammed into place behind the hole.

Mingo dropped the cactus needle.

"What do you think you're *doing*?"

He seated himself again on the squeaky black cushion and poured himself a cup of tea. After taking a sip, he spoke as if into the cup: "Making a point."

From behind the screens came muttered sibilance, a hot, whispered debate, followed by a long pause.

Then the voice of Kosinus addressed Gansevoort again. "Mr. Gansevoort, please pay no heed to our petty squabble. It happens all the time. Mr. Mingo will be in contact with you about those security arrangements," Kosinus told him. "That's all, dear fellow, you may go now."

Nonplussed, Gansevoort got up, stealing one final glance at Mingo, seated contemplatively, like a gecko on a branch. "Thank you," Gansevoort said, although he wasn't sure who among them he was supposed to be thanking. "I'll put together a team for you right away."

"Nothing to it. Thank *you* for agreeing to see us." As if he'd been offered a choice.

But I didn't see you at all, he thought as the lift door opened. Before it had closed, the arguing began again; the man Mingo had turned back into statuary.

Gansevoort stood in the silent lift, his head swimming with open-ended implications and a feeling that he'd just stepped through a mirror. Something very strange was going on. He had been stuffed into the middle of it—led into a very real lion's den and come out the other side miraculously intact. For the moment that was cause to celebrate.

Later, in his apartment across the plaza, the worrying would begin, followed by a fatalistic certainty that everything, including the carrot of a promotion, was a heinous trick of some sort perpetrated upon him by the four Invisible Gods.

Good news *always* preceded disaster, didn't it?

4

A New Assignment

"The best model we have for explaining the effects of Orbitol derives from a theory of wholeness more than half a century old," said the mustachioed man on the TV cubes. "But in fact, it's about the only model we have so far that fits."

Rick Nebergall sat in a large, converted walk-in closet. He wore a flannel shirt with rips in the shoulder seams, black denims, and gray point-toed boots that he had propped on the CG shelf. A multipurpose keyboard lay in his lap, allowing him to shift through the effects spectrum from character generation to resolution pegging. Twenty-one small, high-resolution TV monitor cubes surrounded him. Fewer than half—a large cluster in the center grouped around a single, larger screen—displayed the face of the speaker. The remainder offered Nebergall still frames of altogether different images, most of them moody and dark, in the piece he was editing; as the speaker continued, the various stills kicked into motion one at a time, threading smoothly into the final mix.

Nebergall watched the various displays, nodding at the time counter as each bit of footage began. Each part intersected with the next fixed moment, which had gone into motion, fading up into the master disk, which played on the central monitor. It was all pretimed; nevertheless, he toggled between them, stopping and backing up when he didn't like where or how a segment came in, seeking ways to F/X the fade up—allowing specific visual elements to rise first or dropping them into place in jarring contrast to what had come before, the quick cut timed to a key word. He paused, backed up, and launched the recordings again and again, lasers turning light into bits of speech that he would hear a thousand times before he'd finished. Images would burn like woodcuts into his synapses.

He rewound to where the speaker's face was on the main screen, the face vaguely sad, the eyes hollow, tired, absolutely sincere; then he recited the man's name and credentials aloud. The CG located the words, which manifested in blue across the recording: Doctor Matthew Mussari, Research Chemist, Ichiban-Plokazhopski. Using the keyboard trackball, Nebergall captured and moved the words to where he wanted them, considered the color a moment, and opted for an off-white instead. Satisfied, he faded the lines of type down and let the recording run again. On his signal, the words magically reappeared. Nebergall grunted.

"If we consider ourselves as individual expressions in four knowable dimensions," said Dr. Mussari, "which are derived of a universal cloth, then we can theorize that in some way Orbitol-affected tissues are shrugging off that fabric for one we've never seen. In other words, the body tissues in question have changed into matter we can't see or feel, but which still exists somewhere, and which the poor bugger of an Orbiter continues to sense in some way, much as an amputee receives ghost data from his lost limb.

"As for the world described by some of the final-stage addicts, this is very likely hallucination, a common property of the drug expressing itself, rather than actual reportage of what the new fabric might look like. I mean, blue trees and crystalline landscapes. It's too much pulp fantasy—the Alien News Network is more believable, and that's pure bunk. There's plenty of data to support this—studies of the drug phencyclidine in the last century pointed up a commonality amongst hallucinations."

He paused the disk, backed it up again. Nebergall had been editing without a break for more than forty-eight hours. Once he got started on a final edit, he found it nearly impossible to quit before the piece was complete. The closet smelled like an ashtray in a litter box.

Under the best of conditions, two people could not fit comfortably in Nebergall's icy workroom (he jokingly referred to it as his "edit suite"), and Thomasina Lyell could only imagine what the best of conditions might have been. So much debris littered the space beneath the rails on which his chair rode—cables, old CDs, scripts, cigarette butts, Coca-Cola bulbs and wrappers from creme-filled cupcakes (Neeb's favorite), even a few ancient magnetic tape cartridges—that the trash had become the floor. With Nebergall stretched half the length of the room, all Lyell could do was prop herself in the open doorway and watch. His two cats, Gargantua and Badebec, slept on the small bed behind her.

One by one as the screens went dark, they reflected her. He knew she was there, but he would not acknowledge her until he'd finished the sequence. It could go on for hours; it had, before. He tilted to the left, comparing numbers logged into his keyboard against those displayed on one of the screens.

Dr. Mussari went into motion again. "Each of us, then, can be viewed as a subtotal of the collective implicate expression, the same as a subtotal on a grocery bill. Carry the analogy out, and Orbitol is just changing the price of one or two items, so that the subtotal changes. No other substance has ever done this, so far as we know. The final effect and impact cannot be estimated yet. Frankly, we've no idea how many people have simply vanished into this unknown 'twelve-space,' or if their transformation in some way destabilizes the fabric of our reality. That's why my colleagues here and at Bickham International have petitioned hard for a ban on Orbitol's manufacture. Naturally, ScumberCorp is fighting us on this, but there is a sincere concern that we might wake up some morning to find half the world missing, or time out of joint, or something unimaginably worse."

Three colorful corporate logos shared the screen briefly as he spoke, like the pennants of opposing sports teams; then the scientist's face returned in close-up.

"It has nothing to do with our contempt for ScumberCorp as a business entity, or its pernicious subsidiary, Stercus Pharmaceuticals. I freely admit to such contempt in light of what we suspect. This petition, however, has to do with the untold loss of life among the lowest of the underclass that's occurring as I speak. By some estimates, because of Orbitol's remarkably addictive properties, at least one entire stratum of society will be obliterated within the decade. Human beings, I fear, have finally made the endangered species list."

The image froze, then slowly zeroed into the black pupil of his right eye. Nebergall typed in codes to identify and protect the composite master. Lyell knew he would look at it again later and be dissatisfied with something that no one else could see, and start over from scratch. It was no time to voice an opinion.

When he was finished, he hung the flexible keyboard on the left arm of the chair. He unclipped what looked like a knobby black ocarina from his shirt, began clicking the top of it with his thumb. His legs drew back in increments with each click. He groaned as his knees bent for the first time in hours. Clamping the ocarina between his teeth, he loosened the strap around his middle and then quickly grabbed the arms of the chair, taking the weight of his body upon his wrists so that he could swing his folded legs down. His boot heels slid into place on the footplates. He took the control again in the palm of his hand and tapped two of the raised knobs. His mechanized chair glided forward on its track to give Lyell a little more breathing room. "Close the door, there, will you?" he said. "Don't want all the A/C to leak out and contaminate the pure Philly air."

Lyell closed the closet door behind her. Then she leaned over him and set three video disks on the desk where his feet had been.

"Nice to have you back. How'd we make out?" he asked.

"You're now the proud owner of a couple hours worth of jiggly stock exercise footage should you ever have cause to take a poke at obesity."

He craned his head back and looked at her upside down. His graying blond hair needed shampooing, and darker stubble graced his chin. His blue eyes had gone mostly red. "I wasn't planning to make any sitcoms. No story, huh? That's too bad. Now and then you're gonna get that kinda job, you know that." He leaned forward and picked up the disks. "You found the Tamiami kid, at least. You haven't lost your skill there. Have you told the client?"

"No, only you. I'm meeting with Mr. Trayle this afternoon."

"He's gonna be *real* happy. Promise me you won't beat him up in public."

"What a funny joke. Listen, Neeb, I want you to take a look at the number three disk for a minute. Go in about two-forty."

Nebergall selected the disk. He ejected one small drive, and replaced its contents with Lyell's. Leaning back, he scratched his head with the keyboard, then typed a few strokes. The twenty-one screens lit up with a single image—a still of the Geoplatform bar ceiling with a large, distorted semicircle at the bottom of the frame. "How many times I got to tell you to keep your head straight?"

"I was in the middle of taking a drink. It gets better."

He gave her a skeptical look, then started the video. Blue on-screen numbers began running through sequence. Three figures walked past. "You want speakers on?"

"Not for this. He doesn't say anything, anyway."

"Who?"

"The middle one."

Nebergall typed a few more commands. The picture froze and a dotted square closed over the torso and head of the middle figure at the bar. The bottom three monitors filled with that segment of the picture, and continued tracking the image as he let the action continue. "What's he got on his head?" Nebergall asked. "Looks like a swim cap."

The camera rose up and approached the bar. It focused on the bartender, but abruptly turned, filling the screen with the nearest man, then swinging back to look past him, capturing the other two faces in profile.

"There," Lyell said.

Nebergall marked the spot, and glanced at the bottom row of images. He straightened up, leaned forward. The screen showed a tanned or a dark face, one sharp cheek with maybe a trace of acne in the hollow, a prominent nose emerging from beneath the headgear. "Spanish or Arabic," he guessed. "Some women like that kind of dark, rawboned look, don't they? Been in an accident. From his expression and that bypass gear, I'd bet on major brain damage, too. Hmm." He lowered his head in thought for a moment before releasing the freeze frame.

The third man—a redhead—stared hard at the camera. He snarled a few choice words.

"Not exactly Athos, Aramis, and Porthos, are they?" commented Nebergall. "What'd you do to piss them off so fast?"

"I don't know exactly. Just asked a few questions about the Moon."

"Did you ask nice?"

"I imitated how my editor would ask the questions if *he* were there."

"No wonder." The view swung away from the three men and returned to its previous perspective on the other side of the room. "That it? Doesn't he ever face you straight on?"

"Wait a little."

He scooted the disk along a little. A short, muscular woman with close-cropped ginger hair came and sat in front of the camera.

"Now, who's that?"

"She's a trainer in the weight loss place."

"This doesn't have anything to do with that crap, does it? Your musketeers are out of SC's lunar setup. You tumbled to something here, right? Bet I know something you don't about these bozos," he taunted.

"Hang on. You can't sit still for anything, can you?"

The picture moved away from Nance's freckled features, back to the bar. The three men were heading straight for the table. The black man nodded casually to her and the redhead scowled and pretended not to see her at all. The one in the middle stared right into the lens with his one good eye. Nebergall backed it up, froze it, chose a first shot that he dumped, digitized, into the still-store unit. The full-face portrait appeared on one of the wing cubes. He nudged the disk forward, selected a second, closer image of the face, keyed in another digital snapshot, and then repeated the process twice more before the men on the screen passed the table and headed down the outside corridor. The monitors offered four sharp portraits of the man in the middle, suitable for framing. In the last, his full right profile had become almost entirely machine. "Beautiful," commented Nebergall. "Gorgeous, and that's without decompressing the RPEG—look at that."

The camera focused on Nance again, who had also turned to watch the threesome leave.

"They escorting a prisoner?" he asked.

"Not according to them, but it sure comes across that way in body language, doesn't it? They said his name was Angel Rueda and he was 'cycling down,' which I take to be their euphemism for being shit-canned. They mentioned they were coming here."

"Headquarters. Well, they would be. I'll look into it." He typed *Angel Rueda* across the final image.

"Yup, pardner, I know you will." She slapped his shoulder. "You can shut it off—the rest is irrelevant."

"Maybe I just like to look at muscular women with freckles."

"I'm sure you do. Now, you want to tell me what it is you know about those three that I don't, or do I wait for Christmas?"

"Nothing, for certain."

"Then make something up."

"Okay. About seventy-two hours ago there was an explosion at SC's lunar mining facility. The extent of the damage and other specifics have not been forthcoming. Don't know how many, if any, are dead, don't know what part of the place blew up. Last I'd heard, the official leaking story was that the infamous *Xau Dâu* are to blame. Another attack by little Scumber-gremlins. Probably there's more by now—I haven't checked since I came in here to work on the Ichi-Plok piece— but your date and time code put this at just over a full day later, and that kinda fits." He stretched his arms, flexing his shoulders.

"I don't know. The man looked pretty good for somebody who'd suffered extensive brain damage only twenty-four hours earlier."

"If that's what it was. Maybe he *is Xau Dâu*, a one-man sabotage operation. Those brain-boxes can be misused, you know. Remember the *Pensamuertos* in Chile? Torture with a smile."

"Think you can find out more?" she asked.

"Most likely, but don't ask me how. That way you can't be tortured into revealing any secrets. Even if they screw one of those things on your head." He glanced wryly back at her. He had hundred-year-old eyes, she thought, in his fifty-one-year-old face. "It'll take some discreet inquiry. Too bad you couldn't get his prints, too. I don't think I can unpeg them off this image. He's either holding something or his hands are out of the frame. Try me tonight, anyway, and we'll see. What's on for your morning?"

"It's afternoon, Neeb," she replied. "I've got business to take care of in the Undercity. Haven't been seen for five days, people'll be wondering if my box is vacant."

"I meant to talk to you about that, Thomasina," he interrupted. He hung the keyboard up again and swung the chair around. "The fast-food story isn't happening."

Her brow knitted. "Why not?" she asked defensively.

"Well, Ichi-Plok informs me, off the record naturally, that they don't want any stories on the chemicals in Happy Burgers—because they, and everybody else, have introduced psychoactives into *their* fast-food items, too. Isn't that nice to hear?"

Lyell stared at him in disbelief.

"Yeah, I know." He gestured toward the monitors. "Mussari at I-P there played 'throat' and revealed that Odie and Congress have quietly passed legislation over the past two years allowing the inclusion of certain CNS drugs in all categories of fast-food to, quote, 'insure the safety and maintain the stability of our society,' unquote. He read it off to me just like that. All sorts of bullshit tech . . ." He stopped. Lyell was smiling, and shaking her head. "You wanna tell me what's so funny?"

"Just a remark someone made, about how nobody's covering reality anymore. It's the truth, isn't it."

"It's tough to pick out the leading edge when most everybody experiences their world from a chair, yeah. Who said that?"

She was too furious to let him change the subject. "I can't get a buyer for a story on how the underclasses are being kept docile and dumb by the world's largest manufacturer/distributor of cheap foodgoods—all of which is irrefutably verified!— and the reason is, the competition wants to dump their own tranquility shit in the soup?"

"Exactly. Look, some battles we just don't get to fight." He put his hand across his heart patriotically. "It's not economically viable."

"And I used to admire you."

Nebergall grinned. "All the same, I strongly advise against patronizing in particular the fast-food kiosks with the smiley big buns on them. Look just like those wrappers on the floor over there. Maybe we oughta start a campaign—rename the stuff 'slow-food.' " He rubbed his eyes, yawned. "Hey, I'm sorry and you know it, but that's where we hang at the moment. Unless Bickham or some smaller corporation wants to play whistle-blower and ante up, we don't have a story. Probably that ain't gonna happen, since the law's already two years in place and they'd be fools not to take advantage, too. All we'll do is piss off every potential market we have. If you're so hot to find out who Mr. Rueda is, I think you shouldn't start by sticking it to all our benefactors." He let that sink in for a moment, then asked, "So, what *are* you going to do, Tommie?"

"I'm going to go ahead with the story, is what." She held up her hand to stop his protest. "All right, if no one buys it now, at least the footage will be archived when finally it does go public—maybe my grandchildren can use it next century. Besides, I killed myself to establish this identity and I'm not going to toss out all that goddamned work. I didn't like going up on the Geoplatform, either, but we'd contracted. Now that's finished, I'm going back to what matters. Maybe I'll find some other story we *can* use."

"You always do. Just don't ignite when I remind you later that we can't do this particular piece, no matter how nice the footage is. And be sure you take some shoes with you—should be a few pair left in the bag in the other room." Somewhat cheerlessly he added, "You're the only *'jin* I got who ever uses 'em."

It was Nebergall who, while investigating a story about street gangs in the Undercity, had discovered the value of a good pair of shoes in the barter market. The fresh-faced idealists he usually had to work with didn't seem to appreciate his revelation.

"Okay," she promised.

She didn't move, and he finally glanced up at her again. "What?" he asked.

"Oh, it's a crazy thing, Neeb." She grinned. "Did you record Odie the night before last?"

His gaze went to the ceiling as he thought back. "Probably," then he added, "*I* wouldn't have watched it, though. Why? He finally show us Schnepfe's circumcision?"

"Oh, there was a bit in the middle about this Orbiter who's risen from the dead and—"

"You're kidding? Jesus, Odie's approval ratings must be slipping if he's sticking his hands in that kind of shit."

"Yeah. But I'd like to take a look at it sometime."

He glanced over at the clockface buried in the mass of digital recording equipment. "I should have lunch. Also breakfast, and dinner from last night." He began backing out. She opened the door and stepped into the bedroom. Badebec, the gray female cat, looked up at the sound.

"What about the 'Happy Trayles'?" Neeb called. He backed into the doorway.

"You know that trainer you fixated on in the video? Well, Tamiami's been cohabiting with her for three months. According to her, she skipped home because the old man made her 'play with his mushroom' regularly. Don't look at me like that, that's what *he* called it—daddy's mushroom. Tamiami ran to momma, who predictably denied anything so unthinkable could ever happen under her roof. So the kid snatched a credit card and ran away. Now she's in what I'd call a comparatively nurturing lesbian relationship and I have no intention of reuniting the nuclear family unless that includes shoving a fuel rod up Mr. Trayle."

Nebergall said, "Yeah, but how do you really feel?"

"I promise I won't touch him. I'm just going to give him my bill. You wouldn't believe how many hidden expenses lurk in shuttle travel. The chewing gum alone . . . I was amazed, myself, at the inflation." She closed the closet door after him.

Nebergall drove over beside the bed. Badebec climbed across the arm of the chair and into his lap. Her brother looked at him balefully and didn't move. Lyell went over and stroked Gargantua. His tail flicked and he stretched lazily.

Neeb said, "You know, Tommie, you've got the best instincts of any *pijin* I ever worked with. It's like you can feel a story unfolding someplace and find it. That happened to me exactly once in all my field time. I'd hate to think that such a goddamned clever investigator had to send me her disks from behind bars on Corson's Isle in between gang rapes. Not every father's gonna turn out to be *your* father, Tommie."

She turned, her eyes wide in a shock of violation.

He went on before she could say anything. "You take these jobs personally the same way you take nailing SC personally. It's a vendetta with you, and that's the *one* fundamental error in your primary motivation. If you ever do break them, it'll be the result of your instincts, not because of the screaming avenger. I keep telling you—"

"You don't kill corporations, they kill themselves," she quoted. "I know. In my sleep I recite it. Don't worry about me, Nebergall—I'm not entirely rabid yet. I won't have myself arrested again. Promise. And you know why? Because it wouldn't be economically viable. I'll overlook the comment about my father, which was shitty. But all the same I'm bringing you back a bunch of nice Happy Burgers." She bent down and kissed him on the forehead.

"Yum," he said.

5

The EAP
and the INRE

In her mind, she was seventeen again, about to go off to Princeton. . . .

Her father, Thomas Lyell, sat beside her on the floral-patterned porch swing and handed her a tall tumbler of iced tea. She could hear the rattle of the cubes against the glass and taste the mint leaf he'd dropped in. Wisps of gray had begun to curl through his hair. His black face looked sad in a way that cut into her heart, even all these years later; he thought he'd masked it.

It was the beginning of his downfall. He had only just begun to suspect how his own staff had been suborned by ScumberCorp. The enormous infochemical giant wanted Atlanta for its own—it had used up the last of places like the Oriente in Ecuador, and was starting to collect cities. No individual mayor would dare to interfere with that process.

Except for her father.

Reporters had begun hounding Thomas Lyell daily. They were cutting the legs out from under him already but he didn't see it: his every move was being videotaped, his expressions of anger and annoyance in response to goading questions had been captured on disk—images that would later "appear" in places he had never been.

In his peculiar way of dealing with such pressures, he channeled his frustrations into a story for his daughter. He'd been a storyteller to her ever since she could remember. He never used a book; either he knew a thousand and one tales by heart or else made them up with ease.

"Once upon a time," said her father, "there grew a many-mouthed monster, separate from the rest of the race but living right along side us, called the Eating Press. You've heard of it, honey, 'cause its name is legion today.

"This big hydra had a million heads and every one of them spoke the language of entertainment. The Eating Press—we'll call it the EAP—thrived in hotels and casinos; it interviewed the stars of nightclubs and rock concerts and videofilms. It acquired its name because the EAP heads gathered information over free meals—huge, fabulous after-the-show feasts to rival the bacchanalia of ancient Rome. None of the other hydra-headed press monsters paid the EAP any mind. They hadn't any reason to. After all, its words described mere entertainment—wasn't even real entertainment itself. The EAP told what the entertainment looked like, between bites. The heads' language ran to hyperbole. Nothing they spoke of actually referred to any tangible part of our lives. It was a big fantasy, but this country, my dear, has always preferred its fantasies and fables. Christopher Columbus is more fun as a great explorer than as a man who tortured the natives for a little gold.

"Now, America, at the time, was pretending to be the stellar economy of *all* time, separate from and never codependent upon any supposed world economy. Everybody from the tiny grocer to the lead-assed Congress blissfully went about denying the possibility that things couldn't continue much longer.

"Meanwhile, way down in the shadows, like a tiny mammal hiding out from the prowling carnivorous dinosaurs, a second creature, related to the EAP, languished in near obscurity. This one was called the Investigative Reporter, the INRE. This much smaller hydra lived and wrote and spoke its words around political centers of the country and the world. It saw corruption and felt compelled to expose it. It located subversion of power and focused public attention like a spotlight. In earlier times, people had slept well knowing that the INRE was out there, like a costumed crime fighter, doing battle against the evils of their society. But the more the population leaned hard away from reality in order to maintain their delusions, the less and less interest they had in seeing evil exposed, and the more interest in hearing fairy stories like those the EAP told, which made everything glittery and everyone beautiful and sexy like on TV.

"One president called the INRE puppets and laughed at them to dismiss what they said about him. A few years after him, the staff of another president began subtly to reshape the heads.

"Now, this particular president couldn't tell the difference between the INRE and the EAP. He'd known the latter most of his adult life, which he'd spent in the entertainment field. To him, a hydra was a hydra. He made nice and fed them all.

"I guess the INRE didn't really notice at first how it had been remodeled; some heads had been lopped off, but new ones always grew. Before long the important thing had ceased to be facts and information, issues and answers, and we had us a whole new mess of media heads jabbering endless speculations in the face of nothing. The new heads had turned out to be EAPs.

"The officials of the government now controlled the INRE. They threw the parties, after all, and they told the beast what they wanted it to know. The INRE then went out and told the world what it had learned, which made the people in power *very* happy. In this way, properly nurtured, the creature's career could now float along amicably for decades, and only its wardrobe suffered.

"Meanwhile, the political parties of our tired two-party system became like two big diet soft drinks—indistinguishable from each other and without any substance. Their candidates evaded confronting all the issues anyway, replacing intelligent discourse with snappy bits of verbiage that *sounded* like something without being anything at all. They learned this from, of all places, the videofilm. Entertainment. The EAPs.

"The INRE maintained a dignified air of false objectivity as it reported every pat premasticated phrase. It still doesn't know what happened to it. A party is a party, after all." He sighed.

"I fear, my beautiful, wise daughter, that reality is lost for good this time. News shows are vaudeville. However old the act, there's an audience for it. Stories about ugly little saucermen and children like you possessed by demons, and women who hate men who hate women who hate a basic food group, and people who tattoo their fannies and pierce their unspeakables are a thousand times more interesting than society's *actual* ills." He'd looked off in the distance and smiled then. "The trouble is, that's the truth. You like your flying saucer stories and your music makers. I know. Even *I* know that, and I'm an old fart who thinks it all stopped at Miles Davis. The difference—I hope—between you and that purblind public out there is that while you're loving such goofy things, you know your history. You know your truth. You know there are things that are important, that the EAP doesn't touch, and they aren't quiz shows or talk shows or spacemen or pixies. You know to question everything, even your old man. He would like to be, but he's not perfect. Things do get past him from time to time."

He had touched the tip of her nose then, the way he had since she was a little girl. *Things do get past him.* He had no idea how prophetic a comment that would turn out to be, she thought now as she rode across the city.

The electric shuttle lifted her out of the old section in which Nebergall lived. Below the blue trestle, the convex south wall of the city slid past. Hundreds of people milled around the checkpoint. Maybe half of them would get work today—mostly on or around the market docks. Some—ones with craft skills, for example—would have permits and already be inside, many up in Overcity shops. An even luckier few would have maintenance jobs there. The people lining up below lived from one day to the next, some getting far enough ahead to buy a medical checkup or the fare to some other city where they might try their luck again. In the Midwest, out in the broad plains between urban centers, there were corporate-free zones—independent county-clusters where people grew their own crops, produced their own power with wind and water and recycled manure. A skilled craftsman or guild member was generally welcome, so she'd heard. It would be a subsistence existence, but more dignified than knifing your neighbors for a promise of work or, at best, work of limited duration. These people outside the wall were better off than those who lived on the ground inside, who had effectively been sealed in; but just barely: they had sanitation, running water, electricity, and homes. They'd been born into that middle stratum of inherited debt that could almost never be conquered, just passed down to the next generation.

The shuttle took her to Market Tower Station. From there, breezing through security, she entered the Overcity of Philadelphia—two million people, their whole lives lived in a hive of towers between the Schuylkill and Delaware rivers.

Before the slide of the fossil fuel industries, the city had sprawled far and wide. Now it was condensed, its constituent parts drawn in as if to a magnetic core. The older city

remained, like the ruins of Troy and Londinium upon which
the modern world had set down, referred to disparagingly as
the Undercity, and within the walls as the Box City. Like the
encampment of a besieging army, it appeared to be completely
cut off from the airy fortress towers she now strode through,
which were accessible through skywalks, and all but sealed up
at ground level.

From experience she knew that the two halves were still
connected, and not just in the way that the Alien News Network and Happy Burger represented. Revelations did filter
down over the wall. To Nebergall, to others like him. Robin
Hood nowadays stole information from the rich. She was such
a connection—a live wire between the upper and lower strata, a
covert line of communication. Spawn of the INRE. She figured
it would have made her father proud.

6

Wearing Disguises

The dark man lay back on a tangle of blankets inside his
prestigious plastic box, his digs, and idly rolled one tip of
his mustache between his fingers. He was tall enough that his
head touched the rear wall and his feet the moth-eaten yellow
blanket that served as a door. He passed the time in leisurely
fashion by listening to the squawking of his neighbors. From
the containers fronting both sides of the narrow alley—the
alleys like canyons in miniature—conversations intertwined
on the breeze.

At the moment, right across the way, Mad John and Celine
were balling hard enough to jolt the adjacent boxes, their
neighbors stirred up like hornets and bellowing every foul
word and threat they could think of. The tall dark man just
grinned at the sounds.

The digs consisted of opaque seaweed-plastic sheeting
stitched together over uprights into a two-and-a-half-meter

cube with an opening at each end—a comparatively high rent box. He couldn't stand upright inside it, but the blankets made reclining quite comfortable. He'd brought the blankets along upon moving in rather than trusting the former tenant's bedding, which at the very least had been lice-ridden.

What really made the digs prestigious was their location. They butted right up against the Liberty Bell enclosure; specifically, the rear wall of the box pressed against the low marble wall in back of the little building.

The Bell had become both symbolically and physically the heart of Box City. Only a handful of lucky Boxers could look at it whenever they pleased; it was the equivalent of a title, a knighthood—presuming anyone other than the dark man still remembered what a knighthood was.

The Liberty Bell was hardly the only historical site overtaken by the underclass. Congress Hall and Independence Hall—the white bell tower and cupola were visible from the alley outside—had been engulfed by hovels. So had the First Bank, the Second Bank, Library Hall, and Carpenters' Hall. A veritable Sargasso Sea of tiny domiciles stretched from the Vine Street wall at the north end of the Mall all the way to Penn's Landing, where the southern and the Delaware River walls met.

A few scattered boxes stood as much as three levels high, like scale model trinities, but most were no larger, sturdier, or more elaborate than Lobly's digs. At night, through plastic foam walls, a thousand little TV screens flickered like fires, most of them hooked up to nothing and hissing with white noise, but curiously comforting somehow, like a memory of the womb. The electricity was stolen.

ScumberCorp would have liked to reclaim the monuments of Independence National Historical Park, if only to have them on hand as corporate iconography. The Liberty Bell would have looked great in the lobby beside the logo case containing the COs' heads. However, the company did not dare try to take back the buildings for two simple reasons. First, any attempt to wrest the Bell away from the Boxers would have been met by fierce resistance and followed by riots throughout the Undercity and maybe even (in the worst-case scenarios) storming into the towers. It had happened once before—the charred ruins of the Westphilly Conflagration of '31 could still be seen across the river as a reminder of what the dispossessed could do if they got out of hand. People who might ignore the subtle clipping of their civil rights one by one would scream and go raving, foaming mad over some ridiculous bit of filched iconography: a bell, a flag.

The second reason SC left the Bell alone was fear of the inevitable outcry that would follow close upon the heels of the riots as all their competitors aligned against them. Even the Odie U.S. government might be pressured to take a stand against the company. So ScumberCorp pretended that the icon of liberty wasn't *that* important; maintained the opinion that the whole thing was a myth among the underclass; and went ahead with an end run around the filthy beggars in the form of Orbitol.

As things stood, anyone who dared ask would be escorted through the confines of Box City to view the Bell. For a small fee, even people from the towers could visit it; they were not molested or harassed in any way as long as they maintained the proper air of respect, which was more than any "Over" could say about treatment at the tower checkpoints. The Bell had about it something reverential, almost mystical. No one would have dared to interfere with another's time inside the enclosure. Such action would have resulted in quick banishment to the Snake Pit, or worse. The dark man, who went by the name of Aswad Lobly, had already seen that happen.

Of contrary parts was Aswad Lobly: a curiosity in an encampment full of oddities. So tall as to be almost hulking, at the same time he evinced grace and balance—an almost feline agility. He had chocolate skin and curly black hair plaited into something like a bound cylinder off the back of his head. His mustache was thick, and he kept the tips oiled to points like barbs. Above the right nostril he wore a large sapphire nose ring, and in one ear, six hoops of silver. His voice was milky soft, nasal if you listened closely; the accent in his speech would have been hard to pin down. He disappeared sometimes for days on end.

When he wasn't around, Lobly's neighbors speculated that he was maybe homosexual and selling himself to clientele in the towers, or a pederast, or a procurer for pederasts, none of which was uncommon in Box City. He claimed to have arrived from the North, fleeing some trouble there that he refused to specify. No one had to ask about that. He wore layers of loose robes, red sneaker-boots, and either a tarboosh or a turban on any given day.

What none of Aswad Lobly's neighbors remotely suspected—as he intended—was that he was a woman. Thomasina Lyell, to be exact.

Lyell made no attempt to check the gossip about her alter ego; conflicting stories served to act like an extra layer of camouflage to protect her. All that was known about Lobly was that he might have been an Orbiter once but had taken the cure before he suffered any obvious tissue damage. Maybe he'd lost a couple of toes, maybe not—the stories varied because she never spelled out anything. Lobly could discourse quite knowledgeably about the *effects* of the drug, and that was really all the proof anyone needed. The Boxers' inherent reticence to talk about their former lives or the families they'd fled, deserted, or slain helped her in this. Past lives didn't exist in Box City. Box life was timeless.

The knowledge of Orbitol and some of Lobly's appearance Lyell had borrowed from a lifer she'd met while serving time on Corson's Isle. The lifer's name was Poleby.

At some date prior to his incarceration on the prison island, Poleby had mixed up his drugs with volatile, even suicidal, abandon. He had mistakenly assumed that site-specific drugs couldn't conflict with one another. The result of Poleby's experiments was a permanent, degenerative rewiring of his salivary glands.

In the cell he shared with Lyell, he spent most of his time with a bucket between his knees to catch the waterfall of drool that ran ceaselessly down his face. It dripped from the tips of his mustache and out of the cleft in his chin. Poleby kept a two-liter pitcher of water on a table beside him to keep from dehydrating in the night, and slept with a plastic tube hooked over his lip. The first few weeks, the sucking and trickling sounds had nearly driven Lyell crazy.

The supply of the drugs in the prison astonished even Lyell. From Poleby's stories, she figured out soon enough that as many as five dozen pharmaceutical companies were using the prisoners on Corson's Isle as test subjects for experimental substances and practices. According to Poleby, the first unnatural effects of Orbitol had come to light there.

"It was a girl, one a their first users. (Slurp.) Her toes, you know, went away. When she refused to take any more a the shit, they strapped her into her cell and shot it into her— bang, bang bang! (Slurp.) Well, ya know—after awhile she's begging for it, can't stand to be without it, and she didn't care no more that she didn't have no legs or hands." He paused dramatically to spit. "Didn't matter to her half so much as gettin' fucked up. She let the bastids do anything just so she got fixed. They gouged samples outen her, trying to see what was goin' on, and every day there's less and less of her. One day she just faded right out from under 'em—they's so fuckin' dumb they thought she'd escaped. And they's *right*, too, ya know." He laughed, but self-consciously glanced at his empty sleeve while he sucked saliva. "Now, ain't I a fine one to talk?"

One night, while he flew high on Orbitol, Poleby described quite lucidly for Lyell the vision he had of another reality. According to him, it was a vision he shared with all other Orbiters.

"It doesn't come every time right at first, ya know, like gettin' a signal from a pirate satellite or somepun," he said, "but when it comes, it's a message from God. Glimpse a heaven, gettin' stronger with each visit. That's why I come back to it—why that girl did, why they *all* do—get another peek at it, 'nother look at God. Ya don't know that it's got its hooks in ya till it's happened. And then you're the fish and the other world just reelin' you in.

"It's a place where everything sparkles like that little jewel in your nose," Poleby said, tapping her nostril, the disconnected lens system.

He'd never possessed the least imagination, never once hallucinated anything coherent, and so he concluded that the drug had transported him to a real place. He speculated that it was Mars-to-be—the terraformed Mars that ScumberCorp's ads referred to. "*Not this generation but someday soon*," went the motto that even President Odie had been known to recite. "*A new world is about to open to us that will return mankind to greatness.*" The ad ran ceaselessly on Knewsday and ANN, and the images of Mars in the ad looked so much like his vision that he figured the artist must have been an Orbiter, too. He swore there were thousands of addicts in the upper strata of society all across the world. One of the drug testers monitoring him had said so. Lyell remembered wondering at the time if SC's whole Martian colony might be nothing more than a widespread hallucination. How could anyone be sure?

Poleby believed that the world he saw was real. He had a theory that he told Lyell, "God, ya see, finds His recreation in creating variety. That's what my ma used to say." He slurped, spitting. "She was a Hindu, had all kinds a notions about God an' stuff the old man couldn't tolerate. He was starch-stiff Catholic. I mean *stiff*. He had a miter on the head a his dick. Don't know why in the hell the little prick married her, either. I figure they was doing battle to see who could convert who. If she'd'a had a snake, she woulda put it in his bed, but she didn't. He'd go to confession, then a tavern, then come home broke and beat the shit outen her. She finally run away."

A few years later Poleby had killed the old man himself with a screwdriver. "Carpenter's lobotomy," he called it, lopsidedly grinning with his chin bright and wet. His laughter had gone swirling into the bucket.

Lyell forged many connections to get her Box City digs. The box was one of a number of locations she frequented in the hope she might pick up information about any of SC's unusual offers. She'd acquired it, to Nebergall's joy, by trading pairs of shoes.

The location of the box played a crucial role because information flowing through the Box City tended to cluster in pockets around the Bell and the cooking fires. The fires burned to the north, up on Judge Lewis Quadrangle. Lobly had become a familiar sight there, too, always supplied with extra food to share and always willing to listen to any story.

It was while seated at a cooking fire that Lyell had learned about ScumberCorp's food-testing programs. The first time she'd heard it, she doubted the story. Free food was rare enough, but free food from ScumberCorp was a holy miracle. However, when she mentioned the giveaway, she found too many people attesting to it, and solid details filling in.

From time to time, SC's subsidiaries—Happy Burger in particular—invited some Boxers to a private party. This inevitably involved free food or drugs. The exact purpose of any event was not revealed to the participants, but they were always rewarded, sometimes with coins that they could use for barter, but often as not with other drugs. Occasionally, some of the participants didn't return. A few times, none of them had. That might have scared off new participants, except that there were always Boxers who hadn't managed to find a meal or who had been robbed by a gang.

A legend had evolved that the lost Boxers had been awarded special positions up in the towers. The fervor with which the people she spoke to embraced this nonsense was testimony to their ability to deny reality utterly. She knew better. If people from the Undercity were living full-time in the Overcity, they were doing it in an urn.

She would have compiled a terrific story for Nebergall if he hadn't turned off the tap. It burned her that she couldn't use it. She couldn't have imagined the unprecedented turn that the story was about to take.

The sounds of Mad John and Celine's sex act had degenerated into groans, followed by silence. Background conversations drifted like body odors along the narrow alley—people debating the best way to get rid of head lice, somebody else claiming that Knewsday had pictures of the sea creatures that were coming ashore to rape women in Italy. The weird mixture always surprised her.

The dull murmurous voices lulled her brain and combined with the warm, confined air to send her drifting into a light doze.

She jerked awake as there came a rap on the roof of the box next to hers. She leaned up on her elbows and listened to a conversation in hushed tones.

"Ya ready to go, Pete?"

"Jist lemme git on my boots."

"Naw problem."

"Hamany you figure you can eat?"

"Fuck do *you* care how many? What you don't, I'm eating. Bet on that. I axed Bucca and he said it's gonna be a major feast, like hundreds of burgers an' stuff."

"Oh, *man.*"

When their voices drifted away, she counted to five, then ducked out under the blanket. Mad John's foot protruded beneath Celine's curtain. He'd managed to keep on one dirty sock.

The two speakers—her neighbor, Pete, and the other—were heading along the nearest east-west aisle. Pressing her elbow, she strolled after them, disking the sights and sounds of box life. Only the smells eluded posterity, which in its own way was a pity.

The two men led her far up Market Street and around City Hall to an office plaza of broken concrete pavement and the skeletons of dead trees in big, poured-stone pots. Blocks of pink granite lay here and there as if spilled by some giant infant.

She counted three dozen Box City dwellers milling about aimlessly, and more arriving. Word had gotten around.

Lyell hung back at the edge of one building. The two men she'd followed went up to a short fireplug of a character and began chatting with him.

She recognized some of the people from the fires up on the quadrangle. Among the Boxers there were a few deranged characters. Tended by friends, these examples of untreated madness were settled on the granite blocks, where some immediately engaged in conversation with invisible companions or made faces at nothing. Many of them had open sores, and most wore one or more meals, like embroidered designs, down the front of their clothes. A bald man, with suppurating stigmata at his temples and invisible bare feet, crawled upon one of the blocks and began castigating everybody around him. His cause could not be fathomed and no one but the other "mads" paid him any mind.

Through a slit between two buildings, Lyell glimpsed the statue of William Penn atop the Gothic City Hall building, but almost at once turned her attention overhead, where the others were looking and pointing.

Between the towers directly above, skywalks formed a dark cross against the gray clouds. Out of the center of the cross, a tube was descending. Lyell, who had never seen such an emergency exit in operation, was as transfixed as the derelicts by the telescoping vertical tube.

It touched down lightly, with barely a thump. A big, curved door revolved halfway around to one side. On their feet now, the beggars held back. Even the mad ones had fallen silent. Fearfully, they shifted from one foot to the other and twitched and flexed their hands, ready to stampede at the first sign of treachery.

Four armed guards emerged from the opening.

The wave of Boxers ebbed. Some wasted no time in deserting the square. Lyell pressed back against the wall as two characters came scurrying around past her. When she looked again, she found that the vast majority were hanging on at a distance, waiting to see how things went.

The guards set up a perimeter. They nudged the majority of the mob back farther but ignored the truly demented, most of whom were left seated and incoherent on their slabs of granite. As the mob backed toward her, Lyell stepped into its midst and slipped through to the front ranks.

Five more people emerged from the tube, two of them pushing long carts piled high with Happy Burger foods: surimi rolls, Spuddies, burgers, and malts. Her stomach, unfed so far this day, reacted to the smell of the hot food, even as her mind reminded her of the risks. The carts were positioned in a semicircle. The four guards drew aside, effectively leaving the food unguarded. Too hungry not to take a chance, a few of the derelicts edged up to the carts. For a moment, faced with so much choice, they hesitated. Behind the table, men in shiny suits stood smiling. One of the derelicts heisted two burgers, still wary for the slightest response from the guards. No one batted an eye; the man behind the table, wearing dark glasses like the rest, nodded encouragingly. At this sign dozens of people sprang forward, pushing and shoving toward the carts. Lyell let herself be carried along, concentrating on smooth pans back and forth to capture the entire scene. Once he saw this performance, she figured, Nebergall would have to change his mind about the show.

In front of her, a derelict named Bindlestiff edged along the table, unwrapping and devouring his first burger while he stuffed another, along with bags of Spuddies and *cha gio*, into every pocket. She recorded it, savoring every detail: the blotchy ruin of a face offering a rapturous expression straight out of a Rubens painting, his eyes rolled back as he stuffed his mouth full of food. Stubby fingers grabbed, wriggling; wrappers rustled like a dozen crackling fires; the black plastic glasses of the guards sealed their eyes in obscurity above their carved smiles. She felt like Nebergall's still-store machine, capturing one after the other remarkable frozen image in her retinas.

An advertising jingle danced through her head: "Why worry when you can eat Happy? So eat—*Happy Burgers*." A cartoon family devoured the cartoon icon. How many times she had heard it.

The mob became entangled in its feeding frenzy. Here and there, minor skirmishes arose. A fight broke out between two men over possession of a cherry soda, the contents of which had already exploded over both yanking contenders. One of the perimeter guards stepped in to intercede, and Lyell sidled in that direction to record the episode. Out of the corner of her eye she noticed a tall figure emerge from the tube and move swiftly around the carts, into the thick of things. The guard stopped and returned to his position, and let the new man handle things.

He was thin, blond, leonine, with a smile so absolutely genuine and noble of character that she distrusted him instantly. He slid into the center of the fracas, between the two dripping contenders. "Now, now," he said, "settle down, there's plenty to go around. Take all you want, take some for your friends. No reason here to fight." His tone reminded Lyell of a brother who ran St. Anthony's Hospice—firm but friendly: admonishing. It was the voice of someone who expected something from you, the priest wanting penitence. What the smooth reptile in dark glasses before her wanted remained to be seen, but she had the feeling she was in for a conversion. The two opponents separated, one on each side of the blond man. He led them back to the carts and gave each his own drink.

Lyell snatched up a chocolate malt and some wrapped foods from the cart, then moved away from the table. She pulled herself up onto a stone block from which she could record everything in the plaza. She disked a few more images of the SC staff, noticing another corporate type, who hung back by the tube. He looked uncomfortable with the proceedings, maybe frightened by his nearness to these unholy creatures. He certainly wasn't security.

One of the mad Boxers slid over beside her, and began babbling about something to do with castrating dogs. Lyell offered her one of the Vietnamese spring rolls. The woman snatched it and began immediately to try to peel it apart; it crumbled in her lap. She piled the bits back on her hand, hovering over it, then edged away distrustfully while she gnawed at the mess spilling through her fingers.

The mob, now that they had their food, behaved much as Lyell did, picking spots where they could sit and enjoy it. The security force looked on, unmoved.

Lyell had made the acquaintance of their like before. These would be the cream of the crop. Most often they guarded the checkpoints between upper and lower cities, where they very rarely had to deal with anything more demanding than an expired work pass. She'd long ago learned how to handle them. To the guards she was an inspector of some kind, which was what the words "truant officer" on her biocard meant to them: somebody who went after Undercity workers that didn't show up for their Overcity jobs. Undercity workers were notoriously unreliable, so it was easy to believe that someone had to keep track of them. They figured she fitted above them in the chain of command, and that, she knew, was all they had to think in order for her to sail through the checkpoints without a ripple. To those they perceived beneath them in the scheme of things, the guards had developed a certain dismissive attitude. If they hadn't worn uniforms, their behavior in that regard would have been indistinguishable from the corporate executives they guarded. Like the tall blond crusader. Even from across the plaza, Lyell could tell that smile of his was a fraud.

He was strolling amongst the feeders now. He sat for a time with each little group, speaking to each individual who had enough sense to listen. Whatever he was offering, most of the gnawing, chewing horde nodded emphatically when he finished. He gave each of them a tiny object, gave each one an avuncular pat on the shoulder, and then moved on. In his wake, another man sat down. That man carried a black canvas pouch out of which he pulled a small black atomizer bulb. He was handing out Orbitol. Recording the transaction, Lyell found it difficult not to smile. What could they be doing—testing a new formulation? Something to make the junkies burn up faster?

As the blond man drew near, she unwrapped and ate a little off the edge of a burger. Intellectually she knew there wasn't enough chemical in it to affect her behavior even slightly, but she still had to make herself swallow the pulpy bread and meat.

Finally, the smiling man sat down beside her and made introductions. His name, he said, was Mr. Mingo. He grinned as if the name alone should have made her joyously happy, as if she were his long-lost cousin, a prodigal returned to the family fold.

Up close he had a nastier face. Not that he wasn't handsome—no mistake about that—but when he flashed his perfect teeth, the skin of his jaw tautened unnaturally, as though any sense of decency and honesty surrounding the smile had been liposuctioned out. Lyell nodded back. In a soft voice, she told him her name—"Aswad Lobly." Then, in a thick accent befitting her disguise, she said, "Whatever you're peddling, you're wasting it on Orbiters. Unless it's a better Orbitol in that bag."

The smile was put away, like a handkerchief in a breast pocket. Behind his dark glasses, Mingo's eyebrows arched. "You think so?"

"Look. Look at them leave. Two hours from now, they be grinning like cats, babbling like monkeys, big red spots on their heads, here." She touched her temples where spots of makeup had manufactured old scars. "Maybe when they come down, they remember what you want from them, maybe not. Tends to mix up past, present, and future, Orbiting does."

"Well, Mr. Lobly, you sound like an expert."

"Could be I am. Throw it away how you like. You want everybody to do something for you, that's for sure. You want me, my price is shoes, not your drug. Don't want it. Get me a good pair of shoes—the kind to keep your feet warm in the cold. I'll get more from that one pair of shoes than any of *them* will, what you're handing out."

Mingo stared at her for a few moments, then broke into a huge, toothy smile. "What size?"

"Big, that's all. I don't know who's going to wear them before I hear what it is you want."

The man with the pouch caught up to them; he had an atomizer in his hand, all ready to go. Mingo pushed it aside and sent him back into the elevator tube with orders to get some shoes.

That was the point at which Mr. Mingo quite literally promised Aswad Lobly the Moon.

He revealed what ScumberCorp wanted in return for the free repast. It wasn't to be a test of new chemicals in the meat. It wasn't an offer of new, chaotically improved Orbitol. It was a notion that would have had Nebergall falling out of his chair with laughter.

"We think," Mingo began seriously, "we *believe* that there's a nest of aliens living in the Undercity."

At first Lyell didn't grasp the whole picture. "From what country?" she asked huskily.

"No, no." Mingo smiled, appreciating her confusion. "Aliens from a different planet, a different solar system. From—" he paused to fix her squarely in the black lenses over his eyes "—*outer space*."

"You mean like on Alien News Network? Like 'Alien City on Mars' or 'The A in AIDS Stands for Alien'? Alien, like those shows?"

Mingo seemed to swell with pride as Lobly recited real ANN titles. "I'm delighted you know the programs we sponsor so well. I didn't realize you saw much TV in your boxes." She couldn't tell if he was really so ill-informed.

"Oh, sure," Lyell/Lobly replied, "Watch them 'round the clock, Orbiters do. If they got a TV." Then, as if realizing what this implied, she added, "I seen them a few times, too." She brushed at her coarse black wig, made a nervous smile.

"Haven't we all? But, that's not quite the alien story we're looking for here. I don't believe we need to go looking for the brain of Elvis Presley, now do we? These aliens I'm speaking of, they are the real McCoy, *real* beings from another world. Who knows where?"

"They're really here? People from another planet are among us?"

"We think so. We've reason to believe that a group of them has arrived here, and that they're in hiding someplace in the city."

"Hiding, why? What does a Happy Burger got to do with aliens?" she asked, as Poleby might have. She made as if to offer him a bite of her polluted sandwich, but he politely pushed her hand aside.

"They're hiding because they're confused," Mingo said.

"Let me explain. Our parent company—naturally not Happy Burger itself—was in contact with an alien outpost on the surface of the Moon. That's right. They were in the process of negotiating a treaty of sorts when some of the aliens became suddenly ill. We're afraid that we might bear some—how shall I say—responsibility for their illness. We may have contaminated them, you see. We're hoping that maybe we can help them if we can find them in time."

"But why would they come here if they met you on the Moon?" she asked.

"An incisive question, my friend. We believe they would come here because our corporate headquarters is located here"—and he gestured toward the tall black and gray skyscraper behind him. "What we need is someone we can rely on. Someone who won't tell people about this. Someone with the connections in the Undercity to locate these aliens and then inform us of that location. Someone, Aswad—may I be so familiar?—who's looking for that chance of a lifetime to prove himself worthy to exchange the degradation of the Undercity for a new life, a new beginning, totally at our expense. Life in the towers. What do you say to that?"

She withheld what she wanted to say, but stood up and announced, "I'm your man is what I say."

"Oh, I know you are." He snapped his fingers and the man with the pouch hurried forward, carrying a pair of shiny white-leather walking shoes. Lyell's eyes watered at the sight of them. She didn't have to act—the retreads Nebergall got were usually barely glued together.

She reached for them but Mingo stuck his hand in the way. He was holding something shiny between thumb and forefinger. It was an antique coin, a dime. He placed the dime in her palm. She looked it over. It had a man's profile on it and the date 1967. Quizzically, she glanced at Mingo.

"Remember the date, close your eyes until you can see it. The date of your coin is very important—"

"Nineteen sixty-seven. This a contest?" she asked in Lobly's voice.

The corner of Mingo's mouth twitched the tiniest bit: he didn't like being interrupted. He said, "You must keep that coin with you all the time. It isn't like the other coins you've got, that you all barter with. This one you must not lose. If you find our friends, I want you to give that to them or else deposit it where you find their camp."

Lyell recalled an old expression, long out of vogue, but obviously the little joke Mingo had in mind: he wanted her to drop a dime on the aliens. She almost said it out loud but knew that knowledge would have been far too esoteric for someone like Lobly.

She pocketed the dime, then took the white shoes and got up, but as quickly stopped and sat down again, confusion pinching her features. "But what do these aliens *look* like?" she asked. "How'm I going to know them?"

"They look like you or me, Aswad. They're really *very* human on the surface. They may look like people you've known before. However, they'll reveal their differences to you quick enough, believe you me. For instance, they won't care to be around other people. You must be careful not to be taken in by their appearance. They can seem very gentle, even kindly, but they're powerful creatures when aroused, and they have reason to be aroused, as I've said.

"You leave it to us how to handle them once they're found. The plaza here will be monitored day and night. All you have to do is run right back here and we'll come down and get you, and take you up. After that . . . well." A broad sweep of his arm promised luxury, a fantasy life in a fantasy world for the one who found the aliens.

More likely, SC would hand the lucky winner a one-way ticket to an asteroid, where he would work as slave labor till the worn-out suit they gave him ruptured or an accident buried him. Didn't have to hobble them the way they had done to some of her ancestors; on an asteroid there was no place to escape to. Not when the company owned the very breath in your lungs.

Mr. Mingo shook Lyell's greasy hand and patted her shoulder as he had done to those before her. He told her to make sure and get some more food before she left. Then he continued on his rounds while wiping his hands on a napkin.

Lyell got up shortly and walked between two towers, far enough that in turning she could get a shot of the entire weedy plaza, the security people, and the skywalk vertical lift.

Many of the Boxers had already scattered, in a hurry to seek out the indistinguishable aliens or put themselves in Orbit.

What a clever exercise, she thought, *to sic the underclass upon itself. "They don't like being around other people."* *Really*. That merely described the entire population of Box City. There would be countless murders as a result of this idiotic game. Innocent people accused of alienness; they might as well accuse them of witchcraft, and there were definitely practitioners of dubious dark arts scattered through the boxes. Even outside the walls. Nebergall had a self-proclaimed "seer" in his building, and there must be a thousand more scattered around the fringes. Desperate people believed desperate lies.

What would Nebergall think of this now? It had stopped being a story about chemical pacification, but she had no idea what it was becoming.

Not long after, Mingo departed, followed by his assistants and the nearly empty food carts, and then finally by the security soldiers. The door curved around to seal the tube, and the whole of it retreated smoothly back up into the sky. A few clusters of feeding derelicts remained, already discernibly less friendly, already contemplating the competition.

The old bum Bindlestiff shuffled past her on his way out. He was munching toothlessly on two thin hamburgers, one in each hand. "Kinda like the pyramids there, ain't it?" he said of the view overhead.

"Not really," Lyell answered. "I was thinking, more like a kind of spaceship."

Bindlestiff laughed so hard he started to choke. He hacked and spit out a clot of bread. He gestured at the SC towers. "Now wouldn't it be a hoot if *they's* the real aliens?"

Lyell studied the ornate deco detailing high up the building and replied, "Frankly, I wouldn't be the least bit surprised."

7
Horrible Woman

Amerind Shikker turned and rolled in the semidarkness of the pit and wakefully dreamed of a strange world. However she lay or covered her eyes, the hallucinatory images assailed her.

A landscape all crimson, its substance nothing like dirt or grass or anything exactly, unfolded and undulated around her. It made her think of being glued to a cat's tongue—stuck on something spongy, wet, and budded.

Things—huge things—roamed about on the rolling surface. Masses of some almost indescribable flesh. She lacked a vocabulary to cope. Her senses were engaged in creating shapes for things that had no shapes. Her mind, her chaotic human mind, had to assemble something concrete or else go mad entirely as the gelid masses came lumbering past.

Whatever they were, they seemed not to notice her. When they passed close, she smelled something familiar—the reek of old boots that had been worn until tanned by the body's natural oils and the cracking leather began to exude a fulsome vinegar pong. She'd had clients who smelled like that.

She wondered where the squishy beasts had picked up the stench—or maybe they hadn't, and she was putting form to smell as well as vision.

The shapes—she strained to find a sense to them. Globby fat rabbits turned inside out and tied in knots; some, particularly the smaller ones, dangled from the sky, attached to nothing, reminding her of meat hanging out of the holes in a grinder. They should have dripped down to the ground, but did not, as if gravity had been suspended. Clearly she had no control over the substance of the hallucination.

She couldn't imagine having hit upon such images on her own. The bestriding creatures took no notice of her. They appeared not to have eyes. If they sensed her in any way at all, they gave no indication.

Secure in her seeming invisibility, Amerind looked for Glimet, but he was nowhere, excised from the vision.

When the lumpish shapes and the world they inhabited began to fade against the darkness, Amerind felt a growing itch at her temples. Soon it became fierce, like flame. Her other aches disappeared against it. She clutched at the blankets and began to rock back and forth. She would have scratched at the agonizing itch, dug the flesh off her head, clawed through her skull if she could have moved her arms; but Glimet had tied them to her sides—the broken one, carefully, to protect the knitting fracture.

She lay in the wooden booth that was his home, where he'd fed her and tended her wounds for two days. He'd cleaned her the time she shit herself, an event that would have recurred except that Orbitol tended to speed up the metabolism, consuming most of the body's fuel. There were no fat Orbiters, at least not for very long.

She screamed a wordless, frustrated cry.

She wrestled against his bonds, and he floated out of the darkness and crawled atop her. He whispered, "It's all right," over and over as he would have to a dying dog. "A few weeks and your t-temples'll scar over and the itch will get small. Then you're okay."

His body had become increasingly difficult to maneuver, and he took great care not to press on her broken arm. She responded to his voice and grew calm. Her muscles relaxed. He eased off her. She still did not struggle, so he untied her arms, then sat back against the wall. The candle flames flickered from his moving. She turned her head and peeped through achy eyelids at him.

His eye flashed like sunlight in a mirror and something huge and awful passed between them, drenching the room in its sour smell. It made her cough. He seemed unaffected.

"Yeah, my time's coming real soon now," he said, as though she'd asked him a question. "You'll be a light-year behind me, even if you can get supplied all the time. That's okay, though. I know you're gonna f-follow someday. It's the same for you, isn't it?

"When I close my eyes, my mind focuses somehow. I can see me in the Other Place now—least, I think it's me. I'm like twisted ropes—like plastic, like taffy all gooey or melted candles. Don't know what I am anymore. More there than here, but you saw that right away, too. Sure."

Amerind babbled under her breath. He crawled up and leaned close, knocking the atomizer gun onto its side. She watched it, an onion-shaped bulb with a ring trigger, rock back and forth, then magically right itself—his invisible hand picking it up. She could imagine the hand well enough almost to see it.

Wonderful, she thought, to be invisible and move through the world, to spy on anything you liked. Glimet could almost do that now. Just that little bit of him left—his eye, his forehead, and that piece of smile. She blinked herself conscious. What had happened to the rest of him? Where was his right arm? *Gone, already?*

"You're awake, then," he said, crawling back to his spot, and after a moment, "I'm worried, sweetie."

"Don't be. You're okay," she replied, misunderstanding.

"I've been through the concourse while you slept. Trying to hunt up some medicine for you, to make your bones knit fast. Need to get something with zinc in it, see." The blue eye shifted, glancing around as though jungle animals lurked outside the perimeter of the candles' light. "I found out that topsiders made a foray down today."

She did not know how to react. His tone suggested concern, maybe fear. But exhaustion from the Orbitol was depriving her of body heat, and gathering warmth took precedence over everything else. She got a hold on a rug and dragged it across her. She drew her knees up. Her stomach gurgled in hunger. Glimet began nattering again.

"—never happened before—both halves of the city stay away from us. They don't know what we got down here. These ones charged right into a camp. They tore up some curtains, broke down a wall and smashed Tecato's larder, see, and he wasn't doing anything, he's real quiet. Way up to 15th Street they say a group's k-killed two people since morning, no clear reason for it. Tortured 'em. There's a rumor the topsiders were looking for somebody and promising anyone who helped them a big reward."

"Who's it they want?"

"They're after somebody—somebody *new*. I thought, I mean, it could be you."

Wearily, she tried to puzzle that out, but she was losing consciousness, and her thoughts tumbled out of order. "No," she slurred. "They threw me down 'ere, don' want me back."

He said, "I didn't say anything. Nobody knows you're here. I told 'em the medicine's for me. Big rewards'll work on anybody. Maybe I'd go for one if it was someone I didn't know. But, see, I do know you, and I couldn't give you up, sweetie. I love—"

He leaned up and stared hard at her. She had passed out. He sighed and pressed his invisible skull against the wall.

When Shikker awoke, he was still sitting there and the last of the hallucinations had left her. So had the hunger that had been a craving earlier. Maybe it was an effect of the drug. Awareness of the implications of that dripped like a distilling liquid into her consciousness—a gauzy memory of his babbling, of the little bulb-shaped gun pressed against her head, and then a fire, a flame, searing her brain.

She sat up and wildly kicked the covers back. In the dimness she counted her fingers, her toes, rubbed her good hand over the hair on her legs—everything in order, everything still there. Someone had washed her.

"There a rat in the bed?" Glimet asked. "They get in there sometimes, 'cause it—"

"Goddamn you, you crazy fucking Orbiter! What you think I am? You think I want to be like you? There's hardly any of you left—you got a piece of a smile and a nose and an eye. Where's the rest of you, huh? You don't even know!"

As she berated him, a huge tear welled up in his eye, then spilled down his cheek. The tear clung to his invisible chin a moment before it dripped into his lap. He made a tiny mewling sound.

She fell silent, gaping. No man had ever behaved like that in front of her. Usually they hauled off and smacked her if she got mad at them. This was more like the response she would have expected from a little kid. "Hey," she said more gently, "c'mon, don't be that way. Glimet? Goddamn, Glimet, stop."

He wiped a wad of the cloak across his cheek. For a second it masked his incompleteness, and gave a sense of a whole face, unutterably sad and lost. "I was—was just . . . I knew you'd want to see, because you'd like it once you did."

"Sure." What she saw was the atomizer in among the blankets. She reached for it. A stabbing pain gouged her side. The wound—she'd forgotten the knife attack. She checked herself out. Even in the low yellowish light her breast looked bad. He'd set the arm well enough but all he'd been able to do for the gash under her tit had been to sop up the blood. The line where crazy Jack slashed had crusted up and was tufted with bits of cotton. It was seeping. When she pulled up at her nipple to get a better look, the abrupt pain made her stop. "Infected," she said.

"That's why I went to get you medicine," he explained, sniffling.

"Where is it, then? *That's* not any fucking medicine." She slapped the atomizer away. He made a grab for it, whining, scooping it up into his cloak.

"I t-told you, I couldn't *get* any medicine because the people from above's come down after you."

She nodded, remembering enough. "No way there's anybody wants me back up there. Better have another guess." She glanced around, taking in the tiny room as if for the first time. "You got any smokes here?"

Sluggishly he rose up and hauled himself over to the little rack beneath the barred window. He looked like a jack-o'-lantern set on top of a sheet to scare kids, she thought.

At the juvey center where she'd been deposited on her fourth birthday, they'd carved pumpkins and stuck 'em on sheets like that. A grower from Ceebco-Jersey had sneaked a cartload in off the Vine Street docks. Just that one time. She'd forgotten all about it till now.

Glimet sat down beside her and offered her an open tin. It held two real cigarettes and a collection of discarded butts. She looked into his blue puppy-dog eye, then took one of the longer butts. He turned to put the tin away. She crawled over to the nearest candle, then balanced upright on her knees to light it.

The first puff tasted ten years old and as wonderful as a fuck. She hauled it deep in her lungs.

"You got beautiful skin," Glimet said.

She craned her head, looking at him, then at her own naked ass and legs. She said, "Well, Glimet, at least I *got* some," and laughed even though it hurt. His expression clouded up and she thought he was going to cry again. She quickly asked, "What about the medicine?"

"I brought you clothes," he announced excitedly. "I did that. I know where to get them. May be they're too big, but I kind of had to guess." He gestured into the corner past where she had been lying.

She climbed the rest of the way to her feet, expecting dizziness, nausea—some kind of nasty reaction. When none followed, she walked back beside him and started rummaging. Glimet continued staring at her body.

She found a shirt and pants. As predicted, both were too large. The bulky shirt didn't matter—it would be warm. For the trousers, she took the rope he'd tied her arms with and looped it around her waist. Glimet had to tie it for her. He was as clumsy as she would have been. He hadn't found shoes but there was a pair of ragged wool socks that she let him put on her, too. She watched the excitement in his expression while she finished her brief smoke and wondered if he'd ever fucked anything alive in his life.

He brought her out of her reverie suddenly by announcing, "I know who it is."

Amerind looked up from crushing out her cigarette. "What?"

"I know who the topsiders wanted."

"Who?"

"Horrible Woman. It's gotta be."

"Who's Horrible Woman?"

"She's the one I got to go see now, to get your medicine. Nobody'll have gone down to her camp. Hardly anyone knows about it. She only appeared a week or so ago maybe. Nobody else much goes down there in the all-dark. But I like it, see. The Other Place comes through real good there. I've traveled all through it."

"Wait now," she ordered. "If you're going, then so am I."

"But you're hurt, sweetie. And it's a long way."

"Sure. So the sooner I get helped the better. If I'm with you then I won't have to wait till you come back to get my first dose."

The truth was, she didn't think he would be alive much longer, and she wanted to learn everything she could about the Pit while he could still teach her.

He scrunched up his remaining features while mulling over her argument, finally giving in. "Okay," he said, "but we got to have some barter, though." He groped around and came up with a small canvas sack from beneath the blankets, then turned to his small pantry. "Here. Can of beans and one of potatoes."

"That's all? Two cans of food?"

He nodded sagely. "Doesn't take much down here, and food's worth a lot. She's plenty hard up from what I seen. Her people got funny stock to trade—things nobody else has. Like the medicine. They live way way down in the deepest tunnels, like maybe under the river, so probably they found an old place in the west city that was closed up and forgotten. It happens sometimes—I got most of my cans of food from one of those, a little teeny store that had got overlooked. Got a lot more squirreled away."

"Really?"

"Hauled them myself. I was more 'here' back then."

She smiled tenderly. "You'll have to show me where you keep them."

He gave her a troubled look and made no commitment in reply. She knew better than to pursue the issue.

They set off at a slow pace, Glimet trudging along and Shikker, aching, being careful not to step on anything sharp.

Horrible Woman had twice emerged into the upper tunnels. Like a go-between from a subterranean realm, a troglodytic guardian of some unfathomed Symzonia deep inside the planet, she appeared and then vanished again.

The two who claimed to have bargained with her, an Orbiter named Chemosh and a schizo called Tecato, said she had a cache of rare supplies that they argued could only have been stolen from the Overcity—drugs and unusual tools, flashlights and things. All Glimet knew for certain was that Horrible Woman had traded her supplies to Chemosh and Tecato for cans of food.

By their description, she was so grotesque that, upon her first appearance, she had put the passively drugged Market

Street encampments to flight. At least twenty people corroborated the sighting, although descriptions varied wildly as to what exactly had been seen. Chemosh, who'd been in Orbit at the time, claimed she had multiple, pink, gummy heads with big, stubby tentacles around her eyes.

Glimet believed he had followed her sound through the darkness of the lower tunnels. He had threaded his way along at a respectable distance, wary of her untried powers, until he had come upon her camp.

It wasn't a half-bad camp by underground standards—a glowing oasis on the banks of the Styx: a few sheets hung on cables, yellow lights burning behind them. Clearly, she was not alone. Others were in there with her. And something more.

Even now he couldn't be sure if the shape he had seen far back in the recesses of the camp had been part of this world or the other. If it were alive or not. If the Horrible Woman had known of his presence all the time and had deliberately never moved too fast to lose him.

As if he had called to them, six figures had come shambling out of the tents. They had all fixed their stares straight through the blackness at Glimet.

A wind had come up then, belched from out of the sewers— a stench of such nauseating decay that he'd covered his face, turned and run from it. . . . At least, that was the way he recounted it to himself—he'd run from the smell.

Glimet and Shikker wove their way quietly through the upper strata of underground. At the station stop she was surprised to find tiled walls and pillars that looked as though they had only recently fallen into disuse. Tiled walls led along the narrow corridor to which Glimet led her. He pointed to a side tunnel labeled with an old sign: "SEPTA Police Vehicles Only."

"There's a big somniferum camp down there," he explained, "a whole bunch of room. Cleaner than most."

"What's a somnif—what you called it?"

"Somniferum. That's a d-drug name. You know."

"You mean *kif*?"

"Naw, opium. We're not allowed, down there, most of us. The Somnis come up sometimes. Even up to your level, to give shows with their puppets in the teahouses. Very well connected there, very secretive about it, with ties to outside plantations where the poppies are grown." He shook his head at the inexpressible possibilities, and turned away. "They won't t-talk with us," he added. "I just wanted to show it to you. We should go on."

Numerous entrances to the underground concourse dimly lighted their way. They encountered few people on the trail, although the walls were lined with abandoned shop fronts, behind which Shikker guessed there must be some inhabitants. Glimet pointed out where there were, according to him, encampments far back in the limitless recesses of the concourse; she couldn't see a thing. "Lots of camps in there," he said.

Eventually, they descended a stairwell to a second level. Three high turnstile gates blocked their way, but he went directly to one that rotated freely. They entered a darker realm. She commented, "I smell smoke," but Glimet made no reply.

At first they crossed a long platform. There were tiled walls again, orange ones this time. Each platform so far had been tiled in a different color. Shikker began to understand how Glimet took his bearings. A chrome fire hose valve glinted where it jutted out of the tiles. It still had its little wheel, although there wouldn't be any water pressure. In the distance the glow of a fire revealed a busy platform camp. Glimet suddenly dropped down off the platform and crept along in the shadowy rail pit. She had more trouble getting down, and had to run to catch up.

Once they had skirted the camp, he climbed back up. This time, he helped her up. "Not a friendly bunch back there," he told her.

The walls soon changed to graffiti-covered concrete. She couldn't read the strange symbols and weird scrawls, although Glimet nodded at it from time to time.

They chanced upon a few other nomads wandering through the murk; some greeted them and some ignored them. And once Glimet led her into a thriving camp that even had a pen for a couple of scrawny goats. He introduced Amerind to everyone, making it very clear that she had been living with him for some time. Nobody questioned anything he said. Some of them acted dopey, and she figured they were drunk or Orbiting. Many of them—even those she saw only from a distance—were missing body parts, although none was as comprehensively abstracted as Glimet; in fact most of the others seemed to hold him in great reverence. He had attained stature bordering on sainthood among the Orbiters, poised as he was upon the lip of that final transubstantiation. She'd never given much thought to what Orbiters believed in. Mostly, they seemed docile—like the bear things in Australia that lived in trees and chewed some kind of drug—harmless to everyone but themselves. To that extent they were no different from anyone else she knew: everyone trying to die, just calling it by different names.

Breezes commingling through various tunnels brought her the smell of foods cooking. Not all of the odors appealed, but she started salivating. She said nothing of the tight hungry knot in her belly. Mad as he was, Glimet probably would have insisted they join some group for a meal, shot himself in the head with that lousy bulb of his, and been sucked right out, the last of him, into the stratosphere, leaving her lost and without her medicine.

Staked-out territories grew fewer and fewer. They came to a blue tile station stop, labeled "22nd Street," where they went around a narrow bend, then descended a stairwell into a smoky cavern.

The single point of illumination was a grated vent to the surface. Debris from numerous cave-ins blocked the walkway ahead. Elsewhere lay mounds of dirt and concrete, and bent iron rods sticking out of the walls like the broken feelers of giant insects. Farther back lay the yawning mouths of multiple lightless tunnels. A diesel smell hung in the air.

Glimet turned away from the debris, journeying across the cavern. She followed him to where the floor ended abruptly. Below lay a greasy pit, and in it, the rails. Despite the fact that subways hadn't run for more than a decade, the railheads still shone in the gray light. *Maybe*, she thought, *all the oil kept them from rusting.* "All the oil" was something she had never seen, something which had existed a couple of generations ago. Old people still sometimes talked about "all the oil."

Glimet eased his invisible body into the rail pit. "You gotta c-come down here, too," he wheezed, once he'd gained his footing. "The platform is blocked off where the roof fell over there. You can't use it anymore." She glanced nervously back along the track and Glimet laughed. "There's no SEPTAS. They all stopped. Ya got to get down, sweetie. I'll help you."

Once in the pit, they strode down the center of the track. The rails were attached by large blocks to a relatively flat bed. Between the rails she found all sorts of things—the crooked handle from an old umbrella, plastic silverware, even a few old aluminum cans that she gathered up, knowing that she could trade them. Glimet seemed to take no notice, although it was difficult to see him now.

They bypassed the collapsed area and entered the tunnels. The track did not appear to curve, but soon the lighter point of entry vanished behind them and the rails became all but invisible. "We have to go this way," Glimet insisted. His voice smothered her. The air had become still, oppressive. The odor of diesel enshrouded her. She splashed through a pool of water, cursing it. After the third or fourth, she stopped worrying.

Blindly, she scuffled behind him.

Things moved about in the darkness, skittering away at their approach. Rats, probably. Rats didn't scare her.

For what seemed like hours they pushed through the blackness, at first toward nothing. When a small spot of light appeared before her, Amerind thought it was an illusion, a false image in the retina. To her right, she discovered that she could see pale lines appearing as if in the air and she had time to be afraid before she realized that it was real, not magic at all—white-painted graffiti on the black tunnel walls.

Ahead, the light source grew, and she found that she saw it more clearly when she didn't look directly at it. Shadows lay inside it, lines and planes that soon solidified into a concrete wall with a broad recessed niche above a rough dirt floor.

The light came from another street level vent. A faint buzz, as of insects, came to them as they neared the vent. Not surprisingly, the area stank violently of human waste; someone had been using the vent as a makeshift outhouse.

Shikker held her nose and cautiously squinted up through the rough circle of dripping metal grid work through which the light spilled like milk. She could make out the edge of a building in the background, but it might have been any one in the Overcity. She guessed that they'd crossed to the far side of the river. What buildings might remain there, she had no idea. The west gate had a reputation for being the one where more people got waylaid, beaten, or went missing. Here, however, was a sneaky way in, if they could find a ladder, and the vent up there wasn't welded. Given its other use, no one was likely to investigate it too closely.

She turned aside, intending to share this with Glimet, but found a monster standing before her. She cried out and jumped up into the putrid vent shaft. Glimet lay on the ground. The monster ignored her. It was closing on him.

It was squat, and broad around the middle. Wild hair stood out like oily weeds over its mushroom head. Layers of loose clothing covered up most of the body—just the hands and face showed in the gray light, but that was enough.

Huge, purplish knots jutted from its dark skin, protruding randomly across the surfaces of both face and hands. The entire body was probably covered with grotesque, seeping nodes. Shikker couldn't even see any eyes because of the knots. The eyes were pits into which no light fell.

The monster paused and considered her briefly before addressing Glimet. When it spoke, the voice was so compassionate, so feminine, that Glimet looked around at Shikker. "You're nearly lost," it said.

The name suited her—Horrible Woman. Chemosh and Tecato had done justice to her ugliness in their stories, but they'd said nothing of the accompanying aura of unimaginable pain held in check by sheer force of will. The woman must have been in agony every moment. Shikker could sense it, smell it, like a ripe perfume coming off her, and she responded instinctively. She jumped down out of the vent.

Horrible Woman glanced toward her, sizing her up. After a moment, she asked, "What are you doing so deep in here?"

"Looking for you," Shikker replied.

Glimet raised the canvas bag. "You have supplies we need. I have some for you, to trade." His head bobbed, then rose with considerable effort, into the air. All the while he babbled about Amerind, about her wounds, her need.

Horrible Woman considered what he said. Shikker noticed that each time they spoke to the woman she hesitated briefly before replying, as if each question and answer had to journey past her pain.

She said, "So much disharmony. And you, doomed even now. Even now."

"Do-doomed?" He floated fearfully back.

"Irreversibly. How did you let so much of yourself go? How could you watch yourself be devoured? How could you choose it?"

Her questions were not dismissive; she seemed genuinely to want his explanation.

Glimet faltered. He looked to Shikker for guidance but she shook her head. Already she had begun to doubt that she knew anything true about Orbiters.

He tilted his head back. " 'How' is because of the Other Place," he said. "When I look at it, when I'm there, it's the sweetest, the best thing. I don't want to be anywhere else. I'd—I'd put the bulb to my head and fire and fire and fire if it would get me there quicker, if that wouldn't kill me. I *don't* want to die; I want to go to the Other Place. It's so good there."

Horrible Woman considered him for a long moment before turning to Amerind. "You'll want your medicine. Come." She swung heavily about and headed out of the light, into a different realm of darkness than the one they had just traversed.

"I brought potatoes and beans both," said the Orbiter. The bag floated forward in his invisible grip.

"Reliable nutrients," she said after a moment. Glimet floated like a buoy in her wake. Amerind tagged behind.

As Glimet had related of his first encounter, they followed Horrible Woman by listening. Shikker caught hold of his cloak and let herself be pulled blindly along. In places where another vent or a hole flooded an area with light, the woman burst into view like a nightmare.

They came upon another group of rails, two sets of tracks divided by a wall of vertical girders. Glimet stumbled in, crossing them. Shikker helped him to his feet. In the pitch dark, he had substance, a spongy reality.

By the time they were ready to move, they had lost their guide. Shikker cried out, her voice echoing.

From off to the right, the gentle voice replied, "Here! This way." Horrible Woman had sensed their mishap and had lingered.

Now Shikker led the way. Glimet held onto her shirttail. She reached out, patting at the darkness, then running her hand along the edge of the raised platform, using it as a guide, until her fingers closed around a cold metal handrail. She stubbed her toe against the first step up. She ascended. Something crunched underfoot.

Soft fingers brushed her arm.

"Jesus!" she shouted, and stumbled back against Glimet.

"What?" he asked.

"Nothing," she snapped. "I just wasn't *ready*." She closed her eyes, summoning her will against the phobic dark. Trembling, she made herself reach forward again. She felt the knobs, soft as marshmallows, covering the hand. Against her blind terror, she let herself be touched, pulled, guided along a narrow ledge, and through a door, which, when it opened, revealed a dim light the color of brass. The woman let go of her.

Beyond the door, the light defined a narrow landscape of broken concrete and sewer pipes. Where the walls had crumbled, the black bars of iron appeared as ribs.

They followed the squat figure through all the debris, and finally around a high mound of sand, concrete, and brick.

On the other side was the small makeshift camp that Glimet had earlier described. Cables had been strung across the room and wide sheets hung across them to make the walls of a deep tent. The glow came from inside the tent. The sheets were alive with the silhouettes of other people propped up within.

The monster lingered at the edge of the tent, motioning for them to enter. Glimet lurched to a stop, and Amerind saw from his look that his nerves were frayed to the limit. He probably would have run if she hadn't held onto him.

"The supplies that you want are here," Horrible Woman said. "What is it you're afraid of?"

He stared at the shifting shadows of the others behind the sheet. "Come on," Amerind urged.

"I see," said the other. "Then you don't trust. I'll take you back if you wish."

"No," he shouted, jumping at the loudness of his own voice. "I mean, I—we—need the medicine." He closed his eye, shook his head. "What is this?" he asked, almost in a whisper.

Amerind pulled him along. His terror had made her forget her own. She told him when to duck beneath the cable, and, walking backward now, towed him inside the long, low tent.

What happened next seemed to her to occur in a waking dream.

The smell choked her, the air was gangrenous, as if the tent itself were a rotting skin. They didn't get up, the dozen or so bodies lying to either side. Only a couple of them made the effort even to look up. At once she dismissed Glimet's story about these people pouring out to stare at him. They couldn't have climbed to their feet much less made a mass effort to spook a wayward Orbiter. They suffered from the same disfigurement as Horrible Woman. A few had degenerated to the point that Amerind could no longer identify individual facial features. They had become purplish lumps of tissue. She walked through their midst, and remembered pictures she'd seen of Japanese people who'd been atom-bombed. This was like that. The skin of their distorted faces hung slackly as if all the meat underneath had been sucked away. Some were bloated, the way dead bodies got after awhile. She'd seen some who had died in their boxes and not been found right away. What were these people doing down here?

The tent seemed to draw a breath. The sides flapped in like the sides of a giant lung. Amerind Shikker turned around.

Glimet's head swayed from side to side. He edged back, stepping on a man, who cried out shrilly. Glimet leapt away, but swung around to see the man's leg jetting blood where Glimet's invisible foot had squished it. His one eye rolled like the eye of a horse, and he turned in a circle, whining throatily, seeking a point of escape but trapped in every direction.

Amerind ran over and touched him, trying to calm him. He swung the bag at her, knocking her aside.

One of the disfigured invalids said, "Easy, Glimet." He whipped around to confront a wet, pulpy horror. "Long time, no see," the horror said with grim humor.

Glimet knew the voice, and enough of the face. It was impossible. The man was gone. Orbitol decay. He was in the Other Place. *"Dead,"* he admitted, and recognition of that fact tore it.

Glimet bolted. His invisible body knocked Amerind aside. His cloak slapped her face. He hurtled down the aisle between dying, supine figures; the end of the tent—like an open, shrieking mouth—swelled before him. Amerind and Horrible Woman both called for him to stop, but he didn't hear them above the shrill siren of terror in his head as he sprang through the opening.

Had he been able to hover in the air in this world as he did in the other, it would not have mattered that the ground dropped away outside; he simply would have sailed to the far side. Instead, the bag of cans he carried snatched him, like an anchor, to the bottom.

Shikker watched his cloak flutter from sight. She heard the scrape and crash of his descent, followed by a final splash; and she ran through the tent and out. It took her a moment to spot him among the dark debris. He lay in the wet groove of an open drainage pipe. The smell rising was sulfurous and vaguely excretory, but as fresh as spring air after the confines of the tent.

She climbed down to get him, careful not to fall and tear up her already broken body. The water defined his naked form as if he were a figurine of glass. His forehead had been scraped raw, and blood trickled over his eyelid and down his face, disguising the line between what was left and what had been erased.

Shadows from above shifted across them, and Amerind looked up, her mouth open with amazement, to see Horrible Woman joined by four others at the top, backlit by the glow from the tent. She thought of mourners gathered around a Christ Church Cemetery grave. She'd attended a few funerals.

But how had they gotten up? she wondered. How had those seeping, rotting, dying people gotten to their feet?

Glimet groaned, drawing her attention away. She crouched beside him. He was barely conscious; his eyelid fluttered. Light glinted on his eyeball as the shadows retreated.

She looked around, and the five figures were gone. She stood on her tiptoes, climbed onto a mound of dirt, and searched in vain for them.

That was the moment she saw the faintly glittering shape hanging in the deeper darkness far beyond the tent—an enormous, petaled circle, as if the shadows themselves had taken seed and closed together and sprouted from a concrete wall, folding back, layer upon layer—a bloom, a blossom, a black and shimmering rosette of ice.

Glimet spoke up thickly from where he lay. "Sweetie," he called. "Got your medicine. But I forget, was it the p-potatoes or the beans that did the trick?" He tried to sit up, but toppled back into the stream.

8
Glimet's Passing

"What's happening to you?" Amerind Shikker asked Glimet.

He opened his eye and stared at her, kneeling beside him. He had been humming—not a song, more of a half-conscious utterance of discomfort.

He yawned, and she could see the tent through his mouth as if he were a ghost. "Jesus Christ," she muttered.

One of the others limped up behind her. "It's his time. It's coming now."

"I—I know you," said Glimet. "You're Alcevar, aren't you? D-damn, I heard your voice and knew it." He became puzzled, adding, "I thought you'd gone over, way last year."

The afflicted man nodded. His skin was splitting like a sausage sheath in places on his hands and face. The tissue underneath looked red as lava. "No longer," he said.

"Oh," said Glimet.

The sound of the syllable was odd. When Amerind looked back, Glimet's mouth had disappeared entirely.

The final stage would be a race to the last bit of him, the corpus callosum. He began to thrash inside his cloak. She tried to grab him with her one hand, but her fingers plunged straight through to the pad beneath him.

The man called Alcevar brushed her back. "Let him go," he insisted weakly. "You have to."

Horrible Woman was sitting down, exhausted. She called to Shikker, "You can't interfere. No one can this late. The chrysalis unfurls."

Amerind allowed herself to be walked back a few paces, but pulled loose then. "It ain't right," she argued. Her voice tightened. "We came here to help me, not to lose him."

"*He* came here to die," one of them said.

This wasn't fair. How would she survive among all the nests in the underground? She hadn't even found out where Glimet hid his secret cache of food tins. She forced a sidelong stare his way.

A swipe of pink cranium remained now, hovering, shrinking. His huge blue eye faded away as she watched. The others sat rigid in anticipation. "Wait," she pleaded, and no one paid attention.

Then Glimet began to yowl. The sound emerged from far away, from some other tunnel, from some other level, from inside the pith of the black rose on the wall. She heard her first name shaped within the cry—the first time ever he had said it—and she tore loose from Alcevar. She ran back to the heap of bedding. The cloak lay rumpled and empty. "Glimet!" she wailed, and dropped to her knees. She plunged her hand into the space he had occupied, grasping at anything. Her knee struck something hard beneath the cloak and she fumbled for the buried piece of him—any part with which to draw him back into this world.

She pulled out the atomizer bulb.

Here in the palm of her hand lay the plan he'd had for her. She had only to put the cursed thing to her head and pull the trigger to take her first step toward wherever he had gone. His Other Place, his Eden. That was what he wanted her to do—join him.

She set the atomizer on top of the cloak. "I'm sorry," she told him, shaking her head, knowing he couldn't hear her any longer. "I won't do it, Glimet. I won't do it even for you."

She began to cry, and she willed herself to stop, but the tears continued, raining thickly. She had never had cause to cry over any man. No man had ever deserved that much compassion.

Men had used her all her life, drunks and abusers—all claiming they just wanted a taste, a fuck, a little nothing she had that they coveted. Glimet hadn't been like that. He hadn't even been interested in it. From the very first, he had shared his space, what little he had, all that he had. Never spoke a word in anger. Hell, even in Box City, most of them had hankered after her digs. Glimet had left his to her. He'd left her everything. She remembered the pride in his voice as he had announced to others that she was living with him. She squeezed her eyes shut.

"That's good," said the Horrible Woman. "Throw away the drug. Leave it there and we'll see it disposed of."

Amerind wiped hard at her eyes with the cuff of the shirt as she got up. They were all watching her. She strode through their septic midst to Horrible Woman. "You do what you want with the junkie shit. But we gave you food," she said. "You owe me medicine. That's our deal, you and me."

Behind the fungoid features, something changed. It might have been the face pulled into a scowl or a smile—the features were too distorted to tell which. "We have nostrums," said the woman. "They haven't helped us, but they might work for you. Here." She indicated a large octagonal box on the floor, like an old-fashioned hatbox.

Amerind knelt down. One of the invalids, seated beside the box, watched her with childlike fascination. His skin was hideously burned, charred like wood after a fire. She couldn't believe he wasn't screaming. He sat rigidly still; only his eyes moved, following the lid as she lifted it.

The box was filled halfway with tubes and capsule dispensers. Every sort of drug was represented, a pharmacological heaven, a selection right out of a Geosat or some other manufacturing enclosure. She imagined what she could get in Box City—or better still, in street level shops in and outside the walls—with this kind of barter. She could buy a teahouse room, set up for life.

They weren't going to oblige her that much. They weren't handing over the box. One-handed, she rooted through the pile, picking out antibiotics and anti-infection creams for herself and slipping everything else that looked promising down the front of her oversized shirt, trapping it against her splinted arm.

Movement caught her attention. Instinctively she ducked her head—a lifelong reaction, cringing from her father's vicious backhand. Figuring she'd taken too much, she ducked.

But the movement belonged to the charred invalid. He had fallen back. His mouth was open. The breath rattled like dice in the well of his throat.

Quickly, Shikker scooped up what drugs she had in her hand and jumped back from the box. She bumped against Horrible Woman.

Ignoring her, the monster moved forward and spoke, "Leave, brother, hurry." Amerind stared at her, at the pulpy face and the black pits of her eyes, and finally, against all instinct to the contrary, down at the invalid.

His body shook. His jaw stretched wider than seemed possible, and Amerind anticipated his shriek. Instead, there emerged a series of snapping sounds, like chicken bones breaking one by one. His jaw slipped off center. His body shook harder, his breaths came in mad gasps. He began vibrating so hard that she couldn't really see him anymore, every part of him a cracking blur. Then, as quickly as that, it ended—in one final, brutal snap.

The body sagged down, deflated, deliquescing before her eyes. It looked like a human glove from which the hand had been removed. Invisible, a charnel stench billowed through the tent. She choked, her throat knotted against a surge of bile. She pressed her face against her shoulder.

"He was in time. He'll be back," Horrible Woman stated.

The sides of the tent drew in as though its atmosphere were being sucked away.

Amerind heard herself say tightly, "I'm leaving now. Don't try and stop me." She edged around the grotesque woman and along the central aisle of the tent. "I mean it. Nobody try."

Her implied threat was unnecessary. Nobody moved. Clearly, they lacked the energy or the will to stop her.

She ran back into the darkness, where no one pursued her and where, within five minutes, she became utterly lost.

9
Isis

The man named Mingo found a company car waiting for him on level three of ScumberCorp Tower—a bright blue, front-wheel drive Saracen. Mingo was wearing a black suit with a black silk stock around his throat and a pair of dark glasses.

The attendant unplugged the car from its curbside jack while Mingo slid open the trunk. A stack of six, long, innocuous tubes lay there, taking up most of the space. The word "Maps" was stenciled in black on each. Mingo smiled. He sought efficiency and, most of the time, because he worked for a corporation, was not rewarded. As he closed the trunk, the attendant came over and handed him a flexible keycard.

Mingo climbed into the Saracen and slid the card into its slot. The interior lights flashed once to let him know that the car had come on. He would have known, regardless of the built-in safety feature, because the car had over twelve thousand miles on it, and every knob, handle, and screw in the interior began rattling. To Mingo it sounded abominably like a dozen Box City beggars playing songs on silverware for a handout.

Electric car technology had advanced very quickly, but even at a mere thirty miles an hour God help anyone who had an accident in one. The campanulate car bodies were made from Knitinel and would flex back into their original bell shape when heated, but the same could not be said for the bits of the driver. So far as impact protection was concerned, one might as well have been surrounded by margarine. Air bags—once standard equipment—had been abandoned as unnecessary in the slower-moving electric vehicles. Very simply, you weren't supposed to have accidents.

Mingo prided himself on how expertly he drove. He had never been in an accident yet, not even as a passenger; but, then, he never allowed anyone else to drive when he was in the car.

He took the skyway loop that carried him over the Free Library and alongside the Rodin enclosure. In the darkness before dawn, the small square building with its fountain and unconnected front wall looked like something out of a Poe story, Mingo thought as he headed north.

He liked Poe's stories. They were short.

Today he felt good. His plan to have the Box City scum do all the work for him had been another stroke of genius, he had to admit. Let them paw through the stinking cesspools for the damned creatures' lair. If they got too rough, accidentally killed a few, what was it to him? So far as he was concerned, they were all aliens.

Mingo's destination wasn't too far away: the ICS-IV youth education fortress, referred to colloquially as "Isis-four."

The indigo sky looked clear overhead. A scattering of stars was still visible, the sun somewhere below the skyline of the Vine Street wall. Mingo found himself pretending he could smell fresh, clean air instead of the recycled, ion-charged atmosphere that surrounded him. Things were working, falling into place; it was going to be a good meeting; it was going to be a *good* day. Not for a moment did he conceive that anyone, anyone at all, might have cause to follow him.

Skyways, laid out as they were in mostly straight stretches, offered few opportunities for eluding pursuit, and none at all if the car you were driving had been left unattended for a few minutes while the valet called to let you know it was ready.

ICS-IV had its own entrance off the skyway, a brightly lighted, high-security entrance in keeping with the nature of the student body who dwelt as virtual prisoners behind the school's formidable stone walls. There was a parking lane at the entrance, into which Mingo scooted the blue car. Once out, he stepped up onto the pedestrian walk, from where he could look over the west fortress wall at the starred array of buildings below.

Seven long arms radiated from the central, lighthouselike tower, seven narrow buildings like spokes on a wheel. It was an ancient design, one that had caught on in penal systems the world over, but this one, formerly called Eastern State Penitentiary, had been the first, the template all others copied. The high-security blocks on Corson's Island still used the plan, with ten spokes in the wheel, easy to segregate, one from another. This place, this prison, had been unique in 1829. ESP was the single most-emulated piece of architecture in Philadelphia. For one hundred fifty years, it had operated successfully as a grim hive, row upon row, of solitary cells. Although made over as a medium-security institution of learning, to Mingo's way of thinking, ESP or, rather, ICS-IV still resembled a medieval stronghold around which a modern city had arisen, and it still provided the same service as before—it exiled a dangerous few for the good of the many.

The pedestrian walk led to a steep flight of stairs. A blue wire cage barred descent halfway down. Mingo headed toward it, his hand already sliding into his inner jacket pocket for his biocard. The card had been coded to identify him as an ICSS inspector, a position allowing him free access to any part of any school—including the students' quarters.

Two guards lounged inside the cage, waiting for him. They wore striped, gray and violet uniforms and each looked as if one, if not both, of his progenitors had been a tractor.

The students called them *bullgods,* making a joke both of their gargantuan proportions and their nearly unchecked dominance. Almost all of the bullgods were veterans of prison isle incarceration. Most had chosen guard duty as an extended vacation away from such hellholes as Corson's Isle. Survival odds weren't vastly improved here, but the accommodations and the food—most of the latter donated by Happy Burger and its competitors—were heads above the shingled shit the overpopulated prison isles had to offer.

All Mingo cared was that the megatherian guards did exactly as he instructed them. He had been here before. By reputation they would know him.

Reaching the blue cage, he smiled coolly, first at one and then the other juggernaut. With his thumb in place on it, he inserted his biocard into its slot. The door thunked open. The bullgods twitched and, with downcast eyes, edged aside to let him in.

*   *   *

A few minutes later, the two guards went lumbering up the stairs to Mingo's car. As they neared the top of the steep incline, a jogger passed them—not an uncommon sight to the general Overcity populace, but bullgods tended not to get into the Overcity. They drew up as one and admired the jogger's long legs and wide shoulders. She was a big woman, but that intimidated neither of them, one of whom had carnal acquaintance with bovine life-forms twice his own weight. He watched the jogger's sizable breasts jouncing under her loose clothes and felt a confused sexual heat in his lower abdomen. "Hey, dollin'," he said, "I got a exercise you can do." His buddy chortled and added, "Yeah, me too, sugar."

The jogger glanced slowly their way. She was dark, smoky, exotic. A little jewel in her nose, catching a first ray of sunlight, seemed to wink invitingly at the guards.

They watched her go by.

"Geez, now I got a hard-on," said the uppermost bull.

"Geez," agreed the other.

They shuffled up the steps to keep the woman in sight as she bounced into the distance. Had they been on their own, allowed to act on their urges, they might have pursued her and exacted their satisfaction. But Mr. Mingo was waiting below, and he would not have been understanding.

He had told them how to operate the Saracen's trunk, but it was already open. That had no effect upon the two guards, who wouldn't have known a discrepancy if it had bored straight through their forebrains. All six red and blue tubes lay where they were supposed to be; one had popped open at the end. The black butt of a little assault pistol was sticking out, and the nearest bullgod unhesitatingly reached down and pulled it the rest of the way out.

"Yo, loog a' dis," he said. "Dis no map."

It was a hot little item to be sure, an Ingram Model 30. They, armed with meter-long, metal-headed *lathis,* would have loved an Ingram. The telescoping sticks were nice, and could easily bash in somebody's skull, but an Ingram just poking out of a bull's belt would have kept most of the little toads in line. The two guards slid their hands over the black metal like blind men seeking Braille.

"Why ya suppose he's bringing these in, Tackler?" asked the second guard. He picked up another "Map" and shook it to hear the gun rattling inside.

"Maybe it's like a secret cache, ya know, case of a riot. Ooh, boy, makes you hope they fuck up soon, don't it?" He held the gun a moment longer. "Think he'd miss one?"

"What, like keep it?"

"Yeah," Tackler grinned.

"They's only six."

"So?"

For a minute they just stood there, unable to choose, with no real sense of what they had blundered into or what consequences could be served up. Then the bull with the gun leaned into the trunk and recapped the tube. "If he don't say nothing, then I won't neither."

"An' if he does?"

"Then I say, 'oh, so sorry, we found dis lying in the trunk, you know, and, bein' duty officer, I dint wanta leave it there in the open."

"*You'll* say it."

"I will. I got the gun, so I will."

His partner nodded, having now safely distanced himself from any retribution that might occur if the gun's absence were discovered. Mingo, although he was physically unimposing, was a spectacularly venomous quantity. It was the glasses, the scarves, the swept-back mane of hair, and the way he'd dispatched an overweening bull on his first visit, using nothing but a ballpoint pen.

They scooped up the tubes, closed the trunk, and descended the steep stairway toward the open, empty cage. They had forgotten entirely about the runner.

In the bowels of the school, Mingo had presented a list of names to the guard in charge, and was waiting for his sleepy-eyed guests to be rousted and brought into his commandeered classroom. His program disk was loaded in the podium; displayed on the wall behind him was the LifeMask face he wanted them to recognize. The arsenal was on its way down from the car. He began to hum "The Pirate King's Song" from *The Pirates of Penzance,* thinking that it was his song today. Everything was absolutely splendid, everything was really *good.*

10

Pirate Air

"Neeb, are you around?" called Thomasina Lyell.

The edit suite was deserted, the cubes all dark. She thought of how it would be if he were killed: it would be like this. She retreated to the outer room. His four-room apartment was hardly vast, but there was enough space for Nebergall to get lost among the clutter. So fastidious as an editor, he was anything but tidy personally. The outer room—the one ostensibly for guests—looked as if it had been detonated. Cast-off clothing covered the furniture in layers. Empty soda flasks fought with wrappers from fast-foods (which Neeb still ate, even knowing what he knew about them), cassettes, loose A/V disks, ancient videotape cartridges, and cables and connectors of every sort for possession of the floor. On one wall shelf were two plastic commemorative "ANN: 5 Years Watching the Skies" drink cups that had not moved in at least three years. A few footpaths had been cleared through the debris. She checked the bedroom—deep in shadow but otherwise in much the same overwhelmed condition—before being satisfied that he wasn't home.

On more than one occasion she had found him passed out after two or three days straight of editing, when a smoke alarm pressed to his ear wouldn't have roused him. She knew network corsairs—she had lived with one briefly. They all behaved much the same as Nebergall. They did not seem likely candidates for long life, nor were they the sorts of people given to trying to accommodate others. They were iconoclasts, dedicated to the precept that the applecart needed regular upsetting if one was to keep an eye on all the apples. To Nebergall's way of thinking—and to hers, she admitted— society, thoroughly unaware, needed them. It needed their perspective to maintain its equilibrium. "Harmony," he had proclaimed more than once, "derives out of conflict."

She wondered what he would think of the conflict she was encountering. ScumberCorp was arming ICS guards (she could not conceive of the more dreadful notion that it might be supplying students), while its representative bribed the Box City squatters to hunt down real live aliens, who had supposedly taken refuge in the city. She questioned whether the man, Mingo, actually represented the company's interests. But of course he did—they were, all of them, mad as hatters.

ScumberCorp was the largest corporate entity in the world. Its nearest competitor, Ichiban-Plokazhopski, was barely half its size; next came Bickham Interplanetary, a fresh contender as likely to be absorbed into one of the other two as to survive. There were others, thousands of them—a tower here, an industrial complex there; little companies that had become entrenched in a technological niche and managed to ward off the competition for a time. This became more difficult each year. SC's lobby groups had for decades been guiding Congress through seemingly innocuous legislation that was in fact deleterious to the smaller elements in the business world— specific fetters embedded deep inside impenetrable bills, the means to cut off a targeted company's legs (or worse) legislated so that there could be no question of legality. There were millions of pages of nearly nonsensical bureaucrababble to wade through each year, and even if you ran across the particular paragraph tailored against you, you probably wouldn't recognize it unless you could afford to hire someone (at enormous cost) specializing in congressional encryption. Unprotected both financially and legally, companies in one arena after another succumbed to the grinning behemoth.

ScumberCorp had accrued whole cities, entire states. They owned pieces of everything in every country on the planet, and now in lunar and Martian outposts.

Thomasina had been reared to be a part of it. Her widowed father, the mayor of Atlanta, had sent her to Princeton, where she trained to be a CAD/CAM 3-D animator. In all likelihood, she would have been working for an SC network right now if her father had not uncovered a system of bribery running through his own staff and the city council, who were greasing the local machine for an SC takeover of the entire state. Without hesitation, he blew the whistle. He was a political realist and thought he had prepared for the tough consequences of his actions, but he had underestimated the unscrupulousness of the menace he was attacking. SC savaged him.

They used the very 3-D systems on which his daughter was training to create videos of her father receiving his own payoffs from Ichiban. SC controlled Atlanta's media, and they impaled him with new footage of his reprehensible crimes almost daily for weeks, offering him no avenue of rebuttal or retreat. Soon most of the country had seen Mr. Thomas Lyell take money and drugs, and fuck three different whores—one in a suite in the Peachtree Center Plaza, and two in the tawdry bullet-vans out of which they operated, looping the Omni. It was as if he had brought along his own camera crew wherever he went, just to incriminate himself. Some people besides his daughter must have recognized the unlikelihood of this—but not the obtuse majority. Certainly not the eighteen members of the city council, who were well-compensated in advance for the stress of having to call for the impeachment of their once-beloved mayor. Helpless, Thomas Lyell resigned in disgrace.

The night he quit, his daughter had spoken to him on the phone. He'd laughed away her terror—her fear that he might take his own life. He had said, "My child, don't be so melodramatic. Don't you see I'm free at last? Thank God Almighty, free at last." Then he'd laughed again heartily, as if at some private joke.

She wanted to come home; he said no, she was to finish her schooling. His career was over, hers not even begun. Two months later, Thomas Lyell was dead of a fall from the landing in his apartment. Accident and suicide were both mentioned publicly by way of explanation; one psychiatrist on a talk show had even suggested the possibility of a "subliminal suicide" in which the victim unknowingly seeks mishaps as a means of punishing himself. The word *homicide,* on the other hand, had never once come up.

Since then, Lyell had done a lot of stories on ScumberCorp, catching them in any number of petty lies, from covering for a kleptomaniacal manager to denying outright (as they had done for two years against indisputable evidence) that there was such a thing as Orbitol decay. But nothing as insanely bold as this. Forget tranquilizers in the fast-food; this looked like elective slaughter in the Undercity schools. If Neeb could get good data on this Mingo freak, they might presumably sell the pirate air to every competitor ScumberCorp had. They could damage the megacorporation and make a fortune at the same time.

She went into the edit suite and sat down in Nebergall's swivel chair. She drove it along its rails until she reached the disk drives. Neeb was prickly about letting anyone touch his equipment, even his favorite *pijin*, but she needed to review her two days' worth of disking and there was no telling when he would show up again.

The slots on all the machines were empty; it was a precautionary quirk of his that he never left anything in any of his decks. Where he kept the more incriminating disks, even she did not know. Thomasina inserted her own disk into the "A" drive.

A voice behind her shouted, "It's all or nothin', boys!" and Nebergall burst upon her like an explosion. He smashed open the door and rode his motorized chair in like Longstreet leading the charge at Bull Run. She swiveled around as he swung his satchel at her. His flaming eyes went wide and he deflected his own swing as the corner of the satchel brushed by her cheek. He skimmed the satchel over the arm of the rail chair. It tore from his grasp and skidded beneath the right-hand bench, where it flopped over on its side.

Nebergall said, "Damn it, I thought sure you were the enemy, Tommie. I mighta killed you if I wasn't sober." He paused, his glance flicking from his chair to the disk drives and the two other silver disks she had in her hand. "You moonlighting on me?" Then to prove he was joking he smiled broadly, rolled forward, and gave her a huge kiss. Contrary to his claim of sobriety, he tasted of whiskey.

"It's beautiful," he said. "You woulda loved it."

She understood intuitively what he meant, what his entrance had been about. "You disseminated your Ichi-Plok piece?"

" 'Disseminated'—now there's a word you don't hear enough of anymore."

"That's because so many of our fine university graduates are still learning primary colors."

"God, I love it when you get pissy."

"I'm not pissy, I just speak better than you do."

He laughed, leaning back against the wall. "Yeah, you do, Tommie. You're the consummate actress, *pijin*. Me, I put together images to melt in your mind, and the Orbitol stuff I did is fucking beautiful."

"I gather from what you're not saying that ScumberCorp's a tad upset."

"Oh, yeah," he said proudly. "They're hunting all over Albuquerque for the perpetrators of this heinous attack."

"That's where it went, Albuquerque?"

"I piggybacked the whole forty minutes onto the Knewsday signal and coded its release so that it scrambled when it hit New Mexico, came loose and spread out in about three seconds to cover the whole West Coast. All the way from Barrow to Manzanillo. By the time they figured out to shut down and strip their signal, the Mussari interview was screaming up their asshole from Paris, reattached to a Jerry Lewis film festival. Seemed appropriate. It shot off the satellite and clamped right back onto Knewsday, as programmed. Whole goddamn world saw it and SC couldn't turn it off. People sitting in their cons, drooling at their usual dose of Hollywood shit, all the sudden found themselves staring at *my* subjective reality. Mine's real ugly, and it names names.

"SC's on the warpath. They gave up trying to handle it, just let it run, and whipped up some quick damage control about the unreliability of competitors' speculations. They've spent the last two hours trying to trace the signal back to its source. I had to stay with my nervous buddy to prove they wouldn't twig him. He's got a weak stomach, but they won't come anywhere near *him*. You can't trace a piggyback. It's like trying to track a DNA chain backwards to the Mesozoic. All the same, some of it musta rubbed off for me to think you were SC doing a B&E." He laughed again, then glanced affectionately at her. "You don't know what the fuck I'm talking about, do you, Tommie?"

"Enough of it. You get paid?"

"Tomorrow and next week and next month, slow and steady minipayments. Just so SC doesn't draw a connection between my sudden increase in wealth and the *dissemination*"—he grinned—"of subversive information."

"They're watching your credit account? Even in an I-P bank?"

"I have to pretend they are, don't I? Hey, if Mussari's singing for me, somebody else is singing for them somewhere, every hour of the goddam day. They're *bigger*'n me. Besides, they're suing Ichi-Plok's ass for false accusations. Part of the damage control. Surprise, surprise."

"Sounds like it's time you thought of relocating again."

"Yeah, I've been considering it. Been a purloined letter long enough—sooner or later they're gonna notice I'm in town. I was thinking maybe Seattle, before they buy it." He pushed his blond hair out of his red-rimmed eyes. "Anyway, what's on your agenda? You got something to show me?"

"I think so." She swiveled around to start the cartridge playback. "I think maybe we have something extremely dangerous here."

"Will it sizzle on screen? Let me see it."

She let the pictures roll, turning up the volume so he could hear all that Mingo had to say in the plaza. She added no commentary of her own; Nebergall never wanted to hear explanations. The images on the screen were all that mattered. People remembered what they saw, not what they heard. Take, for instance, Dr. Mussari's informative lecture. By itself it was nothing. Nebergall had added powerful footage of Orbitol decay personified—people in clinics with whole pieces of themselves missing. People blinded when infection from the atomizer guns they used spread to their optic nerves; children with no arms or legs, bedridden torsos born of two worlds; Undercity halfway houses crammed full of diseased creatures who could no longer recognize their surroundings, who saw only some fabulous other world as they slipped into total madness, fell into oblivion. The images delivered the punch necessary to capture the attention of the mentally anemic audience.

The images were what had SC in an uproar. A lot of it Lyell had brought him—he didn't ask how she got it. He knew in a roundabout fashion that she disguised herself; she would ask for IDs, for biocards, and he always filled her orders, but he didn't pry. All that mattered was that people talked to her, opened up, and confessed. She was the best *pijin* he had ever known. He adored her.

She popped in another disk. After black leader, the view came up of somewhere along the skyway over the Free Library. After a few moments of shadowy footpath footage, she climbed down into a parking lane behind a blue car and popped open the trunk. The compartment contained half a dozen red and blue tubes clearly stamped with the word "Maps." Lyell opened one. A rolled up map slid partway out; but with it came something else, bulbous and dark. Using only her thumb and forefinger, Lyell dragged the object all the way into sight. "Ingram 30," Nebergall muttered, nodding to himself as she turned it over, recording every inch of it. Later, he would be able to peg in on the serial number, maybe trace it.

She shoved the gun back into the tube suddenly, and stepped back from the car. The tag under the rear bumper was clearly delineated for a second. Then as she leapt back up on the footpath, the picture began to bounce. She was jogging. The lens gyro quickly compensated for most of the jiggle.

She ran along past a stairwell, looked down it. Two figures were approaching the top. Behind them, larger than the lens could take in, lay the unmistakable fortress of ICS-IV. One of the figures—men in gray uniforms—called out "Hey, doll" or something like that, followed by what Nebergall supposed were rude suggestions, but by then the men were out of the picture and well behind her. The rest of it was of running, followed by more black leader, followed by a return view of the parked car, approached this time at a more leisurely, smoother clip.

Lyell stopped the player.

"The car?" he said.

"Saracen. I gave you the tag, but probably there's no point in trying to establish a link—I mean, anybody can lease a car. They just happen to own the company. But you've got Mingo getting into the car after identifying himself as the great benefactor of SC and making with the loaves and fishes. That should be worth a lot."

He nodded, but said, "Might get him buried. You know all they'll do is sacrifice him and say they had no knowledge of his endeavors, and they're *real* sorry, tightening security, it won't happen again. Someone else immediately takes over. Mingo ends up as part of a sewer system in Bombay."

"So it's nothing."

"I didn't say that, Tommie."

"SC's stockpiling arms in a weapons-free school zone. God knows how many lives they've put at risk."

"But, provided it's contained, it's all in the Undercity, in a scummy reformatory about which nobody gives a shit. If you blew it up . . ." All of a sudden his brows knitted. He grabbed her chair and pulled himself across her lap. "Holy Jesus," he muttered, and grabbed his satchel out from beneath the bench, sliding back into his seat. He dug around in the various pockets of the bag. After a minute, he drew out a scratched-up clipscreen, took a stylus from his pocket, and tapped it in the corner of the screen to flip through pages of notes he'd logged in.

He paused over one, considering, his lips pursing. "This is *it*," he said, in some awe of what he had found. "I made the inquiries on your other footage," he told her, still looking at the screen. "Got an answer earlier."

"That was quick."

"That's what I thought. Like maybe the info was in place, in case anybody asked."

"I don't like your preamble already."

"No kiddin'. Here's the inside scoop. One Angel Rueda was rotated down from the main SC lunar cluster pending a hearing and possible sentencing with regard to his responsibility in the deaths of an entire crew and skimmer pilot in a dockside accident. Some kind of chemical explosion. Rueda was the foreman on the job, the only survivor, and suffers from a kind of hysterical amnesia, like shell shock, which is thought to be due to his guilt over the incident. That's plausible, seeing as how twelve people died."

"Oh, God." She thought of the expression on his face, the way he had looked at her in the bar.

"Wait, that's not the part you have to hear. Since he's out of work for an indefinite period, SC's got him assigned a job in the Undercity. He starts tomorrow, teaching for the Inner City School System. Guess which school?"

Lyell felt her scalp prickle. "Isis-four."

"Now, how'd you know that?"

"They're going to kill him. That's what Mingo's doing."

"That's something of a jump, don't you think?" Nebergall argued, yet found himself elated at the prospect. Tommie looked ready to scream.

She said, "Offer me a better guess and I'll listen. No, they mean to kill him. They've picked the perfect place, you said so yourself—'a scummy reformatory about which nobody gives a shit.' And nobody on the outside save you and me even knows. And the story's already in place. The rest of it, too, I'll wager, ready for airing the moment they take him."

"Amazing what comes with a decent pair of shoes these days, isn't it?" He laid the clipscreen across her lap. He stared blankly at her legs for a minute, then sighed and said, "I'm trashed to steam. Gonna grab some sleep now. You should, too."

"In a while." She was thinking of ICS-IV and her contact inside the school. She would have been much happier if she'd known how long they had. Or if they had any time at all.

11

Adjusting to New Faces

Shikker wandered lost for a day or more. She stopped at one point to piss, but then sat down and fell asleep. She couldn't tell if she slept for an hour or for ten.

When she awoke, she panicked, and ran around in the pitch blackness until she slammed into a vertical girder and fell back between the rails. Semiconscious, she lay there for another indeterminate period, then got up and, with hardly more awareness, went stumbling off, guided by cold, unseen steel rails, into the belly of the earth. She found herself calling out to Glimet to slow down.

By the time she regained her wits, there was no hope of finding her way out.

Recalling the colors of the station stops she'd seen, she pressed on, every moment expecting to spy the blue or orange tiles. Without Glimet charting the way, one tunnel was the same as any other.

She decided that she must still be on the lowest level of tracks, and imagined endless station stops slipping by on higher levels. But when she tried to climb out of the rail pit, she couldn't manage it. One-armed, she could not pull herself up onto the narrow ledge along the wall. She sobbed in frustration, seized with the awful fear that she was doomed to wander in the rail pit for the rest of her life, which wouldn't be all that long as a result. Then she remembered how Horrible Woman had hauled her up in the darkness, and she put her hand on the ledge and followed it. Walking on the uneven slope of the rail bed, she tripped a few times, but got up and resolutely continued on. It didn't take her long, feeling her way, to find an opening in the ledge, a flight of steps up. Then it was along the ledge she crept, pressed hard against the wall for fear that she might slip and fall into the pit again.

The ledge widened but she continued to walk with tiny steps, always testing the unseen floor ahead. She brushed against a pillar. Her eyes manufactured phantom shapes out of the darkness, but she refused to give in to terror. There was nothing there.

The echo of her footsteps changed, dulling, closing in, and she knew she'd entered a passage. It curved around and eventually she realized that she could see a little bit, enough to make out a stairwell dead ahead.

This time she raced up the stairs. The light leaking in grew brighter as she climbed. She came out at a platform. The tiles were polished gray. There was a long tile bench jutting from the wall, and she collapsed onto it, wheezing with joy and relief. She curled her legs up, clutched herself tightly to stop from shaking, and slept again.

A rat came scuttling up her hip. She awoke screaming, swinging upright and onto her feet. The rat squealed, jumped to the bench, and skittered away.

Shikker collapsed where the rat had landed. Nauseous, she pressed her cheek to the cool tile wall, waiting for her weakness to pass. Her arm and her legs ached; the joints hurt. She knew she was ill.

Bending forward, she scooped down into the front of her oversized shirt and came up with a fistful of medicines. The bad light made her squint to read. She identified vitamins, a package of assorted healing promoters, and a time-release anti-inflammatory/antibiotic; she took all of the *promos*, three vitamins, and two time-release caps, swallowing them all without water. She'd have killed for some water.

While she rested, she reflected on Glimet's death in Horrible Woman's camp. How had those people found their way down here? Since they all apparently suffered from the same affliction, she wondered if it could be contagious. Did she have it? Were the achy joints the first symptom? Would she end up like that—her body dissolving, putrefying? She drew her legs up and tried not to think about food. Her stomach gurgled its protest.

Maybe she dozed a little. Some time later, when she tried to stand again, her legs wobbled a bit but the knees didn't hurt so much. Buoyed by this good sign, she headed painstakingly across the platform and ascended the first stairs she came to.

She found herself in another tunnel, one with a wheel-variety turnstile that she eased past. On the far side was a concrete ramp. The light spilling in was bright; she could smell the air. She turned a corner and was confronted with yet another flight of stairs. The sight of them made her sigh. She felt as though she had scaled a mountain of steps. Well, this one last wouldn't kill her. Bent like a crone, she grabbed the rail and dragged herself up a couple of stairs before pausing to see what lay ahead at the top. It was a metal grid, the kind that unrolled off a big cylinder and wouldn't stay closed unless you locked it. This one appeared to be welded.

Shikker's eyes welled with tears. She slid down the wall and sat limply, a broken puppet. "All this way," she moaned, and beat her fist against her thigh.

When the tears stopped, she stood up matter-of-factly and marched back down the concrete ramp, back through the turnstile, down the stairs to the platform, and into the rail pit again.

She would not be conquered. She had medicine, she could treat herself, and she would find food somewhere. No matter what else, she would not die in this maze.

Blackness led her into blackness. She moved from tunnel to tunnel without concern, letting randomness direct her. Without landmarks, signposts, anything, it was all she could hope to do. She came upon black walls covered in white writing lit by sidewalk grates high overhead. The glyphs made no sense to her and she quickly walked away.

A noise finally stopped her, a sound from far ahead, shrill, like a baby's wailing. She took her bearings from that eerie cry and switched tunnels, patting the air ahead of her, thus adroitly avoiding another encounter with a girder. She located a branching tunnel out of which the wail definitely emanated, and she switched again, driven by an urgency born of fear— that the noise might cease before she reached it.

It rose and fell, louder each time it sounded. She was very near now, close enough to tell that no human child was responsible.

A murky white and blue platform came into view. Using the trick she had already learned, Shikker located stairs up to the ledge and followed that to the platform area. A sign dangling from one hook said "30th Street," and pointed at an ancient staircase that led to a bricked-over exit.

She waited, listening. The mewling came, and she sprang toward it, running stiffly along a narrow, twisting corridor. The light diminished till she was feeling her way along, too overwrought to be sensible and go slowly.

The corridor ended in a small doorway. Through it, as she approached, she could see the long, makeshift tent, glowing with its golden light, whose source she'd never figured out. Beyond it would be the trench where Glimet had fallen. She'd come back to her starting point.

The weird wail rose through the vast cavern. It sent shivers creeping up her back, the more so because she could tell from where it came. It came from beyond the tent, in the deep dark behind the golden light—from the black carnation. Or whatever the thing on the wall was.

She crept out, but realized there was no point in such sneaky behavior with Horrible Woman, and strode the rest of the way forward in the open. She approached the tent obliquely, in order to see down the length of it. Initially, it appeared to be empty, just a long triangular chute with heaps of empty bedding. Coming closer, she saw that it was not quite empty.

An individual remained, lying upon a ragged piece of bedding.

At first she thought the woman was merely sleeping—the gross distortion of Horrible Woman's features disguised the further distortion that had taken place. Then Shikker noticed the woman's hands. How flattened they were. She reached down and pulled back the bedding. The whole body had deflated, as though the bones had melted away. It was the same as with the man she'd watched.

Where have they all gone? What is wrong *with these people?*

She was looking down the length of the tent when she realized that the wailing had ceased. An ominous silence had settled upon the tent like Death hovering overhead. Shikker remembered the first time she had seen the tent, the way the shadows had shifted inside it.

They can see me.

She backed away from the body, to the edge of the tent. All the while she watched the other end. The material billowed slightly. Out beyond the light where she could not see, something was moving about.

She turned and took one step. That was the moment he appeared from beside the tent, lit ghoulishly by the fabric, naked and whole; enormous, it seemed to her. But, then, she had never seen his body. "Jesus," she said, her voice gone dry.

"Back again," responded Glimet.

Amerind Shikker fainted dead away.

"Wake up, goddam you!" bellowed the instructor.

Angel blinked at him.

Tall and stocky but with rather spindly legs, the instructor clung to the podium as if in support against rough seas. Underneath his LifeMask (Angel suspected) he would look like one of the other derelicts in the room.

"Good," the instructor said. "Now, as yuz can see, the mask does not quite conform to a normal face. That it's a projection squeezing your head will be obvious to your class, but they don't give a shit so don't you be worrying about it either. They know you're disguised and they know they're the reason *why* you're disguised. It's a little treaty we have between us— what you call your tacit agreement. They leave the masks alone and we don't tear their fucking arms off." He smiled. It was clear to Angel that the instructor didn't mind the prospect of dismemberment.

Angel sat in a small room at a student's desk. There were eighteen more desks in the room, but only seven other people. Five, seated in the front row, looked exhausted already, as though they had endured hours of interrogation prior to this. Like machinery with too many broken parts, they listened and observed; but their slack expressions lagged behind the content of the instructor's lecture. The other two—a man and woman, a couple—seemed, like him, to be coherent and unaddicted, just down on their luck. He wondered what crimes they might have committed, and whether they found themselves here courtesy of ScumberCorp.

The instructor continued, "The LifeMask operates when you lock the collar. You don't lock the collar, it looks like you're wearing a bag over your head." He switched his off for a second. It did indeed look like a gray bag—like a sieve hugging the contours. How did he see through it? wondered Angel. Before he could figure that out, the artificial face reappeared. It expressed fatherly concern. In fact, he thought, the collar did make the instructor look rather like a priest.

"Do not enter a classroom without your LifeMask on. Do not remove it in the presence of students. Not all of the little darlings are confined to the premises, and if they know you by sight they might be persuaded to take care of you on the streets, where nobody's gonna help you. Enough 'accidents' have occurred for us to know what we're talking about when we say this.

"Also, don't concern yourselves with how you look to everybody else, okay? When you smile, *it* smiles. You're going to look so happy they can't stand it. Plus, you get mad, it tones things down. It's interactive. That way, if you're scared shitless, you're protected. Maybe you look a little confused, a little annoyed. They won't know you're ready to bolt and run. Remember that. It could save your life." He was staring at Angel and the other two; they were the ones who might actually heed his warnings. The rest were grist for the mill—lumps of raw nerves without the sense not to panic.

"Now we come to the lectures themselves. Hey, you're no geniuses, but that's been taken care of. Among all the other things, the LifeMask is a hyped-up BAM circuit that overrides certain parts of your brain and lets in the prepared information we have on whatever subject you're going to be teaching. In fact—" now he zeroed in on the derelicts—"the less gray matter you have left, the better it is for our program. Most of you are gonna make real great teachers."

"What's a BAM?" asked one of them.

"What do you care? All you got to know is that you'll know everything you *need* to know. Some smartass kid asks you some question he dug up to show off, the mask'll have the answer. You just let it do the talking."

He pushed away from the podium. On the floor behind him squatted a brown, recycled box. His heels kicked it and, for an instant, he wobbled like a slowing top. The mask face remained bland, unconcerned. Maybe, Angel thought, he was giving them a demonstration of the mask's immutability in the face of fear.

"Now's the time we try out the system for each of you," he said calmly. "I'm going to ask you, one at a time, to come up here and receive your mask. I'll show you how to program it, and we'll run a test lecture so you can get used to the feel of it. Your faces are changed every day, so don't expect to see the same people twice after this. Nobody is gonna know nobody. Safer that way all around." He nodded as if deciding that he'd covered some salient point. He opened the box, took out a gray lump that looked for all the world like a dead octopus. "Okay," he said, "who's first?"

The entire front row leaned away from him as one.

12

Chikako Peat

Thomasina Lyell had an escort through the hallowed halls of ICS-IV. A big, gray-skinned bullgod led her down the steps. He had hands bigger than her head. Riding in his wake, she breathed his brewery scent and watched his undershirt pop into view like mattress ticking where the seams at his shoulders had burst. She pegged him as Circus-fodder—genetically manipulated for use in one of the combat games. The games were broadcast on so-called private channels, frequencies owned and operated by the rich; but as no channel was truly private, plenty of bootlegged disks existed—sold in the black markets of the Undercity, where the brutish fighters had come from in the first place.

Combats were events of gross cruelty and mutilation, death served up like popcorn. Nebergall owned illegal copies of two. She'd watched one long enough to appreciate the ugly magnetism of the event and to feel cheapened by her own immediate reaction to it. The hulking bullgod beside her resembled too closely the composite image she carried around in her head—of a near-rectangular face, the cheeks gashed, the lips swollen and empurpled with blood, the teeth smeared with it. For some reason she had zeroed in on the teeth.

The other bullgods leered at her as she went through their checkpoint. Packed together in a group, they seemed grotesque, like the semi-intelligent offspring of another species. Polyphemus and Ymir, Gog and Magog.

She recorded their thick faces against the peeling paint, the cracked plaster and concrete, the barred shadows and the rot.

Her red-haired escort might have been one of the two who'd watched her jogging, but she could see that he didn't recognize her any more than she did him. She looked from guard to guard for the armaments Mingo had smuggled in. There were no guns. No one appeared to be armed with anything other than the standard-issue metal-tipped *lathis*.

Students mingled in the long hallways, behind gates. She saw no teachers. From research she knew that the teachers had their own access corridors into the classrooms. Interaction with students outside controlled environments was regarded as certain suicide.

Knowing that, she was surprised when one of the gates opened up and the bull led her into a hall full of them. Some of the students paused to appraise her, and their leer was no different than that of the guards. No doubt given time they would become their keepers.

Another generation of compost, she thought. Many of them had severe scars, burn marks, or bruises. One couldn't open her left eye; another didn't have a left eye to open. A few had their arms in slings, their fingers taped to splints. At her approach, they stopped talking and jostling. None dared cross her path. The clusters parted for the guard; the students moved back out of reach of his riot stick. Occasionally someone said something to him or to Lyell, mostly in languages or euphemism she didn't know, but sleazy by inference. One kid called her "*Cô Cát*" along with which the others made meowing noises. These followed her along the hall for some distance. Hands reached out and brushed her arm, her hips as she passed. She would never have run this gauntlet alone.

Eventually the crowd was left behind. She and her escort passed through another checkpoint. The guards' ogling hardly bothered her at all.

Lyell tried to locate herself in the complex. She had studied a map of ESP but the ramp they entered after passing that second gate had not shown on it. As nearly as she could determine, the bull was leading her underground.

The ground floor consisted entirely of classrooms. Living quarters for students classified as permanent residents lay on a second floor above the classrooms—converted cells that could easily be sealed off in case of a riot. Each of the separate arms could be contained as well, isolated in minutes. There were gates everywhere. From her protected lair, wherever it lay, the administrator could accomplish everything from gassing any individual room in the complex to calling in an air strike.

The bullgod led Lyell through a narrow door and into a room off which half a dozen similar doors opened. He crossed the room and entered one of them. Inside was a curving wall that rose up into total darkness. It might have led to one of the corner bartizans or the central rotunda. Metal steps led up the side of it, but the bull walked past them, to a door that unlatched electronically just as he reached it.

They stood in a small entryway, a room that clearly could be sealed off. The bull halted before the armored door on the other side of the enclosure. The door stood ajar. "Dis the twitchers' lounge," he said sharply. "I don't go in. Principal's on other side—you'll be met."

Lyell nodded.

The bullgod stepped back to let her pass. As she did, he observed, "You look strong."

She turned on him, exasperated by this last comment after walking the gauntlet. Then she saw his scarred face was flushed, and his eyes cast down. He was embarrassed. He was shy and flustered. She wondered if he had ever spoken to a woman up close before. There must have been some who would have given him the opportunity.

"I'm not so strong as you," she said. "Thank you for the escort." Before he could get any ideas from that, she pushed her way into the so-called lounge.

It was not a large room. Seated around cheap folding tables, a dozen people in softly glowing LifeMasks looked up at her. She thought of pictures of apostles that had adorned the Sunday school classrooms of her childhood. The same smiles, the same generous earmarks of divinity.

One of them, at a desk beside the door, got up and bowed smartly. He reached for her hand and shook it. "My name is Mr. *Ong*," he said, and chuckled. "I'm in charge of these goats. You're to go right on through and no bother." Ong's mask was grinning delightedly. His hand was hard and callused.

At the other end of the room, the second security door hung ajar. There was a third metal door in the wall on her right, closed.

Lyell passed among the happy artificial heads. One of them could easily have been Rueda. How would she ever spot him among the artificial idiot smiles?

For all of the faces at peace, some of the bodies, the hands at least, were trembling. A few had missing fingertips. One arm was absent altogether but invisibly filled out its sleeve from the beyond.

Their hands were rough, hard. Some of the nails were broken, some hands scabrous. She tried to recall what Rueda's hands had looked like. She'd been so absorbed with the face, but she had checked his hands, his wrists. She didn't think they matched any she saw here. How many twitchers would already be in their classrooms? How many lounges might be strewn through the complex? Her map hadn't indicated any of them.

She passed through the second door, and heard it shut heavily behind her. The sound reverberated as if through many tunnels.

She stood at the head of a conduit between two rows of partitioned cubicles. The air was smoky, misty. The overhead lights barely fired. A few fluorescent tubes flickered here and there in an erratic pattern, but most, apparently, had burned out and never been replaced.

Lyell walked between the cubicles. Shadowy clerks turned to face her, poised like animals caught in the light of desk lamps and terminal screens. The equipment looked a good twenty years out of date, with big monitors as bulky as dictionaries. She thought that if she were to make a sudden move, the figures would all dive out of sight.

The fluorescents ahead flared briefly, revealing scratches in the mottled black stone at her feet. The sound of footsteps ricocheted like bullets off it. A dozen invisible people seemed to be walking ahead of and behind her. Weird, crisscrossing echoes.

Like a freighter's prow bearing down upon her out of the fog, the principal's desk loomed into sight. On each side of it stood high folding screens covered in Japanese brush paintings of waterfalls and brightly plumed birds. The frames were black lacquer, as was the triangular desk. The arrangement appeared to be an origami construct spotlighted under recessed fixtures and magnified to seem larger than it was.

The screens must have disguised an air-filtering system; the moment Lyell stepped between them, the smoky atmosphere vanished and the air smelled as clean and moist as a rain forest.

The ICS-IV principal, Chikako Peat, reclined behind the desk. She rested her stockinged feet on the top, and she was smoking an aromatic cigarette from a holder as long as her forearm. A bank of thin monitors dangled immediately above the desk, their shifting images like rainwater reflected upon the woman's face. She glanced from the monitors without turning, giving Lyell a stare out of the corners of her heavy-lidded, almond-shaped eyes. It made her seem both mischievous and haughty. The irises of both eyes looked violet, but that might have been a result of the monitors. She had rounded cheeks, a flat nose, and full, painted lips. Her face was as perfect and smooth as a mask, but she, unlike her teachers, did not wear one.

She had traded a life as a rich madam in the Overcity for this job. Lyell had met her once before, in her old job. She placed Chikako Peat at twice her apparent age and extraordinarily well-connected in the upper governing levels of SC-Philadelphia.

"We know each other, don't we?" the principal said.

"I once went seeking someone you'd employed."

Peat exhaled a stream of smoke that plummeted almost at once to the ground. "Yes. As I recall, you found her."

"You'd moved her to another establishment with which you were connected. But, yes, I found her."

Peat nodded in recollection. "Did her family ever take her back?"

"Why would they? She'd made it into the Overcity. They're just lowly shopkeepers in a laborers' quarter outside the walls. They can't even come inside without a permit. They only wanted to know that she was all right."

Chikako Peat laid down the cigarette holder on a tray near her feet. "What's your assessment? Was she all right?"

Lyell leaned on one of the screens. "I'm looking for someone again," she said.

"Why don't you sit? Will I have to hide this person from you, too?"

"You didn't have to the last time." Lyell took a seat beside the desk.

"As it turned out. As it turned out, I'm the one should have gone into hiding. The corporation chose to shut me down shortly after your visit. I hope this isn't going to be a déjà vu experience." Her eyes flicked again across the suspended monitors. Her irises were violet, almost lavender.

Lyell followed Peat's glance to the screens, partly visible from her position. "You don't seem to be very busy."

"With paperwork, you mean. That's what all the clerks are for. Reports. Transfers. Death certificates." She pursed her lips. "There are over a dozen new twitchers going into classrooms today—right now, as we're talking. Statistically, fewer than half of them will survive the course. I don't care particularly to be sending people to their deaths, but that's inevitably what I do every day. How busy must I be?"

Lyell answered, "When I found out you were here, I thought to myself how much power you must wield to get yourself such a cushy job."

Peat's smile curled with irony. "Nothing like it," she said. "I was given a choice between this position with limited prominence but continued residence inside the Overcity, or else whoring in a lunar or Martian colony. Until then I thought exactly what you do—that I knew enough about too many people's predilections, and that would protect me. I suppose it did, after a fashion—they didn't have me murdered. They rightly suspect that I have recordings cached away which could damage, perhaps end, a few careers. That tempered the verdict slightly; but you cannot bargain with the likes of ScumberCorp. If you don't like the offer, then you don't like the offer."

"Another company?" Lyell suggested.

Peat laughed. "What a novel idea."

Lyell nodded. It had been the same with her father. "My visit was unrelated to your change of fortune. I didn't work for them."

Peat leaned forward, touching the edge of the desk. A section of desktop slid back to reveal a small keyboard beneath the surface. At the same time a thin wedge angled up out of the desk behind it. "You are—" she leaned forward to read from the embedded screen "—a social placement officer, an interoffice interloper who decides who's behaving and gets released, who isn't and stays bound to this hell on Earth a little longer."

"It says all that?" she asked amusedly. Nebergall had taken care of her long-standing ID. Inside the school system was the one place where the concept of truancy still meant something, however. She carried a court-appointed officer's biocard in her belt bag as backup.

Peat smiled. "I *know* placement officers, Miss Lyell. I deal with them routinely. Little gods. They never bother with missing persons. On the whole, I would say they prefer to have people missing."

"I had a different job back then. Same as you."

Chikako Peat withdrew her feet from the desktop. "What is it you want that you had to come here in person instead of applying to the *phonet*?"

"There's a new teacher—"

"Twitcher. The nons—that is, the students—call them twitchers. It's a grim but accurate epithet, I think. The name has taken root, as with the term 'bullgod' that they attached to their guards. Clever children."

"A new twitcher, then. Named Angel Rueda. His situation is not the normal—"

"I do not discuss these people with anyone," Peat said. She splayed her hand and studied her polished fingernails. "Besides which, none of their situations could be described as normal. If they were normal they wouldn't be here."

"Nevertheless, there are some deeply troubling circumstances surrounding him."

"For you or for me? I get a list of names and appointments. That's all I know. And what does a truant officer want with a twitcher?"

The point had come that Lyell had to trust this woman. Was her low opinion of SC real or a blind? She was the principal, and it was quite conceivable she knew about the weapons Mingo had delivered. She could have requested them. She could be working for Mingo, by choice or coercion. There was the risk, unavoidable.

"Like you say, maybe that's all you know," Lyell began. "What you might find odd about Rueda is that, purportedly, a few days ago he caused an accident at ScumberCorp's Procellarum facility and may be a member of a radical group within the corporation that's been blamed for dozens of similar incidents."

"*Xau Dâu?*" Peat said softly, her face betraying concern at last. "They would never—"

"You might conclude as I did that SC would keep someone that dangerous totally isolated. Their official report in fact says he's been sent down to isolate him from others in his alleged group. Isolated. Yet you've got him on staff."

Peat typed again on her keyboard. After a moment the report appeared on her wedge screen. She skimmed over it, lingering on the standard head shots of Angel Rueda. "That is the same person? You're sure?"

Lyell leaned forward. She nodded. "Yes."

Peat scrolled some more, reading. "Nothing about the Moon at all. An ex-Orbiter."

"What?" Lyell stood and leaned over her to read the file.

Peat continued aloud, "Suffered minor tissue loss in the phalanges of the feet and some sort of necrosis in the parietal lobe of the brain which is why he wears the cranial bypass unit. Here's his work permit number. An employment history clearly reflects drug use, but, then, most of our twitchers are still orbiting despite swearing otherwise. We're used to that. Nope, no job higher than temporary docker, like a million others hanging on outside the walls—not very probable lunar material here." She gazed up at Lyell. "Why do I have this report in my system if what you say is true?"

She didn't have an answer for that. *Why put one story in place for the likes of Nebergall and then plant this one for the school system? Obviously, because these two elements of society aren't supposed to cross paths. Parallel lines.* She would have loved to tie into Nebergall's *phonet* and let Chikako Peat see ScumberCorp's news release, but that would have established a traceable link between Neeb and ICS-IV, incriminating everybody at both ends.

While she was thinking, Peat called up something else on the main monitor hanging overhead. Laid atop the shifting images of various classrooms and hallways was a list in red of numbers and names. "He's teaching in the third cellblock, in classroom F." The list disappeared, replaced by a different classroom image.

They viewed the room as if standing at the back on a chair or desk. The figure at the front had ash-blond hair and the indefatigable smile of the LifeMask. From this distance its luminance gave the impression there was a soft spotlight focused on his face.

From the dimness around them, Lyell heard a strangely metallic voice: "Nucleosynthesis is the making of new elements out of nuclear reactions—the kinds of reactions that occur within stars. We think the universe might not always have been made of the same things as we see today, precisely because nucleosynthesis has added new matter to the world."

Peat turned down the lecture. "He seems to be handling the program well enough."

"Are all of your twitchers ex-Orbiters? Is there a reason for it?"

"It helps us. He remains asleep for all intents while he talks. The mask program disconnects higher brain functions from the speech centers. It's been described as forced meditation. That's why junkies and drunks—anybody who's already wiped a good portion of their brain—are perfect candidates for this. Less resistance. It doesn't have to be Orbitol necessarily. In fact, dipsomaniacs are preferred over Orbiters. When the lecture program takes hold, it acts as a temporary personality. You heard him talking. He sounds alert, doesn't he? But your real Angel Rueda, whoever he is, won't be back again until the program releases him—at the end, or in an emergency situation, where it would wake him."

Lyell turned that information over. "What would constitute an emergency situation?"

Peat opened her mouth to reply, and an alarm klaxon blared so loud it seemed to have blasted right out of her. The principal stared up at the center screen. The scene had changed automatically, the system targeting the source of the alarm.

They beheld another classroom, almost identical to the one where Angel Rueda taught. Except that this one showed a twitcher hanging by one hand off the podium and a girl standing up in the center aisle. She had a black pistol in her hand, still pointed at the dying twitcher. Her classmates had spilled back from her on either side like the parted Red Sea. Peat typed again. The wedge flashed a warning sign that did not deter her. She pressed a code key at the side of the beveled board, and within moments a grayish mist was spewing into the classroom. The klaxon shut off. The danger had been contained.

"Tear gas?" Lyell asked.

"Absolutely. Where did she get a pistol?"

The alarm shrieked again. Peat found herself confronted with multiple images. Classrooms and hallways and one black screen flicked into view on the main monitor only to be bumped aside by the next and the next. "My God, it's a riot. Somebody's *armed* them. Look at all of them!"

"What about Rueda?"

"You think it's him? He's armed, too. Twitchers all are. Print-fixed weapons of course, precisely to avoid this kind of situation—"

"No, I mean call up his *room*."

A hidden intercom began to buzz insistently.

Somewhere within the fortress, something exploded. The floor shuddered. A distorted roar blasted out of the overhead speakers.

The main monitor pinpointed a fish-eye scene of total chaos—students stampeding into a cellblock corridor while, behind them, black smoke billowed out of a room. Two bullgods fell beneath the crush. So did most of the front line of students. The back line pushed, and the middle churned. More fell on top of the first group, jumped, trying to get over them, more often stepping onto them, tripping, falling, adding to the melee. Their screams clashed with the snap of gunshots.

Peat typed more instructions, sealing off sections of hallways as fast as she could. Gates swung shut. "I'm not going to be able to contain this until I know how many there are. There could be a hundred guns in there. Who would have done this?"

"Look, Chikako," Lyell said, "this is going to sound like a colossal leap, but if I don't get to Rueda right now, we might not ever find out the answer to that."

The images of hallway chaos shifted to a secondary monitor and another classroom scene erupted in the middle.

Another twitcher lay dead, her blood sprayed on the wall behind the podium. Students were doing their best to trash the rest of the room. One of them was trying to tear the bloody LifeMask from the woman's head. The principal's eyes narrowed coldly. "There's an entrance in the lounge you came through, takes you to the private galleries. Use that. Remember—Three-F." She added, "First, though, you tell me why." In the monitored classroom, gas spewed out of the walls.

The desk phone began to ring.

"He's the real target. All of this is a blind. They want him."

Peat paused only a moment, her strange eyes reading Lyell's expression. She typed quickly, eyes on the main monitor.

No image came up. The screen went black and a message flashed along the bottom. The camera unit in Rueda's classroom had been disengaged from the system. Without hesitation, Peat gassed the room.

"It's too late then, isn't it?" said Lyell. "They've killed him."

"You *know* who armed them," Peat accused her. "You knew all about this!"

"I thought it was bullgods they'd armed. I thought there was more time, a lot more, maybe days. I thought it was going to fall out differently. And I couldn't be sure where you stood." She headed around the desk. "Will you still be here when I get back?"

"I'll be here until you've told me everything. Now go, I'm busy."

The ringing of the phone never stopped. The sound chased her as she ran. The overhead fluorescents flashed like lightning. The clerks had vanished, every one.

The exit opened automatically. No one remained in the lounge. Half-eaten muffins and an overturned cup of coffee suggested the speed of their departure.

The third door off the room was locked when she tried it, but a second later some mechanism within it thunked loudly and the door slipped ajar.

On the other side was an elevator cage that might have been as old as the prison. She rode it up to a platform—a railed circular walkway off which branched seven gloomy corridors. Tiles inscribed in Roman numerals designated each one. She circled until she came to the one marked "III," then ran on into the unknown.

The gallery stretched ahead with no apparent end. It smelled of millennial mildew. As she ran, Lyell noted the occasional camera snout overhead, tracking her. She hoped it was Chikako Peat.

To her right, along a wall of crumbling plaster laid over stone, lay the classroom doors. To the left, the other wall alternated sections of plaster with translucent panels of thick glass embedded with chicken wire. The glass had been smeared over with paint and dirt. An oily blue light leaked in around the edges. She thought sourly that it had the kind of ambience Nebergall would love.

She passed doors A, B, and C. She crinkled her nose at a new smell, initially slight but, even so, acrid. Tear gas, leaking into the gallery. How was she going to get through Rueda's classroom if it was full of gas? By the time she took twenty steps, she would be in blind agony.

She passed rooms D and E. Her nostrils stung now. The door ahead was bathed in a dull blue splash of light. She called up the picture of the room as she'd seen it on the monitor, thinking that she might make the podium, even with her eyes closed and her head down. In any case she had to risk it.

The door clicked open even as Lyell reached for it. She was thanking the invisible principal when it swung straight into her face and clobbered her off her feet.

13

License to Teach

He knew exactly how his class felt about their new teacher. They had murdered the last two. The bullgod who escorted him to his room told him about it just before abandoning him outside his door in the shadowy gallery. The bull slapped his shoulder. "Hope you can shoot, Tex," he said, "the last two before you couldn't make the *grade*!" Braying, he walked off into the shadows.

Angel turned to the door. It unlatched automatically for him.

Inside, all conversation ceased. The instant he stepped through, twenty-three steely gazes fastened in him like hooks. No one spoke or moved as he approached the graffiti-covered podium.

The entire room—if not the entire building—reflected the Overcity's disregard for the incarcerated nons. The wall tiles were broken and crumbling. Mildew grew where leaks had been patched or ignored. In the back lay a pile of broken furniture—desktops and shattered terminal screens, chairs that had been twisted into abstract shapes resembling tubular sculptures. In one corner sat an engine block that must have been twenty years old. Rust in a brown puddle had spread out slowly from under it. The only thing, in fact, in obviously good condition was the door he'd entered through, but that was steel plate, difficult to damage beyond the odd dent.

He unlocked the podium by typing in a code on its number pad. The podium's processor connected to the thirty desks in the room. Each one had a small flip-up screen—provided it hadn't been broken—and a keyboard.

Angel's introduction had been etched into small program cubes he carried—three of them, two as backups. The lecture was interactive.

The program could field any relevant questions and ignore nonsensical ones. Should the mask perceive an emergency, the podium relinquished control instantly—at least, that was what it was supposed to do. In any case, he should be sufficiently aware of events unfolding around him to override the program if need be. So he'd been told. Much of what might happen rested on untested promises.

The final safety net consisted of a hidden camera focused on him. He'd been warned by his instructor that some twitchers, embarking upon their first lecture, experienced cold sweats and an unshakable terror of certain death as they went under. Angel looked for these elements in himself and found only a blank wall, a strange detachment from the events unfolding. Fear as an option had been occluded by the cranial bypass unit, the *crab*. He wondered how the podium's program would recognize an emergency when it gauged such things from his emotions, and he had none.

ScumberCorp's interrogators on the Moon had described for him how he had broken laws and harmed innocent people. Of the various misdeeds attributed to him, he recalled not a thing. All memories of his time on the Moon had been wiped clean along with his emotions. There might be other memories surviving but, so far, every attempt at prying into them had triggered in him a massive phobic attack, a panic that wrapped around him like a suffocating plastic bag. When it had stopped and he had regained his equilibrium, he could not find the terror within him, could not touch the fear again . . . until he tried remembering the Moon.

Of his childhood, he'd found one scene that had somehow escaped the axe. It had about it a curious transparency, as if he had caught it just at the point where it was about to slip away forever. Like an old photograph, it had lost its color, its definition. He saw two people—his parents? There was a lake glittering behind them, but no specifics—no smells, for instance, no sounds. No names for anything. His parents had no names. *He* had no name.

He tried to bring that memory into focus, as if he could take it in his hands and warm it, make it glow.

His eyelids fluttered. His head lolled forward.

He snapped upright, found his hands clutching the sides of the podium, and took a step back. He'd been thinking of something, daydreaming about a place, but it was gone now. The thing was (and the interrogators didn't know this), he did have memories; he just didn't know how to hold onto them.

He stood in front of a hostile class of children, described as "nons" because to society they were nonentities. He felt nothing either for them or their predicament. Their cruel circumstance lay before him like the ruins of his classroom; he could see it and the hopelessness of it. There was no escape, no ladder up. All of which meant nothing to Angel Rueda. For all the sense he had of it, he might have been viewing the class through the hidden camera lens.

He drew his hand from his pocket. In his palm lay an iridescent cube no larger than a die. It contained billions of facets, each coated with information. This was his program. He dropped it into place in the lectern of the podium. A small cover slid into place over it and a green light came on. That was the last thing he saw.

Something without substance but dark and impenetrable— what the instructor had called *squid ink*—enveloped his consciousness. Where he'd been an empty vessel before, he shrank now, withdrawing altogether. It was a feeling akin to the moment the phobia of memory opened to devour him, except that it never opened. As he shrank, the program swelled like an entity into the abandoned space.

He began to speak. "Good morning," he heard himself say. "My name is Seraph. I'm your astronomy and physical sciences teacher."

"That's twitcher, *borracho*!" called out one of the nons.

The program ignored the jibe and sailed right along. He listened to its drone—his voice, but not his words. He knew nothing in particular about how stars were formed, which was what he talked about. The manner of speaking, the dull cadence, belonged to someone else.

From where he dangled, he saw the classroom as through the wrong end of a telescope, across a wide black chasm. With effort he found he could assemble what he saw into recognition patterns, but it took all of his attention to accomplish. He could see but he could not realize.

He was saying, "Low mass stars are cooler and have very long life spans. The high mass stars burn hotter and quicker. If our sun were a high mass star—an O star, say—it would already have burned itself out."

"Kinda like you, hey, twitch?"

The class laughed.

Unperturbed, the program continued, "Given that, we can predict that these hot O stars existing in our sky are fairly new additions to our universe, and that, right now, as I'm speaking to you, more new stars are being created."

Suddenly, he couldn't see the room anymore. The black chasm pushed up like magma to block his view. Its shape conformed to something like a human head—a LifeMask without features inside his mind. The chasm spoke to him. "Angel," it called, "Angel, do you hear me?" The voice was much louder than his own mechanical recitation.

"*Sí.*" He spoke, but only in his mind, a word he had not known until that moment. His mouth continued to babble science. "Yes, I do."

"I feel you quite near. What has happened to you? Have you freed yourself of them?"

Monitoring its host, the program must have sensed a disturbance in the field with which it surrounded him. Angel found himself abruptly damped down. The room vanished altogether. Only his internal self remained, pressed in, sealed shut. "*¿Quien?* Who do you mean?" he managed to ask.

As if from a great distance the voice answered, "*Piensan matar. . . .*"

"Wait," he called, but the presence evaporated, taking with it his new language.

He was wrestling against the shackles of the program when the first shot went off.

The speech aborted. The program flung him into full command of himself. He pitched forward as if thrown into his body. Reeling to stay upright, he clung to the podium. The room tilted and came back to true like the deck of a ship on rough seas. His rubbery legs braced against collapse.

At the back of the room, a tall Latino non turned to face him. The kid held a nasty, short-barreled black gun. He had fired a burst high into the back wall, blasting a line of tiles. One tile had splintered, revealing a pocket of embedded, ruined electronics. Somewhere, distantly, a klaxon was honking.

"Hey, hey, twitcher," the non said, "it's lights-out time for you. You're the guest of honor today and I collect big-time. *Adios.*"

The non stalked him down the aisle. Others to either side crouched down, some terrified, others grinning.

The non raised the black gun to take aim.

Angel drew his pistol and shot the non through the bridge of the nose. The body kept marching, but the head snapped back; a net of bloody tissue erupted out behind the kid, who all at once seemed to slide. His left foot snapped up too high. His dead arms flailed as if grabbing for balance. The gun spun away, skittered two rows, and banged off a desk leg.

More alarms went off, much closer. An explosion shook the whole room. A chunk of wall plaster crashed to the floor. Some of the kids screamed. A few leapt to their feet as tear gas jets around the ceiling hissed to life.

In the confusion, a second non dived for the black gun. He grabbed it and came up firing at Angel, who promptly shot him down. He had been watching the weapon, anticipating a second attack, with what instincts he could not say. *They mean to kill,* the voice had warned. Didn't they, though?

The second killing ignited the class. Shrieking and coughing, a herd of them scrambled for the door. Others, too terrified to move, crouched under their desks. The gas settled like gauze over the room, thickening. There must have been a dozen alarms going off, so many that they sounded like a single throbbing horn.

The nons threw open the door as a second explosion rocked the foundations. Tiles fell off the walls. The first non to the door was shot as she stepped into the hallway. Some of the murderous barrage pinged off the door.

"Stay in here!" Angel ordered. He choked and lowered his head for a second. The mask filtered some of the sting from the gas. It would be worse for the nons. He heard the door slam shut and glanced up. His eyes were flooding.

Trapped, the students bent double, covering their heads. They retched and cried, glared hatefully at him, glared as if he were the cause of this nightmare.

He had to act. They could not stay here. A few minutes more and he would be blind and sick on the floor beside them, where anyone could pick up the gun and succeed where the first two assassins had failed.

He could think of only one reasonable alternative. He hoped Peat wouldn't kill him for it.

He waved his gun toward the gallery door and said, "Come with me!" He glanced back at the second non he'd shot, to make sure the black gun hadn't taken a walk, then ran past his students to the steel door.

It didn't open.

He looked at the shattered tiles in the back wall of the room. The non assassin had done a very good job. No one on the other end of the monitor would know he had survived, and without knowing that, they would never open the door.

He hammered, his fist thundering against the metal. When that didn't work, he called to unseen microphones, "This is Seraph! Let me out!" The class huddled around him, wheezing and sobbing. The noise from the hallway jumped in volume as another student risked that exit again. Resolutely, he pounded away with both fists.

The door clicked open. For a second he couldn't believe it. Then he launched himself against it before it latched again. The door swung out, struck some obstruction, but yawned the rest of the way open. He wedged himself in place to keep it from closing and dragged the nearest kids into the dark gallery. He counted a dozen of them. Where the rest were, he couldn't be sure. They could be lying unconscious in the middle of the room for all he could tell—the gas had thickened to an impenetrable soup. He could hardly make out the shape of the podium.

When he stepped into the gallery, he found the class gathered around a dark woman. She lay on the floor, leaning back against the wall, one hand cradling her forehead.

Her expression was creased with pain. One eye scrutinized him from between her fingers. She muttered, "Next time, I'll knock first."

With a queer feeling of recognition, he said, "I know you."

"You—you're Angel?" The woman straightened up, wincing. "My God, I'd taken you for dead." Her eyes dropped to the gun in his hand.

He glanced down at it, realizing that he had killed two people with it, and that he felt no remorse, felt nothing whatsoever. His only reaction was to wonder when he had learned to shoot. "We should leave," he commented, and put the gun away.

One of the weeping nons interjected. "Seraph? We ain't supposed to be in here. The bullgods'll do us, they catch us in here. You don't know . . ."

He looked all around the gallery. No idea came to him. He'd gotten them out of the room, and that seemed to be the extent of his captaincy. "We should leave," he repeated.

From the darkness overhead, the disembodied voice of Chikako Peat spoke up like Jehovah addressing Moses. "He's right, Seraph, they're in trouble, get them out of there. Take them to classroom E. It's not in use—there's no gas in there and I'll unlock the gallery door. They'll be locked in from both sides, safe till this blows over."

Angel nodded to the ceiling. Before he could move, a loud report sounded from the classroom. Angel spun around and fell.

Lyell cried, "Jesus, he's been shot!"

An erratic hail of bullets shattered one of the dirty glass panels in the opposite wall. A swath of sunlight sliced across the gallery floor. Peat's voice shouted, "Get him out of the doorway!"

Lyell grabbed his foot, but he rose up on his own and slid out of the line of fire. Another burst of fire spanged into the glass and plaster. Angel kicked the door closed and climbed to his feet. Dust smoked around him.

"They couldn't see me through the gas," he observed. His upper left arm was dark with blood. "It's okay, I think— went straight through the muscle." He touched the wound, and jumped, hissing.

"We'll play doctor later. Get out of there now," said Peat. "I don't have any more time to devote to you. And, Miss Lyell, you will have *all* my answers when you arrive."

Broken glass cracked underfoot. Angel could see the glow from the LifeMask on the wall beside him as he led the nons to classroom E. Behind them someone pounded on the door.

When they had been locked in, he asked Lyell, "What did Chikako Peat mean, Miss Lyell? What answers do you have?"

"She meant that I knew about this riot beforehand. I know who orchestrated it. I still don't understand why."

"Oh," he said, mildly surprised, "I thought maybe this happened every day here."

Lyell started to laugh. "Not every day, no. Just on the days they let Angels teach."

He supposed that was a joke.

As they hurried down the dark corridor, he listened with growing unease to what she had to say.

The doors to the teachers' lounge hung ajar. In the principal's office, ceiling fluorescents that were dark before had been ignited, lending dimension to what had been smoky void. The space was a huge warehouse enclosure with corrugated walls. Where they saw entrances, the doors hung open, offering sanctuary to those who managed to work their way in from the chaos above. The cubicles had been sealed up like rolltop desks all in a row. In the vast room, only Chikako Peat remained.

She watched her monitor screens, paced back and forth, and once picked up the insistent desk phone and yelled obscenities into it. The sounds of a full-blown assault echoed from the speakers above the monitors—a ghost army doing battle in an empty room.

As Lyell and Angel neared, Peat swung around and watched them. She switched off the cacophony from the speakers, pointed at Angel's head. "Take that damn thing off. I want to see when anything penetrates the lock on your brain."

He reached up with his good right arm and fumblingly unplugged the throat latch. "I thought the whole idea was to avoid that," he said.

"Not with me."

The false face vanished, replaced by dull gray mesh, like a fencer's mask. Behind it, his features were a smear. He pushed the mask over his head, dropping it on the triangular desktop. His face glistened with sweat, and his skin had turned milky. He dabbed at his left eyelid.

Quietly, Lyell said, "He needs medical attention."

"He'll have to wait in line. As things stand, the containment gates for sealing off the sections of Isis are blown, almost every one. Circuits are cut. There isn't a single corridor in here left undamaged. We don't know how many guns are floating around free, but by my count we have five dead twitchers, thirty-five dead nons and climbing, twice that many injured, and no idea *how* many bullgods left, because they're too motherfucking stupid to call in and *tell* me!" She regained her composure before continuing. "I've sent home anyone I can find. I called in reinforcements the moment you left, but they seem extraordinarily slow to arrive. If I'm going to go down with the ship, I would at least like to know what sank me."

Lyell said, "You know there won't be any reinforcements. ScumberCorp won't release them till it's confirmed his death."

Peat asked, "Are you *Xau Dâu,* Señor Rueda?"

"I'm not sure."

"Funny, I knew you were going to say that. Maybe we should shut off that goddamned skullcap of yours and see what emerges. You get a lot of mileage out of that fucking *crab,* don't you? Poor Angel Rueda, *qué lastima.*"

"*Lo siento mucho,*" he responded automatically. He knitted his brow, hearing himself speak words he didn't know.

"Did they bring you down from the Moon?"

He glanced at Lyell. "Yes. I was escorted down. May I sit?"

Peat nodded, staring into Lyell's eyes. "So, *your* story is true."

"Would I have gotten myself locked in here otherwise?" Lyell asked. "Why don't we leave Isis now? Why wait?"

"It's my duty. There's no one else."

Lyell leaned forward. "Look, your duty's done here. When the reinforcements finally come in, there will be a blond man named Mingo at the head of them—"

"Mingo? I know about Mingo. He's an ICSS inspector, thinks he owns the school, the assho—"

"He's not an inspector, it's a cover, a blind; it gets him in places. He works for SC, sub rosa. Understand? If he finds out that you know what you know, he's going to shoot you. Probably if he finds out that Angel's escaped, he'll kill you anyway, just to hedge his bets. No one is going to know that you didn't die in the riot. No one."

Seeing the implications of that scenario, Chikako Peat's composure finally slipped.

"I told you," Lyell said, "this entire event was concocted to eliminate *him* in a way that disguises what's really going on"—she tossed the LifeMask across the desk—"the same as this thing does. Mingo will wipe out the entire school if he has to."

"Who in the hell are you?" Peat asked her.

"I'm a very good *pijin*."

Peat sat back in her chair. Her perfect eyebrows arched for a moment, then dropped. She began to chuckle, and continued as she lit a cigarette. She said, "So. Now everything's in its place. That's what you were the last time, too."

Angel looked from one to the other. "The last time? You've met before?"

"Just like you and me," Lyell replied. Turning, she said, "There's an escape tunnel out of here, isn't there?"

"Naturally. One of the few safeguards required by law."

"Does it take us into the city or route us onto a skywalk?"

"Into the city, one way in and one out," Peat told her. "Don't worry, once we're in the Overcity, I've got connections. We'll be fine."

"Only if we survive. We're going to need a different mask for him. I'm sure they're watching for this one."

"All right, then." Peat stood up and slipped her feet into a pair of solferino sling-back shoes. "I resign my post."

From across the room, a voice shouted, "Hold it!"

Lyell turned, expecting to find Mingo in dark glasses, but it was one of the nons, a blood-streaked, bristle-headed, pink-skinned, and tattooed punk. He held one of the black guns, and he came forward from between the clerical cubicles.

"How did he get this far?" Peat asked no one in particular.

The non gestured at Angel. He said, "*He's* the one, isn't he? I made it to that room, and he wasn't home. *No*body got him yet. He's mine. Yeah." He stared at each of them, training the gun on each in turn. "Yeah, you're *all* mine," he said.

The first shot cracked the air.

14

Tunneling Out

The sound of the shot rebounded like hammer blows.

The non leap sideways, landing on legs that no longer supported him, but the shots kept coming. He started to crumple, was hit again, the bullets "thwack-thwack-thwacking" like rivets, jumping his body as if with current. The firing ceased but the echoes had not died out entirely when the non flo
pped
over on his side. His outstretched arm clutched the gun as if in a salute. He lay still afterward.

Across the room to the right, one hulking bullgod stood in an open doorway. He, too, had one of the black weapons. Lyell recognized him as the one who had escorted her into ICS-IV. He moved awkwardly into the room. He limped, and his right heel left bloody imprints.

He waved the gun. "Toog it off my duty officer. Don't even know where Tackler got it—same place as the nons, huh? Dead now, anyway."

Lurching around the triangular desk, he all but fell into Chikako Peat's chair, which squealed under him. He placed the gun on the desk and pushed it aside before making hesitant eye contact with Lyell. Then the bank of monitors caught his attention. "Real hell everywhere. Nobody knows who's in the soup and who ain't, so we're taking out everybody what's loose, and so are they. There's all that gas, too." He sneaked a shy glance at Lyell again. "You okay, though. That's what counts."

"We wouldn't be, without you," she agreed, having no idea what should be done with this gentle monster.

Peat stepped in. She asked, "Are you trained on the system? Can you work it until SC sends reinforcements? I . . . have to get these two people to safety." The bullgod tried to stand, but

Peat pushed him back in the chair. "You've saved her life. But you're too hurt to keep up, and others might follow the same trail as he did."

"That's right," Lyell agreed. She kept the desk between them, but touched his huge hand beside the gun. "You can protect us better from here."

He flushed at her touch, which highlighted the white scars like erratic war paint across his cheeks. Nervously, he shifted. "I know how to work this stuff, is simple." He picked up the handset as if to show it off.

"You see? You *are* the right person to take charge," Peat said, as though someone had argued otherwise. She leaned down, cupped his jowl, and gave him a kiss on the cheek. "Thank you," she whispered, and stared into his startled blue eyes.

"I never . . . nobody ever—"

"Hush," she said. She squeezed the muscles beneath his collar. Then she joined Lyell, taking Angel's arm and helping steer him toward the exit.

Peat muttered, "With any luck, he might buy us a few extra minutes."

"We're going to need 'em all," Lyell said, glancing remorsefully back at the bullgod. She waved a final time.

Angel looked from one to the other of the two women supporting him, and managed to ask, "What is going on?"

Lyell held out little hope of getting through the checkpoint. She anticipated there might be dozens, even hundreds, of uniformed Philadelphia Security Force officers at the end of the tunnel, waiting for the signal to pour in. Conceivably, even Mingo might be on hand. It all depended on how he had organized them. What she and Peat had going for them was the LifeMask they had taken from the twitchers' lounge—the one Angel now wore. It showed an Ethiop-black face, a fringe of gray hair. The features bore an unsettling resemblance to her father.

Troops had not been stationed at the checkpoint. No more than a handful of extra guards had been called in, as well as a small medical unit.

Most of the surviving ICS-IV staff milled around in the area outside the gateway, where they fell prey to different teams of interviewers. One large contingent was from, of all places, the Alien News Network. Between these competing factions, the area outside the checkpoint was utter chaos.

A young PSF guard came rushing up as the trio neared the tunnel mouth. He grabbed Angel, bearing his weight. "Are you all right?" he asked the two women. Before they could answer, three female medical personnel in uniforms closed in around the guard and Angel. Lyell thought they looked young enough to be students. Avoiding the worst of the melee, the group shouldered Angel behind other guards, where there were three cots set up. A few black body bags lay beyond the cots, reminders of the carnage at the far end of the tunnel.

Staff members recognized the principal and surrounded her; their excited chatter alerted the newsteams, who, having used up most of the survivors on hand, scrambled into the throng. Lyell heard one of the doctors call out, "Does anyone know this man's blood type?" She glanced at her own shoulder, where his spilled blood had soaked into her jacket. She was thinking of Nebergall.

The young guard returned. He patted her back. "You're fine," he said, as if her condition had been in doubt. He started back to his post by the gate, but she grabbed him.

"Isn't anyone going in to clean this mess up?" She gestured at the tunnel.

"As I understand it, they've already gone."

She looked at Chikako Peat, who was trying to hear what he said over four or five other opposing conversations. "*We* didn't pass anyone in there," she said.

"You wouldn't," he replied, pleased to share his inside knowledge. "They went in the front, down the skyway and through the gates." He must have read her incredulity, because he shook his head doubtfully and added, "I know—you'd think the tunnel would be the safer route, easier to control. Hell, that's the contingency plan I was trained for. But some polished-ass Scumber volunteered the company's antiterrorist SWAT team to handle it." Conspiratorially, he leaned closer to her. "Don't tell these cam crews, but, frankly, that's okay by us."

Lyell turned and wedged her way through the ICSS people to Chikako Peat's side. She related what he'd said. "I'm convinced," said Peat. "At least we got out in time."

"Not enough. We have to get Angel out of here. Mingo won't waste two minutes once he figures out who's missing. Look at how far they've gone. You think they'll worry about a little thing like executing him in full view of a crowd? They'll take the crowd out, too."

"Why? Who would go to such lengths?"

"I wish I knew all that. Just like I wish we'd put that damned mask of his on someone else's body, not that I think Mingo's fool enough to have fallen for it."

"Just a minute," Peat snapped at one of the staff people who was tugging at her. To Lyell she whispered, "Didn't you bring some form of clearance for him? They're not going to let him in, you know."

"I didn't know they were going to take out the school, remember? I wasn't prescient enough to come packing extra biocards."

"Can't you get him something now?"

"Eventually, but not now. Not in *time*."

The ANN crew suddenly turned and splashed light across both of them. Somebody in the ICSS group had pointed out Chikako. The staffers closed in, and Lyell tried to edge into their ranks. Chuck Soderburn, one of ANN's better-known reporters, came in chatty.

"Hello, there," he said, "You ladies are the most recent escapees from the hell we used to call Inner City School Number Four. What was it like?"

Peat stared icily at him and at the camera hovering at the end of its thick cable behind him.

Undaunted, he said, "You're shaken, of course. I see they're working on someone who was wounded. Was he shot by the student terrorists? How many were there?"

"Chuck," said Lyell, "you have no idea." She pushed past him. She did not desire to be recorded.

Soderburn watched in dismay as she escaped. Quickly, instinctively, he closed in on Chikako. "And you would be? . . ."

"Looking for work," Peat replied. She took a step to the side but he wasn't letting any more fish get away.

The hovercam operator snaked the digital camera right up beside Soderburn's ear. The interviewer chuckled mechanically, then said, "You're the school's principal. Tell the world now, did you experience the evil, extraterrestrial hive mind controlling your attackers?"

Peat stared smolderingly into the floating lens, then at the reporter. "Part company now," she said, "or the world gets a provocative look up your lower intestines." She made a move toward the hovercam and it dodged back like a cobra. The operator withdrew both it and himself beyond her reach.

Behind her, Chuck cried, "But don't you want to get on TV? Everybody wants to get on TV. Where's your sense of *warhol*?!"

She didn't immediately spot Lyell, and her staffers stuck to her, unshakable. At least they offered her a wall of defense against the other interview teams.

The doctors had given Angel various atomizer injections and dressed his wound. By the time Lyell reached him, they had also removed his LifeMask and discovered the hardware glued to his skull.

She knelt beside the low cot, all thoughts directed toward protecting him. He seemed strangely unprepared to protect himself. In light of the fact that he had dispensed with the first two assassins, she was at a loss to explain why she felt this.

His eyes had gone glassy, and she supposed he'd been given a site-targeting sedative.

One of the medical staff came up, and asked, "Are you a coworker?"

She nodded, then gestured over her shoulder at Peat. "That's the principal."

"Your friend's going to be okay. His wound was clean. I don't expect any complications, but to tell you the truth, the tissue sampler's gone wacky all of a sudden and—"

"Can he be moved?"

"Well, I wouldn't, unless you have to, for a couple hours."

"We have to."

"He'll be kind of loose, if you know what I mean."

"I wish . . . do you know anything about crabs?"

"Excuse me?"

"*This* kind." She pointed at the skullcap electronics.

"What, bypasses? Yes, I was going to ask you about that. He must've been in some other accident not so very long ago, right? Certainly, we use them. You know—car accidents, things like that. All the time. I just assumed that was why he'd been assigned a bottom-rung job. No offense."

"How do you take them off?"

"There's a small circuit at the back that can be unplugged with a digikey—any standard one, really, should do it. It's not something you want to do casually, though. Depending on the type of dam—" She had eased Angel's head to the side, where a small display of red LED numbers indicated neuronal activity. "That's odd. This one doesn't have that circuit."

"How surprising," Lyell said, not surprised at all.

The doctor said, "It's going to be bolted to the skull, that's standard. Hang on a minute, let me check with a technician, he'll know more," and wandered off to find one of her colleagues.

"Excuse me," a male voice said from behind Lyell. She glanced up at a tall, thin man with sandy hair and a light mustache. He sported a spongy, white "ruff" collar of the sort that had caught on lately with the corporate set. From the look on his face, the collar might have been a few sizes too small. "This man here," he said, "is he going to make it?"

"Do you know him?" asked Lyell.

The man bobbed his head. "I'm kind of in charge of him."

Feigning ignorance, she asked, "School official?" She glanced askance for Chikako Peat in the crowd.

"No, actually, I'm with ScumberCorp. Ton Gansevoort, Human Resources." He held out a green dialer-card. She took it and read his name. "Mr. Rueda here is a—well, I guess you'd say he's a former employee of sorts. We—the company, that is—got him this teaching post so he could keep working, and I've been keeping tabs on him since . . . that is—"

"Does the head of HR usually handle that kind of thing?" She got to her feet.

They traded looks for a minute. Clearly, he didn't know where to draw the line on what he should say, and was uncomfortable about deciding. She guessed that the ground he stood on wasn't too solid.

"Doctor?" he asked.

"Yes?" she lied.

"Truthfully, no, I don't. He's kind of a special case, and I've been worried that something might happen to him. When I heard about the riot, I ran right here."

"I'm impressed—I don't often see such concern between corporate strata. But I was wondering; you see, I was just examining the cranial bypass unit to make sure it hadn't been damaged or displaced when he fell, and I discovered that there's no obvious digikey release on it. How does it come off?"

His mouth hung open. He didn't know what she was talking about.

"Mr. Gansevoort, I have to tell you that he may have suffered brain damage beyond what this simple bypass covers. My colleague over here, Dr. Peat, wants very much to get him up into our clinic in the towers, away from this chaos, but he lacks the clearance. We really don't want to put him in one of those Undercity chop shops—"

"Oh, clearance is no problem. I can get us emergency pedicab routing if you need it."

"That *would* help." She gestured to Peat, who blatantly sized up Gansevoort as she approached.

Lyell introduced them, slipping his green business card into her hand.

He gawked at Peat. Lyell thought him the most transparent man she'd ever seen. "*You're* a doctor?" he asked her.

Without missing a beat, she replied, "I was at a cocktail party when the word came. Naturally, neither of us wasted a moment hurrying here. Do I need a surgical gown in order to work?"

"Yes, I was just explaining to Mr. Gansevoort about Angel Rueda's brain damage," Lyell said, "and he tells me he has clearance to pass him through the checkpoint."

"How considerate of you. We should get him up right away. Is he awake?"

Lyell crouched beside him and whispered to him. His eyes shifted, focused approximately on her, then beyond her. "Hello, Gansevoort," he said. With Lyell's help, he sat up.

"How's the head?" Gansevoort asked.

"My *arm* is much better." He pointed to the sodden dressing on his shoulder.

Gansevoort eyed him with obvious misgiving.

Peat said, "It's just the sedatives. He's still a little muzzy."

Once on his feet, Angel shuffled along, supported by Lyell and Gansevoort. The real doctor came running back, but Peat stopped her. "SC's taking over responsibility for him," she explained. "They insist he be moved to their facilities, so you've one less problem to worry about." She flashed the green card. "I'll see you're commended."

"I didn't realize," said the doctor, her glance flicking briefly to Lyell. "I thought he was just another teacher."

"No, not quite." She dodged another news crew and caught up with the other three in time to slide through the gate on Gansevoort's corporate clearance.

Once through the checkpoint, the biggest factor in the trio's favor was Mingo's procrastination. He would stall until the last possible minute any incursion into ICS-IV.

Gansevoort proved to be a compulsive talker. While they rode an escalator and then boarded a pedicab—the women seated side by side across from the other two—he babbled at a manic clip about the prestige he'd acquired as a result of this assignment, all the while adjusting and readjusting the inflated white collar.

"Aren't there supposed to be studs in the front of that thing?" Peat asked him at one point.

He flushed with embarrassment and said, "I haven't had time to pick out a set of studs. I know that's where all the prestige is with these collars—the personalized studs." Then he blurted, "I never would have bothered with a . . . a fashion statement, before this. The CEOs selected me personally."

"You met them?" asked Lyell, incredulous.

"Yeah. Angel, he got shunted down from SC's Procellarum facility. Mingo says—"

"Mingo." The two women traded wary glances.

"You know him?" he asked.

"It's an odd name," Lyell replied.

"Yeah, he's a troubleshooter for the company. Efficiency expert." He bit at a fingernail.

"Uh-huh."

"He says, since Angel was hurt through no fault of his own while working for the company, we owe him special consideration. It's our duty to see that he has work, no matter how menial. That's why I went down to the checkpoint. A week ago, I wouldn't have bothered—I was closed off, sealed up; everything happened to everybody else and none of it affected me."

"That's easy to slip into. Most people—"

"Sure is. There are damn few people as concerned as Mingo. The thing is, he has the freedom to act. Why, the other day, he delivered food to some of those box-dwellers down in SC Plaza. The CEOs let him do it. I mean, this is a whole side of ScumberCorp I'd never seen before."

"No, I shouldn't think so," Lyell said. She glanced past him thoughtfully. The pedicab driver, seated in a nearly reclining posture, pedaled steadily, as if hauling their combined weight took no effort. He had a TV screen on his left handlebar, bringing in perfect images of some idiot sitcom that he somehow managed to keep track of while weaving in and out of the taxi lanes. He squawked with laughter at some joke. He must have sensed her watching, and turned to share his grin with her. She smiled in reply, then leaned closer to Peat. She whispered, "Keep him occupied a few minutes."

"I'd rather switch him off," muttered Chikako Peat.

Lyell turned to the side. She took her personal phone out of her belt bag and placed a call to Nebergall.

The phone—an earpiece and throat mike, linked with a satellite feed into the *phonet*. She could speak into it and be heard almost without moving her lips. Nebergall had custom-fitted the phone with an illegal microcircuit that automatically tumbled the net's ESN, allowing her call to pass through, effectively, without a location-tag: the call that never was. The compact-sized case it fit into contained the call buttons.

She let his number buzz a dozen times before giving up.

She had seen him ignore the phone for days at a time when he was editing; but he behaved like a phobic paranoid when she suggested he get a call-retrieval package, arguing: "Those goddam things pose a clear and present danger, since anybody with a gnat's brain can loop themselves in, take your calls off the circuit before you do, and run off with half your business while you squat in your jammies, waitin' for doo-dah. Yeah, put me down for *three* of them things." Even though he had a small handset built into the arm of his chair, she couldn't make him understand that, if he didn't flip his phone *on* when it rang, he wasn't going to nab any business, either.

She folded the set back into its case.

Gansevoort was still talking about corporate charity. Peat nudged her and nodded at the unit. "I should make a few arrangements for our arrival," she said loudly, and took the phone.

Gansevoort said, "This situation is an example of how we at SC need to work more with the Undercity populace."

"That's only fair," Lyell answered, "considering the enormous part Box City plays in your company's test programs." He hesitated. She said, "You didn't know that? You didn't know SC routinely drafts them as white rats for drug and additive testing? Sure—that way, nobody complains if something goes wrong. In fact, there's an unfounded Boxer myth that if they don't come back, they've won a place in the Overcity."

"I don't believe it."

"Some other time, remind me, and I'll show you evidence."

Troubled by her ready offer, he glanced sidelong at Angel and fell silent. Peat winked congratulations at her. A few minutes later, nodding, she handed back the phone.

Angel appeared to have ignored the conversation. With the borrowed LifeMask staring flatly out at the multitude of passersby, at the clipped trees and shrubs adorning the edge of the skyway, the shops and cafes clustered where the skyway entered a tower, it was impossible to tell to what extent he was paying attention.

When the pedicab drew up, he glanced around as if waking from a dream.

"Hey, your clinic's in *this* tower?" Gansevoort asked. "So's my apartment."

"Quite a coincidence," Peat observed. She helped Angel down from his seat, and instructed him quietly as to what they needed him to do.

They grabbed an elevator and managed to keep it to themselves. Lyell pressed the button for the thirty-second floor.

Before the doors could close, Angel gasped, clutched his head, and dropped to his knees. All the while, his projected face grinned.

"My God! He's not going to make it to the clinic," Lyell exclaimed. "Quick. Where's your apartment?"

"Ten, tenth floor," Gansevoort said, and hit the button. They shot up.

The doors opened. The three of them dragged Angel upright. They might have been hauling a drunk between them. His head lolled, and he made hissing noises as if each jounce pained him. Feverishly, Gansevoort fumbled out his biocard and inserted it into the door of his apartment.

Like most single personnel at management level, he had a tiny one-bedroom affair. The word "couch" would not have fit in the outer room, and the bedroom was no longer or wider than the bed itself. The single large window offered a view of the blue, shining tower across the plaza.

They placed Angel in the only stuffed chair in the place. He hunched up with his head down, groaning every few moments. Lyell stepped back and scanned the room, recording everything she saw—DATs of Frank Sinatra and other crooners of that period scattered atop the built-in stereo system; one recessed bookshelf half-filled with out-of-date college business texts, their bindings already rotting from age; two tiny Turkish rugs hung as tapestries that must have set their host back a fortune unless he'd actually bought them before the viral-bombing of Istanbul; and three clumps of cast-off clothing on the tile floor or draped over a folding chair which made it appear that previous guests of Gansevoort had dissolved.

He tossed aside the clothes. "I haven't had time to get them cleaned," he commented.

Peat knelt beside Angel, appearing to take his pulse.

"I think I'd better call in," Gansevoort said. "SC'll give you any assistance you need. Besides, they should know where he is." He took a step toward the phone in the bookshelf, but Lyell blocked his way.

"You don't want to do that," she said.

"Excuse me?" He adjusted his collar.

"You can't call."

Peat interjected, "You know what they did to my school? If you tell Mingo where all of us are, what happened to Isis will happen to you."

Gansevoort stared at them each in turn. Angel raised his head and looked placidly back at him. "Your school? Who are you? You're not doctors."

"She might be. I'm not. *He* sure as hell isn't."

Gansevoort cried out and dived toward the bookshelf. Lyell grabbed his wrist as he went past and spun him around. He slammed into the wall, swung about, and backed against it. "You're *Xau Dâu!*" he cried.

Peat snorted. She got up and approached him. "Where would you get a crazy idea like that? Of course we're not *Xau Dâu.*" Passing, she glanced at Lyell. "Right?"

Lyell shrugged, snatching away the phone. "I'm beginning to wonder, myself."

"You're going to kill me!"

"Gansevoort," Angel said, "why would you think such a thing?" Mildly surprised, the women stared at him.

"You could be the ringleader—I've heard the rumors about the Moon, I put things together. You don't even *know* what you are."

"What is *Xau Dâu*, will someone please explain it?" he asked.

Peat said to Lyell, "Your turn. Why don't you explain it to all of us."

"Including myself."

"What are you going to do?" Gansevoort asked.

Peat patted his shoulder sympathetically and he flinched away. "Not exactly an action figure, are you?" she said.

"I head a personnel department!"

"Yes, as you've overstated."

Lyell said, "Mr. Gansevoort—Ton—I need very much for you to go sit in that other chair."

"What?"

"Please."

Leaving him under Peat's supervision, she turned and strode into the bedroom. There was an armoire built into the corner opposite the bed, offsetting by design the bathroom door. A revolving shelf in the armoire produced suspenders, belts, and a few socks. She tossed Gansevoort's small phone into the depths, then gathered up a few likely looking items. She also grabbed a fistful of ties and a pressed gray jacket. Carrying out her booty, she snagged the folding chair in passing and hauled it along beside her. "Right here, if you would."

Peat nudged Gansevoort forward. Like a condemned man, he walked to the chair and sat down. He gave Angel a look of utter betrayal. "I don't understand."

Lyell looped a belt around his wrists, and then a tie that she fastened to the dowels in the chairback. She explained, "I don't want to tie you, but I have to prevent you from telling anyone about this for a while. Besides which, your associate, Mr. Mingo, would not be pleased to hear that you helped Angel Rueda escape the siege Mingo went to such trouble to prepare."

"Mingo?" The enormity of the accusation struck him dumb.

"Mingo's going to kill us if he finds us. So, if I were you, I would spend my time considering very hard what I could say to minimize my involvement in our escape. For instance, I wouldn't mention using my clout to get us through the checkpoint. No, I wouldn't do that."

Peat tied his ankles. Angel looked on, his false face ever passive.

"Otherwise," said Lyell, "Mr. Mingo will probably feel the need to kill you, too. He hasn't exhibited much restraint in that pursuit."

Gansevoort's mouth hung open.

"You seem like a nice man. Be very careful around him." She turned to Angel and offered him the clean jacket. "Here, it's probably too big for you, but put this on. You can give it back later."

Peat got up and gave him a kiss on the cheek. "I didn't believe her at first, either," she said.

They went out, leaving him in the center of the room, from which vantage point, looking over his left shoulder, he could just see the tinted windows of his office.

He had been told to wait and to protect Chikako Peat and Thomasina Lyell, and that was what he did. He sat at the triangular desk, shifting the screens overhead from one working camera to the next throughout the school, observing the silent slaughter.

To the extent that he could hold any thought for long, the bullgod found the task dissatisfying. Violence robbed of its sound and fury wasn't much fun to watch, worse than a video. Back in his arena days . . . now, that had been excitement.

Taken from an orphanage as a child, genetically engineered to be the bone-crushingly biggest of middle-heavyweight wrestlers, by the age of fifteen he'd stood like a mountain on top of the world. His two English managers had once told him that his image adorned flags in Japan and posters on the Moon.

Kids watched his exploits on satellite broadcasts and dreamed of him; "The Mick" was the arena name he went by.

He'd defeated opponents from every country in fair combats. He'd never thrown a fight because neither of his managers had ever asked him to. They both knew he was too witless to be relied upon. Even if they had been able to explain the financial benefits of purse manipulation, once he got in the ring and got smacked a couple of times, he set about relentlessly crushing his opponents' vertebrae. A tremendous combatant, yes, but too single-minded. In a word, a cretin.

The drugs had done that—constrained his mental capacity. He had muscles as big as most men's fists, but not much else on the ball.

Above all else, he was terribly, blushingly, shy; speechless in the presence of the opposite sex. His managers saw a way to divest themselves of The Mick and make a killing in the bargain.

The Belgian combine, Aubépine, owned a female fighter named Mouche who was tearing up Europe. A deal was struck to pit her against him. Both sides, knowing of his Achilles' heel, bet heavily against him, the odds-on favorite.

He went before the cameras in the Circus Supremus of Rome, into the ring, and found himself confronting what appeared to be a beefy transvestite. Her face had a vaguely feminine aspect if he ignored the prognathous jaw; but her breasts, and other traits that The Mick identified as female, were buried within numerous swollen chemical enhancements, muscles like tectonic plates. *His* breasts were more prodigious than hers. She might have been a woman but he couldn't see it.

In the first round, during which time he liked to warm up, grapple a few times, get the heft of his opponent, Mouche split his lip and broke two of his fingers. She tried to rip his balls off, as well, but there he was grossly underdeveloped—again, because of one very miscreated chemistry—and, though she hurt his shriveled up scrotum, it was not the thing she'd intended.

Between rounds, his managers reminded him of how unforgivable it was to strike a woman. The Mick licked salty blood off his swollen lip.

The bell for the second round sounded. The Mick got up, walked out into the center of the ring, and hit Mouche as hard as he could in the throat, crushing her larynx. The crowd loved it. His managers and numerous executives of Aubépine promptly filed for bankruptcy.

The combine sued, forcing a reluctant investigation into combat rigging. The two managers fired The Mick. Subpoenaed for the hearings, he inadvertently learned from a solicitor that he had virtually no money left—his managers had squandered it, stolen it, spent every credit dollar on pleasures that should have been his. He dully considered them across the judicial arena while various barristers droned on. Perhaps because he stayed still long enough, an idea crawled into his brain. It was to be the most creative idea of his life.

He turned to the solicitor and explained that he had to go to the lavatory, then got up and started out, around the rear of the courtroom, but instead of exiting, he came down the center aisle. He crossed the row in back of his ex-managers and, when he was right behind them, slapped a meaty fist on each of their skulls. With surprisingly little apparent exertion, he shoved their heads straight down through their collarbones.

In the Circus Supremus, such a move would have won him a standing ovation. In the law courts, it had won him a steamship voyage to Corson's Penal Isle, where ICS found him. In retrospect he liked his life in Philadelphia. He supposed now that he would be sent back to the prison. The ways of the world confounded The Mick as much as did his own stirring feelings about these two women. Impotent he might be, but also bedazzled. The one woman—never mind it was the wrong one—had touched him, tenderly. Her eyes had promised things. The memory of it made him sigh.

For her he would have abandoned his principles, if he could have thought of any. For the two of them he would lay down his life.

At one-fifteen, having subdued virtually everyone else in the place, the security forces of ScumberCorp, led by the shadowy Mr. Mingo, charged into the principal's offices. They found The Mick seated at the controls.

"Good work," Mingo told him. "Way to go, Ace. We'll take over the helm now."

At which point, The Mick shot Mingo through the left thigh. He would have ventilated him, but the overused gun ran out of ammo with that first shot.

Perhaps in his simplicity, The Mick could see through Mingo's false camaraderie. Or maybe it was the instinct of the ex-fighter that told him this man meant to murder his newfound love. Somehow, he had put it all together where better minds were deceived.

The security team gaped at the insuperable Mingo rolling on the floor, clamping his fingers around the jetting femoral wound, considered with newfound respect the titanic redheaded bull behind the desk, and, without a moment's hesitation, executed him by fusillade.

The Mick's final, ennobling act, inadvertent though it may have been, was to smash the keypad with his forehead as he fell. Doors and gates throughout ICS-IV suddenly swung shut and magnetically bolted.

It would take Mingo an hour and a half just to get out of the school. He left it in a stretcher, unconscious from the loss of blood.

15

Bordello

Thomasina Lyell had never visited the twenty-third floor of Rittenhouse Six. She'd heard of Grofé's, of course, and her introduction to Chikako Peat had taken place in similar surroundings.

The exterior room resembled an 1890s restaurant, smugly steeped in fin de siècle atmosphere. There were imported mahogany tables clothed in the purest white linens that, like the draperies, were trimmed in silver embroidery. The walls were divided horizontally, with a pastel green upper half, and a dark, ornate tulip dado along the bottom. Thick carpets covered the floor. One could spend an afternoon in Grofé's, eating and drinking in pleasant company, and never have the urge, or the suspicion, to penetrate further.

The maitre d' approached as they entered through the double doors. He wore a purple silk suit and had waxed the tips of his mustache. "Lunch—a table for three?" he asked, as though they were dressed with the utmost taste. Peat, whose attire came closest, took the helm.

"No," she replied, "just *tea*."

He bowed stiffly and directed them toward a set of crushed velvet curtains at the far side of the room.

A few heads turned as the three of them made their way across the carpet—a LifeMask was uncommon enough at these levels to attract some attention, but nothing compared to the stir the bypass would have caused. Reaching the far corner of the room, they slipped between the heavy curtains into one of the most popular tearooms in Philadelphia.

The intricate dado relief, in the second room, had been expanded to cover the walls in a dark green arabesque of swaying stems and tulip bulbs. Small palm trees in large, diagonally striped vases framed the doorway and shaded the various booths around the walls. The air was smoky and smelled of something sweet that wasn't perfume. A few bright impressionistic paintings added to the decor, drawing the eye away from the booths.

At first glance, Lyell failed to notice the booths' odd configuration. She focused on a man and woman sharing one. They were facing each other, but they were both lying on their sides. A low table separated them and an attendant seated on a stool in the middle was pouring cups of tea for them. Padded cushions supported the couple, concave pillows propped up their heads. The pillows and the reclining figures told her the rest. She looked then for the telltale pipes. One woman was smoking hers while an attendant kept the flame going beneath its pregnant bowl.

Scattered about the center of the room were larger tables on pedestals for parties of three or four at most, for those who merely wished to sip tea or an aperitif and enjoy the ambience of the den, the smell of the opium perhaps. It was a scene torn out of time, nothing at all like the dens she had visited in the Undercity.

A new headwaiter, dressed (by comparison with the maitre d') for a funeral, asked, "You will be dividing up?"

Peat said, "We've business with Mallee."

"Ah, you're *special* guests." He flashed a broad smile.

"Old friends," she corrected. "Tell her Chikako's here."

He nodded, muttered "Chicago" into a throat mike that he pressed, then nodded pleasantly again. "You're expected."

"It helps."

"I'm Lalep," he said, although no one had asked.

Beaming with bonhomie, Angel shook his hand. Lyell dragged him aside. "What did they give you downstairs?" she asked. "A joy-buzzer?"

"A lot of healing is attitude," he told her. He looked drunk.

"You should be recovered in about ten minutes, then. Try to remember that we don't want to stand out more than we have to, okay? Try not to plunge across somebody's table."

The mask face bobbed up and down.

Concealed behind a second set of heavy drapes, a long hall led off the tearoom and into the bordello proper. Had they taken a seat at one of the tables in the smoking room, they would have been offered menus depending upon their predilections, listing a variety of proffered pleasures. Everything was discreet, tasteful. What transpired behind the closed doors was to remain a mystery . . . or would have done if Angel hadn't started his own inquiry.

They were walking along, calmly enough, and Lyell had enough on her mind that she did not at first hear the rattle of doors, Angel trying each one he passed; or maybe it was the wind chimes and birdcalls, reminding her of the Geoplatform fat farm that drowned out the noise. Had it really only been a matter of days since she'd been up there? It seemed like months had passed.

All of a sudden, a door behind her opened, and she turned to find Angel standing on the threshold, staring dumbly inside. She stepped back to where he stood and peered over his shoulder.

It was a large room, sparsely furnished in pseudoteahouse fashion, with a floor of tatami mats, various bamboo and rice paper screens standing about, and silk flowers in vases on low tables. In the middle of the room, eight people dressed in baggy gray one-piece outfits sat in two rows along benches fitted with curious saddles. Other benches before and behind them contained empty saddles.

The saddles encased their hips, their crotches. They each

wore a pair of goggles that covered their ears as well and also plugged into the saddles. All eight people held their hands out in front of them and, as if performing some warming up exercise, rhythmically reached forward and drew back, reached forward and drew back, each bench in unison.

To the right, in a tokonoma alcove that would normally have displayed a lovely scroll, a man in what looked like a flight helmet sat in front of a thin monitor screen. He held an F/X control board on his lap but he was watching TV. On the screen was displayed the belly of a huge, ancient galley, replete with naked, underfed oarsmen. Flaming lamps rocked back and forth on chains not unlike those that secured the oarsmen to their seats and each other. A muscular woman in red leather trousers and nothing much else strode the deck between the slaves and flogged them mercilessly with a cat-o'-nine-tails. She spat on them and made threatening gestures. She might have spoken, but the speakers appeared to be turned off. It might have been a scene from a truly dreadful pirate film, except that the oarsmen on the screen and the people in the room were rowing in sync. And when the lashes bit into the backs of the poor wretches in the galley, goggled people in the baggy suits jerked and cried out.

Lyell closed the door. "Come on, Angel," she said, "and don't do that again. You might have to stay here a while, and the next group might notice you sticking your nose in."

"What *was* that?"

"That was *virtual*—all the excitement and the pain without the risk. Just the expense. More than that, you don't need to know. You don't want to know." A far cry from the Undercity teahouses she had been thinking of, where the patrons and the cockroaches shared paltry accommodations, and where the sheets—when there were sheets—didn't get changed. She had never visited one of these places before. Probably it was because Knewsday and their ilk already ran too many shows on the virtues of virtual sex. It wasn't, she told herself, because she wasn't interested. She just tended to focus on the streets, that was all.

Certainly there was some client overlap between the two levels: the Overs enjoyed occasional slumming expeditions out of towers but inside the walls. The rakes still progressed, if that was the right term for it. Degressed? She shook her head. One of the reasons the walls had gone up where they had was to maintain a captive population which could imagine itself better off because it was inside something. People who were happy just to be indoors.

Orbitol pervaded the towers through places like this. Drugs of all sorts were included on the menu, along with the arts of pleasure; mostly opium, but also endorphin-triggers to induce pleasure. Orbitol wasn't promoted nor, strictly speaking, was it supposed to be available here. It was on hand in case some-one asked for it, like the dusty, expensive bottles of Lambic Framboise under the counter. Orbitol was for the masses. The dingy dens on the street had lost much of their trade to various engineered, site-specific substances over the years, but Orbitol was the worst. It had decimated their clientele, transporting its victims to a different Xanadu, transporting them literally. In order to survive, the dens had been forced to buy into Orbitol's distribution. How ScumberCorp had finagled it all—an end run around every competitor—remained a corporate secret as closely guarded as the formula itself. Reported cases of Orbitol decay in the Undercity were a thousand percent higher than among the Overs, and climbing. Her story on fast-foods had begun out of a theory that some of the foods had been laced with Orbitol, creating instant addicts and cementing a drug habit to specific foods, creating totally dependent customers at the trough, at least until they decayed. That picture didn't seem to make economic sense, but she refused to give up on it entirely.

The hall stretched on forever. She wondered how many clients Grofé's handled. Maybe this Mallee was someone she should interview once things quieted down. And Peat, who obviously knew things about ScumberCorp that no one else was likely to know. Like maybe even the sex fantasies of some of the Gang of Four. Now, *that* would make for interesting viewing.

Around a corner, Lyell and Angel caught up with Chikako. She waited just inside the open door of another large room, filled with exercise equipment. It reminded Lyell unpleasantly again of Stardance.

A nearly naked woman was working out on a small tram-poline to one side. Lyell directed Angel to a bench and sat beside him. He fidgeted like a child who couldn't hold still.

Lyell scrutinized him quizzically. Peat walked over to the trampoline.

The jumper reduced her bouncing until she could safely spring to the mat, then performed a tight inverted twist, landing precisely on the balls of both feet. Her perfect, compact, and tanned physique gleamed. She wore a formfitting bikini bottom and a bright red breastband. She had drawn her coppery hair back into a coil. She looked like a bull-dancer from Minos.

From another bench, she swept up a towel and mopped her face, then hung the towel around her neck as she approached Peat.

The two women embraced; everything about the casualness of the gesture told Lyell that they were indeed old friends. They said a few words, then laughed together, then chattered happily. Lyell rested her eyes, longing for a stimulant and a massage.

When she finally directed Mallee toward them, Peat was smiling and more relaxed than Lyell had yet seen her. Mallee's presence had cracked the facade.

"So, this is the Angel," Mallee said admiringly, and Angel crossed his arms, stroked his chin, looked down, and otherwise behaved embarrassedly. She said, "Thomasina," and nodded in greeting, then glanced back at Peat. "You say he's got a *crab* unit under there? What'd he do, land on his head?"

"He can't remember."

Mallee pursed her lips. She had worked out a plan: they were to stay here until evening, when she would have a fully charged car ready for them. Then they would take the club's private exit down to the skyway level, pile into the car, and travel to her Spring Mountain villa.

"I didn't realize," Lyell commented, "that a teahouse operator was in the class that affords villas."

"Actually, it's a perk of the job. Came with the title. Don't ask me, ask Ichi-Plok's subsidiary. It's more for the executives than it is for me—I'm just another piece of furniture with a *virtual* license. At least you'll be out of the city and in a villa owned by a competitor, so you're a lot less likely to be twigged by Scumbers. Meantime, I've got you a suite here—I already took it off the menu. Sorry there's only the one room, but we're busy today."

"Yes, we saw the rowing team."

Mallee smiled. "Would you believe me if I told you that program has a waiting list?"

"Probably."

"We have sixteen *virtual* rooms, more than any other local teahouse." She spoke with obvious pride.

A buzzer sounded. Mallee walked to the bench where she had gotten the towel. She picked up a blue palm phone and spoke into it. After a moment, she pointed it at the wall. The paneling slid aside, revealing a portion of a larger screen. There was a small set beside it—an all-purpose, diskROM entertainment center. The phone doubled as a remote control.

Wryly, Mallee said, "Looks like you've made the splash internash."

At first the entire screen lit, but she quickly reduced the image to correspond with the space she had opened. The view was of an overhead shot of ICS-IV, showing the center tower like a hub and the cellblocks like seven spokes off it. From that shot, no one would have guessed at the chaos reigning within. The sound came up. " . . . estimates as many as three hundred deaths. Believed to be included in that total are the school's principal, Ms. Chikako Peat, and a man ScumberCorp officials have linked to the terrorist group *Xau Dâu,* which has plagued the megacorporation for years. It is now believed this man, Angel Rueda, subverted the school's security in order to arm students, fomenting a bloody revolt."

First they showed a photo of Angel without the bypass, and Lyell almost didn't recognize him. Before she adjusted to it, the picture switched to a tracking shot of Angel entering the school unaccompanied. He was glancing around as if making certain he had not been followed.

"That's not me," he complained. "I *never* went in there alone. I've only been to the school once."

Lyell gripped his shoulder reassuringly. "We know."

"However," said the television, "Knewsday now believes he fell victim to his own plan and was shot in the chaos of the riot. ScumberCorp city officials say it will be many hours before more specific information is available. Reached during rehearsals for his evening show, the president ordered an immediate investigation into the event."

President Odie looked sincerely into the camera. "We have tolerated the monsters behind this subversive group long enough. I know that all of America is behind me when I state that we will tolerate no more. We are going to stamp out *Xau Dâu*. And don't forget to watch my 'Best of Odie' show Tuesday—"

"Please," said Peat, "shut it off before I vomit on the flag." She dropped down beside Angel and took his hand. "Well, dear man, how does it feel to be a monster?"

The mask's black face looked her way, expressing mild perturbation. "I did none of that," he said. The agony in his voice killed the humor in Peat's expression. She took his hands in hers and faced him.

"Angel, don't you see? It just proves what Thomasina told you. The only way that footage could exist is if it was simulated in advance. It would have taken someone hours to doctor up." She looked around for confirmation. "Right?"

Lyell nodded.

Angel leaned his head back. All of a sudden, he unplugged the LifeMask and peeled it off. "I've had enough of that."

"You've got blood on your shoulder, Thomasina," Mallee observed. "Are you wounded?"

"It's his."

"Ah. You'll want to clean up."

"Actually, no, thank you," said Lyell. "I need to leave, and the sooner the better. There are connections that need forging, and I need to find out what's really hopping before they change that report and slap my picture up there, too. If I go out, will there be a problem with my return?"

Mallee smiled at her. "Lots of women do."

"Not exactly what I meant." She turned to Angel. "I want you to hold this in your hand," she said, and gave him her phone case. He stared at it as at some alien artifact. "Close your hand around it. Press your fingers hard against it." When he had obeyed, she daintily took it by its edge and slipped it back in her belt bag.

"Fingerprints?" Peat asked.

"And blood." She ducked her chin toward her shoulder.

Peat mulled that over for a moment. She said, "Don't be too long."

"A few hours only, I hope." She got up and, with a grateful nod to Mallee, said, "I'll find my way out."

She made it halfway down the hall before giving in to the temptation to try more of the doors. None of them opened. She wondered whom she had recorded seated at the oars. Nebergall, the sick bastard, was going to treasure that footage.

16

Virtual Recovery

The woman in front of him wore an elaborate leather corset. She had on laced brown boots with a line of spikes down the outside. Her bright red hair was cropped short. Her eyes weren't human. They glowed with barely contained power that he could actually feel against his bare skin like invisible hands slithering over him, the power pressing him down, down to his knees.

The corset pushed the woman's tattooed breasts up impossibly over the top, making them jut forward. Her pierced nipples were as sharp as cones. She grinned maniacally with teeth that had been honed to points as sharp as the nipples. "Slave," she said.

The word hit him like a slap in the face. He jerked back but couldn't move far. Chains held him naked on his knees. His penis, of its own accord, had stiffened, extending to a prodigious thirty centimeters. His skin was bronze in color, his body narrow-waisted but massive across the chest. He could flex the muscles, feel them ripple. His erection, when he touched it, was definitely attached, the real thing despite his knowing that it could not be so.

The room was an oubliette, its exit a hatch in the ceiling. Looming to the right stood a black vinyl bed fitted with straps and devices of unimaginable intent.

The dominatrix approached him. She had a coiled whip in her left hand. The leather of her outfit creaked like saddlery as she moved. He could smell her strong perfume—some erotic mixture to lure him. "You'll do everything I tell you," she said sternly, then giggled. "Sorry. But the look on your face . . ."

"What does it look like? I can't imagine it's even my face."

"No, it's not that, and anyway half of your head is missing because of that bypass. Really, it's your expression. You looked like a little boy watching his first puppet show."

He glanced down at his aroused member. "A little boy? What about this?"

"Oh, *I* did that. It's fairly standard, an automatic aspect of the program to salve the male ego. I can tweak you a good deal larger if you like, Pinocchio, but you'll have to tell me some lies first. I wanted you aroused because I thought it might bring back a memory of someone, some place, some time when you got laid. You must have made love in your closed past, Angel, a man who looks like you."

He tried to conjure up an appropriate image, then shook his head.

"Ah, well," she said, "I tried. Maybe someone else."

Her shape dissolved into that of a blonde princess in a gauzy gown. Her hair poured across the floor in back of her like a wedding train. Around her the room and the bed reshaped, breaking into squares, each of which transformed. The room became a huge stone chamber with vaulted ceiling and a fireplace large enough to stand in; the bed, a feather cushion. "Perhaps Rapunzel will do it." The voice was no longer Chikako's. It was a soft, singsong of innocence. The accompanying scent expressed milk baths, virginity. Her gown parted as she came forward, and he saw that she lacked any pubic hair. She said, "I would give most anything if my gracious lord would let me lie with him for a night." Her eyebrows danced. "Or is that 'gracious knight would let me lie with him, oh lord'? It's been a few years." She sat on the cushion, and was nearly absorbed by it.

He didn't know what to say. He found each transformation vestigially arousing, but ascribed his feelings to the last traces of the inoculation he had been given earlier. It was as if he stood outside himself, watching his arousal but not actually aroused.

Earlier, before he had regained his composure, Mallee had presented Chikako with a gift—"*ibogaine*," she'd said. After taking the capsule, Chikako had confessed that it was a chemical she loved, and hadn't enjoyed for years—Mallee had given it to her for old times' sake. They had time to kill, and she didn't know any better way to pass a long stretch of time. The *ibogaine* gave her pleasant waking hallucinations that she could manipulate, and a decided sexual appetite. He could appreciate the former from experience. Still, while they talked in the bare little *virtual* room, seated on a small futon, the cool principal vanished and a remarkably fiery woman took her place. She insisted that she would show him what a sexual appetite was—after all, here they were in the perfect place for it. "Not for real sex," she'd sworn at the outset. "Just for fun. I'll demonstrate it to you, that's all. Who knows, maybe it'll jog your memory. Maybe you've used *virtual* before and don't remember. We'll rattle that damn bypass of yours." For that chance, he agreed.

The suits were lightweight, if as ugly as trash bags. They included soft boots and gloves. "You're supposed to have a shower before this," she explained, "you know—good hygiene." She handed him a codpiece unit, then had to explain how it fit on. She had a corresponding unit of her own. "Easy to clean," she said. "Much cheaper to replace if anything shorts out."

With the hood on, he expected a rush of claustrophobia, but before that could happen, Peat snatched him from the room and into a three-dimensional fantasy world. Initially, it didn't look real, but like a computer model. Its depth conflicted with his senses, and she let him wander around in it a few minutes to orient himself before she shifted into the libidinous programs that Grofé's clientele used.

Now he couldn't feel the suit at all, and experienced a pit-of-the-stomach clench if he tried to override the program by will and locate his own body. Was he, for instance, erect in reality as in fantasy? No way to tell from within the suit.

She made the room an eighteenth century palace. He could feel the thick rug beneath his bucket-style boots. The new woman with him wore a blue satin gown with a ribboned echelle front. A canopied bed stood beside her. She climbed onto it, her breasts spilling like fruit out of her deep neckline. He knew the bed was nothing but the futon pallet. He knew how high it was, how small. Yet, when he rubbed the quilt between his thumb and fingers, he could feel the embroidery.

"Come and talk to me, Angel," said her new voice.

He, wearing a red and silver knee-length brocaded vest, climbed up beside her.

"Take off your boots, goodman."

He sat up and tugged them off. He appeared to have on two sets of stockings, the outer one ending in lace at midcalf.

"Can you feel the silks underneath?"

He watched his toes wriggle. "Yes. It's remarkable."

"So now you see why this is so popular. Most of my clients could afford their own suits, and had sets at home to connect us up. A few had sets in their office. We could be in different buildings, sometimes different states or countries, although satellite signals aren't as reliable. Plus you run the risk of having your sex play accidentally broadcast into the middle of a conference call or a few households, or monitored and recorded by outside parties. It's never been exposed, but it probably goes on all the time. I've disks of my own of some very peculiar SC execs' fantasies. Not the kind of personal expressions they'd like to see available as alternative viewing. That's why an establishment like Grofé's does so well. It's a thousand times safer. Really the safest sex possible. You experience the fantasy completely but no one is really touching you or fucking you. No one even has to be in the room with you. But, then, you aren't in the room, either."

He wondered, "Why not dispense with the second person altogether?"

"Because," she said as she eased her hand up under his vest, sliding her palm down around the bulge at his groin, "a computer simulation won't surprise you like this. No matter how it's programmed, it's programmed, and you'll end up aware of it. Two of us makes it livelier. I can change anything you want. I was expert at this. I handle all the intricate details and you don't ever know absolutely what I'll do or when I'll ease you back into reality for the real thing." She saw that she was getting a response from him, and withdrew her hand, lying back coquettishly on the pillows.

"There are still plenty of people who want to have it all, you understand—the fantasy character *and* the person behind it. The danger comes with that kind of individual if they don't see where the fantasy stops. On the other hand, they pay the most handsomely, for the extras. The trick is remaining more exotic than all the virtual femmes anyone concocts. And darlin'—" She jumped out of bed, shape-shifting as she landed. The room cubistically turned into a hayloft. The bed became dry bales of hay. She faced him, a honey-haired cowgirl entity with a set of six-shooters strapped on her ample hips and nothing else on at all. "—I've been every one of them at one time or another."

Her nudity stood out here, the more so for the shock of the change, the strangeness of the environment to which he couldn't adjust. He sat up on the hay, naked and lean. His body looked very much like his own, real form. He studied his hands, the musculature of his arms. "How many are there?" he asked.

She spun a pistol around her finger, then reholstered it. "No idea. They're always changing. Sometimes, people want the fantasy to be of a parent or someone they can't have but desire. I've known of Jesus fuckers, and Elvis fuckers, and even one dimwit who fucked only presidents. He finally gave it up after fixating for too long on Ronald Reagan. Maybe the whole thing's therapeutic. People are far stranger than textbooks let on."

"You make it sound like something has been opened that would've been better off closed."

She shrugged. Her breasts bobbled. "I'd never advocate that. It's better for the likes of Mallee than what came before. Prostitutes were a dying breed. Bad drugs and killer diseases amidst our otherwise lethal society, that about did them in. The johns need you but they don't *want* to need you. You understand? They won't help you. Not even to themselves do they want to admit that need. It's very neurotic. Mallee calls it 'The Victorian Deathgrip' partly because of all the 1890s trappings of this place. Underneath all the electronics, it's still there, but at least we're more in control now. Otherwise, we might all have died off, like buffalo."

"What's a buffalo?" he asked.

"Okay, I think that's enough *virtual* for you today," she said. "Let's get out of here. I should have a bath, anyway, a real bath before Lyell comes back."

The next moment she was gone. Angel waited for the hayloft to disappear. When it didn't, he grew uneasy. He realized that if anything happened to her, he could not get out of the program. He called, "Chikako?" He got to his feet and padded across the dusty boards to the open hay doors.

The view was of a western town, nestled against purple hills beneath dark scudding clouds. There was a windmill spinning slowly to one side. While he watched it, the wooden tower and spinning wheel warped sideways. The legs bent as if the top half were toppling onto its side. Angel took a step back.

The clouds behind the tower bent the same way, and he could distinguish the features of a face poking into relief. A face carved out of non-reality.

"You hear me?" it asked as softly as a breeze. "*Oigame.*"

He did not understand the word, but knew the voice. It was the same one that had spoken to him in ICS-IV.

"Yes."

"They mean to kill you."

"They tried and failed."

"No, it isn't done. Others continue it." The face loomed larger. The edges of the "blocks" that made up the virtual world in transition appeared, as though the program were about to transform. The view behind the jutting face looked as if it were being projected on a brick wall. The face stretched the virtual fabric further. Angel stepped back, and it snaked in through the hayloft door.

"Who are you?" he asked.

"You," it echoed.

He wished that he had closed the doors to the loft, as if that could have kept the head out. A pressure like that thrown off by Chikako's dominatrix persona encapsulated him. The room contracted toward him from all sides, the illusive world collapsing all around the face. Unperturbed, it asked, "Who is on your side? Who can be trusted?"

"This woman with me, Chikako Peat. And Lyell, Thomasina Lyell. She's—I don't know what she is. Listen, you've got to back away or you're going to destroy me."

"For just one moment, let me in, *por favor*," it begged.

He tried to relax, to deny the fragmenting false world spinning like a disk behind the head. He dared to close his eyes, relinquishing control. Nausea fisted into his throat. The room ripped loose from its moorings, snaring him as it collapsed down to a single point like the universe regressing through all of time in a split second. He spun into the face, dropping between bright pixels toward a wine-dark ocean that he could never reach in a million years of falling. "Come back," called the voice above him.

Invisible hands slid over him again, tearing at him. They wanted to rip him apart.

"Angel! Angel!" called the Sirens from the rocks below. The dizzy endless fall stopped.

He sat on the floor of a bare gray room. Chikako Peat, naked and drenched with perspiration, knelt on top of him, cradling his head, holding the *virtual* hood in her hand. Terror twisted her features.

"It's really you?" he asked, and she nodded, just as she might have done in false reality. He could not keep from scanning the room behind her for the invasive face. For the moment he could distinguish reality only in terms of expectation and the appearance of certain body parts.

Some aspect of the other, intruding persona had remigrated with him. He could almost see it—a swimmer under the surface, a shadow broken by the ripples in his consciousness. When he focused on Chikako, the swimmer sounded for a moment. Surreptitiously, it slipped into control.

His hand reached up to touch the beads of sweat on her cheek. His fingers curled around her neck, slid into her hair, and he heard himself say her name as if the word ached. He pulled her to him and kissed her. He had no idea where his actions were leading—he was the teacher in the background again, distanced by a program that steered itself. His body obeyed new instructions, and arousal flooded through him like a new injection. Chikako, for her part, reacted chemically, if no less instinctively. "Let's get you out of the suit first," she said.

She made love to him a second time in a green sunken tub. The bathroom alone was as large as the *virtual* room. Chikako explained that the bathroom represented reality's last hold on virtual sex; there were all sorts of water sports in virtual reality but none that compensated by actually making anyone clean.

Mallee walked in on them at one point, set down a covered tray, and walked out again without a word, just a penetrating look at Angel. Peat seemed not to notice her presence. He would have been embarrassed except that he was too bound up in his own continued arousal.

He soaped and kneaded her breasts while she rode him, and she leaned down and licked salty sweat from his shoulder above the wound that he had quite forgotten. The shoulder was a little swollen, and warm to the touch. They were careful to keep the bandage out of the sudsy water, but that hardly restricted their passion. They moved together with feral fluidity. He sat forward on a submerged ledge, and wrapped his arms up around her back; she hooked her ankles carefully over his shoulders. The water buoyed her. He concentrated on her body and avoided looking into the bathwater around her, where the swimmer in his mind might appear, bending reality again, proving this experience to be another mirage, another layer of deception. He wondered if he could ever entirely trust reality again.

She had, he saw, a curious tattoo on her left buttock—a small block of six straight and broken lines. He wished to ask her about it but didn't want to stop moving.

Finally, he came, in one great, agonized shudder that made him cry out. Afterward Chikako clung tightly to him, letting him shrink inside her before she eased off. He lay back with his head resting on the lip of the tub, almost in a light doze, the fearsome alter ego forgotten for the moment. He was barely aware of her leaning over the edge of the tub, surprised when her fingers slipped around his mouth with something slick and cold. He jerked away instinctively, opened his eyes to find her offering him a green chunk of melon. He let her feed it to him. The juice dripped over his chin.

Next she came up with an antique shaving mug and a brush. He stared at it, clearly unaware of what it was, and she laughed.

"It extends across the board, doesn't it, this memory block of yours," she said. "Or maybe you only used electric razors in your previous incarnations." After swirling the brush in the mug, she raised it, covered with thick foam, and began to soap his jaw. Quite carelessly, she asked, "What happened to you after I left *virtual*?"

He recalled the sound of the wind. "Someone else came in."

"Who?"

"I don't know. It said it was me."

They traded a look, trust passing in motes between them. She broke the tableau to finish lathering him. "Something more happened. You're different now."

"I am. That is, I was."

"It's gone, you mean."

"I'm not sure. I didn't know what it was while it was happening. When I looked at you there was nothing else in the world. After all that fantasy, you were real."

She smiled edgily. The direction he was headed made her nervous. "You're the most dangerous kind of customer," she said, "the one looking for the real thing. It's fantasies we sell here, remember." She reached for the razor. "Don't hand me any future dreams, okay? You can't even tell me who you'll turn out to be. Now, what else happened?"

He shook his head. "The image collapsed and I was falling into a kind of void."

"What about now? Do you still sense it there?"

He tensed. In her relentless pursuit of the face behind the mask, she had no idea what she was asking of him. "I don't know," he said, "I don't know, I have to . . . to look."

His eyelids fluttered closed. He waited, silencing the fear that welled up like the roar of blood in his ears. When nothing came, he pushed a little to recall his life. A new smell blossomed: corruption, something rotten right under his nose. The smell opened up his vision: he saw a narrow alley behind a cantina kitchen, discarded food decaying in mulching bins all around him. It was the first glimpse he'd ever had of his life before the Moon.

The memory slammed shut, and he was tilting off-balance, the chasm yawning below.

Chikako's weight doubled, tripled. She spread out, smothering his face. She would drown him! He fought to fling her off, kicking and splashing wildly.

"*Angel,*" she shouted.

He opened his eyes.

Chikako sat naked upon the lip of the tub, nowhere near him. Foam like a milky tear slid down the side of the brown shaving mug; it clung desperately to the bottom, then plunged into the bathwater where it spread out in rings.

She eased back into the tub. "They really did a job on you, darling," she said.

He pressed his face to her breasts and made himself breathe slowly, calmly, banishing all but the here and now, inhaling the clean and wonderful smell of her. The alley's stench lingered somewhere across the room. "I just remembered a place," he confided. "I don't know where it was, or what exactly, but I know it was from my life before. Who did the job on me, what did you mean?"

"ScumberCorp, Angel." She clinked the mug against the *crab* unit. "*This* is no accident. You've been programmed. They've used this to curtail your memory. Every time you try to access it, the *crab* overrides you.

"I just watched the numbers racing on this little panel on the side while you were thrashing around. You triggered it. *Virtual* must have found a chink in the armor, until the processor recovered and shut it out. Medical technology misapplied."

"They *don't* want me to remember who I am?"

"Put simply."

"Then, why did they ask me all the time to try? Why?"

She stared at the brush in her hand. It was becoming kaleidoscopic, courtesy of the *ibogaine*. This was not the time for serious talk. *Ibogaine* augmented spontaneity, rebelled against linearity. She was losing her grip on the conversation. "I should shave you so we can eat."

"Chikako. *Please.*"

"They were testing you. They had to make certain your programming took. If you remember suddenly now, there's nothing they can do about it. Then again, maybe this thing has an alarm in it, to signal them if that happens." She set down the mug and brush. She was thinking, *Maybe it detonates automatically.* She kept this to herself. The conversation was making her queasy. "Whatever it is, they don't want you coming to it on your own."

"Why?"

"That," she replied edgily, "is the big secret. We can't get the answer without Thomasina, so we should wait till she gets back. I predict this thing"—she tapped his head—"comes off when it happens."

He shook his head. "No. The voice that speaks to me—I know it's not me, despite what it says."

He tried to get up but she held him down with surprising strength. "Okay, Joan of Arc. It's something else. Let Thomasina find out. She'll be back when she has answers. For now . . ." She twirled a gold safety razor. "Don't move." Slipping in close, she began carefully to shave him. The foamy stubble had a pearlescent sheen to it. "I believe," she said softly, "when she gets back, the heat will be turned way up on all of us. Maybe there won't be any more time for you and me alone. When you're hungry, Angel, you should eat. And you're a cornucopia. I know you don't know what that is, either, but you don't need to." Smiling, she set down the razor, then turned and kissed him hard. Underwater, anatomies shifted. Chikako sat back with a foamy mustache of her own and laughed. "I'm absolutely famished. That's a way I know I'm alive."

Nebergall rolled in late. He drove his chair through the hallway of his apartment like an Indy 500 racer from out of his childhood. He had been only eleven the last year the race was held, and he had witnessed the end of an era. His parents had brought him all the way from Lexington because they thought it was important. In one sense it was—it was the strongest memory he retained of what it had been like to walk on his own two feet.

After banging along one wall, he suddenly swung across and clipped the opposite corner. A neighbor, Mrs. Rhozdetsvensky, the clairvoyant, looked out into the hall.

"You are all right, Mr. Neighbor-gall?"

"Jes' a li'l inebriated, darlin'. Don't fret it." He laughed to himself. Mrs. Rhozdetsvensky claimed to have seen him in a future where he was no longer out of work. She had seen him selling fruit-flavored water ice.

He drove up to and unlocked his door, wheeled around to give her a wide smile the way Hopalong Cassidy might have done while his horse reared back and he waved his hat, then zoomed inside in reverse.

Thomasina Lyell lay stretched out on his unmade bed. A cat slept against her hip. A bath towel almost covered her.

"Tommie," he said. He shook her arm. "Your wake-up call's here."

She stretched. "I'm already awake due to some seismic activity out in the foyer."

"You mean me."

"Did you know there's moss growing on the north side of your bathroom?"

"You mean that old saw's for real?" He laughed and belched.

She winced at the smell of his breath. "I wish corsairs took a tiny bit more care of their appearance. Everyone you ever introduced me to had bad skin, greasy hair, green teeth, or body odor—usually in combination. By the way, you're drunk, Nebergall."

He nodded solemnly at her pronouncement. "If I'm not, then I wasted a ton of pub time. Had to change the pee-pee bottle twice. What a pain. People don't appreciate."

"Why did you get drunk? I *need* you sober."

"Hell, I'm clearheaded enough. But I had to wait, same as you, 'cept I was outside in the heat. I didn't get to nap like some tired-out old *pijin*."

"I changed your pillowcases, too."

"You're too good to me, Tommie."

"That's true, and I expect a reward."

"I wish it was me," he said, and the conversation slammed into the turn.

Sober, he never would have lost control. They glanced at but avoided one another's eyes. Lyell picked up the shoulder harness and disk recorder off the bed. She pretended to concern herself with running a diagnostic on it. She pressed her palm against various pads in the harness that absorbed body heat: the recorder ran off body heat. It was guaranteed to record for at least half an hour after she died—a guarantee that did little to excite her.

Nebergall tried to gain ground by making light of his naked comment. "Well, you deserve your reward," he said, "and it's information I'm bestowing. Quiz show time."

Without looking at him, she asked, "Did the blood I gave you match anything?"

"Blood and prints both."

She set down the harness, and sat up. "And the winner?"

"Señor Angel Rueda," he said.

She cocked an eyebrow. "It's his real name?"

"Yeah, for all that's worth." Clearly he had much more to tell.

"Wait a minute," she said, "what's that supposed to mean—for all it's worth?" She made a grab for him, but he joysticked the chair to pivot on one wheel and she clutched air. "Give, Nebergall, you rat bastard."

He stopped, facing her directly, then puttered back to her side. "C'mon, put your feet up and I'll rub 'em for you."

With a sigh, she flopped back on the bed, dragging the harness with her.

He backed up so that he could slide her feet onto his lap, then began working his thumbs into her soles. He had powerful hands, and Lyell shortly succumbed to the sheer excruciating ecstasy of his deep massage. "That is wonderful," she told him.

"I know. I'm good."

After a minute, he added casually, "ScumberCorp's already tagged his ID with their story."

"So, there's nothing left. I'm not surprised."

"They wish. See, Clarence—that's my buddy with the lab, Clarence Marquardt, who has big dandruff and serious BO by the way, just to make you happy—he gets the backup cartridge from his friends in I-P security once they change 'em over. New one's issued every three months. The old ones are supposed to be erased and recycled but these security guys humor Clarence, 'cause he used to be one of them and there's a sort of bond there. Like with you and me, except you want me to take more baths. What Clarence does is he exchanges the cartridge twice removed for his pals to turn in for erasure, and they give him the one that's just been pulled. The city's down one cartridge forever, but nobody's going to miss the fucker. His data base's always a little out-of-date, but for most of his customers that he *has* a goddam cartridge makes him solid gold. So, who cares? He's retired, this is all money on the sly, anyhow. I figure most of the corsairs on the East Coast check in with Clarence. He's a great old guy, with lots of stories. You get him talking over a few drinks—"

"Yes, okay, thank you, Cowboy Bob, for that wonderful bedtime story. I get the point. Clarence has data on Angel Rueda from prior to ScumberCorp's rewrite."

He stared at her with moist eyes. "God, I adore you, Tommie. You're so goddam noumenal." He went to work on her left foot.

"Am I supposed to guess what you found? Okay, the old data cartridge shows he has no connection whatsoever to *Xau Dâu*."

"Oh, better than that," he replied. "No connection to ScumberCorp, period."

She leaned up on her elbows. "None?"

He shook his head, his smile as wide as a scythe. "Never on the Moon, never worked a day as a docker. None of it."

"But they were bringing him *down*. I saw them. You saw them. That's how this all began." He continued to smile broadly and noncommittally. She cast over the the sea of possibilities without sighting a clear explanation. "According to Peat's records, they were passing him off to Isis as an ex-Orbiter."

"Bingo."

Her expression clouded. "What—that's true?" She withdrew her feet from his lap and sat up, clutching the towel to her. "Him, an Orbiter?"

"Oh, yeah, a serious junkie. But not like you think."

"Like *what*, then, Nebergall?"

"Like 'ex' as in Orbitol decay," he said.

"*No.*"

"Yup. Absolutely and without a doubt. Four months ago, your very own Angel Rueda—blood, DNA, fingerprints, and spit—was stone-cold dead and gone."

17

Going Down, No Mercy

"Let me see now. Angel Rueda was CFO for a company named Nubarrón, which is a Bickham Interplanetary subsidiary," read Nebergall. "He worked and lived in Madrid, Spain, until three years ago when he got hooked on Orbitol. Doesn't say how in the report. His work went to hell—big surprise, huh?—and so did he. Dropped out of sight, you might say."

"You got this from Bickham?"

"From Nubarrón, yeah. This is their bio on him. Even includes a presumed date of death." He dangled it in front of her.

He said, "Your old boy took himself right out of the picture and then came back again. A neat trick, that. No wonder ScumberCorp's shittin' itself over him. They want to wipe out the homeless population, and here's some unprecedented Spaniard in the works, to borrow a great man's pun—an inflato-collar, pegged pants, suit-jacketed worker bee from the upper crust of a competitor, and he comes *back*! Christ, what if everybody who ever decayed is gonna do it? That's like millions of the great unwashed dropping in on SC from nowhere. And not here: on the Moon! I like that as a concept, especially if they're pissed off. Tommie, we gotta do this show, even if there's not a word of truth to it and it ends up on ANN, we *got* to—just to sweat the robber barons." His bloodshot eyes glittered madly.

"Neeb, President Odie."

"What about him?"

"Remember, I asked you if you'd copied Odie's show while I was on the Geosat?"

His brows knitted. "Vaguely," he replied.

"It would have been, what, the night of the thirteenth."

He scratched his chin. "I was pulling the Mussari edit, I remember now."

Lyell stood, tucking the towel tightly above her breasts. "We have to find the disk."

"Why?" He wheeled around after her. "What was on that asshole's show?"

"Evidence," she opened the door to the edit suite and encountered a wall of chilled air. "It's *freezing* in here."

"Not if you're wearing clothes, it ain't." He lingered in the doorway, unable in his inebriation to ignore her. "Tommie, you're gonna have to put something on before that towel opens up again and I go bugfuck. I am not driving in here to be scrunched up against your luscious bare ass, without it having a profound and disastrous effect. I'm sure I do not wish to spoil this relationship we've so far managed to avoid." He rolled back to let her out. Unrecognizable objects crunched beneath his wheels. The cat stared solemnly at him from the bed, and he stuck his tongue out at it.

By the time Lyell was dressed, Nebergall had come up with the specific disk and cued it up on the screens. His reaction upon being introduced to Mrs. Akiko Alcevar and the photos of her late husband was much like Lyell's had been initially—utter disbelief.

"I can do better effects work right here in ten minutes with my toes," he argued, while tapping an electronic stylus against his small graphics tablet. "At least make him look identifiably like himself. They must be hellishly over budget if that's the best work they can produce."

"Exactly," replied Lyell. "A three-year-old with a crayon could do better. So why run such a bad portrait unless it's the real thing?"

"Kinda flaky argument, isn't that? What's to keep you from cleaning it up even if it *is* real? There's an audience out there that's seen the best work available and swallowed it like the good little fish fillets they are. The average Undercity dweller sees one hundred fifty thousand hours of programming in their lives. Most of it is either sitcoms or crap about alien invaders, past lives, and troglodytes. They can't discriminate between tits and toilet bowls anyway, none of 'em. So why bother bein' honest if it doesn't get you anything?"

She ignored his pessimism. "What I want to know is where that second image of Alcevar comes from."

"*If* it's the real thing, you mean. If he's another piece of toast popped up same as Señor Rueda. Doesn't look like he hit the Moon, does it?"

"Where could the widow Alcevar have seen her husband, do you think? It's not likely he was shopping up in Penn Tower Six."

"I don't get the impression *she's* ever been in Penn Six."

"Then, what have we got?"

"*Nada* is what we got. All you know for certain is, he didn't turn up on a sitcom."

" 'My Favorite Gulag,' " she said reflexively.

"Awful show. You have to vomit before you can sit down in front of it—ha-ha, we're being beaten to death with shovels, what a fucking laugh-riot. Who the hell cares where she saw it? Maybe the guy was from Madrid, too. Could be location is a factor. I could go check with Clarence. Then there's the question of how ScumberCorp ended up with Rueda at all."

"Explain that."

"Well," he said, "say the guy fades out in Madrid like Nubarrón suggests. Okay? So, what happens? He all of a sudden wakes up on the Moon inside one of SC's facilities? That is what's implied."

She thought about it for a moment, finally shook her head. "No. That doesn't scan."

"Exactly. We got to get more of the story. Before they bury it."

"Meaning *I've* got to get more of the story." She glanced at the real-time clock. "Jesus, is that the time?" He looked, nodded. "I should have known when you told me how many bottles of urine you dumped. Damn you, Nebergall."

"Y'all needed the rest. Who knows when you'll get to sleep again?"

She shook her head. "Exploiter."

"I'll make you a household word," he promised. "But let's not make it posthumously, okay?" When she didn't answer, he said, "I guess I'll check out the footage so far and try to put something together we can sell. Don't forget to take a fresh disk!" The outer door slammed. He wheeled back, and shut himself in with the equipment.

Angel Rueda ignored the lumps under his back as he reclined on the futon, his feet hanging off the end and his good arm under his head. He'd placed Chikako Peat's gold cigarette case on his chest. He passed the time by watching Chikako sleep beside him.

The *ibogaine* had exhausted her after five hours, with a little help from him. He ought to have been worn out, too, but all he felt was an inner calm, a stillness unlike the void of the bypass. Lyell's absence had begun to concern him.

She exhibited extraordinary self-reliance, was quick and dogged in her pursuit of a story—after all, she'd come looking for him as a result of only a few moments on the Geoplatform. He had sensed something about her then, hard to say exactly what even now. He tried to recall the way she had watched him led out, but the image had evaporated. Odd that he could remember the event but no sensory impressions to support the memory.

Now he was beginning to think he had dragged her into something so huge that it had consumed her, as, sooner or later, it must devour him and Chikako. He had no real comprehension of the vastness of ScumberCorp. The way everyone talked, it was an empire with its grip upon the globe and its fingers stretching into space, ready to seize world upon world. Comparatively, he was a grain of sand trying to withstand the whole force of an ocean.

Without thinking, he opened Chikako's gold case and took out the last cigarette. It was neon blue. He stuck it in his mouth, then hesitated, took it out again, rolled it in his fingers, sniffed the tip. Some kind of pungent herb; he had smelled it in her sweat, where it acted as an aphrodisiac.

He put it between his lips again, then pressed the case closed and held it up. A distorted face glared back at him, its seeming anger the result of the lens over his right eye. Now he was fairly sure that there was nothing wrong with his sight and the lens was phony.

He maneuvered the cigarette around from one side of his mouth to the other, a motion which had a certain familiarity to it. The case had a lighter built into the side. When he touched the recessed button, it clicked twice, then lit. He inhaled, tentatively, one puff, and began to choke. Swinging upright, he kept coughing. He reached over and stubbed the cigarette out against a dirty plate on the discarded tray.

By the time he regained control of his breathing, he thought his lungs were coming up. Tears had pooled inside the lens and he had to shake his head to clear it. He sniffled, wiped his palm across his cheek. Glancing up, he found Chikako watching him.

"I just had a dream," she said softly. "You were in it, but you were changed. That contraption had been taken off your head. I was standing on a bridge and you came by, and I saw that you had a new face but it was still you."

"What happened?"

"When you came up beside me, you said, 'Forgive me,' and then you pushed me off the bridge. I landed on the bed and woke up." She slid out, golden, from under the single blue sheet. "I should get dressed. Or—" Slyly, she tilted her head.

"Please, no more. I'd like to depart here under my own power and with the few working parts remaining to me."

She smiled. "How late is it?"

"After eleven."

Worry crossed her face. "Thomasina never came back?"

"Not yet. I was just wondering what we do if she hasn't shown up by one."

"We fly, Fleance, fly. No matter what, when Mallee says it's time, then it's time."

"Could be this Mingo character has found her."

"Probably. It's not a very free society we live in these days. You don't know that, do you?" She picked up and put on a black chemise she'd discarded earlier, then began looking for her other clothes. She had left them hanging in a changing area behind a bamboo screen. "People without your excuse don't know it, either. The difference is, you need to find out more and they don't want to. Where the devil's my dress?"

"Mallee brought it back while you were asleep. And a jacket for me. They're both behind the other screen," he said.

She crossed the room out of sight. "In the last twenty years," she said as she dressed, "SC has become part of everything. The vegetables in that stir-fry we ate probably came off SC-owned land, or from their seed or was fed their fertilizers. Same with the melons. The railcars that brought them to Vine Street. The shots you got today—they *definitely* owned that formula. The president—hell, the president's nothing but a corporate foreskin. He's been signing laws year after year, slicing away individual rights that most people didn't even know they had. The kind of rights that won't kick in till SC decides it likes the property somebody owns or the product they're selling . . . like with Mars."

"Mars?"

" 'If not today, then tomorrow, a new world awaits you.' Ever hear that?"

"I think I saw it on a poster, on the Geoplatform."

She nodded. "The promise of Mars. We can't even live on it for another generation at least, but guess who's got the rights to all the shopping malls?"

He pursed his lips. "I was wondering how big they were."

"You have no idea. Neither have I." She stepped into her red-violet shoes and adjusted the straps, then looked in one of the overhead mirrors. "Ah, the hair's a hornet's nest, but I'll still turn a few heads, eh? Come on with me."

"What are you doing?"

"I've been held hostage long enough. Besides, you just wasted my only remaining cigarette, oaf. Those things are obscenely expensive, but at least Grofé's is attached to a shop."

"Chikako, you can't go out. They're sure to be looking for us. If they got to Lyell—"

"Well, fuck them, Angel!" She walked over to him, then bent down and kissed his cheek, looked him in his one dark eye. "Eventually, if they don't kill you first, you're going to reach a point where even you say, 'fuck them.' It's as American as subverting justice." She grinned.

Troubled by her tone, he asked, "Are you all right?"

"Actually, yes, I am." She straightened up. "I've gotten extremely laid and bathed, and I've eaten and slept. All of a sudden as I speak to you, I realize I've been ScumberCorp's hostage for years. I said 'Thank you' when they gave me the Isis post instead of shipping me to a mining station, which is the equivalent of fucking in Hell till you die. You know, I've been cringing on the inside—for years! You think I'm brave, but that's because you haven't discovered yet how people disguise fear. They make it come out looking like fury. Angry people are mostly scared people. Stupid, isn't it?"

"Chikako—"

"You put on that shirt and jacket, señor, and come meet me for a drink. Let's take a little risk." She opened the door and stepped into the hall before he could think of a way to stop her.

In a mad rush he put on the pink shirt Mallee had brought for him, then the charcoal gray jacket of Gansevoort's. He had to drape it over his bad arm, which had developed an acute ache in the shoulder joint. He supposed the injections had worn off. The shirt had one of those collars like Gansevoort's that expanded into a sort of ruff, but he didn't know how to manipulate it. He rolled it loosely down.

As he was about to leave, he saw her gold cigarette case on the divan, and snatched it as he went by. He tucked it into his inside pocket.

Before the door, he stared at himself in the mirror and remembered the LifeMask. Dutifully, he went back for it. He pulled it on clumsily, one-handed, as he strode down the hall.

In the shadow of the curtain he lingered, surveying the tearoom. A dozen or so people, mostly men, sat or lay on their sides in the room, each booth with its own efficient attendant. He couldn't see everybody but recognized no one.

A television screen had been lowered in the corner on his left. Some kind of CD-I program was displayed, a lined game board with black and white circles on it in clusters. He couldn't tell who had the remote responder.

Two women pushed through the curtains, and he stepped aside to let them pass. He saw Chikako then, just past the opposite doorway, standing at the bar. After making sure his mask was on straight, he stepped out, and, head low, started across the tearoom.

He kept his eyes on her. She must have sensed him. She turned toward him, stuck her hands out and parted the drapes wide, rustling the palm tree, smiling broadly. She had a fresh red cigarette in her fingers.

Her expression stiffened, eyes shifted, going wide.

"No, Angel!" she cried and sprang at him. He stumbled back against a table in alarm. Instinct made him reach for the gun he no longer had. The doctors had removed it. His knuckles rapped against the gold case.

Hand outstretched, Chikako Peat slammed past him. Her shoulder hit him hard enough to turn him. He saw, past her hand, the muzzle of the gun—black like the ones in the school—coming to bear on him. He stared into the eyes of the familiar, placid, blond face, and realization dropped through him like a cannonball.

His own face, *his* assigned mask from the school, had come to kill him.

The killer fired, and blood ripped out of Chikako's hand. Two fingers and the cigarette were gone. She gasped. Someone else screamed. He tasted her blood on his lips.

The maskface fired again, this time into her body. Her right arm swung back, slapping Angel's head. He stumbled into the table again.

The crowd dived for the floor, crouching in their booths. Tabletops flipped up to shield them. Silverware danced through the air. The third shot flung Chikako back into him. He wrapped his arms around her, trying to prop her up.

Past her neck, he saw the gun swinging, the hole like an iris open wide, looking for a spot in him to bore into.

Suddenly, she pushed off him, wrenching free of his grasp. She pounced on the killer. The gun fired. The bullet buzzed past his ear. Chikako and her adversary crashed against a booth, then into the nearest table, flipping it off its pedestal. Drinks and food flew like shrapnel, skittered, and shattered. She slapped at the charming electronic face, glimpsed Angel still there behind her, and screamed, "Get away, goddamit!" An awful, bloody gouge had torn her cheek.

She stabbed with her lacquered nails into the LifeMask's eyes. The false face flickered like a tired fluorescent bulb. The gun fired again. Her body bucked, her back tore open. Screaming in rage and pain, she hammered her fist into the gray mask.

Someone took hold of Angel and yanked him away. He swung around, but did not recognize Mallee for a second. Her horror amplified his own numbness. She had the presence of mind to act. She shoved him through the curtains, dragged him out past the diners, crouching like mice under their tables. Out the front entrance. "Run and don't stop," she ordered.

"Chikako—"

"No chance. She's dead. It was for *you*, you bastard, now *go!*" Another shot went off. "*Get the fuck out of here!*"

A small crowd was gathering outside the door. They stared at him as at a cornered beast. He bolted, and they jumped aside, shrieking.

Mallee slammed and bolted the door.

Furiously, Mingo shoved the dead woman off him.

She had been nearly impossible to kill, as if she had been wired up on drugs. He ought to have opened up on full automatic and leveled the place; but he'd thought it was going to go smoothly.

He crawled to his feet and looked around. No one was about to come near him, but no doubt security was headed here right this minute. The mask, he could tell, had shorted out, useless, incommodious; but the cringing customers all would have seen—they would all recognize the face well enough to identify it. He could take that little satisfaction away with him.

Painfully, he stepped over the corpse, then fled, limping, through the rear curtains, into the deeper reaches of Grofé's. A few doors hung open, people looking out, some so disoriented that they still wore their *virtual* goggles. Many yanked their heads back in as he ran past. Some of them were naked, but their perversions did not interest Mingo at the moment. He'd memorized the club's layout, where other exits lay.

His left thigh burned each time he put the weight of his body on it. In the center of each flash of pain, he pictured Angel Rueda, dead and dismembered.

That dimwit bullgod had actually changed sides, thrown in with the enemy! No corpse of Rueda's and the damnable guard on duty *shoots* him. Well, it was all too much.

He ought to have been in a hospital with a wound that severe—everybody told him that and he even agreed with the diagnosis; but he was going to finish this thing first, tonight. No more unexplained phenomena on the Moon, and no more mingling with the stinking, shit-covered proles. After this, *Xau Dâu* was going into retirement.

Once he'd gone far enough, Mingo unlocked the mask and peeled it off. He tossed it aside as he ran. It still carried a code assigning it to Angel Rueda. That should finish him if nothing else did. Even Overcity security would know to hunt him down, provided Mingo didn't get him first. God, but the man was slippery. Mingo was beginning to think he was hunting some kind of trickster.

Mingo touched his face where it stung and found congealing blood on his fingertips. The Peat woman had shredded his cheek right below the eye. The tiniest bit higher and she would have torn out his eyeball. He smiled grimly, reliving the triumph of having silenced her. That leak had been patched permanently. There remained only Gansevoort to eliminate, which could wait until all the other loose ends had been fixed. Gansevoort—he had to laugh—they'd left the naive boob tied to a chair for six hours. Heaven keep him from honest men!

Mingo slammed out the exit door, ignoring the alarm he set off. He glanced around immediately for any sign of Angel in the deserted corridor. Stranger things had happened, but not this time. He hurried along the alleyway.

He asked himself where a man with no memory would run to. As an intellectual exercise, it intrigued him. Peat had obviously selected Grofé's—that had been a simple enough puzzle to solve. This, now, would require more existential contemplation.

Mingo straightened his jacket, tucked away the gun, and put on his dark glasses, then walked quickly but not obtrusively around the corner and into the main flow of late evening traffic. He dabbed gingerly with his scarf at the gouge in his cheek. From behind the tinted lenses, he stared intensely into people's eyes, believing himself gifted with the power to read in their look any confusion or dismay that a running man would have left, as though he could peer into each retina and locate an image burned there.

A team of security uniforms charged past, and most heads turned to watch them. Mingo pretended to rub at his eyelid.

He could not refrain from a self-satisfied smirk. That whore had been nothing other than a cool gadfly, yet she had succeeded in squeezing the company for years with her threat of "private files." No doubt there would be some fallout as a result of her demise. Naughty picture disks or some such. A few heads would roll. People in power could not afford to exercise their perversions—when would they ever learn? It made the work of people like himself so much more difficult. This way, at least, the equation balanced out. SC might lose some executive material, but they would gain in the end.

"If you'd only listened to me. . . ." he muttered.

After a few minutes' search, he concluded that Angel had fled the twenty-third floor. There weren't enough people about to conceal him.

Mingo took an escalator to the nearest skyway level—the eighteenth—and hailed a pedicab. "Locust Walk Tower," he said. The cyclist eyed him suspiciously but as quickly started pedaling.

Overcity security resided in Locust Walk. He would use their facilities to track his prey while their people sorted out the mess he had just left in Grofé's. If they were pleasant, he might even help them to connect the one with the other.

A large group exited from a theater court. Through the crowd he glimpsed a LifeMask and went for his pistol only to discover, as the cab rolled past, that it was someone apparently crippled, probably disfigured, walking via a CNS-stimulating prosthesis.

He clucked his tongue, tucked the gun away, and contemplated how accidents happened every day. Angel Rueda's being alive was thus far a series of enormous accidents—who could have predicted it?

Security would turn up Rueda, however. There was no place in the Overcity he could go that their lenses weren't scanning right now. If only the bastard had kept his original mask, Mingo could have tracked him anywhere on the planet. If only he hadn't had to go deal with that errant skimmer pilot on the Moon while Rueda was fitted with a cortical calotte, he would have had the stupid surgeon place a tracking device inside it. He hadn't really expected that he would ever need it, and had let the matter drop. Accidents again. Nothing but accidents. Too many accidents and none in his favor.

He took solace in the hope that Rueda would lead him now to the third party, the uninvited guest—the woman who had aided in the escape from ICS-IV, who had seemingly evaporated afterward. She wasn't one of the twitchers nor one of the staff. No one who'd survived had any idea who she was. There would have been a record of her visit if the rioting children hadn't destroyed every active disk in the place. There ought to have been security images of her, only that fool Gansevoort had come along and used his clout to escort her around the checkpoint. *Accidents.*

She was a ghost, this woman, a phantom. Mingo yearned to meet her. Just once.

18

Underworld Blues

It was raining when he reached the plaza—a steady downpour washing the more recent human egesta into dark crevices and drains. Where hamburgers and *cha gio* had recently been consumed under Mingo's governance, Angel lingered on a chipped stone bench and gathered his frayed wits.

Most certainly, Chikako Peat was dead. A few hours ago they had been of one body; and the memory brought to him her perfume, the scent of those herbal smokes, the voice that mocked him while extending comfort, that hexagram tattoo from her former employ: "*Hsien*," she'd identified it. "Wooing." Her voice, full of irony, rang out so sharp and clear in his mind that he could not help gazing up to see her, a fata morgana riding the hiss of the rain in the dark, lost to him.

He knew he should make contact with Lyell but had no idea where to begin. The Overcity worked by tacit rules, and he was conspicuous however he went. No place offered him sanctuary. He had seen the looks in their eyes as he fled: they would all remember him.

Wearily, he got up and plashed across the broken concrete. His arm throbbed. The skin of his biceps was hot to the touch. All the energy that had attended him with Chikako had swirled away like this rain into the drains. He wished he had been able to sleep alongside her. He wished he possessed more medicine, one more shot to see him through his escape. Without it, he must go as far as he could. Mingo would come after him.

Ahead, past a row of huge pots rooting black dead trees, the plaza narrowed. He passed into a canyon beneath a crisscross of skywalks. Another plaza opened to him, this one encircling the Gothic City Hall building and lit by garish sodium lights. A security checkpoint was installed on the far side. He could see a few figures inside a conveyance tube beyond it, riding an escalator up to the skywalks. He hung back against the sealed ground floor walls of the buildings that circled City Hall plaza. He was a solitary figure in shadows cast by the walkways, cut by the lights. The rain helped, keeping the guards inside their gate. At that distance it erased identity: the guards nothing but faceless ciphers.

Edging along, he caught sight of his own lambent reflection in a polished buttress. Where the rain had spattered the mask, it appeared to have holes in it. Splotches covered the top of his head like some fungus or the exposed bones of his skull. Across the crown, the mesh of the mask emerged clearly. He glanced toward the checkpoint but no one was there. No one saw him.

Safely around City Hall, he set off more quickly down Market Street to the east. Not far along the broad and broken, debris-strewn avenue, the main cluster of towers fell away, until only a single strip of looming skyscrapers remained. They stretched east almost to the river. Nearby, much older buildings, many abandoned or inhabited on the ground floor only, filled the spaces between ancient streets. Dazzlingly lighted fast-food kiosks surrounded the tower exits off Market and Tenth Street, representative of every conceivable variety of meal. He stared at the twirling orange bun with the hideous grin on its cartoon face and recalled Chikako's remark linking food and ScumberCorp.

He shied away from the kiosks. Many things he was, but hungry wasn't one of them.

The number of people grew the farther he walked. Nocturnal nomads roamed the streets in search of nothing.

He passed graffiti-coated entrances to old underground rail lines, but did not understand what they were; otherwise he might have vanished right then into the sanctuary they offered. But no one else was approaching them, and he stayed away.

Thinking that Mingo might find him on so broad an avenue, he turned left at the next street. There, in the dark, he discovered ahead a wonderfully strange arch. It stood in the street, like the gate to a mythical realm. Brightly colored figures, monstrous heads, and Chinese characters adorned the twin pillars and the crosspieces. It was all the more strange in that the buildings to each side of it were crumbling edifices. Who maintained this arch and why? He could not imagine, but its very incongruity kept him from venturing farther. Whatever dwelled in that darkened domain of shop fronts might have erected the arch as a warning rather than any kind of welcome to would-be trespassers. He must look elsewhere for sanctuary.

Turning, he noticed a rusted and graffiti-adorned green street sign: "Arch Street." A joke?

A passerby stumbled blindly against him while he stood there looking, grumbled at him before shuffling on. Angel forgot about arches and headed away from the solitary figure.

He walked east upon a surface of flattened, dissolving trash made slick by the rain. Crushed atomizer bulbs skittered underfoot like tiny deformed crustaceans. No one passing seemed to mind the debris. People close by watched him, but most looked fearfully away if he turned his gaze on them and gave him a wide berth. Those few who stared longer did so with mad eyes, seeing something of their own making in his softly glowing visage. He glanced past them, at store windows to either side. Against the darkness of the street, the mask was a bobbing will-o'-the-wisp, a phantom light.

As he progressed eastward, each row of decaying buildings that went by stripped another layer off time, each ushered him deeper into the city's past, toward the Delaware River and the oldest stratum. He did not want to be trapped against the river.

Many of the historical sites had been seized by squatters and converted into seedy shops that clung like barnacles to the city's keel: grocers who grew food and herbs in scrubby backyard plots; cheap teahouses where locally grown opium was smoked and Balinese puppets cast their grotesquely flexing shadows across sex-stained sheets; verminous flophouses for those who had moved up from lower levels or fallen from grace. People lined one sidewalk, awaiting the next available room in a four-story flophouse. He kept to the far side of the street. The flophouse offered him nothing, either. Angel needed to descend to places where scouted shades could mask him far better than his dissolving electronic facade.

The buildings stopped abruptly. An open space lay dead ahead, caught in the sodium glare of lights atop a high wall to the north—the wall enclosing the fabled Vine Street docks.

To his left, as far as he could see, stretched a conflux of boxes. A bizarre living fortress. It overspilled a red brick retaining wall, down a few steps and across the street. Rows of contiguous boxes covered the walks on both sides, the broad avenue ahead. A few scattered maple trees stuck out of the mass on his left, silhouetted, leafless, against the lights.

A layered murmur of conversation rolled like ocean waves upon the air, cresting with shouts and howls and peals of laughter. He could smell woodsmoke and things less pleasing.

He crossed the street to where a crooked sign hanging off a Mile-a-Minute-devoured brick wall announced that he was entering "Judge Lewis Quadrangle." Beneath it someone had scrawled "The Judge is Out." He wandered in beside the wall.

There must have been hundreds of people milling about in the cramped lanes that separated the hovels. A cheesy background odor of unchecked bacteria, of bad meat, assailed him each time he squeezed past one of them. Others, squatting on the ground in their boxes, watched him silently with unreadable, feral eyes.

He discovered an opening in the brick wall to his right. Through it he could see a line of lamps, and he made his way toward them.

The lamps were short antique streetlights on black poles. They glowed wanly, hardly more spectacular than his LifeMask. Their light held a certain magic he could not explain—perhaps it was just that they worked. Moths fluttered obsessively around them. The steady rain glistened like gems, falling past. He took in the concourse around the lamps and noticed that some of the people were naked. They stood shamelessly on the bricks, their arms reaching for the sky as if in supplication; a few, armed with soap, lathered themselves furiously and then passed the soap to other eager hands. Others, possibly more timid, rubbed the soap over their clothes. They all gave him defiant once-overs when they caught him staring.

Behind them lay broad steps up to higher ground. At the top, enormous flagpoles pointed into the sky, flying ragged banners he could barely make out. He started up the steps.

As he climbed, farther back to either side of the steps, two tall cloisters came into view. The greasy smells, combined with pockets of flickering light within the cloisters, suggested cooking fires shielded from the rain. More rain worshipers stood scattered along the steps as if in a shared trance. He had to navigate around them; they did not notice him. When he reached the last step, he stopped still, transfixed by the view.

Ahead of him, the quadrangle descended in five tiers to a center channel, wide open at the far end. There it dropped even farther to street level, where there was a large, disused fountain, and trees made shapeless by ravenous vines. And a second sea of box dwellings. He thought there must have been ten thousand. He had stumbled into the heart of Box City.

Like the tents of an army awaiting dawn's early light, row upon row, their irregular lines ran all the way to Independence Hall. That edifice stood like an elaborate battlement or a simple church, its steeple ablaze in reflected sodium light.

People shoved past Angel, nudging him this way and that. They crossed the plaza and went down the steps. He drifted forward, and took the marble steps slowly. In the channel at the bottom, the crowd thickened but he was not watching them. The steeple had hold of him.

With his gaze fixed, he didn't see a small woman in his path; she wore a miniumbrella fastened to her head and, as she tried to climb the step beside him, the umbrella's sharp ferrule poked his wound. He cried out and doubled up, clutching the arm. The woman tilted back her canopy headgear and said, "Sorry, Mac, didn't see ya up there," and started on. He reached out and stopped her.

When she turned again, he asked, "Can you help me?"

She sized him up from the shadows of her rain hat before replying cryptically, "Who's to say." She tilted her head back and stared some more, as if doubting he was real. She had a bristle of curly gray hair on her chin. He noticed that she was wearing red plastic gloves on both hands.

"I need a place," he said, "to . . . to hide." It slipped out as if from his grasp. "A place down there. Who do I ask about it? Do *you* know of any such place?"

"Somebody has to want to move or else has to have moved and nobody else is waiting ahead of you. There's mostly a list, when you don't know anybody. But nearly everybody can be bribed." She reached out to rub his shirt between her fingers. "I could help you, I expect, for a finder's fee. I know a box, got a blanket and only one owner lately. No lice. Well, not many. Plastic's got a couple rips in the side but the water don't get in bad. Unless it rains a lot like now, and then you take your bath with the rest of them." She gestured back the way he had come, and chortled, revealing inflamed gums and no back teeth. "You don't care about the view, do you? No Taj Mahal 'round here anyway. Although you can make out one of the blue towers of Franklin Bridge if you need something to stare at. Vine Street docks is noisy all the time, but you get used to that real quick. Especially as you usually can't hear it over the assholes squawking on all sides a ya."

"Sure," he agreed, understanding little of her prattle.

She stepped closer, clutching his wrist. "Confidentially, I'd drop the disguise if I was you, unless you're into frightening your neighbors to make 'em shut up. Them glowheads look like Orbiters' ghosts. Liable to get you sliced for scaring somebody shitless. You twig me?"

"Take off the mask?"

"That." She nodded.

One-handed, he undid the hasp and drew it off.

Her jaw hung open. "Hey," she marveled, "you got disguises under your disguises." She touched his jaw, turning it to display the readout panel on the side. "I know someone has one of those on his head, saying all the time he got 'crabs.' " She guffawed. "Says it makes him walk sideways."

"*Crab*, that's right, it's short for—"

"He got a speech problem that it mostly corrects. Does a lot better job on you. Now you come on, I'll show you my box." She grinned lewdly, as though she had made a rude joke.

With difficulty she walked back up the steps. Both hips seemed to bother her.

They returned to the street where he had entered, then across it to the raised park. The narrow lanes allowed little maneuvering room. Angel held his hand over his wounded shoulder to keep it from being bumped into.

Most of the boxes had curtained fronts of one kind or another, but many stood open, the people squatting in the entrance, or standing like prairie dogs in the dark doorways of their burrows. He saw no fires in them but a scattered flickering of TV screens.

Someone called out, "He here for the Bell, Lucy? He come awful late," and his guide hollered back, "Could be."

"You gon' need a can opener to git anything outta him," warned another. A lot of laughter followed that.

He watched the lights atop the Vine Street wall grow larger. The sounds from behind it ran across the ground and up his legs. Like the rumble of an earthquake. All at once the woman said, "Here ya go. As advertised." She held back the curtain from a small box. The curtain, looped onto a dowel, had rows of leering President Odie faces on it.

Angel knelt and looked inside. He could just about sit up, and it was long enough for him to stretch out. Not wide, but the smallness, despite his earlier claustrophobia, appealed. It was an excellent place to hide. The aforementioned blanket was more like a large towel.

" 'bout the size of a Jappo hotel berth," she noted, as if this somehow increased its value.

"How much?" he asked.

"Depends. What you got worth pursuing?"

He dug into a jacket pocket, pulling out everything there. He had two program cubes from ICS-IV, and Gansevoort's green biocard. He couldn't recall how he had acquired it. It must have been in the jacket.

The woman swiped the card from his hand. "Oooh, you's a regular jackpot." She thumbed the edge, enjoying the snap. "Pristine, too. Think I'll be sailing now. You enjoy your stay here."

"For how long?"

"Honey, you *own* it, you stay as long as you like. Just don't try lighting any fires in there or they'll drop ya in hell. Otherwise, you'll be left alone, I expect. If anybody comes looking, you tell 'em Lucy moved *up*." She squinted at the card. "Way up," she added, tucked the card out of sight and limped away.

Angel watched her go. Disembodied voices out of the boxes again called to her, and she joked with them in passing.

Other observers got up and tried to hit on her as she passed, but she shook them off. Across the lane from him the curtains were drawn, either no one home or not welcoming interruption. That was all right by him.

Crouching, he tossed in the mask, then crawled painfully into the confines beside it and pulled the shower curtain closed.

The air in the box hung still and muggy upon him. The rain had imbued him with its chemical odor, vaguely sulfurous, and this mixed with the unwholesomeness of the box itself. He didn't care: the place offered him invisibility, nonexistence.

Hunched forward, he stared at the moist floor between his legs, unable to order his thoughts, to make sense of anything. Memories spilled through the gaps in his synapses.

He grabbed the mask and clipped the collar together. It lit up, its beatific features collapsed and distorted, but at least the mesh was drying out. He stood it in the corner, where it focused on nothing, a manikin head that had just popped up out of the ground.

He shrugged out of his soggy coat and stripped off the pink shirt, placing them beside the mask. Taking the small blanket, he rolled it up into a makeshift pillow. Then he lay on his back against the cool plastic foam floor. Sweat gleamed on his torso. He sighed deeply.

The muscles of his belly were stretched tight as a drumhead. In the mask light, the skin of his upper arm looked swollen and dark. He tried to close his eyes for sleep but found that all he could see was Chikako Peat: the way her lavender eyes laughed at him, the way her body leapt as each shot kicked her.

He opened his eyes and stared into the blackness of the ceiling.

"She died because of me," he said aloud. The words were dull in the box. He turned toward the forgiving maskface.

Where were the emotions Chikako had drawn from him? It felt like days but it had been only hours earlier. He remembered pleasure breaking loose inside him. It had no form, the pleasure—he couldn't hold onto it any more than he could find grief within himself. The invasive *virtual* presence had dusted him with emotion and personality, but he'd used them up in his passion play. The bypass allowed no second sampling. He had to get the damned thing off if he ever hoped to vent all that unexplored, untapped emotion. If it was even there.

For the moment all he had inside himself was ice.

Mingo stood between two security officers wearing name tags that identified them respectively as Gus and Eddie. They perched on swivel seats, hunkered at separate consoles, and traded unhappy glances like two schoolboys under the baleful glare of a nasty, crabby pedagogue. They knew of Mingo by reputation only, but that was sufficient to ruin the rest of their shift.

He had made simple, if drastic, demands, and the two security officers were doing all they could to accommodate him. He wasn't being any too helpful. In the first place he insisted they set aside their regular duties and instead devote themselves to tracking a single individual for him, this at a time of night when their normal work load fell off and all they wanted to do was stretch out, remove their boots and relax, smoke a little *kif*. When they asked him why they were to do this, he responded, "It's important."

He offered a rough description of the perpetrator he was hunting and they set to work, loading the characteristics he gave them into the system and hoping it would find a match immediately. The sooner they got rid of Mr. Mingo, the better. Disks whirred.

"What about *this* face, is this maybe him?" Gus asked time after time, and every time to no avail.

Hung strategically between and before the two men, a large screen displayed each face the system selected.

They looked at a close-up of a brown-skinned face. It was oblong, bald on top, with gray puffs of hair over each ear. Thought Gus, it certainly matched his description.

"No," Mingo said with undisguised impatience, "he's not *really* black. You're not listening. It's a *mask*."

"Gray, you said gray, ya see," Gus tried to explain, "and it's factored that in." He wished he knew the words for what the damn thing did, how it stored and accessed imagery. He wished he could have put Eddie in the hot seat instead of him, but Big Ed had the IQ of a belt buckle. Definitely not the person to appease someone with Mingo's clout, not if the two of them wanted to keep their jobs.

"Gray is *relative*, a mere impression due to the LifeMask he's wearing."

"Well, then, what's he really look like?" asked Eddie. Gus fearfully shook his head and interjected, "We can't factor gray as an *impression*, sir."

"What about LifeMasks in general? Let's narrow it to those if your machines can make that distinction." He walked over and glanced out the one-way glass, down a two-story drop to an enclosed patio where hundreds of bodies milled about. As if everything were fine, as if nobody in the room were under the slightest pressure. That calmness scared Gus more than anything.

"Ahm, sure, we can do that, I think," he'd answered, "but there must be, I dunno—what you think, Eddie?" praying, *Please, Ed, don't fuck up*.

"Hunerts," responded his partner.

"Yeah, must be hundreds of them."

"How about," Mingo said without turning from the window,

"you factor in flight as well? A LifeMask fleeing. Running."

"Well, *there* you go." Gus typed.

Eddie meanwhile mumbled into a throat mike, communicating quietly with other security people who were trying to check in, telling them to call the shots on their own for the time being. Gus heard their heated responses, and cringed, assuming that Mingo heard them, too.

The screen offered face after face, spinning snapshots from the master disk, comparing each to the new parameters established, portraits whipping past in an ever-shifting mosaic. It suddenly delivered up a profile shot of a face leaning forward, the angle suggestive of a body running. It was a very dark black face, yet slightly luminous. Gus had his fingers crossed. Behind him, Mingo said triumphantly, "That's him. Excellent work. Let's track him."

"Sneg it," crowed Eddie, clapping his hands. He wore leather gloves without fingers.

Mingo said, "Does he ever speak comprehensibly?"

"Hey, that's good—speak comprehensibly," Gus replied with feigned appreciation. He launched the tracking program, then sat and watched the screen. His stomach felt as if it were being eaten away.

The program picked up the quarry a short distance from Grofé's, followed him down various levels, caught him on an escalator, a ramp, and outdistancing a cyclecab. Mingo was leaning on the back of Gus's chair. His fingers squeezed at the vinyl, producing a creaky sound that raised goose bumps on Gus.

The final image was of the individual in the mask leaving from the Penn Tower Three exit.

"He's got out, into the Undercity. That's that."

"What do you mean, 'that's that'? Switch to external."

"You want to follow him *outside*, too?"

"I want to follow him if he goes to *Neptune*."

So they had switched monitoring systems. The exterior of Penn Three came up on the screen. The time codes raced to match up.

Soon enough, they were watching Angel Rueda cross an open plaza and head toward City Hall. Another lens system, on the far side, another time code matchup, and there was a shot of him passing the Market Street checkpoint with all of its food kiosks. Far along the side street they could see a brightly painted Chinese arch. They watched their prey wander toward it until the rain washed his image into the shadows.

"That's the last of it."

Mingo sighed. "Look, I happen to know there's a whole system of monitors strung throughout the Undercity. Don't try to get out of this. I can have your asses dropped off the globe if I want to. Now access that system."

The color drained from Gus's face as he considered how to express what he had to say next and still live. "I'll connect up if you want, but I got to tell you, Mr. Mingo, that system's been all but a total bust for years. We put in our microcams, they find 'em and rip them out and sell 'em or barter 'em. We got a few teahouses covered still, maybe two, three blocks of the 'Namese quarter around Box City. The rest they located and removed. They took a whole fistful of microcams from along the Delaware and ringed the underside of a toilet seat with 'em without destroying the transmitters. We still don't know where the goddam toilet is, but I can show you it's still in use if you're interested. They make a big deal of it, probably charging admission to shit on the Overcity. You get what I mean, sir? And it's the same, lots of places outside the walls, too, especially west of town, what with everything bein' burned out. Some places ya need an armed escort, which is the same as painting a sign on it. Not worth the trouble to replace the things."

"I see. Seems I'll have to squeeze a few people. I'd no idea Undercity security had gone to the dogs. Thank you for explaining, Gus." He dropped down on the couch, all the steam taken out of him. His leg was absolutely throbbing. He needed to take another painblocker. "What do I do now?" he asked.

Gus replied, "Now you hope he needs to get laid or smoke some 'O' in the right teahouse."

"Or else," noted Mingo, "makes use of the only optically equipped toilet seat in the city."

"You got it, sir."

"Tremendous."

19

Box City

Asleep in the box, he lightly kissed memory's lips. It was his first dream.

Figures in gray hoods and business suits pursued him through a dark, airless landscape that manifested slowly, creeping into view, until it became a distorted image of Philadelphia, its towers like candle wax, burning down; beside the trash-surfaced roadway, he ran past a headless torso that had limbs formed of metal coils and which droned "Yawp, yawp, yawp," through a plastic larynx atop its stubby neck. The sight of it dogged him until he was running blindly to escape. He dashed into a gloomy enclosure and stopped only when he banged his shins against a projecting pipe—only, it wasn't a pipe at all, it was a large cylinder with lines and glyphs etched into it. It had a dirty glass portal in it just below him through which he saw Chikako Peat, stretched out naked inside. He wiped at the grime on the glass and, as it cleared, the face underneath became Thomasina Lyell's. For some reason the metamorphosis didn't surprise him. The cylinder retreated from him suddenly, and he discovered that it was attached to a mechanism in the shadows. It moved like a shell sliding into the chamber of a cannon, loading as he looked on, ejecting an instant later, pistonlike, empty. The body—whose?—had been launched through a network of colorful tubes, none of which had existed a moment before. He followed them to a crack in the wall and peered out. The tubes snaked across the ground, finally gathered together, and connected to the yawping torso outside. Even when he couldn't see it, the voice of the thing continued to bark with clockwork regularity. He knew, if he stayed there long enough, a head would sprout on the body. Already it had begun to develop breasts, take on sexual characteristics, the identity of which he knew because he could see the emerging hexagram on its thigh. As if aware of his attention, the thing rose up on one foot, balanced deftly, hands poised, an idol, an icon, a more-than-human terminal. Its cranium slowly bulged into place, the tubes and cables loose and writhing in a hypnotic dance, a celebration; he swung away in horror, not wanting to see but more specifically not wishing to *be* seen by her, and startled himself, realizing he had no idea what *he* looked like, what sex *he* was . . . while the arms of metal coils glided in through the cracked wall and spun around and around him, mummifying, sealing out light and air, gathering about him in a whirlpool of nullity, the same seething cyclone the *virtual* program had become. Its magnetism seized and dragged him into the hungry vortex.

He awoke, glued by his sweat to the plastic foam. His curtain hung closed; the air encased him wetly. It was still dark outside. He sat up, blinking back tears. His head brushed the ceiling. He wiped at his cheek, wondering vaguely why he could react to events only in his sleep.

His arm, still warm, had lost some of its ache; the swelling seemed to have gone down; he couldn't be sure. He was so hot and grimy in that oven of a box, he couldn't tell if he had a fever or not.

Drawing back the Odie curtain, he scooched up till he could peer down the lane.

From the left, an unsavory breeze flowed along; it enveloped him, cooled him where he sat. He could see others seated in their boxes. They might have been duplicates of him. He thought, *This is what we all are underneath.*

What that meant, where the singular observation came from, he didn't know.

After awhile, he shook out his shirt and put it on. He got to his feet stiffly, but had to hold his jacket in his teeth while he clumsily tucked the shirt into his pants. Lifting the coat, he could only stare at it, unable to identify it as his own. It wasn't, of course, it was Gansevoort's.

In the dream, he had been wearing something blue. . . .

Already the specifics of the nightmare blurred. Angel had no long-term memory in which to house dreams. They fell like coins through a torn pocket.

He folded the humid jacket over his bad arm and then, turning slowly in a circle, surveyed the encampment.

The rain had stopped, but few heads showed above the boxes. Bright lights still glared on top of the Vine Street wall. Machinery still shook the ground: the unloading of supplies for the city continued around the clock.

He drew a deep breath, then began to cough. Sparkles danced before his eyes for a second; he tested his lungs more carefully.

Over the quadrangle, streamers of smoke rose languidly into the sky. What did they use for fuel? Old clothes? Worn-out boxes? The umbrella-woman had warned about lighting fires; but weren't packing crates like these supposed to be fireproof? He thought he might once have known the answer to that question.

He was feeling hungry again. It would be good to eat something.

He dug around in the jacket for items to trade for food, and found the two cubes and a gold cigarette case. The case had been Chikako's. He remembered. He turned it over, opened it. It was empty. Holding it close, he sniffed its herbal odor, and triggered an explosive memory of her. Her face, eyes, lips lit up the sky. He had to lean against the top of the box—his legs couldn't hold him. He squeezed his eyes shut to blot out the vision, and closed the case, fumblingly tucking it away before it could do more harm. Before it could batter him with his own emotions again.

"Lookit that," cried a raw, jocose voice from below. "Finally. Finally, it's Machine Man!" Angel opened his eyes to find a greasy, unwashed, round, and unshaven face sticking out of the box across the lane from his. "I *knew*," said the man, waggling a finger, "yes, I did." He crawled out, chugging. He was barefoot, with his pant legs rolled up almost to his knees. He smelled like a used condom.

Shorter than Angel, covered with wiry hair and thick as a tree trunk, he flailed with his arms while he spoke. Each time he did, the smell of him grew worse. "I told them. They's got plans to turn us *all* into machines, is what I said. Machines what never wear out. It's the only way to get us to Mars, see. The only way. People die, see, if they get too far from the Earth. Ya take those folks on the Moon, they're all dead and buried, but you'll never get wind of it, they been converted."

"Dead and buried . . . on the Moon," said Angel. That sounded strangely familiar.

"Sure! Nobody up there no more. I said they have to make us into *machines*." He grinned like a proud father, arms extended. "And here you are—the next generation. Come to see me, your predicator." His eyebrows went up and his lids fell halfway. "No concept can exist till it's put into words, that is the natural law. Didn't Moses have to have God's commandments writ upon a stone? I don't expect an answer. But tell me when you're leaving."

"Leaving?"

"For *Mars*. That's next in line. Venus would crush you."

"I don't know."

The man nodded as if he had anticipated such a response. "Sure, keep it quiet, the best policy. And I could be anybody, so you can't be too careful trusting me, although even folks from the towers do. I'm Bucca." He stuck out his grubby hand. "Mad Bucca. It's a title of distinction hereabouts. Only five of us in the whole camp called 'Mad.' Be one less after this, won't there? One look at you and they'll know. You're the proof I've promised 'em. Yup. Come on now and I'll take you 'round. Ya ever seen the Bell? Ya ought to once, before you leave. Can't do it afterward. I'll show ya." He put on a brown tweed coat and a pair of boots that had no laces, then went stomping down the narrow lane. Heads withdrew at his careless approach.

Angel followed at a respectful distance. Onlookers watched Bucca and then turned their attention to him, their expressions clouding, becoming troubled and shifty. He passed them by, ducking his head as if in humility. "See?" his guide was shouting to them in general.

Mad Bucca took him back the way he had come, through the rows, up the steps to the top of the quadrangle, where fires still burned inside the archways to either side. Bucca pointed. "Ya see that funny looking thing on the far side of the fountain, looks like a food kiosk what wandered off? That's it, that's the Bell."

They climbed down the marble steps to a pebbled flagstone flooring, then down past the dry fountain. It looked like a giant's cast-off crown. They waded into the street. The ground turned to flat black slate, then to brick around the building.

The front of the enclosure consisted of rows of mismatched drapery, birds and flowers and stripes all thrown together.

At their approach, a man pulled aside one of the curtains and peered out.

"Coming in, you think, huh? With that computer on your skull? I don't know but that you're a spy for some fascistic Communist power. Got any admission price?"

Angel unhesitatingly handed over one of the program cubes.

The man played a small flashlight over it. The cube shone nacreous colors. He sucked air through a missing front tooth. "This'll get you a couple three visits. Bring the whole family."

"There's only me."

"Well, then"—he nodded toward Mad Bucca—"I'll let you take the monkey with you." Stepping aside, he offered the flashlight. "You gonna want it at this hour."

The interior smelled strongly of urine. The walls on both sides had the remains of artwork on them, enlarged images of handwritten documents, forged in a giant's scrawl. At the opposite end of the small enclosure hung the bell itself, from two curved silver supports. He touched it, and it was cold. He rapped his knuckles against it but it made hardly a sound. Ponderous, dark, it connected to nothing, an object of veneration without a history. For Angel, it might as well have been a soup can.

"Does it ring the hours?"

"Naw, just hangs there from its timber. Got a big ol' crack in it." Bucca scrunched up his face and contemplated it a moment. "Useta make a noise, I think. Hung over across in that tower there."

"When?" He pressed up against the Plexiglas rear wall, staring through the camp at the white steeple.

"Way back. Before ScumberCorp and everything. Even before the city had walls—leastways, visible walls like we got now." A few small fires burned along raised strips on each side of the horde of boxes.

Behind him, Bucca recited, " 'Proclaim Liberty throughout the Land unto all the inhabitants Thereof.' It's written here. You had the right idea—I mean, tapping. Someone ought to ring this bell, don't ya think, Machine Man?" He peered beneath the rim. "I'll be. Bastards've stole the clapper." His words echoed dully up inside it.

Angel glanced back at Bucca and the bell that appeared to be devouring him. He asked, "Can we get food out there someplace?"

"Ya still eat, you mean," said Bucca, straightening up. "Got any more of them memory cubes to barter with, we'll be able to nab credit for a week or more, get plenty of food. Them things are golden." He patted Angel, taking hold of him and turning him around; as he did, he let his hand slide lightly across the gray jacket and dip into the right pocket. "There," he said, "let's go now."

They went back the way they had come, Bucca's boots clomping on the bricks. People stuck their heads out like turtles and stared after Angel until the dimness swallowed him up.

Not long after, a tall figure dressed in layers of cloth swept through the same lane, to the rear of the Liberty Bell enclosure, stopping next to a box there. Drawing back the curtain and peering inside, the figure let fly with a hot, blistering, foreign babble, then jerked back, swung around to the box opposite, and started hammering angrily on the top of it, while shouting, "Celine! Get out here!"

The blankets draped over the front parted. A redheaded woman stuck her head out and glared. Her initial fury drained quickly away.

"Lobly!" she said, mixing worry and feigned joy in the name. Her eyes flicked toward the box opposite. She went on, "Oh, I like the blue turban—it is blue, ain't it? It suits, it really does. Why don't you come on in with me and I'll warm your skinny bones?"

"Thank you, no, Celine. I want to know what is that smelly little tick doing in my home?" An accusing finger jabbed from under the ragged bedouin *djellaba* back at the opposite box; silver bracelets rattled. A skinny form lay prostrate on the floor there, the soles of two bare feet like clumps of dirt in the doorway.

"He, ah—that is—"

"You rented out my space, Celine."

She jutted her chin. "You wasn't using it, been gone forever."

"*Two* days."

"Woman's got to make a living," she tried.

"He'll have fleas. You will now offer me half of what you've skinned him for or I'll have you both tried and tossed into the Snake Pit."

Celine stopped arguing. Both she and her accuser knew that she would lose everything if a quick tribunal were assembled. Violating another's space was the lowest of all crimes, with the possible exception of arson.

"Half of it."

Celine let the yellow blankets drop. Sounds emerged of things bumping about. Her feet, then her naked white rear, pushed out, parting the blankets, offering Lobly an unsavory gynecological perspective. She turned around, half-hidden behind the blanket again, and held up a stack of old postcards, but hesitated to hand them over. "Or maybe you and I can work out an arrangement?" she suggested.

Lobly wearily insisted, "Half."

Celine slapped the cards into the outstretched hand and retreated behind the blanket. "You just do it with little boys and everybody knows it," she called out. "Why don't you go get us something to eat, then, while I toss him out. It'll take a few minutes because he's stupid drunk."

Without looking at them, Lobly tucked the cards away under the *djellaba* and turned for the cooking fires on the quadrangle. That was the place to begin, anyway. If Angel Rueda were hereabouts, news of it would circulate by way of the campfire.

Mingo sat on a couch behind the two security officers. Low blue overhead lights made every surface gleam like gunmetal. Gus had turned them down, hoping that Mingo would take the hint and stretch out, go to sleep, quit watching. In the night-dark, rain-spattered window, his reflection stared fixedly like a scowling corpse. The rip down his cheek was black as seaweed.

His reflection had impaled the two men for hours, relentlessly; if he slept at all, it had to be in nanosecond bursts. His eyes seemed never to close, his body never to move. He sat behind them like some ominous kind of toad.

Eddie and Gus had both gotten up a couple of times to answer the call of nature, and both gave the couch a wide berth, doing their best not to make eye contact with its inhabitant. Each would have liked to catch a few winks, to turn things over to his partner for half an hour the way they did most nights, but such respite was out of the question with the stiff sitting there. Apparently Mingo didn't pee, either.

He was like a hot chunk of satellite that had dropped in through the ceiling—you couldn't move him but you didn't really want to get too damn close in the first place for fear he would cook you.

Seated before the console, Gus clicked the throat mike and breathily answered a request for lens surveillance at the Vine Street docks. He hunched his shoulders a couple of times and swiveled his head. His neck popped, but the knot of tense pain between his shoulder blades would not go away. The source of that knot stared flatly at him in the window.

Most nights he and Eddie had a pretty good time. Tonight they were executing their duties, responding to security requests, like two twitchy, voice-activated mechanisms.

It was getting near dawn. At least, once the sun came up, that bilious blue-faced reflection would fade out.

Then Eddie broke the silence, guffawing about something—a sound so out of place, Gus had to look. All at once he stopped chuckling, holding up his hand. "Wait it," he said. His face squeezed as if in pain, then relaxed. "Great one." He punched a button and swiveled around. "You got somefin—colleague you mentioned, name a Gansevoort. Got his card heisted."

"Yes. The idiot," Mingo replied dully. The continuing misadventures of Ton Gansevoort did not concern him. "What does *he* want?"

"Unh-uh. Turned up the biocard right now at a Happy Burger, Chestnut and Tenth exit, street side. Paid for a Big Box meal."

A tiny smile quivered upon Mingo's blue lips. His tired eyes transformed, narrowing into chrome and cunning. "Tell them . . . someone's coming," he said.

"Sneg 'im," said Eddie, grinning.

"I will. Make no mistake." He rose up, stretching, then strode out.

The door closed. Gus and his partner exchanged exhausted looks. "I love ya, Eddie, I wanna have your children," Gus announced.

"Ah, geez," Big Ed replied, and flushed brightly.

* * *

The escalator dumped him at the exit. A small crowd milled around just outside the doors, a mix of those who lived outside the walls being assailed by those less fortunate ones who lived at ground level inside. Mingo ignored the lot of them.

He flashed his security pass as he circumvented the checkpoint, got a nod from one of the security people, and skirted the crowd. He ran into two people conducting a drug sale. They glanced up nervously at his disdainful glare, but he passed them by, marching rapidly into the Happy Burger stand across the narrow plaza.

The shift manager had been watching for someone from security. When Mingo pushed through the revolving door, the manager gestured with his shaved head. "Her," he said.

A high shelf at the far end allowed for eating while standing up. A grimy gnome of a woman stood there, munching on a biscuit, idly scrutinizing her surroundings, and forming silent words as if talking to an invisible companion.

"Her?" Mingo asked.

"That's the one. Straight outen the boxes. Lucy McElveen, and she says the card's her brother's. I wouldn't have noticed even, except . . ." The manager stopped talking when Mingo walked away.

He strolled up beside the gnome. Casually, he leaned on the shelf beside her. "When did you have your last Orbit, Lucy?" he asked.

Lucy hunched protectively over her food. Between her red rubber fingers she held the stringy remains of a crisp spring roll. She watched Mingo with rabbit eyes. She'd stopped chewing when he spoke, but now, as if cued, started up furiously again. Surreptitiously, with her free hand, she dragged a biscuit into one pocket. "Been a while."

"Week, maybe? The scars are pretty fresh." His teeth gleamed.

" 'bout that, I guess," she answered. "I don't check off the days."

"It's a nice world 'there,' isn't it?"

She brightened, and reconsidered her initial opinion of him. "You seed it?" she asked.

"You must miss being there terribly."

"Yeah." She popped the rest of the spring roll into her mouth and spoke around it. "Right now, supplies is dry. I hear they got this big hunt on fer some bogeymen down below, and till they's found, it's like the taps got turned off."

Mingo, having personally turned off the tap, could not help but laugh that this grotesque, stuffed full of chemical-laced food items, could make the connection between any two events, much less these two disparate ones. His machinations were too subtle for the CEOs, but she understood them. Well, well. "How's the hunt going, do you think?"

Wiping at her mouth, she shrugged. "Made everybody fuckin' damn crazy. No supply, lotsa demand. Pretty soon they'll be turning in whoever's around just to git the pipeline up and running again. Don't wanna be stranded here."

Mingo made a single fist of both his hands and bowed his head as if in prayer. "I have the means to tap a supply for you anytime I like," he told her quietly.

She glanced quizzically his way, then turned her head, looking around at dozens of other eaters. "This is kind of a public place for a blow job," she observed.

Mingo closed his eyes, summoning patience. Of course he could understand her misunderstanding. "Tell you what. Here's the deal I'm offering. You show me where you got the useless biocard you have—oh, yes, your 'brother' got you arrested just now—" he flashed his security card in her face long enough to savor her terrified realization of what he represented "—you do that, and I'll not only let you slide, I'll hook you a trip to where you want to go." He tapped his temple. "Enough even to reach 'decay' in, say, a week or two. How about that?"

Frightened though she was, tears welled in Lucy's eyes. "For me? That much? Really?"

"No one else," he promised. "I don't want you—I'm after someone else."

She sniffed, wiped at one eye. "Git my house back," she muttered. "I'll need it, won't I?"

"Briefly."

She began stuffing her food into her mouth, more rabbitlike than ever. Chewing openly, she said, "He's in my box right now, this guy." From out of her clothes, she produced Gansevoort's green card. Mingo plucked it and pocketed it mechanically, without taking his eyes off her. It felt gloriously good to shake somebody down. He could pretend she was his nemesis, that other woman.

"This guy one of the bogeymen, is he?" Lucy asked.

A smile tugged at his lips. "The king of bogeymen, Lucy, dear."

The first faint light of dawn was showing across the eastern sky as Lobly/Lyell climbed up to the cooking area.

An arcade of thirteen arched enclosures stood to either side, and recessed inside each large enclosure lay a second, smaller one—a cubicle mimicking the larger space, with arches all around. The brick floors inside the cubicles had been removed and pits dug into the earth below. The roofs had been designed with round holes in them, and these proved to be ideal chimneys. What they had been intended for originally, no one could say, but they were perfect for drawing the smoke from the cooking fires of Box City.

The larger, cloistral enclosures protected from the elements the piles of gathered tinder as well as the individual who tended each fire. Tenders made out very well in the hierarchy of the Boxers, especially in the winter: they were rewarded for their efforts with a portion of each Boxer's meal. Over the years, the position had gained guild status and a certain mystique.

Perhaps two hundred people stood or sat around on the three-sided marble steps of the quadrangle and on the recessed benches along the walls at the top. Their conversations lay upon each other, disconnected words and phrases sticking out like frayed ends. Lyell could see the glow of a half dozen TV screens. The quadrangle was wired with old video hookups; at one time city pageants had been put on here.

Nearby, one thin TV screen sat propped on a bench, belching out bits of a broadcast—an animated feature with talking dolphins and sea gulls. People wandered in front of the screen, lingered, staring uncomprehendingly at the grainy, stolen signal.

Crouched behind it, and clearly visible through the tilted glass whenever the picture faded, a skinny man was fiddling with the cable relay he had tapped. The picture sharpened momentarily, and a few halfhearted cheers went up.

In the nearest cubicle, a good fire had been built up. This one had a cooking surface over it—nothing more than a stolen sewer grating fitted tidily inside the small square and resting on four heaps of bricks. The grating allowed the tender easy access both above and below, and that seemed quite practical to Lyell. All manner of pots sat atop it, bubbling, smoking, stinking. A few glowing, misshapen globs indicated where cheap pots had overheated.

Lyell did not expect to find Angel himself among this crowd, only information about him. However, the very first person on the steps whom she asked about him sniggered, nudged her around, and pointed. There, up the steps and not twenty meters away, stood the man she had sought through both halves of the city—*a dead man*. She closed her hand over the pads above her elbow. Finally, Nebergall's shoes had paid off.

He had connected up with a short, hairy individual who was leading him along just outside the arcade, making loud introductions, and flashing what looked like a small gem, snatching it away when anyone made a grab at it. Fire tenders emerged down the line to look it over. They bartered and argued. The squat man shrugged and moved on to hear the next offer. He looked unsettlingly familiar to her, but she couldn't place him. She had stared into too many faces during the past few hours and they were all jumbled together.

She climbed up a few steps but hung back, watching it all, recording a scene acted out in nearly every country of the world every day.

Then she heard Angel's companion shout, "Not gonna be humans no more! Not humans no more! This here's the next generation." He placed his hand on Angel's shoulder, Angel looking dismayed by this abrupt pronouncement.

People began to gather around the two men; they got up off the steps and walked past Lyell. Some of them went up and touched Angel, as if he were a good luck charm. They chattered among themselves, ignoring a dozen other conversations going on simultaneously. She lost sight of him behind the press of bodies.

On the bench, the TV controller had gotten a steady picture on his portable screen. He switched to the Alien News Network and received a round of applause and cheers that drowned out most of the noise surrounding Angel. Distracted by the sound, the worshipful Boxers abandoned him and shuffled toward the screen.

The short man began bellowing, trying to retrieve his audience. "My friends!" he yelled. "We're talking about missions to Mars, colonies in space that never come down!"

The first picture that came up on ANN was an aerial shot of ICS-IV.

A sense of dread rose in Lyell. She started through the crowd toward Angel. Each time she glanced over, she saw another chilling image—mangled bodies being hauled away in bags; wounded students limping along in smoky halls, some of them falling and dying conveniently on camera. She knew what must be coming, and shoved harder to get through the crowd.

The next time she looked, the screen had filled with a face: Angel Rueda's face. *Thank God*, she thought, *the sound isn't working*.

A few members of the crowd beside her turned around, too, comparing the screen image with the man being touted as the "next generation."

Somebody shouted, "Shut up, Bucca," and a dozen angry voices seconded the order.

The noise level dropped, and in that portentous lull a thunderous, distorted sound flooded the area. The audio signal had kicked in.

"—responsible for the deaths. His organization, known to ScumberCorp as *Xau Dâu*, has already taken full responsibility for the riot. The incident represents the first time this organization is known to have acted upon an entity other than the corporation itself. Rueda, its leader, escaped the scene, using this woman, the school's principal, to navigate through the city." A second still, of Chikako Peat, dropped in beside Angel, along with fake securicam footage of him shoving her roughly down a hallway in front of him. "We have a report now that he has since murdered her in cold blood and fled into the lower levels of city. At that time, he was wearing this electronic mask as a disguise." Chikako's face was replaced by the all-too-familiar icon of gentleness. "Called a LifeMask, it's assigned to teachers in the high-risk inner-city schools, such as the one Ms. Peat governed." The mask faded, and the original, half-mechanical face appeared.

"It's *him*." The word spread, more and more people turning around, staring at the color screen, seeing Angel there, comparing the image with the reality. "You hear what they said? He's a terrorist murderer—he's killed *hundreds*. He's killed *kids*." Like a cord, the words were binding them together, into a mass. Into a mob.

Lyell found herself caught in the thick of it.

Mad Bucca cried, "Wait—tell me you aren't buying that. You can't be! That's *TV news*. They only tell you what somebody wants you to hear!"

"Our ANN experts have *absolute* proof that the *Xau Dâu* organization is an alien collective," droned the TV voice. "They're bent on destroying the largest, most beneficial corporation on our planet as the first step toward world domination."

"He's an alien, you hear!" someone shouted. "The one they're looking for. Look at 'im."

Insisted Bucca, "Sure he's an alien—he's *Machine* Man. We built him. But you can't have him, I get to take him in. I get my *reward* for him. I'm the one going to Mars colony, not you bastards. Git away!"

Lyell shoved her way to the front row, and the angry crowd propelled her under the arcade roof. Bucca backed in beside her, slapping at the front row.

Lyell grabbed Angel's wrist. Reflexively, he looked from his hand to her; he didn't recognize her. It showed in his eye. She said, "Come on, Angel, it's time to go."

"Lyell?" he asked in amazement.

"It's 'Lobly' here. I'm lots of people today, just like you."

"Hey, he's mine," Bucca yelled. He abandoned his defensive position in the archway and shambled angrily into her path. "*I* seen Machine Man first. The reward belongs to *me*."

Ungoverned, the crowd, at the brink of coming together or dissolving, pressed in under the arch.

The fire tender, who'd been too busy working to listen to ANN's nonsense, stepped in their way, brandishing her cooking tongs, and shouted, "Here, what the hell you think you're doing? Back off!" The mob stopped. She snapped the nasty tongs at them. "You have to *pay* to come under here— get that? Go tear down something else or I'll put a torch to you."

"Let me have him, just for an hour," Lyell urged Bucca.

"Here," and passed him the postcards she had acquired. "I'll *rent* him from you."

"All you, too," the tender snarled to the three of them. "You have to pay." Angel handed her the remaining cube. "Well, *okay*. You bring food in or you want to buy?"

"Buy," Angel said. He knew without doubt that he didn't have any food.

Bucca, his lower lip jutting out, squinted at the top postcard, a sepiatone showing City Hall in its heyday, and then riffled the stack. His face expressed contortions of calculation. He said, "Ah, well, for an hour I guess it won't hurt. But I stay with youse, make sure you don't try to weasel nothing."

She tugged at Angel, who observed drily, "I'm not worth much, am I?"

"Right at the moment, no. The reward he wants comes from Mingo." Bucca started at the sound of that name.

Angel said, "Mingo again."

"Wait, you," someone at the forefront of the crowd yelled. "It's that same bastard, I'm tellin' you. Lookit the screen. The *alien*." But they didn't dare enter the arcade, and they couldn't get the rear rows to cooperate and spread apart to offer the tender a view of the screen.

A grubby hand grabbed at Lyell's shoulder but she twisted free and moved deeper under the roof. The tender was kneeling, tossing legs of furniture on the fire. The fire had little colors in it, no doubt from the chemicals burning.

Lyell said, "Stay with me, both of you."

"What about our food?" whined Bucca.

She still had hold of Angel's hand, and she pulled him away. Bucca reluctantly followed, yelling to the tender, "We'll be right back."

Lyell hurried along, dodging other patrons, ignoring the complaints of other busy tenders. Outside, the crowd moved in pursuit, though not nearly as fast. They netted everyone who stood in their path, their numbers surging and churning. Bucca waved and bellowed fiercely at them to stay back.

Lyell ducked beneath the last arch and ran for the north steps. They had beaten the crowd. She figured they had it made. They dodged between the flagpoles, and made it halfway down the steps before she saw the solitary figure in the narrow lane below.

Even in the crepuscular gloom she knew his shape, his leanness, the smooth way he moved. She'd been expecting him ever since Grofé's but not here, not in the midst of this new nightmare. She was surprised that he would let her see him like this, then reminded herself that he wasn't seeing her, but Lobly.

She stopped, and Angel bumped against her. She gripped his hand hard. He followed her stare.

Mingo's features emerged out of the smoky dimness—blond hair, eyes pale as milk, a mouth set firmly but indicating nothing of the frustration that must be seething within; there was dried blood on his face, which made him look barbaric, like some Teutonic god come for a final reckoning. His black scarf fluttered like a banner. He drew up at the end of the lane, upon the edge of the bricks. *Here*, she thought, *is the* real *Machine Man*.

Four steps above, the denizens of the Undercity towered like the cracking wall of a dam about to burst. The word "alien" stained their speech like a racial slur. Bucca stood in their forefront.

Ahead and below, the pale Grim Reaper of ScumberCorp triumphantly contemplated the execution in progress.

Lyell and Angel hovered midway between heaven and hell.

Then suddenly Angel tore loose from her grip. She turned in time to see him bound up the steps and charge the crowd.

Screaming in fearful hatred, they shoved back away from him. Then, with cries of, "Alien! Get him!" they enclosed him in their roiling mass.

20
Reigning Chaos

All hell broke loose in an instant.

Mingo saw his prey devoured by the mob, and he sprang up the steps.

As he passed by the blue-turbaned figure who'd been with Rueda, the fellow threw a sudden, skillful punch that caught Mingo in the ear. Teeth grinding, he staggered to the side but managed not to fall off the steps.

He charged his tall assailant, grabbed fistfuls of loose, striped robes, and hurled.

Lobly/Lyell tripped up the steps and caught herself against a narrow opening in the wall near the top; then, with a quick turn, shot up the steps and tried to escape into the melee.

Mingo leaped forward and managed to snare the robe's ragged tail. He yanked her back and himself up the final step. One driving punch snapped the dark, mustachioed head around like a top. A follow-up to the midsection doubled the body over, and a third uppercut lifted Aswad Lobly off the ground and straight back through the opening in the wall. The turban unwound, ejecting a bright blue fillet, which lingered momentarily in the air after Lobly dropped from view. The mustache, like a black butterfly, twirled in undetected spirals to the ground. Mingo faced about.

He bounded the distance to the edge of the mob and began hammering at the nearest exposed necks, prying aside stunned figures, flinging them from his path, down the steps. They bowled others over, starting a second ruckus at the bottom. "Not again, damn you, Rueda," he cursed. "This time I have you." Rhythmically, he assaulted each impediment, a fist thrust on each beat.

Somewhere nearby, someone tuned in a music broadcast,

and an electronic orchestra erupted with a crazy Latino beat.

He punched a large, incommodious shape, but when he pulled the man around, a hand the size of a packing crate responded, slamming into his temple twice—ba-boom!—in quick succession. He stumbled across the bricks, barely avoided plunging off the top step, and caught his balance against a rickety table where a scabious little man was selling purloined canned goods. Under his weight the table crashed, and the tinned wares bounced and rolled into the crowd. The owner shrieked, pouncing upon Mingo, spitting in his face, digging at him with filthy nails. Mingo dazedly weathered the assault for a moment. His head rang with whistles and bells. Then the man inadvertently clawed into the deep cut in his cheek, and the pain jolted him like current from a whirring dynamo.

Mingo grabbed the man's hair, hooked fingers under the stubbly jaw, twisted quickly and snapped his neck. A can of tuna spilled from the folds of the Boxer's clothing, rolling across the bricks and down the steps. In the general unfolding chaos of bodies and debris, no one noticed the heap of another victim against the wall, where Mingo tossed him aside.

Mingo put all of his weight on his wounded leg in order to kick the table out of his way, and a hot bolt of agony shot through his thigh. He nearly fell but steadied himself before the leg collapsed.

Unable to manipulate the raging mob before him, he dragged himself up on a stone bench for a better view over them. He searched for the gleaming lines of the *crab*, but he couldn't see it anywhere in their midst. They must have pummeled Rueda to the ground, smashed him underfoot. He could hope.

The turmoil seemed to be spreading like a contagion beyond the flagpoles. Mingo eased down off the bench and limped toward the center of conflict. He drew his gun, checking the grip, where a tiny panel displayed the number of rounds it held. The clip was full—he had filled it while trapped for hours in "security." Nevertheless, it paid to be careful, to double-check. There weren't going to be any more mistakes.

He next calculated the size of the crowd. It was conceivable that he might have to spray them all in order to confirm Rueda's death. Whatever it took. That he might not kill Rueda was unthinkable, unacceptable even as a remote possibility. Suicide was preferable. He *had* to see this pursuit through to the end. The grinding pain in his thigh would keep him alert to his purpose.

Once again he tried to thread himself into the midst of the melee. The steroidal gorilla who had cuffed him had wandered off. Nevertheless, the outer ranks closed tighter before he reached them, as if resentful of his attempted intrusion. He scowled and contemplated shooting the nearest Boxers. Nothing was more demeaning than being ineffectual.

Before he could make up his mind, a wonderful and miraculous thing occurred—the crowd began to disperse of its own accord.

The tight knot of people unraveled slowly, drawing away from the core. Mingo held the Ingram tight by his side, ready for the instant when he spotted his adversary. Nearer and nearer he edged toward the epicenter. More and more people pulled away, like shrapnel thrown off by an explosion. The fight had gone out of them; they didn't know what to do or where to go next. In fact some of them seemed to be fleeing. Whatever the cause, he brushed past them with no trouble. The frenetic dance tune cut off in midnote.

There was fresh blood on the white marble. The dawn's light flashed in it. His heart hammered. His spirit soared. Surely, they had killed Rueda—that was why they were dispersing. There was no reason to continue, they'd torn him apart. But where was the corpse, where the bits and pieces? The last half dozen of them turned aside, disconcerted, their instincts guiding them away from Mingo as well.

Now he could see straight down to the dried-up fountain, to the Liberty Bell enclosure, all the way to the cupola of Independence Hall glowing pink in the light of dawn.

Impossibly yet incontrovertibly, Angel Rueda had disappeared. Vanished into space.

Some cog broke loose and jammed the perfect mechanism inside Mingo. He stood, feet planted, unable to sort it out. For a brief moment he considered putting the gun to his own throbbing, wounded head and pulling the trigger. *Suicide is preferable*. Eyes wide, struck apoplectic, he gaped at the white marble flooring and willed body parts to manifest themselves before him. He wanted severed limbs, crushed bones, heart and kidneys and spine; but most of all he wanted that damned elusive cybernetic head. Wanted to see it hoisted on a pole like an executioner's trophy.

"*Rueda!*" he bellowed, sustaining the last syllable operatically, a raging Alberich upon the stage, flinging his curse so powerful it could snap tree trunks and split mountains: "*Verflucht sei dieser Ring, Rueda!*"

The whole of Box City stilled and a thousand heads turned to look at the murderous black figure on the top step of the quadrangle, lighted orange in the fires of the dawn.

Angel heard his name and looked up, too.

A ghost had rescued him.

The hydra mob of a hundred limbs that he had plunged into had dragged him down to the marble tiles. He had expected to be killed and he hoped it would be swift.

He'd skidded onto his wounded shoulder and cried out at the fresh pain, pinned his elbows against his head and curled instinctively into a ball. Feet and fists struck at him, but the crush of so many bodies enfeebled their actions. A few short jabs stung him, a snapped kick at his ribs barely scraped his side.

One of the attackers directly over him fell prey to phobia, turned on his fellows, and began scrabbling madly to get out, bleating with foam-flecked lips, the sound drowned in the roar of the crowd. When the Boxer started peeing himself, the clutch quickly disgorged him. Music began to play.

Somebody grabbed onto the bypass unit to wrench it free. Angel thought his neck would pull apart, and he tore the hands loose, then rolled to the side. A knee collided with his face, shooting bright sparks under his eyelids. Blood flowed warmly over his lip. Something struck him on the back, shoving him forward. His head dangled over the top step.

Then a woman's voice close beside his ear said, "Quick, get up." A hand slid beneath his arm and managed to turn him so that he could haul himself up by clinging to various bodies, ignoring the rain of blows as some of them tried to beat him away. Miraculously, the mob had spread out a little, allowing him room to maneuver. He absorbed a few more punches, but most of the people were now trying to shove him aside. They seemed to have become afraid of him.

The woman who had spoken steadied him. Her head passed

easily beneath his armpit. She stared up at him with heavy-lidded eyes beneath thick brows. She had broad round cheeks, black hair. He didn't think he had ever seen her before. She explained, "I know a lot of these bastards, see. They all think I died and they did it, so I told them I'm my own ghost, come to haunt them to their graves for killing me." She glanced around. "Word spread pretty fast, hasn't it?"

He understood: it wasn't he they were getting away from, it was *she*.

He wiped at the blood on his face. With her one good arm she tugged him free of the crowd, which, as if in a dream, released its hold and let him go. The battle waged on but the cause was lost. He stumbled down the broad steps of the quadrangle. The collapsing mass of people above still walled him off from his would-be assassin, trapping Mingo on the far side.

When he reached the middle plateau—the narrow channel at the bottom of the steps—the woman tried to drag him to the left, behind a sidewall, but he resisted. He had to look back, to search for Lyell. The woman insisted, "You have to come. I'm taking you to your friends."

"Friends?" The word tugged at him. *Who could she possibly mean?*

"The others like you," she said. "You have to come." She dragged him behind the wall.

Then, from over the quadrangle, his name roared like a jet of flame, like a flare across the sky. It echoed out of the arcades and over the camp, and he stared back in amazement.

"Like somebody screamin' their way out of hell," his savior observed, and with more urgency tugged him around behind the eastern arcade, down two more sets of steps to the ground.

They headed toward a ramp beneath the quadrangle.

"I think it was," he replied. "Tell me who you are, why you helped me."

"My name's Amerind Shikker. Glimet sent me after you. He described what you'd be like, right down to that thing on your head. He thought you'd be here in Box City—don't ask me how he knew it, but he did. He sure did. I guess he must a seen you on TV, huh? Like maybe an earlier broadcast. I saw that one."

"Glimet?"

"That's how *I* know him, not the way you do. When I found

him, he only had one arm left and part of his head. Now he's all back together again, only he ain't him no more. I mean, who he is didn't used to be Glimet, he was somebody else real different." She shook her head. "You better not have me tell it, unless you want to get it wrong from the start. I know it in my head but I can't speak it right. Just come on and he'll tell ya."

She led him down the curving, broken concrete ramp into darkness.

Directly above them, hanging over the wall behind the arcade, Mad Bucca helplessly watched his catch disappear into the underground parking garage. Bucca knew the garage as well as anyone. There was just one place where the black-haired woman could be going, supporting Bucca's assumption that she was one of Mr. Mingo's aliens. He was glad he had thought to use his magic coin when he had.

Getting down from the rail, he shoved his way through the open arches past an enraged fire tender who swung a chair leg at his skull. When he reached the inner plaza of the quadrangle, he found that the crowd had gone back to its general milling about, except for one group that stood clustered around what appeared to be a body over to the right. Where Mingo had bellowed his defiance, the light of the rising sun shone brilliantly, making the marble glitter. The metal tackle of the flagpole cables clanged overhead like morning bells against the tall aluminum poles. The man in black had disappeared.

Bucca pulled idly at his lower lip. Events were requiring enormous efforts at reasoning, an atrophied faculty in Bucca. Complexity and decision making were at the top of the list of things from which Boxers in general had escaped, and Bucca was no exception. The simplest divergence posed a conundrum that could tie him up for several hours or even days.

He was still standing indecisively on the same spot at the top of the quadrangle when the first of a dozen fires erupted in the boxes below.

21

Toward
an Explanation

They wedged their way through a split in the wall of the parking garage, and entered another world.

To Angel the woman named Shikker became a lifeline, and the journey she forced upon him took the form of an endless descent into a sunken realm where sound was the guiding sense. Had she let go of him at any point, he had no doubt that he would have meandered in darkness for an eternity and died in black confusion. What magic guided her in a realm so totally lightless that there was no discernible difference between open and closed eyes? What kept at bay the things scrabbling along to the sides, the things fluttering above him? It was as though the two of them walked a magical path through enchantment, through hell, and so long as they held to their course, the million lurking demons could not touch them. He hadn't known till then that he had an imagination. He was sure he hadn't possessed one the day before.

Once they had climbed through the hole, Shikker did not speak. Angel listened to the crunch of gravel underfoot, the skitter of broken things, the splash of unexpected puddles. Smells of all sorts wafted in and around them on various breezes. There was the obvious odor of urine, the organic stench of mildew, even the smell of smoke from who knew where. None of these offered him anything substantial by which to locate himself, and in fact only caused him to lose track of where he was while he pondered them. He stumbled from time to time, but Shikker did not. Nor did her one-handed grip ever relax. It was forged, welded, seamless.

Eventually, they leveled off. She tugged him over an ankle-high barrier; he nearly fell on his face. The strength in her arm kept him up. Then he started tripping over raised objects set at regular intervals in the floor of the impenetrable tunnel. He developed a sense of the spacing of these and began striding from strip to strip. Every so often the spacing changed, and he stumbled again before regauging his stride. At one point he sprawled forward onto his knees, and she lifted him back up as if he weighed nothing and they continued on—all without a word passing between them.

He stuck his free hand in his jacket pocket and felt something small and hard there. He thought at first he had found another cube, but it was round, thin. It was a coin, and he didn't remember having it when he had searched through his pockets earlier in front of the umbrella-woman, but he closed his fist around it, pressing it into his palm.

Soon the ground became uneven again, and he withdrew his hand in order to catch himself if he fell. He smelled sulfurous gases and a sweet cloacal reek for which he knew no name.

Shikker muttered, "Someone dead in here," and immediately the rebarbative stench of decay burst upon him as if her words had ruptured a membrane. It was worse than anything he had smelled in Box City.

Something rattled just in front of them, and a dim rectangle appeared upon the air. His guide moved as a silhouette upon it, while he automatically blinked, believing it to be an illusion, like the amorphous shapes that manifest before the eyes in total darkness. But it was real enough. He could see her, and the rectangle. He had to step up to go through it, the doorway.

Shortly, they emerged on an old subway platform. Nearby, a defunct escalator stretched two stories into bluish space. Voices and the sounds of clanking metal echoed from above. A flock of birds flittered around the ceiling. Fascinated by them, he tried to walk toward the escalator, but Shikker dragged him inexorably away—through a high turnstile with comblike teeth.

They were going down again, he could tell. Back into unconscious darkness.

From there they wove in and out of pockets of light, like a fever-ridden mind collecting fevered images: a platform strewn with bodies that, at Angel's approach, erupted into thousands of agitated, feeding flies. Underneath, the true corpses could hardly be recognized but for their general shape. He was prepared for the smell this time, holding his jacket over his nose and mouth. The inexplicability of their deaths in this out-of-the-way place troubled him, but Shikker ignored them, as if blind to the carnage.

With mechanical strides, she tugged him again into utter darkness.

The golden tent hung on the crest of a subterranean hill, a curious crown—more like a party hat—upon a rough black skull of earth. Climbing down into a ditch across from it, Shikker and Angel had to jump a wide trench to reach the other side.

He was concentrating on his footing on the precariously loose hillside and didn't see the contents of the tent until he was almost on top of it. Inside, on the floor, lay more bodies— or what had once been bodies—all in a row.

Nothing like the ghastly scene on the platform, these withered, soft-boned torsos lay neatly aligned, their heads bowed and crumpled, their folded fingers like corkscrewed brown papier-mâché stubs. He recollected mummies he had once seen in catacombs, though he could not remember where or when that could have been. They looked as if they had just been unearthed, and their disjointed familiarity shook him as nothing else had.

The Shikker woman stood beside him, her attitude reverential. It was as if she were praying over them. Then she simply let go of his hand. She moved off and sat down on a small rug. She was looking directly at him when her eyelids fluttered shut.

The sides of the long tent fluttered, too. Angel twitched in response and looked from end to end, finding no one else, nothing but heaps of rags, blankets, and debris.

He felt it then—a tickle like an insect crawling across his scalp, except that this insect was deep inside the gray matter, a shifting, trickling chemical flow. Neurotransmitters forging new synaptic bonds. A pain stabbed through his right eye as if a splinter were pushing through it from inside his head. He clutched at the lens covering it and, with a groan, doubled over.

The pain stopped.

Someone said, "No, that's not the way, is it?"

Hunched over, Angel peered at Shikker, but she still had her eyes closed. It hadn't been her voice in any case—this belonged to a man.

At the far end of the tent, an arm arose, a cobra dancing, inveigling. What he had taken for a rumpled heap of clothes sat up. "Over here."

Behind him, Amerind Shikker fell over on her side.

"Don't worry," said the man, "she's sleeping."

He had graying blond hair that was oily and uncombed. It stuck up absurdly. He needed a shave, which reminded Angel emptily of Chikako.

"What is it?" asked the man. "Tell me, what passed through you just now?"

Angel turned inward. He groped for the shape of his feelings and, when he could not find it, chose words that applied, that everyone else used. "Loss," he said. "Sadness."

The other shook his head. "You don't know but a ghost of either of those things. Sadness, loss, joy—they're all estranged from you." His voice itself expressed more sadness than Angel felt. This man *knew*.

"That's so," he admitted. He sat down across from the man. "I don't feel anything toward anyone."

"They've taken it away."

"Who?"

"All of them—the corporation, the government. The great collusion that has never seen light of day but lurks behind the teeth and tongue of those who make promises. Orbitol, by way of example." He reached into his loose cloak and produced a small plastic atomizer. Its silver head gleamed.

"The drug they all take," Angel commented.

"And you."

"Me? No. No," he repeated, adamantly.

The man held him with a look for a moment, then touched the sides of his own face. "And me. See my scars, here and here?"

"I don't have any," Angel argued.

"Under that contraption you do. I've seen."

"When? I don't know you." His stomach seemed to be expanding into a vast pit that his heart would fall into.

"On the Moon I did. Before they got their hands on you."

On the Moon! This man had known him before the amnesia. "Did I," he asked in dawning fear, "did I kill all of those people?"

The man said, "The name I have now is Glimet. To answer your question, we must rid you of your artificial limitations." He leaned forward until his fingers brushed the *crab*. "Then you won't need to ask."

"You can do that?"

Glimet nodded. "Only . . . it will be very unpleasant."

"I don't care."

"No, you wouldn't." He stood, stiffly. His head brushed the glowing side of the tent. "I want you to come with me. And to do exactly what I tell you."

Angel glanced at Shikker. "Did she follow this course?"

A dry chuckle. "No. Light hypnosis is all that was, to enable her to find her way back. Now, please." He offered his dirty hand to help Angel up. They walked outside the tent.

In the deeper reaches of the huge vault, there was a petaled, shadowy shape. At first it looked like a drawing done in black paint on the far wall. Drawing nearer, Angel saw it sparkle, glistening with something like moonlit quicksilver—droplets that cascaded over the petals but did not fall. The ground beneath was unblemished.

The flower shape moved. Its rounded petals stretched wide, exposing a membranous silver center. The beads, or whatever they were, came from there. He looked questioningly at Glimet.

"This will be hard," Glimet told him, and the way he said it revealed the deeper truth.

He was going to die.

Glimet put the atomizer gun against Angel's head. They looked into one another's eyes, trading fear, and hope, and esteem. Then Glimet squeezed the trigger. . . .

22
Dead Is My Body

Imagine a place that is no place, has no ground or sky, no solidity to which you can affix your reason. Where a vortex swirls nearby and your thoughts say "*dust*," the concept of dust being all you have with you. In naming it, you have transformed it, and dust, spit from a whirlwind, scrapes you. It stings, which is odd, since you don't have a form to be spattered in the first place. But "me" is a tenacious concept, able to give life to form and form to life. You manifest.

You have no memory, nor can you imagine a moment succeeding this. There is only *now*, moment to moment. How you came here, if it hurt, who you were or want to be, and if you are content—these things cannot be addressed in a place such as this.

There are others, too. The autochthonous inhabitants of this non-place. They appear to be strands of raw tissue, muscle and gristle without skin or bone. At the top is a lumpish knot of strands upon which your mind's subjective grid identifies the features of eye sockets and thin lipless mouths. Toward the bottom, their ropy essence flattens out into a calyx from which dangle more ragged strands, long deformed fingers. These others float and bob, moving as if by force of will alone. But it is your will at the helm. That is how form evolves here— through the exercise of interlopers. The inhabitants themselves don't require any.

You discover that you have finished taking form yourself, only to find that you're one of them. You are a floating mass of wet and sticky rope; when you try to move your hands and feet you feel a pseudopodal wriggle beneath the basket of your torso. This is not the shape you have grown used to, but that one doesn't seem to be an option here.

Just when you're adjusting to the idea of this physical conformation, you feel yourself begin to compress. Your boneless body squashes down as though the atmospheric pressure is doubling every moment. Boneless or not, the new body cannot compress this way. The other creatures hover near, unaffected by the pressures warping you. You have a mouth but not for screaming. For what then? You'll never know. It's unbearable, like drowning while being on fire, having joints and sockets wrenched apart, in all directions at the same moment. Pain, it grows louder than existence.

"This will be hard," he said. "Hard" doesn't measure this, is your answer.

You've finally figured it out. The hard part hasn't begun yet.

You still have to go back.

Bruised, bloodied, achy, and as tired as he had ever been, Mingo leaned against the Free Quaker Meeting House, Ingram 30 dangling in his hand, and grimly watched the conflagration. It wasn't particularly satisfying, coming as it did after so many successive failures—more an expression of his frustration than of real anger.

His leg hurt as if the bone had split, his cheek was inflamed, his left eye swelling, and there was a ringing harmonic in his ear that had him worried. On top of that he had once more lost the Angel. They had beaten him—the homeless, thoughtless, malodorous swine. They had beaten him bloody. Well, the last laugh would be his. He would go down in history right next to Mrs. O'Leary's cow.

He maintained a tiny, ridiculous hope that his prey was trapped somewhere in the flames along with the hundreds of others. At least that was what he would tell the damned COs. If the truth ever came to light, well, by then it would be old news and he would simply shrug it off. So many charred bodies, so little to work with. If they were lucky, maybe the whole place would ignite, and SC could sweep in and raze it before more squatters moved in.

He had played a complicated game. It should not surprise him that it had failed; and yet he had been so certain. He had considered every variable in advance—or at least every variable he had *known* in advance. They all looked rock solid.

The company couldn't have kept Rueda on the Moon. There

was nowhere he wouldn't have been noticed. Employees would have made the connection between him and . . . other bad business. The story would have leaked—on that point he knew absolutely that he was right. Stories always leaked. Angel Rueda had had to come down to Earth. But they, the asinine quartet, had wanted him alive, as if he were a hostage, an endangered species, a bargaining chip. They actually thought they could trade him for some technological marvel such as a Buckyball opener.

He found his reverie interrupted at that point. A short, squalid man was tugging at his sleeve. The guy had a little tuft of hair on top of his head, like a greasy ski jump.

Mingo decided he needed a vacation. Someplace where ScumberCorp didn't own the works. New Zealand maybe. The little man tugged again. "What?" he snarled.

"Mr. Mingo, my name's Mad Bucca."

"How appealing."

"I found him, Mr. Mingo."

"Found whom?"

"The one that got away. Machine Man."

A bag woman wearing four layers of clothing ran past. Her hair was alight. Mingo thought affectionately of the Statue of Liberty.

He shook his head. He would have liked a nap before his brain dried up. Even the security bozos had gotten to take naps. They didn't have to maintain their facade of superior intellect. Anyway, in all this screaming chaos, where could he sleep?

"What's a Machine Man?" he asked, disinterestedly.

"You know—a *alien*."

Mingo focused on the little man. Yes, he remembered this turnip from the feeding frenzy in the plaza. He dared not hope. Not yet. But energy was seeping back into him, charging him, as he asked, "Where?"

"Down there," Bucca said. He pointed along the wall behind the meeting house.

"What, he's down the street?"

"Naw, he went down the rabbit hole. C'mere, I'll show youse. No, really, come on." And he led Mingo to an old chained ramp that had once had a semaphore at the top.

"A parking garage for people who live in boxes," Mingo commented. He paused to listen to the screams, like Dracula immersed in the howling of the wolves. "Or used to. How long ago was it that you saw him?"

"Dunno. Half hour, maybe longer. I couldn't find ya, and then the fire broke out and I had to go rescue my house."

" 'House' overstates the matter somewhat, doesn't it?"

"You see, mine's fireproof an—"

"Yes, all right." He grabbed Bucca by the shirt and stuck the muzzle of the gun under his chin. "You were given a dime. By some miracle of the ages, did you happen to use it?"

Bucca intended to describe his ingenuity but the words tumbled out in a panic. "I slipped it in his pocket at the Liberty Bell, when he wasn't looking, like you wanted, right? What you said, when we did lunch."

Liquid was spattering on the little man's foot. His bladder had given way.

Mustering control over absolute loathing, Mingo released him and stepped away. He holstered the gun. "What was your year?" he asked.

"Nineteen eighty-four."

"An amusing vintage." He tilted back his head and to the sky cried, "I'm not undone yet!"

Bucca said very quietly, "I was wondering, Mr. Mingo—"

The blond head snapped down like the visor on a helmet. "Your reward. Yes. I have to follow up what you've told me first—make sure everything's as you say. Then, when I've finished, I'll come back for you."

"That's good, 'cause, like, there might not be no place left here tomorrow. Box space'll be a premium, ya know?"

"I think I have the picture." He was thinking: *in the darkest hour of the darkest day, all is not lost*. The plan was going to work as he'd intended after all. One program covered the contingency of another; better still, they coalesced. He was going to triumph! If Rueda was in the tunnels below, then so were his companions. Mingo had them; he had them all.

23

The Evil
That Men Do

The *1984* coin fairly sang to Mingo as he tracked its signal through levels of concrete and iron. Everywhere he went, he found bodies. He covered his mouth with a cloth as he passed them. Some had been gnawed on, and not by rats. There was hardly a living one in the bunch, although he did occasionally hear the echo of running feet. The living had withdrawn before he could catch them. They had learned their lesson well.

He wore goggles displaying a 3-D security map of all the tunnels with his position and that of *1984* brightly pinpointed. He could view them in either or both eyes, from above or in cross section, as a solid grid or a transparent overlay against the night vision lenses of the goggles. The map designated platforms and stairs, doors and even disused fire hose nozzles, by which he could confirm his position on the tracks.

The coin had not moved for a while. Maybe Rueda was asleep. After all, the man had been through hell. Mingo had kept the fires going. They were, he thought, like two men on opposite sides of a mirror. Both of them shot, beaten, running against the clock—the only real difference was that Mingo knew why. He had to credit Rueda for remarkable survival instincts in the face of such incalculable odds. He could afford to be magnanimous now that the game was ending.

A subway platform loomed up beside him. A noise caught his attention, and he had the gun out as he turned.

He saw a derelict shuffling toward him, begging. Mingo shook his head but the Boxer continued toward him. Did the idiot think he was on the street someplace?

Rather than waste time arguing, Mingo shot him. The gun roared, the blast rocketing down the tunnel like a train. He pursed his lips and decided shooting wasn't such a clever idea—

it might warn someone that he was coming. The pathetic beggar toppled headlong into the cinders, and Mingo kept going.

1984 was very strong now.

According to the map, he had crossed beneath the Schuylkill River. He arrived before an old subway security door. The map showed a hallway behind it leading to a sealed up area—what had once been a local subway stop for 30th Street Station. It had been closed off in the last century. Now it was just a vast underground cavern under the old train station, a concrete ruin accessible from at least five different directions, according to the goggles. The coin was in there. He switched off the map.

Alert for anything now, he tried the door, confirming that it was not locked. He eased it open. No one waited for him on the other side. He glided along the musty concrete hall, avoiding a heap of collapsed ceiling. A stairway to the right joined the hall, and he swung around its metal rail, gun at the ready; but the metal-edged stairs ended in a solid ceiling. They had not led anywhere in decades. He followed the map back down.

Mingo reached the opposite end and opened the door a crack. He peered down upon a large makeshift tent. The glare of it made his eyes water. He turned down the goggles. The tent looked as though a lantern were burning inside of it and the canvas intensified the light. That was quite a trick. He liked it, though; liked it fine. Anyone inside there would be blind to the darkness and an easy target.

He eased like oil around the doorjamb, then paused again, bringing up the map for a moment, double-checking as he always did. The map marked his position accurately, showing the doorway, the hall behind him; but in that case the coin wasn't in the tent. Its blip was far off to the right, not far from a secondary tunnel.

He turned up the goggles' penetrating power. Scanning wide, he spotted the shape of the lotus, and almost gasped aloud.

Lotus was what he had tagged the first one, the one they had found and inadvertently destroyed inside the aliens' enclosure on the Moon. It had been as brittle as blown glass. At the first touch it had shattered in a chain reaction that, in a matter of moments, reduced the whole structure to a pile of gritty black dust. He knew it had been some special device, a weapon possibly. Yet analysis of the dust revealed it to have been composed of carbon.

This one had bright dots moving on it. They swirled and danced in an intricate, unfathomable pattern from petal to petal. He had not seen that on the other one—this one was still . . . alive. As if to prove it, the thing moved.

To his dismay, the map placed Rueda right there beside it. And there *was* someone there, standing so motionless that he hadn't noticed before. He held the gun up. His heartbeat hammered. He took each step carefully, placing each foot deliberately. His feet seemed to make no sound; in fact, in all the world there was nothing but the sound of his heart. No one could know he was coming.

The person ahead continued watching the lotus. Mingo moved as close as he dared. From this distance he could not miss, and Angel Rueda could not escape again. No tricks, no surprises, no crowd to shield him. Raising the gun, sighting down the barrel, he said gently, "*Adios, muchacho.*"

The man turned, showing no surprise, no fear. It was not Rueda, and the utter disregard in the man's blue eyes, even upon seeing the gun, unstrung Mingo. He balked. "No," said the man, "you must get back." Mingo, wavering in his resolve, could not stand the calmness in those eyes. He lowered his head and saw, at his feet, the cranial bypass unit. It lay on its back like a horseshoe crab, revealing an intricate, greasy underbelly lined with tiny pins and two studs, like legs, that had affixed it to Rueda's skull. He could even make out the indentation where he had planned to put in a tracer. This was worse than impossible. To remove the bypass was to kill Rueda. He stared questioningly at the other man. Perhaps it was all over.

Beside him the lotus fluttered again. The tepal stretched back, opening up the center. A shiny mucosa there bulged outward. Something like a thick gray mucilage spilled out around it. A shrill, rising sound nearly drove him to his knees—a shriek like that of a thousand Harpies or the gathered agony of all the tortured souls of history, pressed into one devastating wail. His hand, holding the gun, shook so hard that he could barely keep from dropping it. He felt his bowels unplug. He was crying, sobbing, his teeth grinding.

The discharge gathered, transformed. It pushed out hard, like toothpaste being crushed out of the end of a tube. One instant it was gray, indefinable; in the next it had become human, and the bone-crushing scream of agony was erupting from its lungs—the scream not of birth, but of formation.

Mingo wrapped his arms around his head. He collapsed to his knees.

Angel Rueda, naked and slick and whole, fell quivering like a fish beside him.

Mingo shook off his tears of pain. He saw his prey, the cause of his agony and his befouled state, shivering in the aftermath of pain.

Now! Mingo's brain urged. He squeezed his hand around the gun, dragged its awful weight to bear.

The blond man who had not moved till then took one step forward, and Mingo hastily pointed the weapon at him. "Back off," he snapped. The man hesitated; he didn't move back, but seemed confused by the order. Mingo got up shakily. "You just went into the Underworld for nothing," he said to them both, then stepped over Angel and, with both hands to steady it, pointed the gun straight down.

In the last instant, he had a premonition of motion at his back and tried to twist around.

A length of pipe caught him squarely across the chin. The point of his jaw shattered, and he tripped over Angel Rueda and fell into the black heart of the thing on the wall. Tepals folded over him. He screamed.

A force like suction took him, tore him off his feet.

His view of the world sparkled around the edges. It began to slow down. He saw—recognizing the enormity of a fate that would allow it—the blue-turbaned character he'd beaten up on the steps of the quadrangle. A band of light emitted by the tent glistened off the jewel in her nose, split for an instant into a dozen colorful prismatic rays. *Her!* he realized. *It was a woman*! *A woman in disguise*. It had to be *the* woman, of course, the one who'd escaped detection, the one who'd defeated him at ICS-IV. At last he had her and he yearned to dispatch her, but he couldn't feel the gun, or his fingers, or his arm. Blood was in his mouth. The sparks around the edge ignited across the center of his view, and fire seared every thought he had ever had. For Mingo, vision ceased altogether, along with all thought and all being, other than a torment eternal.

*   *   *

"He can't go through," the Orbiter told Lyell, "without the drug his tissues aren't realigned. It won't accept him."

All the same, the flower-shaped conveyance tried. It absorbed what it could of its captive and spat out what it could not.

Before anyone could react, the black tepals opened up and Mingo slid down the wall to the ground. He was barely recognizable. The lotus had reduced him to a glassy-eyed, drooling shell. Above his eyebrows, his head had been squashed in like lumpy dough. Only a few strands remained of his fine mane of hair. A few bubbles of bloody spit popped between his broken lips.

Lyell dropped the length of pipe and turned away.

The man said, "But we have to help—"

Lyell shook her head. She couldn't even look at him.

Angel Rueda groaned and rolled over. Dirt stuck to him like patchy fur, sprinkling when he moved. Groggily, he looked up at Lyell's back and at Glimet, then caught sight of what remained of Mingo. For a minute he stared, motionless. Then he sat up. His hand nudged the bypass unit. It rocked back and forth. He grinned: he was free.

His hair was a short black stubble, the way it had been cut for the *crab*. His body smelled of the sticky substance on it, an odor not unlike that of cilantro.

He got to his feet, testing his balance. "Lyell?" he said.

Wiping at her eyes, she turned around. He stood unabashedly naked. Lyell tried to keep her eyes on his brown face. She remembered the lost look on his face that had claimed her involvement right from the first, and she remarked to herself how out of place it would have seemed on this man. She had to remind herself that he was dead.

"Who are you, Angel?" she asked.

He glanced sidelong at Glimet. "That is a little complicated."

They sat in the bright tent—Thomasina Lyell now shed of her disguise, a groggy Amerind Shikker, and Glimet, and Angel. He had wiped off the sticky substance and put on his shed clothing.

Lyell checked the disk recorder harness above her left breast, then sealed up the seam on her jacket. "Okay," she said to Glimet. "We have five hours left on this disk. Let's try to get it all. Tell me first, who are you?"

"He's Glimet, back from the dead," said Shikker, pointing.

She thought again of the woman Odie had interviewed, Akiko Alcevar. *Her* husband had been back from the dead. "Is that true?"

"In effect," replied Glimet. "Glimet was an Orbiter, who met his final decay right here in my camp. He was deadly addicted but couldn't see it, even at the end. But that's the nature of your kind and your drug. What is also the nature of the drug, but has gone undocumented, is that it is *not* killing those addicts—not as you imagine it."

"Wait a minute, don't we all *know* it is?"

"You know it alters them, makes them go away where you can't see them. Into 'twelve-space.' "

"What's twelve-space?" It was a term she knew she had heard somewhere.

"Well, twelve-space . . . I picked it up from a video broadcast. Some physicist offering theory—a wise man, I think. Very nearly has it all with his theory."

She remembered: the Ichi-Plok spokesperson who had scared Nebergall off the "slow-food" story. What would he say when he found out that aliens constituted part of his viewing audience? Knowing him, he'd love it.

"He said one of your physics proposes that you live in a world of eleven dimensions," he continued, "four of which you know and experience, seven of which you know nothing of and cannot experience. You can only imagine them—seven dimensions around you right this instant, everywhere, throughout the universe."

"And that's where you're from?"

"Not really," said Angel. "He calls it 'twelve-space' because that's an easy tag that we can all comprehend. It's a common concept." He had a decided accent now; the rhythm of his speech had changed, become lilting. "We are right next door, *pues*—that is, therefore—he says twelve. We don't have any idea how many dimensions we are. It never occurred to us to ask. I can't explain beyond that."

"I think I see," she replied after a moment. "It's pretty much what Mussari was guessing. Orbitol acts to alter the nature of the body so that the tissues cease to conform to our four dimensions and become part of yours—some sort of crossover?"

"Yes, that's fairly accurate."

"ScumberCorp thought it was wiping out what it considered an undesirable populace—"

"But in fact it was dropping them onto your next-door neighbors like bags of garbage," Glimet finished for her.

"What happens to the Orbiters in twelve-space?"

"They decay, almost from the moment they arrive. They appear out of nowhere as huge pulpy masses of suffering—it's very hard to convey because the physicality is nothing like here. Say that we share their anguish as our own. Pain and pleasure are open among us—no, not 'open,' what's the right word?—communicable? We're susceptible to them. Their continued arrival fills up our world with their agony. Eventually, we'll drown in it."

None of this talk of pain and dimensions was making much sense to Shikker's beleaguered brain. She asked, "What about the place Glimet seen all the time, that he wanted to go to? That your world?"

Glimet smiled indulgently. "There never was such a place, Amerind. His mind was making up images he could cope with—the way all of you dream by creating images that represent things in your life in some abstract way. He saw pink trees and grass and physical things that don't exist at all in our universe. Or if they do, it's in one of those dimensions *we* can't experience." He turned to Lyell again.

She thought his sharp-eyed leanness and directness alone would persuade many in the viewing audience.

He told her, "This body that I share, I share with a remnant of Glimet's consciousness. His memory is in here—that's how I know what he saw, what he dreamed. So is Angel's memory returned now that the bypass is eliminated. But this—" he paused briefly, then held up his arm, closing his fingers into a fist "—this is done by remote manipulation from a distance too strange to describe. That's why there is that momentary delay when you ask a question of us."

"You're not here in front of me."

Angel said, "No. That would kill us in the crossing, as it has nearly done to Señor Mingo. *Empero*, the remotes are not too stable. The first group of them decomposed here recently." He gestured at the withered corpses. "I'm second generation.

Glimet, having survived the first batch, is third, I guess. There seems to be a time factor that is inconsistent. I know from Angel Rueda's memory that I 'died' some months ago. However, I seem to be one of the most stable of the remotes."

There were matters that, as a reporter, she wanted to make sure they covered. She took control of the conversation, asking, "Tell me what happened on the Moon."

The lightness of his manner collapsed into solemnity. His eyes unfocused upon memories. It was his first opportunity to reflect on those events. Tears welled in his eyes. He lowered his head. The tears fell in silent grief. "They're all dead. I led them to their doom."

No one spoke. Even Shikker grasped what was happening. She crept nearer to Glimet and placed her hand over his. He glanced her way uncertainly, but tenderly. It was a look of sadness, reflecting what he must know of her former relationship with the body he inhabited, and the understanding that she would never comprehend Glimet's subordinate presence. Lyell filmed it all.

Angel raised his head. His eyelids glistened. He spoke softly. "We, that is to say Glimet's first wave, had learned what was causing the appearance of these creatures, these Orbiters, in our world. They found out that the chemical is processed in a factory on the Moon. So we created an enclosure to sustain life and made it blossom beside Stercus Pharmaceuticals' lunar manufacturing plant. We can extrude inert material back through the hole where our space is torn, the crossover you referred to."

She held up her hand to stop him. "Wait a second, on the *Moon*? There was a rent in space corresponding to a location on the Moon?"

"Not one, dozens, close together. Next to Stercus's facility, yes," he said. "It's the factory for making Orbitol. ¿Comprende? There's a mass grave." He stared hard at her. "The guinea pigs were put to sleep before their tissues had totally transformed, at various stages of transformation. We had to stretch some of them apart to come through. The enclosure is built on their bones."

Lyell saw how what he was saying connected up with ScumberCorp's free lunch inducements to the Boxers, especially the ones who went up into the towers and were never heard from again. She grimaced. "And down here. Your first wave was here, you said. A similar situation? Bodies?"

"Yes," said Glimet. "A much higher incidence here. There must be bodies scattered all through this subterranean maze."

"Sure," agreed Shikker, "down here's where most Orbiters come sooner or later."

Angel continued, "We invaded Stercus Pharmaceuticals. A dozen of us, innocently believing we had the power to overcome any obstacle. *Verdadero*, we expected to reason with those we met. What we met turned out to be ScumberCorp security. Mingo led them. Glimet has already explained about the time delay in maneuvering these bodies. We're in no position to make snap decisions. We hoped to negotiate. They executed everyone on hand. Cold-blooded murder under Mingo's guidance, with ScumberCorp's seal of approval on it.

"I was knocked down at the beginning and taken prisoner. Mingo interrogated me himself. I told him why we were there. I informed him that he had just slain not a bunch of reanimated Orbiters but the first ambassadors of a friendly alien race. An intelligent race. Mingo showed less reaction than you do right now. Weighed against ScumberCorp's profit margin that Mingo was paid to secure, we were of no consequence. I was inconvenient, nothing more."

"Nothing surprises me where ScumberCorp is involved," Lyell commented.

"Then, you will understand my horror and repulsion at discovering that Mingo and the quartet to whom he answered were most concerned about their failure to *kill* the underclass people this drug is made for. They didn't give a damn about my people or what they were doing to our world. They didn't give a damn about anything except pie charts. Graphs and pie charts. The room I was kept in was full of graphs and pie charts—projections of population reduction as a result of Orbitol addiction. Pie charts.

"Stercus ran an identity check on me, and the information came back that I was a dead Orbiter from Madrid, and that news sent them right over the edge. *Como loco*, the bastards. The four of them screamed at him across the void. One wanted to kill me, and another to have me dissected to see how I'd been altered, except they already had eleven dead bodies for that useless purpose. Two of them argued for using me as bait, to draw out more of us. Their idea was to establish right off that coming over here was an unhealthy idea. Do you see how insane they are?"

"No problem there. So, then, you really *are* the infamous *Xau Dâu?*"

"Actually, no. *Xau Dâu* is sitting out there."

"Mingo?" she said incredulously.

"Mingo had been milking a phantom for years. His creation. He was fiercely proud of it, he wouldn't stop talking about it all the time I was his captive. *Xau Dâu* allowed him to dispatch anyone who threatened to go public with information about corporate violations, anyone who wanted to make trouble. They either became terrorists posthumously or were made the victims of terrorists. It was a foolproof idea. Everybody grieves for the company's loss. *¡Qué lastima!"*

"Clever. My editor's suspected something like it for a long time, but he's a cynic. Did Mingo want to eliminate you from the beginning?"

"Right from the start, yes. He couldn't do it there—too many people were watching. The Moon was too small a community and the CEOs had other plans. He had to get me out of there, so he fell in with the two heads who wanted to use me as bait to lure the others, and thereafter insisted they had to get me off the Moon as soon as possible and bury the evidence of this incursion before the word spread and public sentiment or an investigation forced them to suspend Orbitol production. Events proved him right. In just the few hours they held me inside Stercus, a pilot of some craft or other flew over, accidentally saw our extruded enclosure, and tried reporting it to the nearside lunar facility. The message was duly routed back to Stercus. Mingo had to clear an entire cargo bay and race halfway around the Moon in order to set up another accident to take care of that one man before he talked to anybody."

"*Xau Dâu.* Another terrorist act."

"That's right. Mingo had it all worked out. How to use the media, how to manipulate public opinion, how to wage a never-ending war on the perceptions of the whole human race. That was the key element: perception. How it looks is a thousand times more important than the truth of an incident.

He was right again. Machiavelli would have placed a poor second to Mingo."

Though she had said similar things at one time or other, Angel Rueda's words troubled Lyell. She recalled her father's faraway words: *You know your truth*. She wasn't so sure anymore.

"While he was gone, I fell asleep. I never woke up till now. I gather they drugged me and installed the bypass. They located our point of control in the remote, maybe with an MRI scan, then shut down that part of Angel, including the core of his memory. Both of us nearly ceased to be. With that calotte on, as they called it, he was a zombie, lacking so much of his identity that he hardly reacted to anything around him. I couldn't disengage, either. I was stuck in the remote body, dragged along with no means of influencing it. I couldn't so much as look through his eyes to see where I was. If he'd been one of the first wave, he would have begun decomposing. We knew that members of the first group were, and I could never be sure he wasn't. I found myself in contact with him twice, briefly, and attempted blindly to warn him of the danger he was in. He seemed to be regaining some awareness, but nothing that could communicate with me for very long."

She pressed a knuckle to her lips. "What happens now? Mingo certainly won't be back."

"Now we must confront the four who remain. The ones in charge. They have a great deal to answer for."

Lyell laughed spontaneously. "Forgive me, but I can't imagine how you expect to sneak into the tower, unless it's through another one of those flower arrangements of yours."

"That would be impossible. Without the corresponding tunnel that Orbiters create, we cannot pass anyone through to your side. There are already thousands of these intrusive wormholes. We could spend years investigating each of them before we found one that admitted into the right tower in the so-called Overcity. We understand that situation well."

"Then assassination's not on your list."

"It's unacceptable," Glimet said. "We're not a violent people."

"Then, how? You can't very well just walk in and announce yourselves to the secretary. Or . . ." She tilted her head thoughtfully, tapped her forefinger against her lips. A wicked smile spread across them. "Or," she repeated, "maybe you can."

"Really?" said Angel, doubtfully.

"Maybe," she repeated. "Just maybe. If it works, it's going to make great TV."

24

The King of Misrule

Gansevoort had only managed two hours of a fitful sleep during which he remained constantly aware of his body tangled up in sheets.

Then a clamorous, nasal *baa* from the outer door drilled with surgical precision right through the thin veneer, hell-bent for his reticular formation. *Baa!* and peptides leapt like dolphins out of the message's path. Wake Up!

He thrashed at the sheets like a man drowning, and came fully, dreadfully, awake. He lay still, and listened, and knew absolutely and for certain that he would never do so again.

This would be it, the confrontation. Death—the ultimate fatalist's dream vacation.

Sweat seared in a wet rash across him. The fear itself was strangely buoyant; his horrific elation would sail him through the room, float him to the door, carry him to his doom. In blue and white pin-striped pajamas, he would face his executioner. *Mingo.* It wasn't the same as being bound and helpless, but it was helpless nonetheless.

He got up. The floor was cold underfoot. He should have put on slippers. What kind of sleepwear, he wondered, did the other executives wear? Well, it hardly mattered anymore—a realization that strangely lightened his load. No more worrying about being out of step, unfashionable, out of his depth.

Standing near the door, he spoke his set password, "Chaos." The unit came on—sound, disk recorder, a flicker igniting on the clear monitor screen. He appreciated the obvious futility of attempting to record his own impending death, but this in no way forestalled him. With aplomb, he was cresting the wave of his fear.

The screen presented to him the face of Thomasina Lyell.

Gansevoort coughed. His fear collapsed like a bad lung. Certain Death peeled off the menu.

She was staring straight into the hidden lens, straight into him. She *knew*. He couldn't figure out how—she hadn't called, he hadn't answered his phone. He touched the intercom key. "What are you doing; get away from here," he ordered.

"Mr. Gansevoort?"

"Yes," he hissed. This was no good. She was not Mingo come to kill him. He wanted Mingo; his whole being had prepared for extinction. This woman was spoiling everything. "I'm calling security right now," he threatened.

"Is that such a good idea?"

The way she said it made him wonder what secrets she kept. "Why wouldn't it be a good idea?" he demanded. "Right this minute they're all looking for you and your friend, the terrorist. I'm just doing my job if I report you."

"Just doing your job, I see. Then, you'd better." She turned and walked away.

He watched her grow smaller and smaller. Her shrinking image sucked his resolve with it. He hastily uncoded the door and threw it open. "Wait a minute," he called.

Lyell turned around. From a distance she considered him, her arms crossed. She strolled leisurely back.

"Who are you really?" he asked.

"You know. A friend of Mr. Rueda's. Of yours possibly, depending on how deep runs your loyalty to the Gang of Four. That is the colloquial SC expression for your bosses, isn't it?"

"You tied me up. Used me to get access to the city. That's no sort of friendship as I understand the word."

"We tied you up to protect you so that Mingo wouldn't simply shoot you. The access, you'll recall, you volunteered on your own."

He closed the door behind them. "Mingo, he . . ." He withered into something small and lost. "I'm dead on account of you, your involving me like that. I thought you were Mingo just now. You know what he told me? While he was untying me? He told me I wasn't to worry. He was taking care of everything and I should wait here until I heard from him, not to go to work, not to talk with anyone, not to be seen by anyone, everything would be *fine* in the end. Fine." He smiled without humor. "The moment he said 'fine' I knew he was going to kill me. I've been waiting here ever since."

"That's taking dedication too far, don't you think? If you know all this, why don't you escape? He's not sitting out in the hall, you know."

"Where to? Iowa? One of those little subsistence farms, those places where they think they're taking back the land from the agribusiness concerns?"

"It's not the worst life I can imagine."

"Well, it'll *do*." He slumped down in the same chair she'd tied him to. He had a Kleenex in the pocket of his pajamas, as if in an attempt to make them more formal. "My whole life, I've expected everything I did to catch up with me. That's the way I see Mingo—final retribution, punishment meted out."

"I don't understand. Has everything you've done been all that bad?"

"Been a lie. A sham. I've never gotten anything right. Only, sometimes people miss it, and I slip by."

She clicked her tongue. "No escape, then, I take it."

"None."

"You're probably right. He'll come for you the same as he did Chikako Peat."

He glanced up. "I thought the news said . . . but, then, it would say that, wouldn't it? He'd make it say that. Terrorists. When he had me act as liaison to get Angel Rueda that scummy ICS teaching post, I knew nothing was the way it appeared. I mean, who would do that to a valued employee, and an accident victim, too? I expect this has been about Rueda from the start."

"Partly. It's about you and the people you work for, too." Lyell leaned forward and placed her hand on top of his. He shivered at the contact. "All the lies you blame yourself for are a speck of sand compared to the mountain of deceit you work for, that disgusts you. There's at least one option to sharecropping among the Mennonites, you know."

"I don't know," he said, and he didn't.

"You could try to blow the top off that mountain."

"What, Mingo? Must be mad. That'd be like fighting a shark with a chicken leg."

"I didn't mean Mingo. Higher than that." She glanced at his work area. "Your set there is linked to SC, isn't it? You work from home occasionally?"

"I'm linked. I have to be, in my position. Secure line."

"Mmm-hmm. Tell me, then, do you have access to schedules—who's assigned what duties, what shift? That sort of thing. It's not protected data."

"Certainly." He gestured at the air. "I don't bother with it much. That's not a concern unless someone isn't showing up as they're supposed to or their account isn't being credited the proper hours or—"

"Cleaning staff?"

"Yes, even them. I can tell you who's got lavatory duty this evening if you want to know. We could run down the procedures list if you've got a few hours to learn the proper way to scrub a urinal."

"There's a proper way, how about that? Listen, Gansevoort, I need your help. Rueda needs your help. Lots of people need your help. I think I can offer you an alternative, a real alternative—what I mean is, a way to salvage that pathetic image you maintain of yourself, God knows why. You might even turn your life around. Or do you prefer to sit and wait?"

"Actually, I do, I think," he answered.

"For Mingo."

"That's right."

"You elect to die."

He almost said "yes" but stopped on the brink of it. That would be admitting too much.

"I don't believe you," she replied. "And in any case, Mingo won't be coming."

"What do you mean?"

"Just that."

"He's dead?"

She stared at her fingers. "More like untroubled by thought."

The implications took a while to filter through his self-recrimination. "It's all gone to hell, hasn't it? The company, even the world really, gone to hell."

"Pretty much. I'm doing what I can. The pay's none too good but it feels better than waiting for the next Mingo to show up."

"And what do I have to do to contribute?"

"Two small things. First I need to browse some company procedures regarding display cases—when they're cleaned, how they're accessed, how to switch off any alarm codes."

"Simple enough," he replied. "That kind of alarm you can shut off from here. . . . Well, *I* can."

"Good."

"Number two?"

"I need you to repeat what you did for me and Chikako Peat."

That brought his head up smartly. He thought it over for a moment and then asked, "Will that include tying me up again?"

"No, nobody will tie you up," she said, adding, "unless you want to be."

The latter of her "two small" requests made him tremble. If he did what she wanted, and failed, there would be no escaping the severest of penalties. But he had been awaiting just such a fate already, and now, according to Lyell, it would not be coming. In one sense, then, no matter how events fell out hereafter, he would advance toward a recognizable goal of some kind. "Why should the Devil have all the good tunes?" he muttered. It was a phrase his grandmother had often used, one he had never been too sure about, but now he understood how it applied. "Let's get started, then," he said, and directed her to the screen of his set.

25

Transported
by Ecstasy

The doors to the lift opened. Gansevoort peeked warily around the edge at the empty rice paper–walled room and, as he did, the long-haired figure of Huston Sherk stepped around him and out onto the bare wood floor. Sherk's chubby visage would have been at complete odds with Thomasina Lyell's Stardance-conditioned body, so she had draped an oversized vinyl jacket of Neeb's over her clothes to bulk up.

Gansevoort watched her with panic in his eyes. He didn't know what sort of nefarious devices protected this chamber—information about the officers' private suite was not accessible to him.

The art deco doors started to close and the three other occupants of the car forced Gansevoort out as they quickly disembarked.

Like Sherk's, their faces glowed ever so slightly—a LifeMask characteristic that might not have eluded Mrs. Fulrod's blue-tinted scrutiny if she had been on duty; as it was, the night guard had been stupefied, struck dumb, and, more to the point, totally persuaded that he was in the presence of his masters.

"You're supposed to take off your shoes," Gansevoort whispered. Lyell gave him a deadly look that the mask mimicked with toadlike sourness. But the damage was already done.

From behind the wall of *fusuma* screens, a dull voice called out, "Who's out there? Fulrod, is that you? It's way too early for tea."

Lyell scanned the black rails along the tops of the screens. There had to be microlenses mounted up there, probably all along the convenient frames, the kind of system that produced a composite "spider-eyes" image; SC could certainly afford such an array—after all, they manufactured them. In that case, however, why the questions? There would be a defense system, too, which no doubt imperiled them. Yet she hesitated, wanting to hear what more the voices had to say. There was something peculiar about this arrangement.

The voice continued petulantly, "Damn it, I said, who's out there. Dorjan, you're supposed to be monitoring the room! Wake up!"

"What?"

"The *room*!"

"What about it?" Dorjan Kosinus complained from farther away.

"There's somebody out there."

"There is? At this time of night? Don't be silly." A pause, while something crackled. "I don't hear anybody. Turn on the set and let's see."

"Gotoh's supposed to be in charge of that."

"Gotoh's barely conscious of anything anymore, or hadn't you noticed. We've been losing him for days."

A woman interjected testily. "Your blathering's ruined my nap. It's the first decent damn sleep I've had all week, so would you both please shut up."

"Huston says the elevator opened."

"He's hallucinating. Here, look at the . . . Oh. Oh, my God, we've been *invaded*."

Lyell grabbed the nearest sliding panel and flung it aside, opening a door to the inner sanctum. Gansevoort and the others barged in right behind her. None of them was quite prepared for it.

An immense glass conference table on gold tubular underpinnings stretched across the middle of the room; but it and the high-backed chairs around it rose, like fabled Atlantis, out of a geological stratum of garbage. Trash lay everywhere. The room must have been lovely once. There were paintings and sculptures lining the walls—Inuit masks and Oriental jades, works by Horunobu and Degas, and even one huge Kokoschka canvas. The debris dwarfed it all, blighting all the potential beauty.

To Lyell it was a colossal version of Nebergall's walk-in closet. Faxes and documents, empty drink bulbs of assorted colors, food trays that, judging from what was growing on them, had been stacked there for months, clothing that included underwear of various persuasions dangling from the "clipboard" terminals and statuary, and still more clothes stuffed into shelves. On the wall dead ahead hung a screen displaying the composite picture of the room she'd just vacated. Beneath it stood an enormous, black, all-purpose set manufactured by one of SC's subsidiaries. The set appeared to offer every possible convenience—the satellite networks, world radio bands, disk formats, private phone fax lines, lighting controls, a thermostat and humidistat, and a versatile security system that probably would have been her undoing if she had waited any longer to enter. They were armed to the teeth but so retarded in their coverture, their utter contempt for all enemies, that probably none of them had ever contemplated bringing those weapons to bear.

The far end of the room was of glass—a breathtaking view over the city. The sparkling spires of three dozen towers stabbed at the sky. Their arrangement formed the walls of a deep artificial canyon which seemed to run all the way to the Art Museum. Between a crisscross of skyways and walkways, as beetling Troy might once have appeared upon Hisarlik, the Art Museum glowed in a shield of light, as though time and space had fractured. It was ancient history and it was the pristine city of the future, the way architects' renderings always looked, with everything idealized, without the litter and the vagrants and the helplessly insane, without the souls numbed to life's possibilities. Not a box dwelling or a weedy, crumbling speck of the true Tartarus in sight at this height. It was the kind of illusional view that windowalls delivered, and the foursome had hoarded it as well.

Gansevoort edged to the front to lead the four imposters over the trash heap toward the seemingly unoccupied table.

Among all the debris, the four COs nearly escaped detection. It was Shikker, under Rajcevich's mask, who stabbed the air with a finger and crowed, "They're just like Glimet!"

Lyell had already seen. " 'Corporate heads' *is* the term, isn't it?" she asked rhetorically. She peeled off the mask of Sherk, then took a careful step back from the rest of the group to capture everything in one slow, steady pan.

"A witty bitch," the real Jean Rajcevich responded. Her corpulent, disembodied head bobbed at the top of her gray chair like a balloon that had lost its string. Her face was saggy, as if the skin had come loose. Her hair, a thinning, unkempt tangle, added to the overall effect of dissipation. "Get out of here, every one of you!" she ordered them.

Her tone of command actually impelled Gansevoort back a few steps: he caught himself, and glanced self-consciously left and right. No one had noticed, but he glared back at her. "You're nothing," he accused daringly, "nothing but a fat head."

He compared her to her mask on Shikker—a slimmer version more than two decades old. And idealized—the modeler had disguised the contour of scorn on her lips, or perhaps the years had exposed it. He compared all of them to their artificial counterparts. The effect was the same—they were all ravaged, every one.

They had aged prematurely. Dorjan Kosinus had gone paper-thin and blotchy. His shaggy hair had turned white. Huston Sherk's jowls had filled out, becoming trembling, wrinkled dewlaps, while his cheeks had caved in. His long hair now stuck out like dry grass off the back of his head. But Masayuki Gotoh could hardly be seen. He had vanished as far as his upper palate, and his shiny black mane blended into the chair behind him.

On each of them were displayed the telltale scars of long-term Orbiters.

What had at first looked like drink containers scattered about might as easily have been discarded Orbitol atomizer bulbs. The truth of it struck Gansevoort all at once: the Gang of Four, the gods of ScumberCorp, were *junkies*.

Realization triggered his anger as if it were a hydrogen bomb. "You two-faced jackals!" he screamed shrilly. "You lying, fucking bastards!"

He charged at the table but the figure—the false image—of Gotoh turned and stopped him. "Calm, Ton Gansevoort," said Glimet, unclipping the mask and drawing it off. "Put your outrage to use." He turned back to the table.

Jean Rajcevich threatened, "I'm calling security."

Glimet replied, "I doubt that very much, mademoiselle. The last thing you want is for senior management, the public, and especially your competitors, to learn of your condition. And without your Mr. Mingo around there's no one to set about eliminating everyone who sees you."

"Gansevoort," she cried, "let's see your team spirit. You swore we could rely on you for anything—we're asking you now, *kill* these people."

Kosinus commanded, "Jean, for once in your life, shut up! *I'm* the chairman here; you're only COO. Try to remember that and let me handle this." His chair swiveled sluggishly. His disembodied head looked weary of existence. "You say Mingo is gone?"

"Yes."

"Of course, he'd exceeded his authority. We all knew it and turned a blind eye."

"You allowed him to continue," said Angel under his mask.

"True," Kosinus replied lightly. "Some of the blame has to fall on us. We'll make restitution to each of you, naturally."

Lyell asked, "What about the people of Box City—the ones who burned up this morning? What was it—at least a hundred dead and ten times that hurt? All the squalid little shacks north of the quadrangle destroyed. Poof, just like that—not very fireproof after all, those crates."

"If that was Mingo's work—"

"It was. I was there."

"Then we'll have to do something for them," said Sherk. "Give away some boxes—big ones, better ones. We could bulldoze the area for them, how would that be?"

"Why not instead," suggested Angel, "stop trying to exterminate them?"

The four heads floated in silence until Kosinus said, "I'm sorry? Exterminate?"

"You dissemble almost as well as you disassemble," Angel said. "Mingo exceeded his authority, did he? ¡*Pamplinas!* You would like it that way. Absolved of all guilt, as much as the victims of your agent as those he ruthlessly killed. I would sing another song were I you. But I'm not." Angel drew off Kosinus's face then. He tossed it onto the table. The neck clip rang the glass top like a bell. "I am he that lives, and was dead."

"Rueda."

"Christ, he's alive."

"No thanks to any of you. You've now obliterated me two times. First in Madrid, with your drug. Then on the Moon, with your clever brain trap. Tried to squeeze out my soul like toothpaste. You can't attribute that to Mingo—remember, I was there and heard your conversations. About me, about my people whom you slaughtered, about the others you buried up there in the airless silence. These people with me know all about it."

"This human refuse?" said Rajcevich with a sneering laugh. Under her head the mechanism of an Orbitol atomizer appeared. It floated down to settle on the table. "Here. Don't you want some? Aren't you all hungry for it? Burning? It's like that, isn't it? Only supreme will can deny such a hunger. Few have that kind of will." The container skidded and rolled across the table. "Go ahead, all of you. There's plenty more. We own the warehouse."

Shikker broke from the group. She made her way to the table and picked up the atomizer with her good arm.

"That's right," Rajcevich urged. "You can't help it."

"What are you doing, Jean?"

"Just offering our friends a treat before we get down to reaching a settlement. How about you, there, in the back," she said to Lyell. "Wouldn't you like some?"

Lyell stared back at her. On what did this woman base her assessment of Lyell as a Boxer? Could Rajcevich even see this dimension any longer? Offering her Orbitol!—she started to laugh. "Once upon a time," she said, "there was a big ugly monster with four big, fat heads. And because it had four big, fat heads, it had four fat mouths, and an appetite so big that it devoured whole cities. Philadelphia, Montreal, Atlanta—ate 'em right up. Ate the whole continent. Pretty soon the world gets gobbled up like that."

"Let's skip the morality tale," Rajcevich said sourly. "You have some specific point to make?"

"You want to jump straight to the moral—okay, here's the moral, the way Thomas Lyell would have said it: you don't need to kill a greedy thing, it eats itself to death."

"Would that be Thomas Lyell, the late but hardly lamented mayor of Atlanta?"

Lyell took the comment like a physical slap in the face. It cemented her position. "Case in point." She turned and made her way down the room as she spoke, thinking bitterly, triumphantly, of all that her lens had recorded. "Here sits the very core of the company, the four COs, with your lovely view, and look at you. Rotting away in self-deception, almost gone altogether."

"Quite the contrary," Rajcevich argued. "Not gone at all. We long ago established a maintenance dose, which for our own reasons we've kept to ourselves. We slowed down the process to where we've held steady for near on a decade, and we can remain like this another decade if we like, long enough to realize our dreams. The real question is, do you want to realize yours? You, whoever you are, do you want money? A large apartment in the best Rittenhouse towers? Better— a villa overlooking the sea? Or even passage to Mars. Even that. We can set you up forever."

"The way you had Mingo set up the Boxers who volunteered for your experiments, the ones who were promised the same Martian colonies but got a mass burial on the Moon instead? You've dangled your Mars colonies in front of so many people, I doubt they exist." She arrived before the window, and peered down at the stepped architecture, down into the blackness that was the plaza at the bottom. "It looks to me," she observed indifferently, "as if you've positioned yourselves on a setback."

Reflected in the glass she saw Amerind Shikker wandering as though mindlessly around the table. She could tell what Shikker intended, and kept talking. "It amazes me you can accept your own addiction so casually. Don't you see the same things as other Orbiters?"

"Hallucinations," the woman said dismissively. "Who cares?"

"This far along and you can still pretend that. That's impressive." She turned.

Coming up beside Rajcevich's chair, the LifeMask image of the ideal Rajcevich produced the atomizer bulb she had been offered. Lyell held her breath, seeing the actions before they came as clearly as a Knewsday psychic.

Shikker suddenly sprawled over the chair, pressed the nozzle of the bulb against the woman's disembodied head, and fired.

Rajcevich bobbed to the side. She made a wailing sound somewhere between ecstasy and agony.

Shikker slid up over the back of the chair and around the other side, catching Rajcevich on the rebound. She pressed the thing against the left temple of the floating head and fired again. Rajcevich shrieked ferociously, primordially. Her breathing went erratic, became trip-hammer panting. She gave her head a violent shake, slammed it first into the back of her chair and then down again and again, hard against the glass tabletop. A smear developed where she struck.

Kosinus rose as fast as he was able, but was too far away to prevent Shikker's third pull of the trigger. His invisible hands clutched at her—the ragged clothes plucked and jumped in his grip, but she wrestled free of his weak hold, twisted, and fired back at him. He retreated from the danger she represented.

Lyell stood her ground. As cold and hard as the lens she wore, she held her place and disked what happened without interfering. Later, Nebergall could zoom in to extract every nuance, every moment he wanted. "You chose," she muttered, "when you said his name—one cruelty too many."

Angel and Glimet stood by like judge and jury, and she made sure she captured them, too. Glimet's eyes were closed as if in prayer. Gansevoort stood trembling behind them, his teeth bared in feral repulsion.

Around the table, Sherk had slunk down in his chair, as if he hoped to be overlooked. She couldn't see the last one, Gotoh. His chair had cranked away immediately from the action.

Rajcevich shrieked in terror. Her pouchy eyelids stretched wide, tracking the approach of a horror she alone could see. "No, no, no, *stop* them!" she called, "don't let them near me."

Of an instant her head ceased to exist. Its disappearance made a "pop" like that of a champagne cork. A tiny spurt of blood, as from a nosebleed, spattered the table in front of where she'd sat.

"Aw, God," Gansevoort groaned.

Meanwhile, the head of Kosinus had begun to bob and weave through the air. He opened his mouth and a yowl emerged, a yowl echoed by Gansevoort, who then slumped down with his arms wrapped around his head.

Shikker's first blind shot must have hit Kosinus somewhere, enough to disorient him. Her second missed his temple and fired into his forehead. His skin reddened where the chemical opened his capillaries. He spun around with surprising speed for an Orbiter, ululating all the while, like a screeching three-year-old trying to make himself dizzy. His wail swelled with fear, and he halted his crazy spin. Shikker ruthlessly gave him a third shot for good measure, and a moment later, he, too, was gone. His cries seemed to continue long after, but again it was Gansevoort, mewling where he huddled.

Huston Sherk had drifted from the table. He stood against the wall. Shikker ignored him, and closed on the chair ostensibly containing Gotoh. Lyell circled carefully toward it. Shikker turned it from the wall.

Gotoh floated calmly, not a hint of fear in his eyes. He focused on the atomizer bulb. "Please," he asked, as if desiring a cup of tea. His eyes closed. Shikker fired twice into his head. His reaction was unlike the others.

He hissed and his face scrunched up. The veins stood out on his forehead, but he was smiling—a grotesque sight, since he had no lower jaw. He faded away like a ghost. Shortly, there was nothing of him to be seen.

Sherk begged. "Don't, I don't want to go over. Please don't let her do this."

Shikker said, "You done this to a lotta people. Been trying for years to make me take it, you and your pitchmen. I don't see why we shouldn't give it back, if it's so damn good. You think you're special, but you ain't special, bastard. You got the urge like Glimet, ya want some of this, don't ya? Hunger that bitch was on about—yeah, you got that particular hunger. I been surrounded by people itching your way. Ain't no supreme will when you got to have a taste. So, I guess I'm giving you my share. I want you to join the party, don't be late for your own funeral." She stalked him around the table. He couldn't move his altered limbs fast enough to escape. He tried to pull himself over the glass. Shikker had him like a Thanksgiving turkey.

Lyell asked Angel, "Are you making her do this? Is he?" She indicated Glimet.

"She's doing this on her own."

"Then what's he doing, communing?" she asked, indicating Glimet.

"He acts as a focus, a beacon. Drawing the others in twelve-space to himself. From him they can locate the transformed COs and be there to take them as they arrive. She's doing them a favor, really. Easing their passage. Best to get it over with."

He stared meaningfully at her. "Believe me, it's a journey better avoided."

"Lying, fucking bastards," muttered Gansevoort.

Sherk cried out, in pain, in pleasure, then in mortal terror for his life.

The tabletop cracked at one end, but nothing remained on top of it.

"What happens now?" asked Lyell.

"Now," said Angel, "I bid you *adios*, Thomasina Lyell."

"You're going to ride off into the sunset just like that?"

"I have no choice."

Shikker was turning, glancing all around herself in search of another head to attack. As she passed by Glimet, he reached out and touched her and she stopped. She gazed lovingly at him. "Never again," she said. "Never again for you." She flung the atomizer against the large screen. It bounced harmlessly off.

"No," he promised, "never." He hugged her to him. The gesture reminded Lyell more of a parent than a lover, and made her ache with an emptiness she had not felt for years. She wondered which side of Glimet initiated the hug, then decided it really didn't matter. Certainly it didn't to Shikker. Lyell sensed more than saw Angel Rueda start to collapse.

He doubled over, one hand stretched out as though clutching for support. Then he pitched headlong into the debris.

She knelt beside him and flipped him over, intending to apply whatever lifesaving techniques she could. He was no more than a husk, his body already collapsing, cast off. The energy—whatever it was—that had kept the spark of him alive was gone. She covered her mouth and nose against the sudden stench, and stood away. Behind her, Gansevoort flopped over, unconscious.

"Glimet," she asked, "what happened, why did he—"

"He told you, he had to. He'd made a promise."

"I don't understand. Promised who?"

"Angel Rueda. His work was done, and he granted release to the human host. So it's agreed, each of us with our hosts. Glimet's time isn't long off, either. I hope you'll help Amerind—she won't realize the true nature of the event as you do."

Lyell bowed her head over the body of the man who had brought her into this, and bade farewell to the soul released from strange purgatories.

A presence moved into the room. Like a shadow passing, it drew her attention.

In front of the wide window, phantom threads unfolded out of a dark core. By the moment these joined and gained in complexity, like a living Julia set, crystalline but somehow supple. The evolving form was familiar to her already—call it lotus or mandala. A circle, vaguely.

Trash on the floor sprang up and danced. A frisson like that preceding an electrical storm filled the air; a glow akin to St. Elmo's fire outlined each bit of flying debris, none of which touched them. Its flight had a pattern to it, or, rather, hundreds of patterns coexisting. The table split its length and collapsed. Its tubular supports stuck up like animal legs in rigor mortis. The trash spun ever more slowly, lower and lower, dying down like dry leaves abandoned by a wind. They skittered to a stop.

Glimet turned toward Lyell and said, "Behold, and I'll show you a mystery."

The dark, thousand-petaled form, flowing in a continuous cycle from center to tips, had fully eructed into the here and now of the room. Held in the air by whatever unseen forces, it blocked the view of the towers. Lyell moved past him to disk it in detail. As she did, the first of its new offspring began to push through.

Epilogue
The Big Broadcast

"It's the President Odie Show! With Veep Schnepfe! The Capitol Hill Synthestra! And tonight's very special guests in an exclusive interview: the Chief Officers of ScumberCorp! That's right, folks, you'll never see them anywhere else. So give me a big assist and say 'To Hail with the Chief!' It's President *Odie*!"

The curtain parted and out shuffled the president of the

United States, Malcolm Odie. His suit gleamed only slightly brighter than his teeth. He waved warmly to his constituency, waved the one-man synthestra down as a Dixieland send-up of "Hail to the Chief" filled the hall.

"Thank you all, every registered voter out there. Good God, you'd think I was in charge of something." Laughter. "Yeah, yeah. Well, here we are, on what promises to be an eventful night, the kind of night that goes down in TV history as the night where everybody remembers where they were. They used to say that sort of thing about Jack Kennedy and the New York nuke and Schnepfe's piles." A synthetic rimshot spanged like a bullet across the stage.

"You get your sets warmed up, you're going to wanna record this. Okay? Ready out there? Schnepfe, show 'em your penis. Ha!—just kidding. No, no, this has to be bigger than *that*." Rimshot, more laughter. "Tonight, four people who have controlled the destiny of our nation—dare I suggest our entire planet and way of life?—are here with us, live on this very soundstage. Because of their unprecedented appearance here, and, really, because ScumberCorp owns the puking network and can do whatever it pleases, we're not going to plug any products tonight, no cutaways, which means Schnepfe'll have to fall off his stool if he plans to crawl off and drink. Yeah, yeah.

"Okay now, let's get this great show moving before Congress thinks up something for me to veto. Let's bring 'em out here. Ladies and germinals, the Chief Officers, the Fearsome Foursome, of ScumberCorporation!" He jumped to his feet and began clapping enthusiastically. The music worked a wild variation on "La Marseillaise."

The curtain drew back on four darkly silhouetted figures. Overhead lights blazed in tight, tracking beams, and the COs paraded out. Shots intercut of an audience on its feet and pounding out a standing ovation.

The foursome, like a caterpillar, chugged across the stage and sat down. Dorjan Kosinus, looking fit and distinguished, sat nearest Odie.

"How's it going, Mr. Chairman?" the president asked. "You and all the other—uh . . ."

"Scums?" Kosinus suggested, politely.

Odie laughed, reddening slightly. Did people so high up

actually make fun of themselves? "Not from me did you hear that. Tell us, what brings you four out in the public eye this first time in, what, ten years?"

"Well, Odie, a very troublesome state of affairs has arisen and we've finally decided to do something about it." The other three nodded. "As you know, we are involved in nearly every aspect of daily life on this planet. There's hardly an industry, a technological advance, that we don't have some hand in."

"Can't spot any flaw in that argument, no sirree."

"Odie, I'll speak plainly. It's come to our attention that government has all but become the utter enemy of the people."

Odie's mouth hung loosely for an instant. He tried to guffaw his way out. "Not me, I've got nothing but friends, Dorjan."

Kosinus did not bend. "Not on the streets, you haven't," he said. "Not where more than twenty million people are living in squalor, many of them mentally deficient, in need of attention of every kind, while we seal ourselves in and build up into the sky to get away from them, away from our responsibilities."

"Well, you know what I say, I keep both feet firma-ly on the terra." He appealed to Capitol Hill for a snare and cymbal but got nothing. He was starting to sweat copiously.

"That's why we've come out of our long hibernation. We've deliberated this carefully. ScumberCorp has decided to turn a few things around. As the largest single employer in the world, we believe we have a voice that will be heard. That *must* be heard if we're to continue as a civilization."

"This sounds *damn* exciting," Odie said, trying to recapture territory. "What's your plan?"

"Well, for starters, Malcolm, we're asking for your resignation on the grounds of unparalleled incompetency. You can take the besotted baboon on the stool there with you as you leave. I'm certain there's a street corner someplace where you and Schnepfe can perform for idiots. We'll see to it that you get a few assigned to you.

"In case you're thinking of fighting this, let it be known that Congress, at our behest, has already put in motion impeachment proceedings against you. I would read the list of charges but that could take up the whole hour."

To Odie's horror, Capitol Hill fired a rimshot for Kosinus.

"Go quietly, Odie. We would prefer to get on to matters of importance, such as tearing down walls, rebuilding cities, and starting a rehabilitation program for Orbiters. As I speak, bulldozers are clearing land here in Philadelphia to begin construction on the Remington Mingo Memorial Rehabilitation Center for the Orbitol-Diminished. It's a big step, I think."

"The who?" squawked Schnepfe in his fractured, frightened delirium.

Before Kosinus could answer, Odie jumped up and pointed accusingly at all four of them. "I *work* for you. Anybody out there watching who doesn't think so, I can prove it. These policies of mine they want to get rid of, these four are the ones who created them! They're the villains! How do you answer that, Kosinus, huh?" he asked gleefully.

"Like this: ScumberCorp pleads guilty to various ethical violations—manipulations of mutual funds and futures markets, crimes against competitors, and a program of cold-blooded elimination of the underclass. We've halted all production of Orbitol and begun the dismantling of the lunar facility where we've been manufacturing it." The other three nodded in agreement on each of these points.

"What about the shareholders, the directors? They'll *never* go along with this liberal crap!"

"Why do you suppose we've made this public announcement, Malcolm? It's no longer a matter of choice but one of setting precedent."

Odie looked as if all the blood had oozed from his body.

Seated beside Nebergall on his freshly covered bed, Lyell said, "This is the fourth time I've watched the broadcast, and I still get chills at the look on his face."

"Yeah, he's special, the little dork," Nebergall replied. "I couldn't have manufactured a better look of panic with a stylus and week to do it. I hear he's lined up a job headlining in an undersea supper club off the Caymans. Let's hope he stays down a good long time."

"I was referring to Kosinus. It makes me wonder if the Gang of Four's true personalities realize what's happened to them, what's going on out here. You remember, on the disk, where we're sitting in that weird tent, and Angel starts explaining about how he knew he'd died before because the part of him that was still Angel recalled it? I was just wondering if that holds true for each of them."

"If it does, then everyone of them's gone through the trip that Rueda went through, seeing as how they're sharing the same puppeteers. If you ask me, it's hellish poetic justice after all they did—fucking up the world for a handful of nothing. Having Rueda and Glimet driving them is just fine by me. Although, I'll tell ya, on a slow day I may actually miss the four bastards. Don't get me wrong, I think the extruded versions are a quantum improvement. 'O brave new world' and all that."

After a moment, she said, "When we finally archive our Orbitol documentary, I think we ought to get away for a while."

"You mean like a vacation? Like they gave Gansevoort?"

"Not like they gave Gansevoort, thank you. I don't consider rehabilitation a holiday."

"I've never had a vacation, Tommie. I wouldn't know what to do with one, except chew my fingernails worrying about being back on the job." He glanced sadly toward his edit suite. "All that technology, and we didn't need to splice in anything to get this."

"Sounds like you're sorry you agreed to let them handle Odie."

"Goes against the grain. Doesn't it for you? Don't you have a twinge of conscience that you've sold out by agreeing?"

She thought about it for a moment. "I think selling out has to do with principles, and we haven't changed ours. It just feels the way it does because this used to be the enemy, and now we're working for them."

They sat without further comment for a time, until suddenly he asked, "Where would we go on this vacation?"

"I was thinking, New Zealand."

"What am I supposed to do, crawl up the mountains?"

"With your salary from ScumberCorp, you can afford one of those exoneural systems now—there's no excuse. You'll outdistance *me* with one of those."

"I don't know about that job offer," he said, and stroked the cat in his lap. "The idea of money and stability kinda scares the crap outta me."

"Only because you've never had either one. Listen, Neeb, something is going to replace the Alien News Network; why shouldn't it be something you and I create? A new entity, a viable one, slapping some real, ugly, naked truth on the screen for a change. God knows, you've got enough of it stored away in there. Hey, we can even do the 'slow-food' story now, with a slightly different spin. ScumberCorp's out of the business and everyone else is in it. Torsion perspective."

He pursed his lips. "Does that mean I have to give up my state of the art, intercutting, image-synthesis animation facility?"

"Move it into your new office."

He pondered that. "No, I think I'll keep it in the closet at home. You never know. Eventually, this new batch is going to rot, and ol' SC will be left in the hands of people again. Somebody'll snort the power and get crazy. The world's still big—they're bound to fuck it up. And even if *they* don't, the competition won't toe the line unless forced to. Naw, I think my secret identity oughta stay secret, same as twelve-space. Who knows when we'll have to *disseminate* by night again?" He grinned crookedly her way but she didn't notice.

She was transfixed by the face of Dorjan Kosinus looming huge upon the screen. His high-definition eyes, so clear and alive, looked out upon a hundred million viewers with the sorrow and the mercy of a Messiah. *Or of an angel*, she thought, and smiled finally upon Nebergall.

THE MAGICAL XANTH SERIES!

PIERS ANTHONY

QUESTION QUEST

75948-9/$4.99 US/$5.99 Can

ISLE OF VIEW

75947-0/$4.99 US/$5.99 Can

VALE OF THE VOLE

75287-5/$4.95 US/$5.95 Can

HEAVEN CENT

75288-3/$4.95 US/$5.95 Can

MAN FROM MUNDANIA

75289-1/$4.95 US/$5.95 Can

THE COLOR OF HER PANTIES

75949-7/$4.99 US/$5.99 Can

THE CONTINUATION
OF THE FABULOUS
INCARNATIONS OF IMMORTALITY
SERIES

PIERS ANTHONY

FOR LOVE OF EVIL
75285-9/$4.95 US/$5.95 Can

AND ETERNITY
75286-7/$4.95 US/$5.95 Can